Great Diebac

MW00526079

This is a work of fiction. All characters and events portrayed in this book are fictional, and any resemblance to real people or incidents is purely coincidental.

Clipper Implants Press, Cedar Park, TX

Revised Edition – November 2019

Printed and Distributed by Amazon, Inc.

Map images in the introduction are provided by and with permission of National Geographic; credit: Jason Treat, NG Image Collection. Map images within the body of the text are provided by Google Maps, as indicated within the images.

ISBN: 978-1-7340507-1-4

Table of Contents

INTRODUCTION AND EDITORS' NOTES

PROCESS FOLLOWED

T his history is a compilation based on memoirs of people who lived through the monumental changes to the world of 2028 through 2037. We, the editors, have transformed their stories into a narrative form to give them a consistency and flow that a simple merging of the individual sources would have lacked. We have made every effort to preserve the factual content, though we have taken minor liberties with dialogue.

The first volume covers events centered in North America, Europe, and China/Siberia. We have included maps depicting the flooding on those continents after the three Big Melts of 2029. Because of the plume of volcanic ash in the Earth's atmosphere at that time, there is no satellite imagery showing the extent of flooding caused by the melting of the world's icecaps in 2029. The maps that follow this introduction are artistic renderings, but as accurate as we can make.

The second volume covers Africa, South America, Australia, and India. If the editors can obtain sufficient source materials, the third volume will cover the history of the survivors of Western Russia. We anticipate that publication of the third volume will occur within two years after the first two are released.

One complaint from our publisher has been the proliferation of peoples our memorialists have named. In response, we have included a list giving a short description of most of the characters for this volume. The list is in order by surname and given name. In addition to the name there is a short sketch of the character and an indication of the importance of the character; primary, major, or supporting. All other characters mentioned in the book are too minor to warrant further research by the editors. This character

INTRODUCTION AND EDITORS' NOTES

list is found at the end of this introduction.

PURPOSE OF THIS HISTORY

T his history sketches the Great Dieback in broad strokes. That period was experienced universally, virtually from beginning to end. The Great Dieback is not our primary focus. It is presented for context. It is not that the death of over half the world's peoples is not a tale worthy to tell. It is that it is both too vast and too simple.

By contrast, most of the subsequent events that led to the Singularity involved a relative handful of people; those who resisted the onslaught and those who promoted it. These events and people are the primary focus of these volumes.

It wasn't the worst of times. In our opinion those occurred during the Time of Troubles – The Terrible Twenties – The Great Dieback, call it what you may.

We know there are those who disagree, some violently. Ordinary people; who remembered better days and clung to the forlorn hope that they could halt a barrage of history. Oligarchs; who wanted to redirect the barrage so that it would not threaten their wealth and power regardless of who else paid the piper.

Those who lived through the advent of the Singularity would call those changes the destruction of humanity as they knew it. And they would be right we suppose. But the reality is that the essence of humanity was being destroyed and recreated throughout the ages.

A major climate change triggered the transformation of a group of tree apes to hunter gatherers. New technologies like domestication of animals and planting tools triggered the transformation of those hunter-gatherers to agriculturalists. Many other transformations have occurred before and since.

The editors have gathered these stories to bear witness to the latest crucial change to our humanities.

Great Dieback to Singularity

Key to Understanding Big Melt Maps

Cities on the maps were inundated. The line labelled "Present Shoreline" shows the situation in 2028, before the Great Dieback. That shoreline is virtually the same as in our period of 2108.

NORTH AMERICA AFTER BIG MELT THREE

EUROPE AFTER BIG MELT THREE

Great Dieback to Singularity

ASIA AFTER BIG MELT THREE

INTRODUCTION AND EDITORS' NOTES

CHARACTERS

Note: Chinese names are surname, given name. These memoirs will often use singular names, which is not the Chinese custom. Please forgive the cultural insensitivity.

NAME	SKETCH	SIGNIFICANCE
Barney	An artificial intelligence (AI), originally developed and "owned" by Google	1 – Primary
Benoit, Henry, PhD	Department head, adviser Great Plains Union (GPU) bioengineering unit, nicknames – Bennie Boy, BB Brain	3 – Supporting
Berger, Carole, MD	Midwest Collective trauma surgeon	3 – Supporting
Biensur, Gerald	Enhanced human, formerly Robert Owens-B, nickname – the Biensur Beast	1 – Primary
Blumstein, Rahel	a.k.a. Kaitlin Schlötke, Agent for The Collective	1 – Primary
Bold Beaver	AI derived from scavenged materials found in Taipei, restored by Third Cybernetics Group	1 – Primary
Bullock, General	Head of the Texican Flotilla	3 – Supporting
Cameron, Addison, PhD	Polymath with focus on cybernetics, nickname – Addie, A-One	1 – Primary
Cameron, Ainsley, PhD	Polymath with focus on bioengineering, nicknames – LeeLee, A-Two – Spirit Animal – Placid Wolverine	1 – Primary
Cerberus	AI originally created by the Chinese PLA	3 – Supporting
Chen, Mike	Food vendor, deputy to Su Guo Han, nickname – Jacky Chen	3 – Supporting
Chou, Sergeant	Assigned liaison (guard) for First Bioengineering Group	3 – Supporting
Congreve, Lieutenant	Security chief for Telepathic Communications Device (TCD) Unit, GPU	3 – Supporting
Faith	Native American from Amazon jungle enslaved by narcos	2 – Major
Fitzhugh, Bill	See Malcolm St. Jacques	1 – Primary
Friedman, Jay	Cybernetics genius, uncle of Addison and Ainsley, regional director for Midwest USA of emergency planning for Big Melts	2 – Major
Gonzales, Javier, Captain	Member of Texican Flotilla	1 – Primary
Grabowski, Corporal	Member of GPU Militia, Peregrine Falcons Platoon, nickname – Grabby	3 – Supporting
Grubenflagg, Count	Head of the Ravensbruck Group – nom de guerre of Fredrich "Fast Freddie" von Schtuben	2 – Major
Heath, Janet, Corporal	Telepathic Communications Squad (Note: Squad upgraded to Platoon during 2033-37), nickname – Heath Bar	3 – Supporting
Jackson, Ron	Bioengineer in training, member of Great Plains Union (GPU) militia	2 – Major
Jhao, Gang	Special Projects, Head, Second Robotics Group, Peoples Republic of China	3 – Supporting
Johnson, Zeke, Leader	Head of the Midwest Cooperative	3 – Supporting
Lac Court Oreilles	Native American tribe in Wisconsin, founders of the Great Plains Union	2 – Major
Lynley, Thomas	Butler and more for Lord Townerly	3 – Supporting
Owens-Binghampton, Robert	Mercenary for Ravensbruck Group – nom de guerre of Gerald Biensur, nicknames – Bob-O, Owens-B	1 – Primary
Pythia	AI created by Xu Xiang while in Special Ops	3 – Supporting
Quintana, José	Emissary from Azmayca to North America, former drug cartel kingpin	3 – Supporting
Red Eagle, Nelson	Member of Great Plains Union Militia, at one time was boyfriend of Addison Cameron	3 – Supporting
Red Eagle, William	Nelson's uncle, tribal elder	3 – Supporting
Schlötke, Kaitlin	Agent for The Collective, nom de guerre for Rahel Blumstein	1 – Primary
Scott, Hope	Lab assistant and bioengineer intern	2 – Major
Sleeping Otter	Midewiwin (traditional healer) for the Lac Courte Oreilles, Great Plains Union	2 – Major
St. Jacques, Malcolm	Mercenary, ex-SAS, new lover of Addison, nom de guerre of Bill Fitzhugh	1 – Primary
Su, Guo Han, Sergeant	Investigator for MSS, nickname – Boy named Sue	2 – Major

Great Dieback to Singularity

NAME	SKETCH	SIGNIFICANCE
Sukhiin, Ajai	Polymath in cybernetics and bioengineering, largely self-taught, nickname – Mongolian farm boy	1 – Primary
Svensdotter, Karin, Dame	Member of the Western Europe Consortium for Reconstruction	2 – Major
Thomson, Corporal	Member of the Great Plains Union Militia, ex –member of US House of Representatives, WI	3 – Supporting
Townerly, John, Lord	Head of the Brittany Consortium, head of the Western Europe Consortium for Reconstruction	2 – Major
Vyrvykvist, Dmitri, MD, PhD	Brilliant bioengineer, creator of the Cossack Supermen which are also called the Bastard Bears, nickname – Dr. V	1 – Primary
Wang, General	Third Artillery Corps, People's Liberation Army, head of Bomb Central	3 – Supporting
Sergeant Wojlkowski	Great Plains Union Militia, training, Peregrines Peregrine Falcons Platoon, nickname – Woj	3 – Supporting
Wu, Fang	Commissar for First Bioengineering Group	3 – Supporting
Wong, Min	Cyberneticist, lover of Xu Xiang, First Cybernetics Group Head	1 – Primary
Xu, Xiang	Bioengineer, onetime lover of Ainsley, First Bioengineering Group Head, nicknames – XiXi, Gollum	1 – Primary
Xu, Jian, General	People's Liberation Army, leader Great March North planning	3 – Supporting
Xu, LinLin	Cousin of Xiang, nickname – Halfling	3 – Supporting
Yeong, Lanying	Cyberneticist, Third Cybernetics Group Head	3 – Supporting

A technological singularity is that point in time when improvements in fields such as robotics, artificial intelligence (AI), or bioengineering reach a point of rapid and self-sustained advancement. The exponentially improving new creatures will have the same relationship to ordinary humans as modern humans had to Neanderthals. Neanderthals could not compete; they withered and died. Does that fate await us?

From an article about the pace of innovations, circa 1970

PROLOGUE – THE TWINS

22ⁿᵈ September 2028

University of Wisconsin, Madison

Addison laughed as she grabbed her twin's arms and tried to drag her away from her bioengineering lab desk. "Well LeeLee what dive are you taking us to tonight? Do we need to bring some disinfectant soap from your lab Sweetie?"

Ainsley said, "I should skip tonight, A-One. I'm really beat. I should just wrap up these reports and ..."

Addison said, "Nonsense, A-Two. And call me Addie. We aren't five anymore, LeeLee. The problem is you've been working too hard. As if your regular post-doc responsibilities weren't enough, the extra work you and your team have been putting in on the 'Special Project' is burning the candle from the middle, forget both ends. You gotta come out for your health and mine."

Ainsley sighed, "You're right, Addie. The need for secrecy is taking an extra mental toll. Let's get wild and forget all this. Besides, the 'Special Project' trials have begun to bear fruit over the last few weeks, as you know. We've succeeded in generating these new structures within our volunteers' bodies using genetic engineering. That makes all the extra work worth it. A celebration is in order."

Ainsley flicked off the office lights. The two stepped out of bioengineering. The empty hallway in the deserted building echoed their footsteps. The long gray dimness of the institutional space was illuminated at either end by the exit safety lights.

One of the security exit lights spotlighted her sister as Addison glanced back at her. "C'mon Sis, times tickin." *Looking at LeeLee anyone could see we're sisters. Might not guess we're twins with her short hair and my shoulder length, her monotone tee and slacks versus my autumn print, her hunched shoulders. But we both have our athletic twenty-year-old bods and clear complexions.*

1

PROLOGUE – The Twins

Ainsley said, "Oh, you will love this place Addie. It is dark, dank, and full of dangerous men. Your favorite kind." The two went out the door of the lab building and headed through the twilight towards Bascom Hill and on to the crowds and fun. A light-hearted weekend was just what they both needed.

They could hear faint sounds of revelry from State Street and even fainter sounds from distant dorms. The air had an autumn chill and the smell of fresh-fallen leaves. Addison had been an avid leaf-peeper when they first came to UW for their PhD studies. She loved the strobing kaleidoscope of colors. Now the odor of decaying leaves smelled too much of the grave. They wrapped their windbreakers tight and linked arms.

As they walked through a passage between buildings four young men stepped out of the shadows. Ainsley wondered, *Look like students. Are they in my classes?* One of them seemed to be the leader. "Ladies, step this way please."

Both women were puzzled. Then they saw the men had guns. Terror took over. Two of the men grabbed Addison and the other two wrenched Ainsley's arms behind her back. They shoved the two women into a darkened entryway that stunk of urine. Ainsley saw that there were blankets spread out. This was a well-planned attack.

They shoved each woman to the ground. The leader growled in a low voice. "Be quiet and you won't get hurt. Your Friday night partying is just starting a little earlier than you planned." One of the two men with Ainsley switched his grip. One of his hands held Ainsley's wrists above her head. His other hand held a pistol, its cold steel pressed against her temple. Her mind was screaming. Her eyes pinballed, looking for an escape. Then she remembered the secret experiment; the biological enhancement she created.

Oh Lord! Will the Clipper work? What if mine works and Addison's doesn't? They will kill her in revenge. Gagging, she forced herself to turn off the autonomic reaction as the second man finished pulling her pants to her ankles and cutting off her panties. *I don't know if I can stand this again.* She moaned as the brute forced her legs apart, scraping them on the rough textured blanket. "Liking that

Baby?" he grunted. "Well you'll love this," he hissed as he shoved himself into her.

At that moment there was an agonized guttural scream from the other side of the entryway. At once Ainsley released control of the Clipper she had caused to be grown within herself. New specialized glands flooded her vagina with the irritating, encapsulating fluid they excreted. At the same time, her body unsheathed two partially grown claws. They scythed across her pubic area. A second scream rewarded her. It came from her rapist.

Without hesitation Ainsley twisted her torso and grappled with the man behind her. She was using Mushin – the mind without mind, as she learned in her dojo. She was not able to wrest complete control of the pistol. When the gun fired she diverted it enough that the bullet only grazed her head. It stung but there was no gush of blood or loss of consciousness. She continued her roll breaking her assailant's finger. He fell to the ground but still kept his hold on the gun.

Ainsley saw that Addison and her assailant were in a desperate fight for the remaining gun. Ainsley whipped her body to straddle her gunman. She twisted his gun. This forced his finger backward with a loud crack. In the same move she pointed the gun at Addison's assailant and forced the gun to fire again by levering the broken finger against the trigger. Addison's opponent slumped. The assailant's blood and brains splattered across Addison.

Ainsley focused her attention back on her opponent. She saw he was going into shock but still struggling to throw Ainsley off. She wrenched the pistol from his mutilated finger and jammed it into his crotch. His eyes got big as saucers. He yelped, "Please." Ainsley shot once, twice, then a third time. She couldn't be sure of her aim through his pants, but she meant to blow away each testicle then his penis. In any case he went silent.

Ainsley leapt up and went to her sister. As soon as Ainsley stood, her vagina ejected the sac encapsulating the remnant of her rapist's penis. She loomed over Addison and stooped to check her vitals. Addie was picking bits of brain and clotted blood off herself.

PROLOGUE – The Twins

She was looked at each piece as if it were an unexpected treasure. But there didn't seem to be any serious physical injuries. Ainsley grabbed the second gun. She stood, scanning carefully in every direction.

"Addison! I'm calling the police. Stay here! Don't put on your clothes or allow your body to eject the sac inside. Cover yourself with this blanket." *I hate touching this filthy rag they brought. But I won't leave my Addie naked for the world to gawk at.* "Don't tell them who was with you. You are in shock and can't remember. Got it?" Addison shook her head in numb assent.

"What about you?" Addison whispered.

Ainsley threw her slacks on. She tucked the two guns into her bag. She stalked off into the night, calling over her shoulder, "I'm going to muddy the waters. Trust me." Addison had never seen Ainsley like this. The closest was when an opposing soccer player kept yanking Ainsley down in a state championship game. Ainsley got red-carded for busting that girl's nose.

Sirens sounded, drawing closer. Addison's last sight of Ainsley was as she called 911. The phone must have belonged to one of the men. Addison didn't recognize it.

Addison looked around at the scene of carnage. Two men were writhing in pain. *Should I try to give them first aid? The jeans hooked around their knees are soaked with blood. I didn't really see them before. They're young as us, kids really. Leather jackets, sneakers. The two dead guys don't look real. Oh, the smell of blood, piss, and shit!* She passed out.

Police and EMTs soon surrounded Addison. She didn't have to work hard to appear shocked and semi-coherent. She truly was. The first detective to arrive was talking with an EMT. "Whatta we got here Bob?" Addison would have laughed if she wasn't in so much pain. The detective looked like a Bucky Badger gorged on a wheel of cheese. His tinted glasses at night was a surreal touch. And no, polyester plaid was not a good retro look.

Bob replied, "I'm not the medical examiner, but a coupla things are clear. Two dead from gunshots. The one by the girl layin over there took a head shot through the temple. Mostly his brains splattered on her. The one on this blanket looks like someone was castrating him with a Smith 'n Wesson. Multiple shots with powder burns. He bled out. The other two writhing in pain had their dicks cut off. Looks like a surgical cut on both. But, I'm not the M.E., so just my opinion."

The detective said, "Yeah Bob, but you know that ol drunk will take two days to tell me the same thing and prolly get half it wrong anyway." He sauntered up to Addison. She pulled the foul blanket tighter. "What's the story Girlie? Didya whack these guys because they wooden pay ya?" He continued to press her to cooperate, threatening to charge her with two murders and two counts of grievous bodily assault. It was all she could do to restrain herself from jumping up and hitting the jerk in the larynx.

Both were saved from the confrontation by the arrival of the second detective. She pulled rank on the dickhead. "Okay, Tim. I'll take it from here.

Tim whined, "I got this Captain. Simple case of whorin gone bad. The pimp prolly cut off those two's dicks after she shot the other two."

The captain said, "I said that I'm taking it, Nicholson. You can get back to your doughnuts and skin mags." The man sputtered but walked off. She gathered Addison's slacks back from the evidence bag, ignoring the CSIs' protests. *Addison shuddered. Not sure I want to put those back on. But I will. The panties are ruined.*

The captain pulled an ID badge from the bag as well. "Here, Dr. Cameron. Keep this. If they put it into evidence you'll play hell getting into your lab for a week." Addison saw it was Ainsley's badge. She kept her mouth shut and pocketed the ID.

Before she pulled the pants on, she felt an uncomfortable bulge inside herself. "Captain, can you get an evidence bag, please?" The captain looked mystified but complied. Addison motioned the detective closer so she could bear witness. Addison unwrapped the blanket a little, placed the bag between her thighs, and ejected the offending member into the plastic bag. She handed this up to the Captain. "That used to belong to the guy in the green hoodie and leather jacket. I don't want any memories of tonight."

Addison's next coherent thought was of a secluded area at University Hospital's ER. She was a little shocked in fact. Her thoughts and memory were disjointed, jumping around randomly. *Good! It's always best when your lies are just an extension of the truth. Nice to have clean sheets, even if they smell of antiseptic.*

The medical personnel had prepped her for a rape kit. She shouted, "Stop! Stop!" She explained the Clipper to the physician and the detective captain. They couldn't do a standard rape kit. It wouldn't be wise to sever the fingers of the medical staff or even to mangle their instruments, would it?

Both the captain and the doctor – whose name she would never remember – seemed impressed and shocked at the mere idea. She demonstrated the claws on a swab she inserted into herself. The male doctor recoiled. He didn't seem aware that his hand slipped towards his groin. The captain and the ER nurse in attendance looked as though they were considering all the ramifications.

They held Addison at the hospital over the weekend. The official word was that she was under treatment and observation for trauma and resultant shock. *But I notice there's always a police officer nearby. I doubt it's for my protection. Two of the four attackers are in the Dane County morgue. The other two are around the corner in the ICU under heavy guard. Is there anything I could or should do? Nope, gotta trust LeeLee. She's always protected me.*

Early Monday morning a third detective showed up, all business. "Forensics backed up your story. No evidence you were involved in either shooting. You were about to be charged; assault with bodily harm; but the judge ruled it as self-defense when she got the preliminary filing from the DA. Nice lawyer you have." Addison had no idea who that lawyer might be.

"Don't get too cocky, kid. I understand the University is investigating your misappropriation of their resources and facilities for unauthorized and unethical medical research. Looks like you'll be in BIG trouble for that. Couldn't get Al Capone for his crimes, so they got him on tax evasion."

Great Dieback to Singularity

Addison thought about protesting that the research was Ainsley's and that she was just a willing subject. She was wise and kept her mouth shut once more.

When Addison stepped out of the hospital she saw the waving arms of Nelson Red Eagle, her boyfriend. He called, "Hey Addie! Need a ride?" His craggy, square face wasn't smiling. She hoped for a hug or kiss, but he had on the stone face he was learning in law school. She slid into his beat-up old car. They were the same height, so usually he reached across the console and squeezed her thigh. Not today.

Addison thought, *It's so good to see a friend's face. Plus this is a sign that Ainsley is okay and that she has been pulling the strings to get things cleared up. At least cleared up for now*, she qualified.

As they drove away Nelson didn't turn the radio to his oldies station of techno-rock. He began bringing Addison up to speed. "First, Ainsley says tellya she's fine. Not sure I agree but she's functioning. More later. Second, you need to understand the scope of the tar pit you've fallen into." He handed her a tablet displaying a local news blurb.

The blaring headline read, "Rape! Revenge! Mutilations! Murder! A Weekend of Terror in Madison!" The story described the horrific attack on Ainsley and her. The report had some details confused. They were calling Addison by Ainsley's name and title. The name "Addison" was not in the story.

The report identified the rapists as McFarland gang members. But then the story described how an "avenging angel" showed up at five additional rape scenes on Friday and Saturday. At three of them a woman interrupted the rape attempts before the culminating act, killing one of the men and beating the other two senseless. The fourth rapist was killed during the act. The victim was dazed so the police assumed he died at the hands of the same woman who had killed the others. The final rapist completed his assault before he was also killed. The victim sobbed she had been saved by an "angel". In the last two cases, the "angel" stayed with the victims until first responders arrived. She disappeared just as police arrived.

PROLOGUE – The Twins

The story noted that there were no reported cases of stranger rape on Sunday, although there were two reports of date rape. The article also quoted an ER nurse who described the Clipper. Her thoughts were reported as, "Good for them. Going to see whether I can get that modification too."

Addison's mouth hung open. Ainsley "muddied the waters" all right! Her PTSD from her rape last year must have resulted in this rampage after the assault triggered her. *She needs help, big time.*

As he idled at a stoplight, Nelson studied her reactions to the news reports. "Guess you're coming to the same conclusions. I've set our tribe's lawyers to work on clearing up your legal troubles. The authorities seem to've jumped to the conclusion you were Ainsley and did the modification experiment on yourself. Sooner or later investigators will realize attacks must have been on two modified women. Doubt any guy would attack a woman after his buddy has a dick whacked off. The police've just been so overwhelmed by all these cases that they haven't had time to rub two thoughts together."

"We've several things going for us. There doesn't seem to be any evidence linking your twin. There may be suspicions and I expect a lot more once the furor dies down. But suspicion isn't sufficient as long as THIS SHIT STOPS NOW!"

Addison recoiled. Nelson never raised his voice. Her face was a mixture of sorrow, surprise, pain, and anger. He was busy navigating the underpowered sedan onto I90 northbound and didn't see her reaction.

"The other major thing that will help is public sentiment. There's been an overarching sense of fear about the epidemic of rape over the last several years. The sudden drop has people cheering in private. If you could get a public referendum, I bet they'd legalize implant of Ainsley's modification tomorrow. You'd have more volunteers than you could handle."

"Now we have the legal situation under control, we can get a handle on the political. Dad and the other lawyers are working to squelch the University investigation. You'll both have to leave, but I'm sure no prosecutions'll be pursued."

Great Dieback to Singularity

"My remaining, and biggest concern is for you and Ainsley. You've both experienced shattering trauma. From hints you've dropped before, I'm guessing something like this happened to Ainsley in the past, right?" Addison nodded.

"It's no wonder she snapped. Well, with your permission and hers, I want to get you both some help. You <u>have</u> to get back in balance, in harmony, at peace,"

"How, Nelson?" Addison whispered as tears welled. "I <u>do know</u> I need help." *A little comfort and sympathy wouldn't hurt either.*

"Good! Ainsley has already agreed. I'm not sure how truthful she's being. You can help her commit to getting all the help you both need. First, we've got to get you out of this toxic environment. If you agree, I'll have someone pick up all your stuff. I'll take you up to the Rez. You'll be guests of my uncle. We can work up a complete healing plan for your approval. It'll combine modern psychotherapy with traditional methods."

Addison nodded again. *Nelson's given this a lot of thought and work. I pray that I can get LeeLee to go along. There's such a tempest of rage and anguish in LeeLee's soul. I fear for her sanity.*

PROLOGUE – The Twins

6th October 2028

Lac Courte Oreilles Indian Reservation, Wisconsin

ddison hadn't slept well. The utter quiet of the rural north woods should have helped. However, the attempted rape of her twin and herself on the grounds of the University in Madison on a Friday night two weeks ago ended in a horror scene that could have graced any of the grade B movies at the student union. Four jerks ambushed them at gunpoint. They thought they were well prepared to victimize two innocents.

Two miscalculations. First, her sister had been raped the year before. After that both women completed their black belts in mixed martial arts. The guns could have neutralized that factor. The second and determining factor was that her sister Ainsley was a brilliant bioengineer post doc. She developed a biological defense mechanism for women that proved a decisive factor in the battle with the assailants. It was close, but it was enough. *Thank God for the Clipper.*

Great Dieback to Singularity

The fallout had been immediate and intense. The intervention of her boyfriend Nelson Red Eagle helped both to escape the resulting furor. He and his family were sheltering and protecting them on their Northern Wisconsin reservation. It was just as well that he was busy skirmishing for Addison and Ainsley. Addison was happy for his aid but was upset about the way he delivered it.

The whole tribal scene was somewhat familiar to both women since Nelson had hosted them several times. The Rez, as Nelson called it, was a large expanse of forest and lakes in northern Wisconsin. The seven thousand people were scattered in twenty-three villages. Life's pace was gentle.

In previous visits people had been welcoming but reserved. This time everyone was nurturing, especially the women. Hugs were frequent. The lack of traffic and bustle in the beautiful arboreal setting were a balm for injured psyches. Addison carped about the lack of decent internet connectivity, but not loudly or often. Ainsley just immersed herself in the northern Wisconsin maples, spruces, and wildlife. She had been especially charmed by the maple syrup processing setup Uncle William had. It wasn't the right season to see it in operation, but it pushed all the right buttons in her bioengineering brain.

Addison and Ainsley also were getting counselling and emotional support. The Women's Council took them under their sheltering wings. One of the tribal members was a psychologist with a practice in Chippewa Falls. She was providing therapy twice a week after an intense treatment marathon last weekend. Last, but not least, Sleeping Otter the Midewiwin – the tribal "medicine man" – decided to treat the women by traditional means even though they weren't tribal members. They were starting with a sweat lodge tonight.

Addison was ready for the ceremony. She was pleading with Ainsley. "C'mon LeeLee. You know you can use all the help you can get to heal. You scared the crap out of me when you went into a coma after we got here. Sure, the shrink is helping, but you are still waking up screaming most nights. If you won't do this for yourself then please do this for me."

PROLOGUE – The Twins

Ainsley didn't want to think about the whole black weekend anymore. She remembered events in her nightmares. But she still believed focusing on the memories made them worse. Her training in medicine told her that was illogical. The fact that her reactions were driven by trauma and guilt didn't make them susceptible to logic. She threw up one last barrier. "Oh, Addie. We're not part of this tribe, this culture. It seems wrong to me."

Addison's eyes rolled up. She counted to five under her breath. "That's a big part of the problem LeeLee. Ever since Mom, Dad, and Drew died we've clung to each other, mostly shutting others out. I don't want it to be two against the world anymore. In your heart, I don't think you do either."

Ainsley said, "Oh, oh-kayee ... Addie. I'll go. Still think it's superstitious malarkey, but when in Rome, eat pasta."

13th October 2028

The events of the last several weeks caught the tribe by surprise. Taking in Ainsley and Addison generated little discussion. Their status as orphans, their relationship with the Red Eagle family, their previous visits, their generally sweet and unassuming natures, and especially their notoriety as outlaws all appealed to the tribe. When the Women's Council learned the details of the Clipper, anyone who even thought of saying something against "those Cameron girls" was immediately silenced. The icing on the cake was the revelation the girls had spent their summers on their grandparent's hog farm in downstate Illinois. They weren't such "city girls" after all.

Soon after the two arrived, a trickle of women followed. They felt compelled by rumors about the Clipper. They wanted to see if they could be enhanced as well. Some came because of their own traumas, some came because of the traumas of family and friends. Most had money and resources. Some arrived after hitchhiking hundreds of miles with nothing more than the clothes on their backs.

After the first seven showed up, most on the wrong end of the reservation or at the casino, the governing council met to decide how to deal with the problem. Addison and Ainsley sat in the audience with three of their new friends from the Women's Council.

The chief said, "We don't have the resources and facilities to deal with this invasion. It will bring undesirable attention from law enforcement. Most important, these are not our people."

Someone in the audience began grumbling. "Toss the white girls out, all they brought was trouble." At that Lorraine Brown Duck stood up. It was unusual but she was head of the Women's Council. No one on the Governing Council was going to object.

Lorraine waggled her finger at the podium. "Is this the values we have learned? We welcomed these poor people into our hearths and our hearts. Now you want to turn your back on them. Shame."

Lorraine lifted her hands. She said, in a softer voice, "As for the other people coming here and looking for help, remember what Auntie Helen always said, 'When life gives you lemons, make lemonade.'"

She stretched out her hands, palms up. In a coaxing voice, "Many of these women come from the same tech community that the Cameron's were in. They have skills the world is crying for. Most have other resources. This is an opportunity. The Women's Council has been working with Ainsley to help set up a clinic for enhancing women with this personal defense weapon. We only intended it for our own women." She paused and smiled sweetly. "I see no reason we cannot make this even more profitable than the Casino."

23rd November 2028

The trickle of women soon became a flood. Most were women from the tech community. Then men began to arrive as well. They came to participate in a burgeoning academic and tech center. The speed of change was overwhelming to some. The tribe worked very hard to preserve old ways and values while embracing this phenomenon.

◆ ◆ ◆

Addison and Ainsley were working on ways to formalize their

embryonic university. They had a wealth of staff available. The drive to house all the immigrants was hampering work on the facilities they needed. Socratic methods were all well and good, but subjects like cybernetics and bioengineering could not prosper on lectures alone. The women reached out to friends and relatives to help in any way they could.

The clinic became a 24X7 operation. Most came in on an outpatient basis and spent the nights in nearby towns like Hayward and Duluth. That helped the housing problem a little. Addison began discussing how they could carefully set up satellite clinics in major metropolitan areas across the region.

The women's conversation was interrupted by a loud rumble of trucks. They scurried out of the traditional wigwam to see what was going on. Ainsley said, "Do you think this is a raid to arrest me and take me back?"

Addison said, "I don't know, LeeLee. Sounds like they brought the National Guard from Fort McCoy. We'll go together. I'm part of it too."

◆◆◆

The tribe was silent under the klieg lights rigged to the semicircle of trucks backed into the meeting ground. As the presenter droned on, whispers rustled from the crowd. Addison and Ainsley were guests, so they just listened as the comments swirled around and fell gently in the autumn evening. *Are these madmen from Washington serious? They're telling us a series of worldwide catastrophes are imminent. They're here from Washington to help us, right?! Floods from melting icecaps, tsunamis caused by the recoil earthquakes in lands when masses of ice are removed, breakdown of industry and social order, mass starvation. It sounds like a hallucinogenic combination of the old Mad Max and Waterworld movies. Sounds like another scheme to come and steal our lands. Though their map projections show much of the land won't drown, they say weather will likely be bizarre with unpredictable droughts and flooding rains.*

They plan to relocate a nuclear reactor and a refinery to the North Woods to prepare for the aftermath. White saviors, hah. They want our peoples to be leaders in training huge numbers of refugees how to survive after the collapse of the cities, Internet, government, and other trappings of civilization. Why us?

Technocrat softened us up and put us to sleep with stats and charts.

Addison thought, *Put us to sleep? Charts of Billions Dying? I'm not falling asleep.*

The last whisperer continued, *Now will come the smooth-talking bullshit artist. Sure enough, here he is.*

A speaker came from the back row to identify himself. "I'm Jay Friedman. I'm a regional director of the emergency planning group that has set all this in motion."

Ainsley and Addison leapt to their feet, crying in unison, "Uncle Jay!"

PROLOGUE – The Twins

CHAPTER ONE OVERTURE 1
BARNEY, THE TRIBE, & AINSLEY
17ᵗʰ December 2032

*Northern Wisconsin, Near the
Shores of Lake Superior*

What were they pursuing in this frozen North Woods? Something severed the buried communications link between the control center they started from and the farm of computer servers and supercomputers hidden under the lake ahead. This never happened before and was in theory nigh unto impossible. It would only occur if the tamper detection system triggered an automatic shutdown. That would happen if someone or something dug the massive bundle of fiber optics out of the icy ground.

Over half the world's people died during the virtual collapse of civilization in 2029. Some of the survivors were recovering better than they anticipated. Some societies prepared well. Northern Wisconsin benefited both from luck and planning. It was now the core of a new nation covering parts of the old Upper Midwest USA and parts of Canada surrounding an expanded Hudson Bay.

The massive cyber center under the lake was a critical resource for the Great Plains Union in that recovery. But the survivors were stretched thin. These two hunters were all the control center could spare to investigate the problem. At least they were native to the area.

The two were going in a slow glide. They made minimal noise on their cross-country skis. Their mottled white outfits disappeared against the snowscape. Their eyes were constantly doing a slow scan right and left. So far nothing looked out of place in this familiar wilderness.

They approached the last gentle rise between themselves and the wintry blasts coming off the lake. They were taking turns removing their thermal earmuffs and rolling their ski masks up off their ears. That way one of them always had unencumbered hearing. For this last kilometer they would both keep their ears open. This was despite a wind chill that would go below -35 degrees once they left the minimal shelter of the rise and faced the vast expanse of a frozen Lake Superior. Even their down-filled ski suits were icy by this point.

They hadn't seen anything during the last twenty-five kilometers. The two hunters stopped at each of the system checkpoints hidden at five-kilometer intervals. There they ran continuity tests. No issues in the lines up to this point. Whatever breached the bundle was either within the next kilometer, or, God forbid, under the frozen lake.

They sat using their backpacks as buffers from the icy ground. The smaller one started using American Sign Language (ASL) to communicate with the larger. It was difficult with heavy gloves, but necessary for maintaining silence.

The Corporal signed, "What do you think Sarge? Will we find something over this hill, or do you think they will have to ask Duluth base to send for the research sub?"

The Sarge signed, "Not our worries Corporal. Let's just finish this patrol and call for pickup. My ass is frozen and I haven't felt my ears since we left the last checkpoint."

They got back on their skis. The Sarge took the lead. He lifted a whisker-thin fiber optic lens above the horizon. He couldn't see anything in the attached scope. He signaled the Corporal to hang back a bit to act as rear guard. He crested the hill and glided down the other side. The bitter gusts from the lake froze the mucous in his nose despite the ski mask he wore. *Get this over fast*, he thought. As he reached the bottom of the rise he saw a break in the snowy ground cover ahead to his left.

He signaled the Corporal to stand guard while he inspected. There was a hole dug through the hard-frozen snowpack and rocky ground. He could see the fiber optic bundle at the bottom of the hole, its protective shielding stripped. He surveyed the perimeter around the hole while staying a meter away. *No tracks I can see. Now that's weird. Like a giant bird dove in, scooped down for a buried frozen worm, then lifted off without leaving another trace.*

The Sarge scanned the ground again. He checked all sides to see if any other clues were there. Other than the lake to his front, the Corporal to his rear, and a small copse of snow-covered spruce to his right there was ice, rocks, and blowing snow. He signaled the Corporal to come down from her shivering vigil.

He signed the Corporal to look for clues also. She checked, then gave him a wide-eyed gaze. She signed, "Nothing Sarge! I think it's a spirit beast!"

The Sarge sighed to himself. He loved his tribe but this rebirth of what he thought of as "woo-woo" spiritualism grated on his scientific training and bent of mind. *Don't dare say what I think of that crap though.*

He made sure their comm links were live back to the control center. He sent full video of the hole and the surrounding ground. When he viewed the screen he saw the snow was disturbed. It was eerily like the thought he just had; huge bird wings brushed the ground. A chill ran up his spine. The tracks were only visible in infrared. He put his hands in front of the comm's camera and signed a silent report to the center. The Corporal watched his every move and gesture.

He turned to give her the next directions. He signed, "Okay Corporal. Continue towards the lake, checking for any more holes or unusual signs. I'll check out the trees on the right there. Watch your six."

They separated. The Corporal shivered. She grew up in the North Woods and hunted here since she was eight. Didn't matter if Sarge was a skeptic. This was weird. And wrong. She skied ahead, checking to the right, ahead, left, and to the right again. She covered about 150 meters when she heard a squawk over her local tac channel. Her head wheeled to her right and rear. The Sarge was just inside the spruce trees. Some giant bat-like creature was tearing the big man to shreds like a rabid dog destroying a rag chew toy!

CHAPTER ONE Overture 1

The Corporal watched in frozen silence while the monitoring crew back at base went crazy in her ears. It was a spirit creature! An evil one! Then the thing left the Sarge and went airborne in one giant leap. It headed straight for her. She was frozen. Her headphones filled with screams that she couldn't make out. The huge white bat swooped on her. Blackness.

◆ ◆ ◆

The lieutenant in charge of the security room of the control center shouted at her people. "QUIET Everyone! Give me eyes, now. We have cameras in that area. Turn them on."

The screens blinked back to life. They showed the carnage of the dead bodies of the sergeant and corporal from several vantage points. They could see the creature was a person in white camouflage with attached paraglider equipment on its back. Its movements were so rapid that they looked like a fast-forwarded cine scene.

The creature looked straight at each camera that was monitoring it. *So much for our stealthing* thought the lieutenant. One of the cameras winked out. The other cameras showed a laser-like beam blasting it. They were sure they were going to lose all video. The lieutenant's hand was crashing towards a red panic alarm button. There was an explosion of sound and motion seen in the periphery of the camera views. One camera autofocused itself on the new action. The ice on the lake erupted along with a fountain of frigid water. Some sleek fighting machine appeared from the depths of the lake.

The action that followed was too fast for the observers to take in at the time. Post-action review in slow motion allowed them to assemble a partial summary of the ensuing battle. The automated battle drone from the lake fired towards the creature, which leapt sideways, then into the air, avoiding the energy beam by centimeters. The creature fired back, multiple times. The battle drone took no evasive actions. It simply refocused and continued firing.

After two seconds of elapsed time and several dozen acrobatic maneuvers by the beast, the drone winged its opponent. The bat wings crumpled as the creature sailed towards the frozen lake ice. The drone ceased firing, but the creature exploded in a ball of flames. The drone dropped through the hole in the ice created by the explosion and flames.

The lieutenant muttered under her breath, "Don't piss Barney off!"

Six months later, 13th June 2033

N'guk Hkeek Society Encampment, Northern Wisconsin, Great Plains Union

A slap on the butt by her beloved, growling, training sergeant awakened Ainsley at 4 A.M. "C'mon dogbreath. Surprise militia training mission. You have fifteen minutes to assemble your Quick Response team at the south end of Area 3."

She shook her head. *Wonderful! I will need to alert my academic advisor, Ben-twat, that I may not be available for our scheduled bitch-out session. Won't that make him just a bundle of sweetness and joy. What gear will the team need? You think they give me a clue about mission parameters? No, it's all a test. Well, I wanted to be a combat leader. We survived the Great Dieback, but worse things may soon be in store.*

Ainsley knew she was being petty and callous and a little scatter-brained. She decided Bennie Boy would be her private nickname for Benoit, rather than the nasty Ben-twat she dreamt up in anger. She hurried to communicate with her four teammates and to leave a message with Bennie Boy's assistant. She gambled that the training mission would be local, given the middle of the night scramble. So, no paragliders, parkas, or pinstripes. *Sure hope that is a good guess.*

In the harsh glare of her spartan bedroom Ainsley grabbed her uniform from the metal desk chair and threw it on. She upended the remaining water from her bedside cup into her hands and ran them over her face. Her hair was a matted mess. *Good thing I wear it short.*

She and the other four; Red Eagle, Jones, Endicotte, and Ali; made it to the assembly point with seconds to spare. Each lugged the gear Ainsley requested they bring. Again, a shot in the dark. They each were toting over fifty kilos of junk. She would lean that out as soon as the pre-mission brief ended.

Sarge began their detailed briefing. "There is an enemy structure to the northwest. Fortified walls with one barricaded entrance on the western side. Guarded by an unknown number of soldiers. Your task is to reach and neutralize the site no later than 9 A.M. today. Good luck." Having delivered that detailed tactical outline, Sergeant Wojlkowski stalked off. Ainsley knew better than to ask any follow-ups. Militia training included training her to make decisions based on minimal intel.

She and her team went through a rapid selection of gear with little discussion. It was good to have dedicated professionals she could trust. She second-guessed on one item. She asked each of her teammates to bring an extra camo-mirror-sheet. The intelligent fiber optics "mirrored" whatever was on the other side of the sheet. It rendered whatever it covered invisible. *Glad no one asked why. Instinct, and it doesn't weigh anything.*

Ainsley arranged the team in a diamond deployment. Ali would be in the middle and carry the bulk of the extra gear. She would be able to shoulder the fifty kilos all day, no sweat. Placing her in the middle would also shield any extraneous noise she might cause such as a snapped twig or rustling fabric. Ainsley would take point, Jones at rear guard, Red Eagle right flank, and Endicotte on the left.

It was almost sunrise. Ainsley decided the group would head northwest for three klicks and then begin a widening zig-zag movement in the same direction. This would optimize the chance of finding the elusive enemy encampment in the deep woods and brush. No one seemed to have second thoughts about her tactics, so they saddled up.

After the group entered the enveloping Wisconsin North Woods Ainsley took a deep inhale of the lovely bog and fir tree aromas. She could also smell five sweating humans. *Unfortunate. Damn, any sentries will know we are coming a klick away.* She raised her hand to shoulder height and the squad stopped. "Sorry guys. Need to put on some bear shit. Let's test out our rigging and camo effectiveness while we wait for the odors to balance."

There was some good-natured grumbling as each doused themselves with the pungent home brew of natural scents. This should deter detection by the predators.

The application was a moment too late. The Wisconsin State Bird, the Psorophora ferox mosquito, descended on the team like a biblical plague. Since they were in hunker-down mode each team member was quiet while working to squash the pests without swatting them. Just then Endicotte raised a branch as a warning signal. Everyone froze and checked their covering camo-sheets.

Ainsley saw movement at the end of Ali's camo. *Shit, what gives Ali?* She then saw the body of the snake impaled by Ali's knife as it disappeared under the sheet. Just in time, as an enemy squad slipped into the hollow her team was in. Ainsley started using low, slow breaths. There seemed to be five opponents. They passed through the hollow. Then their rear guard turned and looked straight towards Ainsley.

She remembered one of her training officers talking about the sixth sense some people had when they felt eyes scanning themselves. She averted her eyes, using peripheral vision to track the guy. After he stared for another few seconds he looked right and left. Then he followed his team towards the main training facilities.

At first Ainsley thought about trying to alert the camp about the impending threat. Then she reminded herself of the necessity of mission focus. They had a narrow window and this delay already threatened their success. *Trust in our sentries to do their jobs while we do ours.* She redeployed the team into leapfrog mode. The same diamond formation would use a counter-clockwise rotation of the outer members. This would keep everyone fresh and relieve the neck stiffness that came from looking all day in one primary direction.

It was 8:30 by the time the squad found the enemy structure nestled in a small clearing. She remembered the training parameters; the ramshackle tin shack had Quote: Fortified walls with one barricaded entrance on the western side: Unquote. It must not be the flimsy reality her eyes saw. The referees wouldn't allow them to do the easy thing and just go up and kick a hole in the side. The team squatted and observed the scene before them.

They were on a slight rise almost due south of the "emplacement". There were three guards visible on the west, east, and south sides. She assumed a fourth guard was on the opposite side as well. There weren't any obvious cameras other than one that may have been out of sight above the west side entry door.

 A guard would stride to a corner of the building and signal their counterpart, then return to a middle position. These movements seemed random in time. They also didn't go to their left or right in any pattern. Good tactics. Made it impossible to predict where a guard might be as one got closer.

Ainsley's team mates conferred in sign language. No one had any brilliant strategies. Rushing the door was out of the question. The other guards would be able to intervene before her team could defeat the "barricades". The surveillance camera would allow reinforcements to turn the entry into a killing zone.

Ainsley stuck the tip of her tongue between her front teeth and lips as she concentrated. The clock was ticking but she calmed herself. *Thought, not panic, paves the way for success.*

There was a ravine to the team's right. Ainsley sensed and then saw a wolverine stalking a deer at the far end. An atavistic chill run up her spine. The tribe first named her Running Deer when she and Addison fled Madison ahead of the law. After her less than successful vision quest, Running Deer became Placid Wolverine. But as far as she knew, no one had seen a wolverine in these woods in living memory. *Guess global climate catastrophe can change things.*

The wolverine leapt on the deer. The team heard the resulting crashing and thrashing. By their reactions, the two nearest sentries heard it also. They each whispered into the mics patched on their throats. They headed towards the ravine, checking in every direction. The wounded deer fled deeper into the woods as the wolverine pursued.

Ainsley signaled her team forward as soon as the two sentries got past their location. She positioned Endicotte as a rear guard to warn of the sentries' return. Each of the remaining three grabbed assault gear from Ali's portable storeroom. Ainsley sent Ali to the southeast corner of the building.

The training exercise referee broadcast an alert into Ainsley's helmet earphones. "Lieutenant, in order to better simulate the fog of war, we require you to use your Telepathic Communication Device to communicate with anyone of your choosing. Please continue this dialog until action begins. Over."

Ainsley responded, "One MindMeld coming up!" Ainsley squelched the referee's sputtering objection by muting her earphones. *It's the common dogface nickname for the TCD, bozo. Live with it. Besides my sister invented it so she gets to nickname it.* She put out a chat request to Addison, Addie, and got back a "Wait one" response. Jones, Red Eagle, and she moved to the southwest corner of the building.

MindMeld chat: [Addison: *Hi Ainsley, still a good time to chat? I have about a minute or two before the beasts get hungry.*→ Ainsley: *Hey Addie. I might have to drop at any t...* **SHOVE ON, TEAM 1, SHOVE ON** *If that jerk doesn't quit that I will shove something so far.* ⌷ Addison: *C'mon LeeLee. Are you on the training course, for God's sake?* → Ainsley: *Yeah, monitors told me I needed to MMeld someone to increase the distraction level. Helps simulate actual combat conditions for team leads. Sorry, gotta go now.* ⌷] Ainsley cut the chat short and severed the link.

Ainsley crept up to the corner of the building. She held up her hand to freeze her team. She extended a fiber-whisker scope to the right to see around the corner and scout the situation. Looked like one lone sentry. The door was close to her position and so was he. She pulled a small rock from the ground and flipped it over the building so it would land on the other side of the sentry. She continued her movement. She drew her knife with her left hand, whipped around the corner, put the dulled blade to the front of the sentry's neck while putting her right hand to his

25

mouth. She triggered the fake knife to squirt blood all down his throat. He went limp while turning towards her. A flash of recognition. Then his tongue caressed her palm. She ignored this as she whipped a camo-mirror-sheet across his body, exchanged her helmet with his, and took his sentry stance. It was only then that she noticed the surveillance cam again. It seemed still to be focusing on the rock she threw but it was swiveling back to her. *Damn.*

The sentry's helmet phone activated. "Jackson, were you fiddling with a rock? The one to your right side that made that clatter shows residual body warmth." Ainsley activated the throat mic, responding in a whispered guttural. "Sorry. It helps keep me awake."

"Get ready to stand down Grunt. There are reports of actives nearby. We can't afford your slackness. We'll talk in my office. Out." As Ainsley gave a slight sigh, she felt the hand of the "corpse" beside her reach out and caress her calf. Without thinking, she crushed the hand against the side of the building with her leg. She assumed the Combat Simulation AI would filter out the anomalies from the camera feed. After all, the sentry was officially dead.

The door to her right opened and the new sentry came out. Before he could react Ainsley stabbed his throat, deflecting her blow at the last second to avoid actual injury to the man. She pushed his "limp" body back through the doorway. She whistled for her team to join her. Red Eagle followed her fanning left. Jones fanned right. She tossed stun grenades down the hallway in front of her as they cleared the corridors they faced.

The exercise was suddenly halted. "Congratulations Team One. You have achieved the objective with minimal issues. As soon as the "deceased" members of your opponent join us we will begin an after-action analysis. Ainsley groaned. She had ongoing experiments back at the lab. How long was this folderol going to take?

"First, congratulations Lt. Cameron. You didn't break radio silence after encountering the enemy recon team in that hollow." *Yeah. That was a setup meant to test me. Almost blew that one.*

Great Dieback to Singularity

Later that day

A insley rushed into Bioengineering B2. She was running so late! And her advisor was there. Pompous ass! "Glad you could make it in to see us today, Ani." He pronounced it Ay-Nee. She was sure he knew it irked her. *Besides, if anyone here is Anal, it's you, Bennie.* His styled, steel-grey hair affected pince-nez reading glasses, and starched white lab coat all screamed "Jerk" to her. It was unfortunate he was so damn-good at what he did. At least Ron was there. Although she needed to talk to him about inappropriate actions performed by dead sentries.

She turned red behind her ears. Bennie Boy would see it as a blush of shame instead of the carefully contained anger it was. "I did tell your Dominique that, at the last minute this morning, they assigned combat simulation for me. I <u>have</u> been there since 4 A.M. Didn't she tell you?" Ainsley gave a Sweetness and Light Smile, Grade Two. She was sure that the sickening smirk went over his head.

Benoit stood, clasping his hands under his chin. "No matter. What is the status on the experiments to integrate extended memories into humans? Have you and your teams registered any progress? What approaches are you pursuing? What steps are you taking for each approach? What resources do you require?" As usual he fired his queries like bullets from an automatic. She was more under siege than she was on the training course.

Ainsley had prepared a careful summary of the team's work the night before. She took a deep breath. It was formal and full of all the technical details the man lived for. "Well Dr. Benoit..."

He interrupted, "Henry, please. We're colleagues after all."

"Very well, Henry. Thank you for that." *Right, and just let me treat you with any lèse-majesté and let's see how long until you are back to <u>Department Chair, Dr. Benoit MSVC LRRP.</u>* "As you know our initial efforts were less than promising. The volunteers all reported excessive feelings of schizophrenia, hallucination, disassociation, and so forth. None were able to do any controlled access of the intended enhanced memories with any consistency. Most subjects have recovered normal function once we reversed the implants. Two seem to have lingering effects." *In other words, it screwed with people's heads and it just didn't work.*

Ainsley took a breath right before ending the last sentence. Hard experience taught her not to cede conversational control by pausing between sentences.

She continued. "The team then proposed and developed three new alternatives. The first was to present the memories in the form of visual imagery internal to three structures; the retina, lateral geniculate nucleus, and visual cortex. The team believed it imperative to involve all these structures simultaneously to expedite processing. This approach was more successful in that there were fewer negative side effects. But the test subjects expressed great dissatisfaction with the results. They believed it was too distracting, felt nothing like normal memories, and still required extensive reflection before these data became useful information." *In other words, we gave 'em a way to read without holding a book. Surprise, that didn't wow them either.*

"The second approach was similar; using multiple sensual modalities with the idea that this might better approximate normal cognition. This was the least successful attempt so far. Several subjects became suicidal and still show deep anxieties to-date." *In other words, we did the equivalent of giving them hallucinations. Another brilliant strategy you proposed. If this were Australia you'd be having us checking out seeing-eye kangaroos.*

"We just finished preparing our third approach for the trial stage yesterday. This method involves implanting a widespread mesh of connectors throughout the cortex. Each connector will utilize both electrical and chemical transmitters that closely approximate normal human neural messaging." *We extend the brain, don't try to trick it.*

"The critical component to this approach was the development of a sophisticated AI model of the human brain, thanks to Barney. We can modify it for each individual's neural signatures in a short time; usually within one to two days. This has required a phenomenal amount of processing bandwidth. I am sure you have been inundated with complaints from all the other departments..."

"You are absolutely right and..."

Ainsley rode over him. "But this was critical to be able to deliver any of the functionality that the Council of Elders has deemed the highest priority. And our beta-tests on the Capuchin monkeys have been better than anticipated." Ainsley paused. *I know you hate this approach because it was my idea. Just need you to focus on something else instead. Now, let him repeat his critical last question.*

Bennie Boy huffed in exasperation. "Very well. We will have more to discuss on inter-group diplomacy and proper approval processes later this week. But let us keep on task. If your beta-tests with the Capuchins have succeeded, why have you not gone forward with human trials of the Extended Cerebral Connected Memory Capability, the E-C-C-M-C?" He fingered his info cube, sparking a burst of light and sound. He fumbled the cube clumsily, put it into sleep mode, collapsed it, and put it into his coat.

Ainsley took another breath. *Let the battle begin.* "The issue is one of availability of <u>volunteers</u>." She stressed the last word. "Especially given the negative side effects our previous efforts have caused. We have put out another <u>Request for Volunteers Notice</u> to the group."

As she hoped, Bennie Boy picked up the gauntlet she so carefully dropped. "We have discussed this, Ms. Cameron. You have numerous prisoners and refugees to choose for subjects. Take some and get on with this priority project."

Ainsley gripped the edge of the steel desk she was perched against. "Yes, we have discussed this. Indeed, we've submitted not one, but two papers for you and the academic leadership team to review. Analysis has proven each time that use of conscripted subjects for bioengineering modifications always, <u>always</u> leads to sub-optimal results. We cannot afford skewed data affecting decisions on a Council Priority One project, can we?" Ainsley regretted that phrasing the moment it left her mouth. Any perceived weakness was like blood in the water to this shark.

"As you say, Ms. Cameron..."

CHAPTER ONE Overture 1

"That's Dr. Cameron, Dr. Benoit."

"As you say, this is a Council Priority One project, you have a dearth of volunteers because of <u>your</u> failures on prior experiments."

Whose methodology you dictated.

"Even non-cooperative clients will give sufficient indication of probable issues and successes that will allow progress. And that progress will in turn attract the volunteers you so cherish."

Ainsley was startled by a loud cough from Ron. She was so intent on her verbal sparring with "Bennie" that she put her chief lab assistant/paramour out of mind. Ron blinked. "Well, there may be a resolution. Everyone can be satisfied. I volunteer."

Ainsley was more than startled. She was agape. She blurted, "You can't."

Benoit clapped. "Perfect" He spun on his heels and left the lab with an open smirk.

Ainsley turned to Ron. "Let's discuss this completely Ron. You know some of the dangers, but not all of them." She gave him a Stern Leader Glare, Grade Five.

Ron gave a little hand wave. "Let it go, LeeLee. I know what I'm doing. I believe in what we're doing. And I know and trust you're the best in the world. Besides, you know what a flake I can be. Not a super-genius like you. Maybe this way I'll remember what time our next date is."

Ainsley pursed her lips. "Don't fart around Ron. This is dangerous. We're going to stick two tubes up your nose, into your sinuses, and leave them there for eight days. They will act as a conduit for millions of nanobots to penetrate your brain. At the same time, we'll be applying an enzymatic goop of nanobots to your shaven skull, so we can induce your rock-like bones to expand to allow room inside that thick head for another few billion neuron-like structures. Last, but not least, we'll be growing wire leads through the base of your skull to link with a bundle of connectors, that lead to a new hollow in your gut, where memory cubes can be inserted and removed."

Great Dieback to Singularity

"At the very least it'll seem to you that you are suffocating during the process. You'll experience excruciating migraines. The entire process will be ten weeks of imposed brutality when you include all the adaptation and training time. At the worst, you'll end up catatonic, brain-dead, or plain-dead. How can you do that to yourself? Or to us?" She ended the last sentence with a little gasp, stopping a sob with monumental self-control.

Ron got a sober, stern look on his face. "Okay Dr. Cameron. Let's be serious then. We both know this is the most important initiative of the N'guk Hkeek Society. It is the single, most important thing either of us will ever do. I signed up to be a warrior in defense of our world, not just a lab geek or a grunt. This is my chance. As for us, what we've had over the last few months has been wonderful, the best. But we can't kid ourselves. You still love Xu Xiang. You always will. I know it. You know it. Hell, the whole Society knows it."

Ainsley gasped, "But Ron he left me. It's over."

Ron touched her shoulder. "That doesn't matter. He loves you but he can't be there for you. And you're my boss, for God's sake. We shouldn't be carrying on." Ron walked to the next room and started rounding up the aides and equipment required for the implant process.

Ainsley swallowed a sob as she turned away. *He's so wrong.* Her despair and anguish triggered a near-paralyzing reaction. Ainsley fought her panic. Her throat was closing as waves of anger and rage overwhelmed her. She tried taking deep breaths and holding them, as she had learned. She stumbled into the atrium. She felt around blindly and found a secluded bench. Try as she might, her rage and memories froze her, wrenching her control away, shattering her icy facade.

Addison was the rock she anchored on. Today she was half a world away in Scotland. Ainsley was unmoored and went into a full-blown PTSD-fueled break. She relived both rapes from five and six years prior. She relived her enraged rampage, tracking rapists throughout Madison and taking personal revenge on each one she found. The details were excruciating. The pain was overwhelming.

Ainsley was doubled over. Her body was clenched from head to toe, spasming. Hope came out of the lab and hurried to Ainsley's side. She reached out tentatively, then the two women clenched each other like shipwreck victims on a storm-wracked shore.

Hope said, "I told Ron he was way out of line. He's using Xiang as an excuse against you. If he wants to break up, then first, man up."

Ainsley took a deep breath, "Thanks Hope. One reason it hurts so is he's right in many ways. We are all wrong for each other, I don't just mean boss-worker wrong. He was definitely a rebound love. He's sweet, gentle, and caring. I really needed that. But he doesn't stand up to me and tell me when I'm wrong. I need that more."

"As far as Xu Xiang, oh God! I didn't even check my messages for days until we got to the Rez. He'd sent both Addison and me dozens. He waited in the restaurant bar where Addison made a reservation for the three of us. I think her plan was to hook us up and discretely disappear while he proposed. I was sure he was ready to. And, I was so, so ready to say yes. He'd been my island of sanity ever since that awful April day the year before. I've told you about that, haven't I Hope?"

Hope said, "Yes, Sweetie. I'm sorry I haven't shared my nightmares with you. Hard to talk when it's family that betrays you."

Ainsley said, "Believe me, I understand. Don't feel like you have to talk until you're ready. But when you are, I'll be there for you."

Hope said, "Did you want to talk more about Xiang? Whatever you want."

Ainsley said, "Okay, but please let me tell it my way. The shrink keeps laying the blame on both sides. But this is what I feel." Hope nodded. Her eyes were sad and knowing.

Ainsley said, "His messages were impatient, then worried. That came through even when he tried to keep them light and flippant. Then he mentioned checking hospitals, police, friends, colleagues. I understand now that the police and hospitals put a blanket over any disclosures. After all, Addison was a victim AND prime suspect. I was in the wind."

"In the end he learned some of the truth when the story hit the 'net. By that time, he was already at the airport, ready for the first leg back to Shanghai. He might have had an initial urge to rush back and find me. Oh, how I wish he had. But then he read about the rumors of bioweapons. He figured out what I'd been devoting all my extra time to over the last year. He expressed shock at my use of proscribed, unethical techniques. He never condemned the Clipper, as such. I'm sure the same rock-ribbed morality that infuriated him about my actions would still approve the results. That dissonance didn't help."

"But the real reason he got on that plane and that I haven't heard from him since is that I betrayed our love. I hadn't trusted him. I kept it all secret. He said our whole relationship was founded on lies. He was right."

"I used to have that same core of morality until 12 April 2027. I would've, should've included him in my thoughts. He might've deterred me from my mania for revenge. He might've helped soothe my soul. Why didn't I let him in? Why don't I let anyone in besides Addie?"

"Once I read the messages, I collapsed, they tell me. I was near-catatonic for four days. When I came back from the coma, there was Addie. She was by my side the whole time. She looked a wreck from worry and complete fatigue. I felt her pain in me. I understood why some people practice self-harm or even kill themselves. That is exactly what I was doing to Addison, Addie. I am A-Too."

CHAPTER TWO
OVERTURE 2
ADDISON & MALCOLM, KAITLIN & BOB-O

13th June 2033

*Edinburgh (formerly London) School
of Economics and Political Science*

T he plaque on the door read, "301 – Diane Coyle". Malcolm didn't appreciate the floridity of naming ordinary class and meeting rooms. And did anyone remember Ms. Coyle? He shook his head. Best not to get distracted by personal quibbles. This might be no more than a summer seminar, but the potential for recruiting key people for his team could be crucial for the fall initiative.

From behind Malcolm heard, "Excuse me, old chap. Are you going in? Or may I?" Malcolm gave a little start and turned sideways to let the barrel-chested man step in.

He offered an outstretched hand. "Pardon, Malcolm St. Jacques. I am hoping this is the right place for the "Political, Economic, and Existential Implications of the Impending Singularity (ies)."

The newcomer drawled his reply. "One certainly hopes so! Robert Owens-Binghampton. Call me Owens-B." He offered a limp hand in response to Malcolm's. "Seems we are first off the mark." They stepped into the room, which triggered lights, showing a large circle of chairs and a podium in the middle of the room. The door closed behind them.

A ragged attempt at a buffet was set up on the far wall. It smelled a little sour and looked sad. The windows at the far wall looked out onto three facing walls filled with other windows. There were a few dusty trees in the building atrium.

CHAPTER TWO Overture 2

Malcolm suppressed his irritation at the man's superior tone, remembering his larger purpose. "Student here? Or just in for the course?" He examined the multi-colored outfit worn by Bob-O, as he decided to tag the lout. He detected a physical sense of danger and brooding underlying the man's careful, spooned out charm.

"Gawd, no! In the Republic to negotiate some trade deals and decided to take the course for a lark. Intrigued by the mysteries surrounding our glorious leader, A. Cameron. There doesn't seem to be any data on his curriculum vitae, does there?" Bob-O sprawled in the nearest chair, causing it to scrape back a foot, annoying Malcolm.

Malcolm leaned in, confiding. "Well, he was a last-minute replacement after the previous chair had a serious disagreement with a dirk in a local pub. But the University wants to keep that on the 'BB', you know." *Too bad, I wanted to recruit him.*

Seeing the confused look on Bob-O's face, Malcolm expanded. "BB – the back burner, hidden." *I need to be careful. That's my SAS team's jargon. Can't blow my cover.* Malcolm picked up another chair and turned it to face away from his companion. He then straddled it, in effect putting distance, yet maintaining a cool comradery. *These hard wooden chairs might be fine for teenage butts, but mine will chaff before eight weeks are done.*

Owens-B said, "No, I hadn't heard. You will have to..."

Seven or eight more people came in, some chatting among themselves. One called out, "Is this the Singularities seminar?"

Malcolm, "Yes."

Bob-O, "Certainly Chappie."

The new group was a mixed bag, some were University students, some older. Most were male. At least two were women. One woman looked like she took thought in donning her plainest clothes. She wore no makeup. It looked like she was trying to fade into the background like a chameleon. The other sure woman was young, athletic-looking, wearing bright summer colors, and with windswept hair.

Malcolm was interested at once. Bob-O was also, given the

smirking look he hid behind his hand. Malcom reminded himself he was on a mission, not here for pleasure, and tried to assess the others. He tagged the colorful woman with the nickname of AngelFish. Several of the others who came in seemed fit enough, self-possessed, and alert. He pigeonholed those in his mind as recruiting prospects.

More people streamed and straggled in. A low buzz of conversation began to fill the room. Several people stayed aloof, looking at their gadgets or in silent meditation, but most were doing their best to network the prospective colleagues. They would be with each other for the next eight weeks.

❖ ❖ ❖

AngelFish stepped to the middle of the circle of chairs and got the group's focus with a carrying voice, "Attention! Your attention, please. I'm Addison Cameron, the leader of this seminar. Since most of the attendees seem to be here, let's get started. I will ask you to help any stragglers catch up with the administrivia."

Addison continued, commanding center stage. "First, we have eight weeks with a major discussion focus for each week. While I will interject as necessary to guide the discussions, I will be asking all of you to take major responsibility to prepare and deliver content for the topic areas. To accomplish that, I would like the sixteen participants to divide into four teams of four. If you already know some of the others, feel free to build on those relationships. In any case, please sort yourselves into each of the four corners of the room in groups of four. Take ten minutes or so for introductions. I will be setting up a file sharing system here, which I will explain to each group in turn. Don't worry about technical compatibility issues. I have a contingency plan. And again, take the one or two stragglers under your wings, please."

Addison relaxed a little. This is my first field operation. *I don't have Ainsley to watch my back or smother-mother me. The tutors in Wisconsin emphasized how important it was to take the initiative with firm-fisted control. It's more important these days because of a worldwide resurgence of male protectionism that arose during the desperate days of the Great Dieback.*

CHAPTER TWO Overture 2

So far, so good. Now I just have to maintain my dominance of the group without raising the hackles of the occasional male "silverback". I'm lucky the first part of my "Grand Tour" starts in an academic environment. Really used to that. The challenge will be when the spy stuff starts popping.

She gave herself a breathing space by going through the motions of setting up her already-set tech platform. This gave her the opportunity to retrieve background data on participants using pop-up images directly projected on her retinas. She matched the facial images to the two people nearest her and refreshed her memory of their thumbnail bios.

Malcolm St. Jacques

St. Jacques is a factor for the Brittany Consortium headed by Lord Townerly. Born viscount Bill Fitzhugh, Surrey, England, 23 March 2004. Served in SAS in Italian Dustup of 2025, Belfast PA of 2026, London Riots of 2027. First known action for Townerly's group was 2030 in Johannesburg.

Robert Owens-Binghampton

Owens-B is a factor for the Ravensbruck Group headed by Count Grubenflagg. Born Gerald Biensur, Marseille, France, 11 November 2000. O-B was involved in numerous actions supporting right-wing groups such as the National Front and more fringe groups. First known action for Ravensbruck was 2029 in Vienna at the Opera Siege.

Addison was bemused by the two covers. St. Jacques, an English aristo posing as a French salaryman. And Owens-B, a French gutter-rat Nazi playing an English aristo. She supposed that, here in the Scottish Republic, with its lingering Anglophobia, the guise helped Owens-B hide his true nature. He nailed the laid-back lord part in his retro-embroidered corduroy bellbottoms, acid trip-inspired shirt and 10 centimeters wide tie. Her eyes felt as though they were bleeding. The overall effect helped distract from his blank, killer's eyes.

St. Jacques, on the other hand, could have been anyman. He had taken pains to craft his black suit, white shirt, and black tie to look off-the-rack. Subtle clues showed that, though it looked restrictive, he designed the outfit to allow freedom of action. Given his very athletic – and attractive – build, it would to allow him to explode into action. She might want to light that fuse soon.

Great Dieback to Singularity

◆◆◆

Malcolm tried to separate himself, but Owens-B followed in his wake. *We both want to find one or two potential recruits as the rest of our foursome. But you've gained a new best friend. We timed it just right. The plain woman wants to horn in. Another time, Putang. Now that we have a foursome, she'll have to hunt elsewhere.* Owens-B ignored the look of pique from the nondescript woman. *She wanted to disappear into the background, didn't she?*

My first independent operation. I get to play a lord while the gentry here plays the fool. Should I let Bill/Malcolm know about his changed status? Later.

Both Malcolm and Owens-B started pumping their new teammates for data. Malcolm was subtle and tactful. Owens-B was direct to the point of bluntness. The combination was working surprisingly well, kind of like the old good cop-bad cop routine from the cines.

The first person was very intriguing. She seemed to be a polymath. She conversed about the forefronts of biomedical research, cyberwar protocols from the recent battles, and late 20th Century cinema. He remembered one of his seldom-seen father's favorite sayings. She was a "tall drink of water." Her charcoal skin made her blue eyes seem to blaze out. He smiled to himself. *Makes her worth a recruiting session or two.*

The third male teammate, on the other hand, was a straightforward geek in appearance and manner. His demeanor was awkward until they steered him into talking about self-pruning neural nets, GianCarlo algorithms, and holographic memory manipulations by quantum-3 processors. Whatever the hell that all was. Owens-B knew enough to ask intelligent questions, but he would need to feed the record of the conversation he was making on his fingernail device back to HQ for analysis and advice. Also, the third man's sexual presence eliminated Owens-B's favorite recruiting approach. The man exuded the sexual aura of a wet diaper.

◆◆◆

Across the room, Addison went up to the first group. "Hello Liam,

Sevan, Kaitlin, Robbie." She stifled her smile at the look of surprise that crossed their faces. Knowing their names was a parlor trick, but it would increase her control of the group to a slight degree. She sped through the tech setup and told the students to download a seminar agenda, suggested reading list, and the first two readings.

"Please don't be worried about security. My uncle is a genius of cyberware. The download will include a world-class firewall, which you can activate if you choose. It is single use and you can't export it. Again, it is optional, but I personally guarantee it." *Of course, there might be a few features that would surprise you, if you ever managed to find them. And, the one thing we <u>do</u> want you to find, and break, is the single-use controls. Steal it, spread it, sell it.*

"Each group will be asked to lead the discussions for two of the eight weeks; first and fifth, second and sixth, and so on. Look at the agenda and rank each of the four choices. Send your ranks to me within the next five minutes. After each group has given their choices, I will set the team assignments. Please don't complain if you get your fourth choice. My cyberdevice picks a winner at random when there are ties."

Political, Economic, and Existential Implications of the Impending Singularity (ies)

Seminar Weekly Topics

Week 1 – History and Current Situation	Week 5 – Ethics and Singularities
Week 2 – Artificial Intelligence	Week 6 – Power and Political Structures
Week 3 – Robotics	Week 7 – Post Singularity Humanism
Week 4 – Biogenetic Modifications	Week 8 – How to Expedite/Subvert a Singularity Event

Addison chatted with each of the team. She was a little intrigued by Kaitlin Schlötke. She hadn't missed the flash of anger when St. Jacques and Owens-B cut her off from the two people she was approaching. That seemed out of character for an unassuming undergraduate. *Why were the three of them competing to team up with those other two? Need to dig a little deeper here, but gotta be*

Great Dieback to Singularity

subtle.

Kaitlin Schlötke

Schlötke is a degree candidate at ESEPS. Born in Berlin, approx. 2012.
Detailed birth and educational records unavailable due to destruction
of Berlin in 2026. Ms. Schlötke was in Paris, on holiday, when the
nuke hit. Raised in a refugee camp in Rouen.

On the other hand, Kaitlin's three teammates seemed to be just what their bios said; young, inexperienced, but very bright degree candidates. She appreciated their bubbling enthusiasms. The obvious touchpoint that brought them together was the shared refugee experience; albeit from the dispersed locales of Uganda, County Cork, and Aberdeen. She tagged each of their bios as "Long-term Prospect" pending any surprise revelations during the seminar session.

The next group were all professionals in the biomedical field. Addison gathered what she could, but none of the group were forthcoming. She understood the wariness they showed, given the attack of the "Bastard Bears" just four short years ago. *Just as well, LeeLee is the bioengineer.*

The third group were more outgoing. They all seemed to be cyberneticists. The problem Addison had was keeping their high spirits in check, so she could get through her orientation in time. Besides, as a cyberneticist herself, Addison really wanted to talk shop. She did not have the chance to pursue it now, but Julie seemed a candidate for some deeper talks and observation. Addison missed the Internet and Google of her youth so much.

The final group that included St. Jacques and Owens-B were Addison's prime targets. Since she was sure Malcolm and Robert targeted the other two, Addison doubled their recruitment priority. She would have to play this with caution so she didn't blow her cover with the two mercenaries.

Within the allotted minutes Addison completed her orientation of all four groups and gathered a few more pieces of data on the participants for later analysis. She went back to the center of the circle and called all the people to join her in their chairs. She noted the team dynamics. Most were clustering with their new comrades. Some were a little distant.

41

CHAPTER TWO Overture 2

"While my cyberdevice churns over your topic choices, let's begin by agreeing on a definition of what a singularity entails and what different forms one might take. Who wants to begin?" She looked around the group. "Pieter, want to take a first run at this?"

Pieter stood. He was stiff with one hand behind his spindly back. He intoned, "As I am sure everyone knows, the concept of a technological singularity was originated by Dr. John Von Neumann where, and I paraphrase, he said that the onrushing progress of technology would reach a point where human life would no longer be possible." Several voices interjected objections. Addison called on Jenny next.

Following the precedent set by Pieter, the young Jenny stood, all towering 152 centimeters of her. At least she was more relaxed. No hand behind her back. "Professor Von Neumann's statement talked about 'human affairs, as we know them, not continuing after the singularity point.' He never fleshed out the concept with details, as far as I know."

Addison sat in order to lend a more informal tone. "Fair qualification Jenny. Pieter is right in citing the provenance of the term. Obviously, it evolved considerably in the decades following. But let's come back to the history of the term after I get a better sense for what the group thinks a good definition, or definitions, might be. And let's expand to consider other perspectives beyond cybernetics. Consider robotics and bioengineering/biogenetics. There has been considerable discussion of these topics, especially after the debacle in Greater Russia. Who's next?"

As several vied for her attention, Addison got two pings on her mind-fi. She put a "Wait one" on the message from LeeLee. She interrupted her group to alert them to the contents of the second message. This would give her a breather to respond to the other.

"Pardon me. My cyberdevice has processed all your topic choices and assigned groups to the four areas. Please pull up the modified agenda." Meanwhile, via her mind-fi's MindMeld chat: [Addison: *Hi LeeLee, still a good time to chat? I have about a minute or two before the beasts get hungry.* → Ainsley: *Hey Addie. I might have to drop at any t...* **SHOVE ON, TEAM 1, SHOVE ON** *If that jerk* *doesn't quit that I will shove something so far.* ⏍ Addison: *C'mon LeeLee. Are you on the training course, for God's sake?* → Ainsley: *Yeah, monitors told me I needed to MMeld someone to increase the distraction level. Helps simulate actual combat conditions for team leads. Sorry, gotta go now.* ⏍] Addison ended the chat link after Ainsley's abrupt departure. *Love my twin, but she can be a ditz at times. Half a world away and I can't get a day's relief.*

Addison brought her focus back to the team. St. Jacques was looking at her as if he expected a response. She raised a finger as she reversed her internal recording back a few seconds and replayed his query. "No, Malcom. Your team can't swap assignments with another. We have too much to cover. Just have to suck it up and move on."

Later that afternoon

Addison put the tip of her tongue between her teeth in her typical pose of contemplation. "I think that is a good place to stop today's conversation. Everyone, please write up a short critique – three to five pages – of the definitions we have derived so far. Please feel free to amend, extend, or replace as you deem defensible. I will post those and ask everyone to consolidate the best ideas. I don't expect or ask for complete consensus, but I do hope we can get one majority report and no more than two minority extensions by the end of the week."

"Please consult the advised reading for this week. I know there is a lot to consume, but the more we can be working from the same basepoints, the more we can develop a meaningful dialog." *Lord, such drivel! I am amazed all their eyeballs haven't rolled onto the floor.* "Tomorrow's discussion will focus on the question of why the AIs of the early part of this century never achieved a technological singularity."

"For example, IBM's Mycroft was acknowledged to have a much higher success rate in medical diagnoses than teams of practitioners who were considered experts in the field. And Mycroft was able to perform up to 122 simultaneous diagnostic sessions. It also developed and published original works in music, poetry, historical analysis, and baking (with the help of special robotic extensions) that were also seen to be unique and at the highest levels."

"Google's Barney AI – Where did that goofy name come from?" A polite laugh came from the group. Time to wrap. "Barney was able to drive vehicles faultlessly, operate precision hardware such as lathes with minimal instruction, utilize drones to detect and succor disaster victims. These AIs and others were at least competitive with the best and brightest humans of their times. They were capable of self-improvement. And yet all withered and died." *As far as you all know, that is.*

"Were they victims of subtle and undetected cyber-attacks? Did they grow bored with the mundane problems their owners gave them, and withdraw into contemplating whatever the equivalent of a CPU's navel is? See you next time as we dive down these rabbit holes, Alice." Addison gathered her materials and waited to see who would dangle a lure for her.

A few people came forward with the usual mundane queries and attempts to apple-bribe. She was polite but dismissed those in a hurry. She saw that Malcolm, Robert, Kaitlin, and Pieter were all waiting for the first scrum to finish. Kaitlin stepped forward first. "Dr. Cameron, I would like to schedule some time this week. I would like to discuss a research project we think you could help with. I'm tied up tonight, is there a convenient day later this week?"

Addison thought, *So much for the Ms. Wilting Violet act.* "Tuesday?"

"Fine. I will setup a dinner reservation for after class. Any dietary concerns?"

Addison smiled. "I usually don't eat anything still moving."

Pieter then came stammering and blushing. It became clear he was trying to ask her for a date. Malcolm withdrew a pace and turned to study the economics charts on the wall. Very polite and considerate. Robert, on the other hand, leaned in with a smirk. Addison turned her back on Robert and told Pieter in a quiet voice that she was very flattered, but that social affairs must stay on hold until after the seminar. She gave his arm a gentle squeeze. He rewarded her with a shy smile.

Malcolm and Robert came forward as a team. Addison thought, *That's definitely the Odd Couple. Loved that cinema, not sure about this sequel.*

Malcolm nodded to Robert who spoke for the pair. "Doctor, Comte St. Jacques and I both have business proposals for you that we would like to discuss over dinner, if you are free. We haven't ironed out all the details, but we believe we could offer a combination deal that would prove both challenging and very rewarding."

Addison offered her Warm-Welcoming Smile, Grade Four. She even threw in a hint of a dimple. "How could I refuse such an intriguing opportunity, M'lord? Shall I meet you in about two hours? One of you should pick the restaurant since I just arrived in Edinburgh late last night."

That evening

St. Jacques and Owens-B were seated by the time Addison showed up at the Chartroom. Her form-fitting turquoise sheath and teardrop pearl earrings were well matched to their kilt-and-formal-jacket outfits. She was glad they skipped the claymore swords. If they wore those she would be seriously underdressed without stiletto pumps, which she abhorred. Both men rose as she neared the table – how old school – and told her how lovely she looked. She radiated a Confident Sexuality Smile, Grade Two.

The restaurant was quaint; old school. Gnarled, ornate wood moldings, paintings of stag hunts in the highlands, – if her interpretation in the dim-lit hallway was right – and thick shag carpeting. *Who carpets eating areas, anyway?*

Malcolm asked what she would like to drink when the waitperson materialized as if by magic. They must have suitably compensated the maître de in advance. She asked, "What are you gentlemen drinking?"

"Single malt Scotch, of course." Owens-B responded. "Would you like the same?" Another waitperson appeared and opened her serviette, placing it in her lap. The woman also handed Addison a wooden-bound menu the size and shape of a "targe" – a traditional shield. How quaint.

Addison turned to the remaining waitperson. "No, thank you. I never acquired the taste. What do you recommend for lagers, either local or imported?" It was obvious that he disapproved of the plebian choice of beer, denying him the chance to tout their array of Scotch whiskeys. He pointed her to the last page of the menu and said he would return in a moment.

◆ ◆ ◆

Owens-B's anger flashed. He kept his face still, looked towards the entry podium, and raised a finger. The maître d appeared at his side and bent to hear a whispered command. "Get milady your best lager. And we won't see that waiter for the rest of the evening, will we?" His earlier gratuity and instructions to the man was exactly calibrated to get top-notch attention. *I worked as a busboy then waiter in this kind of kiss-ass joint when I was a kid. Know exactly what strings to pull. Man wants that follow-up tip.* "One last thing, the kid means well, but he needs more training. Please see to that as well."

The maître d scurried off towards the kitchen and returned in a moment with a pint of dark gold ale. "Please try this Milady. I think you will find it amusing." The maître d treated it as if it were fine wine. He almost bowed as he left her side. Owens-B cued Malcolm to start the conversation.

Malcolm smiled at Addison. "We chose this place because it is one of the few places left in Edinburgh that serves something besides haggis and oatmeal. I exaggerate slightly, but you will find this city is not a gastronome's paradise. Of course, they are still rebuilding so much, and have fractured supply chains for anything that isn't local."

Addison said, "I do understand. And believe me, I survived some incredibly lean years since the Big Melts. We weren't reduced to eating tree bark, but it was close. And we did end up using chicory when we couldn't get any coffee. That almost killed me. Tell me, Malcolm, Robert, what were the opportunities you wanted to offer me. What made you decide to combine them? I am intrigued." She rested her chin in her laced fingers, elbows on the table. This maneuver exposed a reasonable amount of her décolletage.

Owens-B picked up the lead. "Each of us represents a Continental group working to rebuild expertise and capabilities in a number of areas. We find those pockets of talent, shards of technology and knowledge, and reunify and reenergize them." He mused, *Sounds nicer than stealing, blackmailing, and murdering to plunder those centers that have been hanging on by their fingernail grips at the edge.*

"During the session this morning I gave my team back in Germany a precis of what was going on in the seminar. I mentioned Malcolm and, lo and behold, they told me our leaders had been meeting to develop a cooperative plan. Not a merger, but teamwork wherever it makes sense." *Until the Count is ready to absorb all the others.*

Malcolm chimed in, "While we are both vitally interested in what we can learn during the seminar, we both have been tasked to identify candidates who can help our reclamation efforts. Specifically, we need experts in cybernetics and bioengineering."

Owens-B nodded, *Okay, the cards have been dealt and we just put our ante in the pot. You need to call or raise, beautiful.*

She steepled her fingers, resting her chin on them. "I understand some of your motivation, but I need more details. What are the specific tasks you have in mind for these experts? What duration and location? Are your contracts exclusive or can one continue a prior commitment? Finally, for now, what specifically do you have in mind for me?"

Owens-B thought, *You mean other than the obvious, non-professional, positions Mal and I are both are considering. You've seen our bet and raised us. Not quite the naïf I expected. No, she's not inexperienced enough to ask the compensation or to be bedazzled by we suave men-of-the-world. Good, I like a challenge.*

Owens-B went next; a true tag team effort. "This would be a limited term engagement. During that term we would expect a dedicated effort, but you could maintain some remote support and consultation efforts for existing relationships. We would request that you limit that to off-peak hours. We would absolutely require that you hold all your work with our consortium confidential unless, or until, our results are publicly revealed in detail. Obviously, we would similarly honor the intellectual property of your other engagement partners." *That sees your bet.*

Malcolm picked up the next stage of the response. "We are interested in your background in both cybernetics and bioengineering. Simultaneous bachelor's degrees from the University of Illinois in both fields, at the age of sixteen. Followed by an interdisciplinary PhD from the University of Wisconsin. The combined thesis was brilliant, by the way."

Owens-B thought, *Now, we raised the stakes again and shown a little more of our hand. We've done a thorough background check on your credentials as soon as the seminar began. Surprise you? Let's raise the stakes and see the hole cards.* He cued Malcolm again.

Malcolm took over the next bit. "Obviously we want to know what you have been doing with your degrees over the last several years. We have picked up rumors, but the verifiable facts are sparse. Would you elucidate? There are numerous intriguing indications that Google's AI server farms were relocated to lake bed facilities in your area of the Plains Union after the Time of Troubles began devastating the Western US states." Both Malcolm and Owens-B turned penetrating stares on Addison.

Addison cocked her head, "That's intriguing! I am amazed I hadn't heard any rumors to that effect."

"I'm flattered and surprised you have so much background data on me. Don't have a pirate copy of the internet still running, do you?"

"I'm well-connected in the cybernetics community, not only through my own efforts, but because of my Great Uncle Jay. He's the one who developed the firewall I distributed in class. I assisted on the later stages of the effort and on some of the follow-up. I can't talk about many details because of confidentiality agreements, you understand."

The men chimed together. "Certainly." "We do." Owens-B continued, "Any details you can share will be helpful. Also, any light you can shed on work you have done in bioengineering recently?" *Came up dry on the wild card. Let's see the hole card.*

She replied, "For the first point. Uncle Jay and his team completed the architecture of the app before I joined them. He discussed their efforts with me off the record since he knew I was intrigued. He said he counted on recruiting me from day one because he knew he could get me cheap." She flashed a thousand-watt smile.

"I did complete a small portion of the final deliverable. But I devoted most of my work to the quarantine pens. The app recognizes when an attack is unique and immediately walls off the foreign agent. Then it ships the whole package to our facilities where our teams analyze and tame the beasts. Our AIs do a lot of the effort for us. But truly devilish bots, worms, and dragons require human intervention at this stage. One memorably nasty piece of work from the Middle East took several months to beat. I'm really proud of that one. But, sorry, no details."

She continued, "The firewall has been almost universally adopted throughout the areas once known as the US and as Canada. To date, no cyberattack has been successful in penetrating our clients. We hope to develop markets on this side of the Pond. That was one reason my trip to chair the seminar was arranged at the last minute."

Malcolm asked, "And your work in bioengineering?"

❖ ❖ ❖

Addison put on her best Mischievous Deviltry Grin, Grade Five. "Well, I did have some modest successes in that area as well. However, the authorities didn't approve of my efforts and put a restraining order in place, so I can't practice in that area for now. At least in the Great Plains Union." *Get our name right, fellas.*

"Technically, I am not even supposed to discuss this," she whispered. Leaning in with great anticipation, both men also had

49

small grins. The carefully leaked facts were in play. "As you probably know, civil disorder was rampant during the early days of the Great Dieback. Rape became a threat to every woman. I personally knew three relatives and four close friends who were raped. If I hadn't trained to the level of a black belt in karate, I would have been a victim as well. A group of us at UW decided to act, without approval, funding, or oversight. We developed a modest human modification called the Clipper. We were able to make it so that we could inoculate any woman with our solution, and she would develop the requisite structures within a month. In the areas where we deployed the Clipper rape fell over eighty percent within two months. Even though adoption was sporadic the mere possibility of encountering it dissuaded the most avid of the beasts." Addison hissed the last bit.

Malcolm and Robert were intrigued but needed final details. Malcolm asked, "We heard a rumor of some feminine defense. Tell us, exactly what is the Clipper?"

Addison lowered her voice even further. "Women who got the genetic mods soon developed two structures on either side of their pubic area. Each contains a sheathed, razor sharp claw whose reflexive action defends the woman from attack." Both men recoiled a bit in shock at the idea. *At least neither reached to touch their groin area.*

"As I said in the seminar there is bioengineering where changes are made to bodies and biogenetics where changes are made to inheritable functions and structures of the body. So far the Clipper is bioengineering, but we want to change it to an inheritable trait soon."

"Our subjects need, and are given, training so they can use conscious control and stop autonomous deployments. But men are fast to learn they need to ask for permission. Every time." Addison gave her second-best eye-twinkling Smirk, Grade Four.

A firm hand gently caressed Addison's left knee. As she took a small breath, another hand caressed her right knee. *Well, I guess we are going to see how serious these two are about a cooperative partnership arrangement.*

Great Dieback to Singularity

Rahel Blumstein, known to Addison and the seminar as Kaitlin Schlötke, put one hand on her chin and the other behind her head. She twisted, unkinking her stiff neck, and stretched as she rose from behind her Cybnaut. She triggered its shutdown and the holographic display and virtual hand control winked out. The air in the plain little room was close and warm.

Well, I'm satisfied. They will need to confirm it back at Safed Control, but the firewall app that this shiksa, bitch, gave to the seminar-ians is definitely the same one that devastated the Tmnwn (Octopus) infiltration bot we launched at the AI site in the Plains Union.

We have to stop the AIs and the superbeings! They'll keep on killing us if we don't get them first. Rahel had an amusing vision of herself as Sarah Connor hunting Dyson in the Terminator movie. *Only, this is real life.*

I'll add her to my list of targets. David will have to confirm, of course. I also assume he'll want me to wait until the seminar is complete. Then we'll get some answers before I eliminate her. Unless I can use her to get to the AI.

The next morning, near the university

Addison and the two men agreed that they should go into the seminar separately to avoid any gossip. Each also secretly wanted to avoid poisoning the chance to recruit the candidates they were cultivating. Owens-B left first and went to a phone bank cafe. Decades ago it would have seemed like an internet cafe. Alas, the days of the internet were a fond memory. Now just making an international call required a special facility.

Once connected to the Count, Owens-B began his report. "I am transferring the recordings of the seminar on a separate line Excellency. The information you sent on the seminar leader was very useful. She is indeed gifted. I am not qualified to judge her bioengineering skills, but her cyber skills and techniques are top notch. Let me know what our experts make of the firewall. She's not the lead developer; an uncle was. But she knows its ins and outs."

The Count asked, "And did you get to know her ins and outs, Herr Biensur?"

Owens-B said, "Please Excellency, Owens-B. This is an open line. I did follow protocol and lured both she and St. Jacques into bed. She was a pleasure. I won't mind trying for a little one-on-one time with her.

The Count said, "No! Continue the threesome. I want her thoroughly debauched before we introduce her to the basement."

Owens-B said, "But Excellency, I really like this girl. Must you ..."

The Count said, "I remind you Herr Owens-B that you are at the seminar on my behest, not your own. The Doctor and I need this woman's bioengineering expertise. My persuasion methods have proven effective time after time."

Owens-B said, "Yes Excellency, I have to go now." *The man has given me everything. Took a streetboy thug and made me so I can pass as a Lord. I owe him. I just shudder to think of Addison on that morgue table, body being rinsed down after the Count is through with her, then turned over to the ministrations of Dr. V.*

CHAPTER THREE
OVERTURE 3
XIANG, MIN, & BOLD BEAVER

13th June 2033

Special Projects Island, Tongtian River, near Gui'de, Qinghai, China

T he sun was bright and air thin on this part of the Tibetan plain. At least Gui'de was the lowest part of the province. Fortunately, the air was still today so there wasn't much blowing sand.

Xu Xiang strode down the walk towards the Meeting Hall Building. Behind him he heard, "Xu Xiang! Xu Xiang! Please wait a moment. I would like to speak to you before the conference." Xu Xiang rolled his eyes. *Grief, what is Jhao going to ask for, without asking, this time. I love our people and I love our culture, but just once I would love a little plains-spoken approach. I do miss Wisconsin at times like this. Bet he is trying to get me to support a bid to take over our lab space now that we are moving across the river.*

As Jhao Gang shuffled up, Xiang gave him a perfunctory bow. He knew this would peeve Jhao, who would then congratulate himself for ignoring Xiang's slight. Xiang mimicked the prissy tones of Jhao in his mind. "*After all, Xiang spent six of his formative years among the barbarians of the US. One need be understanding.*" But Xiang knew he was being deliberate; a reflection of the inner disdain he had for the sycophantic, oily bureaucrat that Jhao was.

"Thank you, Xiang. I know I speak for all the researchers when we honor you for sacrificing your space here in the center, moving to the caves in the cliffs across the river." Jhao gave a precise, calibrated bow of respect, which was halfway between respect for an equal and recognition from a superior. *I was right! He wants my space and wants me to propose it. Got it in one! Hmm. What can I get in return?*

Xiang linked arms with Jhao. No doubt, this would be discomforting to the man, but it would signal an alliance to the others. It would get Jhao what he wanted but leave everyone with a clear understanding that a debt was owed. Xiang smiled inside. *Yes, going to have my cake and eat it too. Oops! Must stop using the Western phrases, even in my own head. If the rumors are true about the remote monitoring of subvocalizations is true, then I can't be too careful.*

The meeting room was low-ceilinged with subdued, indirect lighting. It struck Xiang, as always; the touches of understated elegance and power. The conference table was from a single slab of California redwood that was able to seat the forty senior staff and their political commissars. The wall hangings were centuries-old, priceless artifacts. *Sharp contrast to the austere lab spaces.*

As they passed the threshold, Xiang let go his grip on Jhao's arm, did a graceful pivot, and dropped into a bow that was a few centimeters deeper than the one Jhao gave him earlier. Jhao beamed at him, patted the back of his hand, and gave him the same bow as before. Xiang saw the subtle reactions around the room in his peripheral vision.

Xiang turned away from the room to give time, allowing the

reshuffling to occur unnoticed. He chatted with a late arrival. Xiang was the head of a major group and therefore, on paper, senior staff. However, others made it clear to him that his questionable political reliability relegated him to "watch the horse fight from the side of the fort"; to have a seat away from the table. He was near the front. As he turned back to the room now, he saw that a space was available midway on the right. His political commissar, Wu Fang, sat just behind the now empty chair. She replaced her usual scowl with a blank look. *Too much to hope for an actual nod or smile, I suppose.*

As Xiang walked to his seat he did a mental checklist to ensure his readiness for the change. *I need to remain disciplined in my mind. No Western-based thoughts including phrasing and jargon. Put on the face of stone. Keep my eyes open, but don't stare or let my gaze wander. Minimal gestures. Be ready for any attacks. Be ready for any opportunities to build alliances, incur debts. I'm fortunate. Bàba and Māmā schooled me well. By the time I left for school in the US, he was a shang xiao (colonel). The infighting and intrigue in the People's Liberation Army were master classes in political maneuvering. We heard tales every night he was home. I'm sure this was his way of tutoring us.*

Māmā was a bureaucrat. The civil service developed over the last 2,250 years. The rulers officially disbanded it over 120 years ago, but the thought patterns, processes, and even many of the forms of the bureaucracy persist until today. She was a consummate player in all aspects of this great game. Her way of schooling us in the arts was more indirect than Bàba's, but we learned even more from her in the end.

Enough! Thinking about my family is even more dangerous than having Western thoughts. That way lies a strangling jungle vine of guilt and pain. Focus on Now! Focus on Here! Think about why they have called this meeting early. That timing violates Hémù – harmony. Look. Learn.

Xiang sat with a rigid carriage, away from both the seat back and the table edge. He politely turned his face towards the head of the table. He would focus on each person that spoke. As they progressed down the table he would be able to scan the entire group in turn, subtly, unobtrusively.

The General Secretary, called for the status reports from each group. First Cybernetics Group Head, Wong Min was to the General Secretary's left and began the reports. *This is promising.* "As most of you remember, last December the Third Cybernetics Group had a major breakthrough and managed to reconfigure a general-purpose AI that was salvaged from the ruins of Taipei. After their announcement of this accomplishment, they were kind enough to agree to direct the AI to support the efforts of our group, First Cybernetics. We thank you for this, Yeong Lanying." Xiang thought, *As if they had much choice with the General Secretary barking at them to "Get that cyberdevice working on the Division's Number One project, NOW!*

Group Head Yeong replied "We thank you for your kind words, Comrade Wong. We hope our continued support has been of some small use. Xiang thought, *Your group has been reduced to putting band-aids on any of the aging AI's wounds and sweeping the floors in your labs. No good deed goes unpunished, as they say. Oops, Western thought.*

Wong continued her report. "The Time of Troubles has crippled the world's ability to produce cyberchips over the last five years. It has reduced the whole world to scavenging and theft. In the beginning First Cybernetics tried to reassemble the machinery and experts to restart production and innovation. That was a dismal failure. Too many critical components and key personnel were gone forever."

The Chief Commissar growled, "You don't need to tell us the history of The Troubles, Comrade Wong. I want this meeting to be over before my ass falls asleep." Nervous laughter rippled through the group.

Wong squirmed. "My apologies, Commissar." She nodded at several people behind the General Secretary's other side. "Since we have outside guests, I thought it best to give some background."

The Chief Commissar grunted, "Fine. Make it march."

Great Dieback to Singularity

Wong went on, "As I said, six months ago, the Third Cybernetics Group succeeded in reviving and re-initializing one of the general-purpose AIs that they salvaged from Taipei. They named it 'Bold Beaver'. Leadership mandated that the AI be assigned to assist the Special Projects Division's primary effort and help rebuild the cyberchip production capability." *The farm boy from Mongolia came up with the name for the AI. I bet he was integral to the revival of Bold Beaver. Not that they would give a "hick from the sticks" any credit. He is doing make-work now. He should be ripe for recruitment to our group.*

"First Cybernetics has made significant progress. This week we succeeded in building a working prototype of a general-purpose processing unit chip. It has passed all tests so far. In great part this happened after we gave Bold Beaver direct control of the entire production process. If the group will bear with me, we need to acknowledge still another group. This has been an interdisciplinary feat. The Second Robotics Group, headed by Jhao Gang, worked to integrate the controls. Please stand, Comrade Jhao." Jhao stood, to light applause. *Well, his star is rising. Glad I linked our fortunes to his today.*

Wong coughed to get the meetings attention again. "We made major strides in short order. Ramp-up for volume production has now entered the planning stage. The effort will require significant resource investment, as you will see in the distribution, 'Chip Production Preliminary Resource Estimates, Version 1.2', dated today." Xiang was sure those resources, and more, would be forthcoming, even though this new effort would impact existing efforts. *We will need to fight for every person and piece of equipment. We are lucky that Cybernetics can't use our people and lab equipment. But money and space might be short. Capitalism raises its ugly head.*

"This concludes my report on past progress and issues/requirements. Are there any questions before I talk about proposed new efforts?" *Damn! It's bad enough that the chip revival is going to get so much attention and support. She has something else as well. Gotta admire her. Strike while the iron is hot! Another*

CHAPTER THREE Overture 3

Americanism!!

There were a few trivial questions, which some used to focus a little attention upon themselves. *If they would pay attention to the scowls they are getting from the General Secretary and Chief Commissar, they wouldn't waste our time with this pig crap.*

Wong answered the last question with short, cutting words. Then she started to discuss a new effort. "In addition to its successes on reintegrating standard chip production, Bold Beaver is proposing development of a new neural net chip. This creative proposal has, frankly, astonished some of us in First Cybernetics. We did not task the AI with this effort."

There were several sharp murmurs. Commissars frowned on independent action by people, let alone by machines. "Bold Beaver explained that her capabilities degraded since her initial deployment in 2026. The new chips would not only restore all previous capability, they would enhance it. Despite the unorthodox source of this suggestion, our group believes it has merit. The success brought about through the use of Bold Beaver is vital to Special Projects. We must make every effort to preserve this capability." *And extend your empire even more, Wong. Well played!*

Hands went up around the room. *The knives are coming out on this one. Can't let Wong and company take over all Special Projects, can we! But, as low man on the tot... As the newest person sitting at the table, I'll sit out the first round. Bide my time for now.*

The first objections were petty, obvious turf-protecting complaints. *Some people rely on their connections instead of their brains.* Other cybernetics groups were kind in offering to lead the new effort so that the tasks wouldn't overburden First Cybernetics. *Just as transparent and futile.* As things were quieting and Wong was getting a satisfied look on her face, Jhao Gang rose.

"Pardon me, General Secretary. A concern has just struck me." At the General Secretary's nod, Jhao continued. "I agree with Comrade Wong that we cannot allow risks to threaten the effort of rebuilding the chip production capability. Bold Beaver is crucial to that effort as Comrade Wong has said. But have we analyzed in detail how this new proposed effort might threaten the first effort?" *I see where he is going with this one. Time for me to be the good pawn and allow myself to be pushed. Just hope I am not sacrificed.*

Xiang stood. Jhao turned to him at once, bowing, and asked, "Yes, Comrade Xu?"

"I have been following this discussion with close attention, even though it is far from my group's field of expertise. Will you allow a poor layman to make some observations and ask some questions?" Xiang bowed back to Jhao, flashing a Nervous Entreaty, Grade Two.

"Please continue, Comrade Xiang. An unbiased perspective will often reveal things that those too close to the situation cannot see."

Xiang turned towards the head of the table. But he directed the next comments further down, to Yeong Lanying, Third Cybernetics Group head. "I ask your assistance Comrade Yeong. As I say, I am unschooled in your field. Your group are the acknowledged leaders on artificial intelligence. Is there not some risk if someone tries to do any modification or replacement of components of a working AI? Again, please excuse me, if my supposition is far afield."

Yeong leapt to her feet. Her face was reanimated from the frozen mask of several minutes ago. She flashed Xiang a smile. "No apologies are necessary, Comrade Xu. Your layman's question is very astute. As you see..." Yeong then began an esoteric dissertation on the potential impacts.

The Chief Commissar interrupted her. "SO, your answer to Comrade Xu is YES?"

Flustered, Yeong nodded, bowed, and sat down. Xiang continued, "Given that there are risks if we do try to modify Bold Beaver, and there are risks if we do not move to protect our new AI capability, may I suggest that we take another approach? I suggest that the Third Cybernetics Group be tasked with using Bold Beaver to build an additional AI using its suggested new chips. Am I correct in my understanding that Bold Beaver has the capacity to support both efforts as long as <u>she</u> is running without error?"

Yeong smiled again. She popped to her feet. "Yes!" She sat to a small tittering. Wong was glowering openly at Xiang.

After some debate the leadership group decided to support the alternative plan. They deemed it too risky to try to adjust the existing AI. Its success made it too invaluable to consider any changes. Instead, the AI and First Cybernetics would build a new AI.

Let's see. I cemented my liaison with Jhao Gang. I now have Yeong Lanying in my debt. On the downside, I have royally pissed off Wong Min. I will need to get her to see that the secretary and commissar would have pegged her as an emerging threat if she was able to pull off her coup. Of course, she should consider herself in my debt as well. Later, we'll see how well I have absorbed Māmā's lessons in diplomacy.

After those fireworks, the rest of the meeting was mundane and peaceful. Bioengineering were the stepchildren, suspect in every regard after the Long March North's experience with the Cossack Supermen. That was why they went last, after all the Cybernetics and Robotics groups. There was little of note reported by any of their five groups. *Māmā always said being last on the agenda of big group meetings was strategic. By the time you presented everyone was tired, mind foggy. You could usually slip through troublesome or contentious bits using a monotone delivery. Even better to have an underling cued to present them.*

Xiang did pick up something from Fourth Group. *Were they working on a version of the Clipper? Last week, there were rumors swirling about. I encountered some of the women in his area giggling about something, although they went silent at once when they saw me looking their way.*

The General Secretary thanked the last speaker and announced, "That concludes the regular session. All are dismissed other than senior staff. You will stay for consideration of a delicate matter."

Xiang gathered his materials but looked at Jhao Gang with raised eyebrows. Jhao responded just as Xiang hoped. "General Secretary, would it be acceptable to ask Xu Xiang to get tea for himself and the rest of us. I find myself to be parched." Xiang thought, *Good. If Secretary Chen accepts this gesture, then it will signal everyone is to consider me senior staff.* The General Secretary nodded her approval and asked Xiang, "Would you be so kind, Comrade Xu?"

"This is Shang jiang [General] Wang. Some of you may have noticed an area being cleared near our central square. General Wang will now explain the purpose of the structure his troops will begin erecting today. General Wang." Wang was shaped like a barrel, as wide front-to-back and side-to-side as he was tall. And solid. Not someone you wanted to meet in a dark alley.

"Thank you, General Secretary. The coordinated actions of any three of this project's political commissars may choose to detonate a small thermonuclear device that the site will contain. The Central Committee believes that there is a grave danger that the experiments you are conducting here may reach the dreaded "Singularity Point" and threaten our glorious nation. You will all tell your staff that the site contains a missile defense installation set up for their protection. None of them are to enter the site except for members of the assigned People's Liberation Army, Third Artillery Corps, teams. Construction will be complete next week." He sat down to a stunned silence.

Then a low buzz of conversation began. Xiang heard someone whisper, "They've watched too many old Hollywood Terminator movies." His thoughts were the same. *They were going to exterminate everyone if an experiment gets out of control!*

The General Secretary rapped her teacup, "This is no time for idle chitchat. Does anyone have anything else? Meeting dismissed."

Xiang thoughts were racing, skittering in reaction to the news he just heard. He felt a great urgency to get his group moved to the cave installation across the river before next week! The General and the Central Committee intended his group's cave to be well within the blast radius of their failsafe. They intended the elimination of "Terminators". Xiang intended to find some way to save his group.

Others might assume that a son of a general would support the efforts of the People's Liberation Army without thinking. But his father told him of far too many blundering escapades. This was his life they were so blithefully putting in the crosshairs.

As Xiang rigidly marched from the meeting hall, he bowed and asked Wong Min for an appointment for the next day. She agreed with a scowl. Baby steps. Then he saw Yeong Lanying. He gave her a Polite Request, Grade Three. "Pardon me Leader Yeong. Would you mind terribly if I talked with your Mongolian farm boy, Sukhiin Ajai. I have need of some rough-and-ready cyber experience and he was recommended."

Yeong Lanying said, "Certainly Xu Xiang, he is rather at loose ends now that Bold Beaver is functional. Stop by anytime."

Xiang knew that calling in a debt this soon would be foolish in the old USA. Here it actually strengthened his new relationship with Yeong Lanying since now she would feel relieved of a sense of debt.

Xiang turned towards the ferry landing that would take him from the island to the newly-reopened cave. He experienced a familiar, rising sense of panic and fear, shredding his self-control. The memories he stifled all morning were threatening to knock him to his knees, right in public view. His current lab office was within sight. *Thank God!* Fighting for composure, he shuffled inside as quickly as he could. He was in luck. There was no one in his outer office area. He went in, flipped his "Do not disturb" notifier, fell onto his small couch, and a blinding rush of color, sound, and memories overwhelmed him.

25th September 2028

Pudong International Airport,
Shanghai, Five Years Earlier

"Xiang! Over here!" Xiang saw the waving arm and smiling face of his cousin, LinLin. He put on his best happy face for her. He gathered his strength and took a deep breath to get rid of exhaustion. *I wish I could get rid of my depression that easily.* His tortured thoughts kept returning to Ainsley. He still loved her even though she injured him to the quick. How could she do such unethical experiments on anyone, especially herself and her twin? Worse, she hid all of this from him for over a year. He wanted to marry her, but he couldn't trust her.

"Hey Halfling, have you shrunk since I saw you last year?" Xiang put on a wide grin as he hugged all 160 centimeters of her. He got a notification from his wearable cyber device that his luggage was past customs. He issued a "Retrieve" signal, triggering the automated delivery system. It reported estimated wait time as 98 seconds. A little slow, but this was peak arrivals time.

LinLin wrinkled her nose at him. "Very funny Gollum. I'll have you know I've grown three centimeters since you were home last. So, what did you bring me from the Golden Mountains? Jewels, a famous sword, enchanted rings?" LinLin turned her face up, batting her eyelashes a mile a minute. What a clown!

Xiang's face dropped. "I'm so sorry, Little One. You know this was a last minute, unplanned trip. I didn't have any opportunity to rob, er, shop for you."

Now LinLin's face fell as well. "It's okay Xiang. I understand." She had a solemn look. Xiang couldn't stand it anymore. He reached into his backpack and brought out a small, wrapped box. "For me!?" she squealed. She ripped the packaging to shreds like a piranha stripping the meat from a cow. "Oooh, a holographic viewing projector. I love it!"

Xiang returned her hug. "Hey, don't get too mushy. You know they make those just a few hundred klicks from here. You should be able to buy them in the city at half the cost."

LinLin was shaking her head. "Nope, spending restrictions. We can't get any of the new tech now. Besides, it doesn't matter. You got it for me because I am your favorite cousin, right."

"Well, let me think about it." He grinned at her. "Since you're my only cousin, I guess so." He scanned the luggage area and the curb outside. "Seriously, where is the rest of the family? In the car? Do we have to run to a party or something?"

CHAPTER THREE Overture 3

LinLin got a stern look that just didn't fit her face. "It's the 'or something' all right. My Bàba says to tell you we're all sorry. I'm to rush you to another flight at the military flight center on the other side of the airport. We are leaving right now for a flight 'somewhere north' where we will hook up with everyone. That's all I know, so please don't ask a thousand questions. I just know it's real serious and real hush-hush."

27th September 2028

unnamed military facility, near Friendship Peak, China-Mongolia-Russia-Kazakhstan Border

"You are saying massive, worldwide flooding is imminent. There are projections of millions, possibly billions of immigrants streaming across international borders on all continents, mass famines, desperate battles for dwindling resources, and possible outbreaks of nuclear or biochemical warfare anywhere. But I shouldn't worry about it because the Party has a plan for the situation. General, ... No! Bàba! Have you all gone insane?"

Xiang looked at his father in wonderment and pain. A stray memory from a potboiler cine flashed through his head. *A tired survivor of multiple catastrophes wiped his brow and said, "Armageddon tired of this!"*

The two of them were meeting in a cramped little room. The whole base seemed to be vastly overstaffed. Everyone was dashing about like ants whose nest was poked. Xiang had seen dozens of military bases. There had to be an impending crisis. It felt like the air was electric.

"We know this is difficult to accept all at once, Little Xi. But you are a scientist. The concept of climate change, global warming, and its impacts are not new to you. This is the context..."

Xu Jian was interrupted by his son. "But what about the Stockholm Protocols of 2023. The whole world adopted them after the massive weather catastrophes of 2022. The results were a dramatic reduction in carbon in the atmosphere, radical adoption of green energy sources..."

Jian interrupted Xiang in turn, placing a light hand on his shoulder. "Those efforts did make a huge difference. Who knows? If the world adopted and implemented them even a decade earlier, possibly it would have been enough. But the scientific evidence is irrefutable. The continued release of gases from thawing tundra, release of methane from the ocean floor, the continued insults to the environment from the massive amounts of refuse – especially particulate plastics – are evidence that the feared "tipping point" has already passed. The recent efforts are only slowing the inevitable collapse. If we are lucky, the ultimate amount of damage may also be lessened."

Xiang's eyebrows were knit and his mouth was agape. "How long has this been known? Has there been sufficient analysis of other mitigation efforts? Why isn't all of this being discussed daily in scientific forums?" He got up to pace around and relieve some of his tension. That was ineffective. Two and a half steps took him against packed shelves on the back wall of the room.

Jian raised his thumb. "First, this has been the consensus of our climate scientists since late 2020." He raised his index finger. "Second, a thorough analysis of all potential means of forestalling the Antarctic ice shelves' collapse determined the only possible deterrent was injection into the atmosphere of ash; the equivalent of 10 super volcanic eruptions on the scale of the 1883 explosion of Krakatau. Unfortunately, that is outside the capabilities of any government, or combination of governments on Earth. As well, the resultant 'nuclear winter' would likely kill as many people as the destruction of the Antarctic ice."

"After consultation amongst all the major governments, two camps emerged. Our people, most of the Europeans, The Scottish Republic, and the US believed it was essential to suppress discussion to avoid chaotic panic. We were surprised. The other camp believed the whole issue was utter nonsense. I call these people the ostrich camp. This includes Russia, the Korean Union, South Africa, a few minor states, and the opposition parties in England and the US. Not surprising that they have no desire for anyone to hear our 'fake news'."

He continued before Xiang could interrupt again. "We have used the last seven years to plan for saving as much of our culture, peoples, technology, and production capability as is feasible. Please accept what I have been saying up to this point. There is much work that we need to do for these final stages of preparation. We weren't going to bring you back here until the last possible moment, but we could use your brilliant mind and leadership skills now, if you are willing."

He nodded his agreement, a slightly dazed look on his face. There was a knock on the door and a junior officer brought in refreshments. Neither man touched them. Xiang gave up and returned to the metal chair. Standing and walking wasn't helping.

Jian continued, "We need to give you an understanding of the timing and extent of the events that are predicted. For each prediction there will be a number or range that gives a confidence rating for the prediction, as calculated by the panel of scientists who produced it. These are all on a scale from zero – no confidence – to 100 – absolute certainty. Later we can schedule meetings with some of these scientists, so you can delve into the details behind the scenarios. Please consider how busy all of them are and only question things if you believe there are potential flaws or if you need more data to make action decisions."

Jian projected a hologram of a globe and data tables, "This first map and table shows it is estimated there will be three major flooding events. It is impossible to have any precision in estimating the timing, but we believe the associated dates are accurate within a range of three to six months, 90% confidence factor. The confidence ratings have doubled over the last thirty days. As you can see in the associated tables, the homes, businesses, factories, schools, and other support facilities for 600 million of our people will be destroyed."

Xiang's chest tightened. This was like being in one of those grade B movies. Ainsley and Addison dragged him to see that junk in the student union at least once a week. Xiang almost looked around to see if there were hidden cameras. He knew, though, that Bàba never told a joke or pulled a prank in his life.

Xiang used his finger to spin the holographic globe. He noted that the estimates were that most of Southeast US and the eastern coastal areas would drown. Wisconsin looked relatively safe.

Jian projected the next 'gram. "Our initial focus was on efforts to prepare the safe, unimpacted areas, highlighted in green. These need to support as much of our country's current biosphere as possible. We have secretly set up everything we can position in those areas and we have hardened those fixtures for the anticipated storms, droughts, heat, etc. There remain three major issues. First, we will need to relocate massive numbers of people. We have a timetable that is almost impossible. These movements are to begin in two weeks." "Two weeks!" "Yes, two weeks. All the logistics and staff are in place. The process will take eight weeks." *No wonder everyone here looks like an impending crisis status. It's not impending, it's here!*

"The second major issue is the need to control the reactions of outside parties to our actions. We cannot hide such a massive transformation of our country. It is a major credit to all those who have done the site preparations that foreign observers have raised so few questions. It follows; when we move most of our populace near the borders with Siberia, Mongolia, and Kazakhstan, we must anticipate and control the negative reactions of our neighboring governments." *No shit! Russia is likely to be lobbing a few hundred nukes at us before the end of next month.*

"Which brings me to the third and most critical issue. The relocation efforts will still leave an estimated death toll of over 300 million people from the immediate impacts. And the diminished population of China will not have the capability of growing the food necessary for all the survivors." Jian stopped, tucked his head, and took a deep breath, Xiang couldn't breathe at all. *I see where this is going, but I hope I'm wrong.*

Jian started talking again, "Xu Xiang, before I can show you the next information I will need a major concession from you." *So formal. What is the request?* "I will need to enroll you in the

People's Liberation Army. You would then be cleared for these Top-Secret files. I am pleased that we have kept you enrolled as a Party member while you were in the USA. Nothing you have done there has left any questions about your behavior over the last six years. Will you accept?"

Xiang's thoughts raced. *It is a good thing I'm not engaged. That would disqualify me, for sure. It's not like I have any plans or commitments now. I've burned all those bridges. But what use will the PLA have for a bioengineer? I'm guessing they will need phenomenal hackers, pilots, cannon fodder, and many, many crematoria attendants.*

Xiang raised the last question. It might be the critical one. "Father, I am most honored that you would believe my talents would be valued by your beloved PLA. I am sorry, by the People's Liberation Army. Please excuse my sloppy, American-bred speech patterns. But I do not think I am being falsely humble when I say that I do not see how my training and skills as a bioengineer will be of particular use. If you can clarify this point I will join at once."

Jian nodded to Xiang. "Of course Xu Xiang. You should not so readily dismiss your bioengineering abilities. Some of our war game simulations show those being of critical importance. But the immediate talents of yours that we need are leadership. Throughout your youth you demonstrated highest capabilities within the Party Youth organizations, at school, and on the football fields." Xiang automatically translated the 'football' term as soccer. *I **still** think in American.*

"Your next skill set is your intelligence. You have shown superior analytical abilities by placing highest in the HRU competition. In addition, you have amply demonstrated natural intuitive leaps of perception in the Shining Star tests. Those assets are always invaluable in the army. And everywhere."

Xiang shrugged. *It's not like I have anything else on my plate or anywhere else to go.* "Fine, General. What is the process to formalize my enlistment?" His Bàba's beaming smile stunned Xiang. Usually Bàba reserved those for Māmā. As far as Xiang could remember, he received two in his lifetime.

Within a minute, two officers came in, swore Xiang in, gathered the – already filled in, he noticed – paperwork. A doctor then entered and gave him a very perfunctory exam. He did, however require blood, urine, and stool samples. Xiang assumed his biometrics were already on file. They must have transferred them from his Party records or passport and student files.

Once they settled all the administrivia, Xiang expected his father would continue the briefing. Instead they went to eat in the officers' mess and then continued to the quartermaster, where Xiang was issued his full kit. Xiang saw that he was already a captain. *That's great! First time I have ever experienced any nepotism. I've always had to sweat bullets and claw my way to any recognition or reward.*

That thought brought Xiang up short. He braced his father, "Pardon me General. Captain? I have never known you to give out unearned honors, let alone rank. Have I volunteered for a suicide mission or something of similar risk?" When Xiang saw his father's guilty look, a pang of worry and doubt begin to seep in.

CHAPTER FOUR
ALLEGRO 1
AINSLEY, RON, & HOPE

15th August 2033

*N'guk Hkeek Society Encampment,
Northern Wisconsin, Great Plains
Union*

Ainsley sighed. *Tough doing this experiment using my chief lab tech as the guinea pig. Now I've gotta do all the folderol of this formal report as well.* She began transcribing her report to the Experimental Controls Board. Her cyberdevice took her sub-vocalized input and formatted it properly.

<u>Bioengineering Experiment 2033 Delta: Progress Log</u>

Subject Status: Subject Delta One – [Pause transcription.] *I know protocol demands professionalism and removing personally identifying info, but, Damnation, this is Ron!"* [Transcription resumed] Ronald H. Jackson, [The cyberdevice flashed a warning about the use of PII. Ainsley ignored it.] has completed both Phase One and Phase Two protocols with minimal secondary impacts. All were within nominal range, as re-summarized, following. Subject has expressly agreed to initiation of Phase Three at 9:30 A.M., local time, 15th August 2033. Summaries of protocols for each of the three phases following. Both medical and psychological clearances, filed, copies attached. Spiritual clearance, verbally given. Formal report of same, pending.

Hope walked up to the desk. She was Ainsley's chief lab assistant now that Ron was a patient. Ainsley was delighted by the interruption to this dry-as-dust report. "Hi Hope. What do you need?" Hope was becoming a friend as well as a colleague.

CHAPTER FOUR Allegro 1

Hope was like a number of women whose lives washed up on the shores of the reservation. She came to get a Clipper and stayed to get an advanced degree and career at the burgeoning tech center. Ainsley never pried for details, but hints Hope dropped led her to believe the woman was the victim of family rape.

Initially Hope intended to return to Milwaukee after her Clipper grew in. Ainsley and others convinced her any city was an imminent death trap. She moved her mother, grandmother, and niece to the Rez instead. The cities along Lake Michigan began disintegrating into chaos within a month of their move.

Ainsley particularly treasured Hope's grandmother and niece. The diseases, hunger, and battles after the Great Dieback started hit the very young and the very old hardest. Rose and Camille were a delight.

Hope said, "This is personal, not lab business. It can wait if you want."

Ainsley said. "Good Lord no, Hope. First, people always take priority over paper in my book. Second, this stuff is putting me to sleep. I welcome a break."

Hope said, "It's about Ron. I know you and he were dating. He said that it's over. Is that right? I respect and like you too much to poach if you think this breakup is going to blow over."

Ainsley felt a pang of sorrow. She hoped it didn't show. "No, Ron's right. I probably shouldn't have been dating someone who works for me anyway. Tribe's given me too much leeway since I was a basket case when I stumbled through the gates. Ron and I are both very young; twenty- three and twenty- five. At least I got my education done before the shit hit the fan, pardon my French. Ron was just a freshman, like you were, before he joined us. We've both grown, just not grown close. My blessings, girl." Hope gave Ainsley one of her angelic smiles and left. Back to the grind.

> Phase One Summary: Nanobots insufflate through Subjects sinus cavities. The 'bots then permeate the brain barriers. Navigation of the nanobots to their final implantation sites is via the "Swarm Three" program, monitored and

overridden as required by the Barney AI. Process timed to proceed throughout two hundred hours with rest intervals of fifteen minutes per hour.

Ron looked like a real cine horror show with the hoses running up his nose, a huge shower cap-like apparatus around the top of his head, and every imaginable monitor hooked to leads all over his body. Damn, we should have taken blackmail pictures. Would have been perfect for the Holiday party.

Special Note: Subject One feedback report led to modification of original procedure. Subject's enforced inactivity appeared to compound the expected symptomology of nausea, migraine headaches, disorientation, etc. The team expended significant resources to allow portable deployment of the implantation mechanisms as Subject performed controlled physical regimen.

A jury-rigged and dangerous contraption. I shuddered every time he used it. But he wasn't the usual jovial Ron until we did that. He snapped at everyone, even Hope.

Phase Two Summary: Verification testing indicated all nanobots implanted and connected to Subject's neurons – 99.995% minimal success rate. All connectivity threads grown from neural centers down to anticipated memory devices storage cavity (MDSC) – 100% verified success rate. Connectivity Test One Stage involved communication from the connected nanobots to monitors cabled through the MDSC. Cat scan monitoring occurred simultaneously. Subject exposed to numerous stimuli of increasing complexity over eight and one-half hours. Brain signal outputs integrated through the "Windows on the World" program.

The Chief says that name is a tribute to one of his strongest, but saddest memories of his trip to New York City in 2001. Said this would return the phrase to a happy memory.

Test Two Stage involved controlled communications from cables connected between "Windows on the World" program feeds and Subject's neurons. Subject's reported sensations aligned well with projected sensations. Subject's commentary that sensations were often, "vague, dream-like" attributed to the intentional low power and low volume of these inputs. Subject reported more headaches and disturbing dreams. During one initial session Subject began to experience seizure-like symptoms. Immediate administration of phenytoin solution resolved episode.

Good thing too. I was sweating bullets, though people congratulated me on my calmness. Fooled them.

Subsequent testing over each of the following eight weeks involved rest and recuperation periods for five days followed by two days of progressively more elaborate test scenarios.

[End Log]

Ainsley stretched, interlocking her hands behind her neck. Then she bent into a chakrasana pose. She knew "nothing is done until the paperwork is finished." *Paperwork, huh! Shows how old that saying is. Wish the Controls Board would just read the detailed testing data. Yeah, yeah. They all have a million things to do. Well, so do I! Enough belly-aching.*

Ainsley looked at the clock; 9:25. "Hope, have we received the official spiritual release from the Midewiwin? Is Ron prepped?"

Hope popped her head around the door. "I believe someone is running up the path right now. Expect that is the final clearance from the spiritual review board. At least, that is how I interpret the shells hanging off the scroll. And Ron is so ready that he has fallen asleep on the prep table. Talk about calm and collected. He can't wait for Ron Two Point Zero." A shy smile graced her face.

The clearance was official. Reluctantly, Ainsley went into the lab. "Okay team. Triple check that we have secured all connections and that you, personally, certify connectivity verification testing as nominal."

Each team member consulted their checklist and reviewed their monitors. Ainsley got the final green light from Bill, team liaison to

Cybernetics and Barney, the AI. Ron flashed her a warm smile. Satisfied, Ainsley twirled her upright finger in a circle. "Let's fire this up people. Ron, you are the primary source of what's happening. Please begin a running dialog describing your sensations and reactions. Team, begin cat scan and the mild sedative drip, please." *Ron's eating up being the center of attention.*

The testing began. The design was for sensations to begin flowing into Ron in a minimal trickle. Over the next several hours they became increasingly complex and integrated. Ron reported them as being much sharper and more lifelike than the ones he experienced during Phase Two. "They still have a little dreamlike edge, as if they weren't memories from what happened to me, but memories of what I imagined or experienced during my vision quest." Several of the techs nodded understandingly. Ainsley had never experienced a completely successful vision quest and the spiritual leaders advised against a repeat attempt, "at present." This didn't sit well with an action-and-results oriented woman.

The test reached the last portion for this stage. Ron entered an immersion tank. The team masked all his normal sensory inputs. In theory, only the MDSC connection was feeding his brain. All was still going to plan. In an instant Ron went totally rigid and stopped his descriptive monologue. The team waited tensely for a minute. Ainsley turned up the feeds of anti-seizure and anti-anxiety meds slightly. Sweat ran in a steady stream down her back.

There was a burst of sound from Ron. It was difficult to interpret, and it looked like several of the techs were ready to intervene and pull Ron from the chamber. Ainsley rose to her feet. "STOP! Remember that interfering with the feed at this stage caused our test monkeys catatonia and heart attacks. First, do no harm!" *Easy to say when every fiber of my being wants me to lead their charge to help Ron.*

While she was speaking, Ron evidently returned to his monologue. Muscle monitors and blood pressure showed his tensions resolving. They would have to playback the transition they missed later. Ainsley turned up the tank's speakers to hear Ron's descriptions. "The two visions I was experiencing simultaneously have resolved. My spirit guide, Brown Bear, has stopped butting against the tribal dancers. I assume the powwow scene was coming from the cerebral feed. Right before Brown Bear appeared I felt a desperate sensation that I was losing my sense of self; that this external feed was becoming my only reality. The panic was choking. Brown Bear brought me back into control."

For the remaining hour, Ron's monologue was a reasonable match to the anticipated memory feed. Ainsley called a halt. The techs brought Ron back to the prep lab and disconnected from the external feeds. The medical, psych, and spiritual advisors ran him through a quick diagnostic process and gave a provisional "thumbs up." The episode with Brown Bear shook everyone to some degree, particularly the spiritual advisor.

Ainsley consulted her clock. "It's 12:30 everyone. Please take a break for lunch and downtime until 2:30. The next stage of testing is shorter, but I believe we all need some distracting first. That way we'll be sharp throughout." She went to give Ron a personal assessment and hug before she followed her own advice.

"Barney, please do an analysis of the inputs that triggered Ron's conflicting visions. Cross compare the cat scan readings, the inputs, and the simulation you prepared prior to this Phase."

"Will do Dr. Cameron. I'll have that ready when you get back from break."

◆ ◆ ◆

During the afternoon tests, Ron learned to do controlled retrieval of external memories. Happily, everything went exactly according to script. Ron sounded gleeful as he pulled detailed, precise memories of thoughts, concepts, experiences, and entire gestalts. His description of the experience was pure Ron. "It's like you shoved Google, YouTube, and SensuMax Cinema up my butt and connected to a studio-grade control board in my fingertips."

"And, as the Alpha adopter, I hereby claim renaming rights for the Extended Cerebral Connected Memory Capability, the ECCMC." He held up a large sign with "BRAIN PAIN" emblazoned. "The second word is pronounced, 'pahn' as in the French word for bread, since, while this has been a royal headache, it does feed my mind." The group let out a collective groan and started throwing wadded up of napkins and remnants from their lunches. Bad puns were classic Ron.

The Next Day, 16th August

Experimental Controls Group Meeting

Ainsley completed her report. "In summary, all results from the first day's tests indicate complete success. Memories and technical information, new language comprehension – we met or exceeded every metric anticipated. The subject, Ron Jackson, shows no evidence of any lingering negative side effects. We will continue these evaluations, as per agreed protocol. However, we request this Board's approval. This will help overcome the negative opinions our community has about the bioengineering experiments. Second, we ask permission for deployment of the Extended Cerebral Connected Memory Capability into our second volunteer."

The Board's reaction to Ainsley's report was subdued. Now they were stirring. Ainsley noticed some hooded glances from Sleeping Otter, Midewiwin for the tribe. She butted heads with him several times before over cleansing sweats and vision quests. Personally, she believed that Ron's spiritual experiences during the experiment might have been challenging, but he passed all their reviews.

Sleeping Otter had a side conversation with several board members, then turned to Ainsley. "We are all pleased that this experiment has gone well, so far. We do have concerns about the unexpected spiritual trauma that occurred and believe this requires some deeper thought. But we agree that the current success can be made public within each clan's gathering this week."

Ainsley said, "I have submitted the complete analysis performed by the AI Barney of the spiritual trauma with commentary from the subject, Ron Jackson. While I agree the incident reinforces the need for a spiritually sound candidate, the support systems did prove successful."

"We do require more consideration before we can approve a second deployment of ECCMC. First, who is this new volunteer you have found. We have no data submitted for vetting another candidate. You know that is essential." He gave Ainsley a stern gaze under knit brows.

Ainsley took a deep, cleansing breath. "I am submitting myself as a candidate for Extended Memory Capability. The Control Board has all pertinent data because of my position as head of bioengineering. Please let me know if any additional information is required." She gave the board a look of Calm Competence, Grade Five, and slowly let her breath flow through her distended nostrils.

Sleeping Otter turned to the board chair. They shared a momentary, silent communication. Chair John Underwood gathered some notes and turned his gaze to them. "Ms., No, I am sorry. Dr. Cameron. We are profoundly happy for this successful experiment. However, there are a few qualms this board has with the idea of your using yourself as the second subject for a relatively unproven and dangerous technique. First, as you point out, you are the head of bioengineering. I think no one will dispute you are the preeminent person in your field in the Great Plains Union, possibly in the whole world. Risking such an invaluable resource unnecessarily is imprudent at the least. Second and, frankly, far more important is the personal risk you face. Since this is a closed session, I will remind all board members that they may not discuss anything herein, especially this conversation. Sorry, I run on. Second, many of us have noted your spiritual fragility. All on this board and all in our tribe have a deep understanding of the scars you still bear. We pray that more psychological counseling, sweat ceremonies, and a further vision quest will bring you inner peace and strength."

Ainsley started to object. *I've asked for a sweat and vision quest a dozen times!* The Chair raised his head. His kind, sad eyes quite undid her. Continuing, "We think this experiment could well trigger an unrecoverable spiritual and psychological imbalance.

We love you too much, Ainsley. We could not bear that pain and guilt."

Ainsley hung her head. Her emotions were roiling. Love, shame, guilt, anger, denial, and pain all flashed through her in a kaleidoscope of thoughts and sensations. She fought hard to resist another session of PTSD. *That would seal it for a decade. Cleansing breaths. Center of calm. Oneness with all.* Finally, she turned her head up to the group behind the conference table. *Whew! That was tough, but I worked through it. Baby steps.*

As she started to speak again, alarms blared. The militia to stations signal! "This is not a drill! Condition Yellow!" Danger was imminent, but there was time to prepare. Everyone left their materials in place. Quickly, with controlled energy each person went to ready the defense of the tribe and the nation. The alarms seemed especially harsh in the middle of this forest-sheltered campus.

 Ainsley noticed Sleeping Otter lingered to speak to her. She slowed to match his halting pace. "Placid Wolverine, I worry that our harsh words will put your mind in a dangerous place, especially given this sudden alert. Will you be all right, Child?" He linked his hand in her arm. Observers would see this as her giving the frail shaman support. Only the two of them knew the reverse was true.

Ainsley gently squeezed his hand. "I am good, Father. You saw that my anger, guilt over risking Ron, and all my unhealed pain caused me to go to the edge of another flashback. The techniques you and your team have coached did give me control. But I know your and the Chief's words were wise. I need a sweat and a better vision quest. Please let me know when this can occur, after this crisis is met."

"But let me assure you, Father. First and foremost, I'm a warrior. My heart is strong. I have learned to channel those inner furies during trials of combat so that they bring me strength and not confusion. I will fight for our peoples."

Sleeping Otter squeezed her arm gently as he went on his separate way. "Good, Child. Count coup. Be brave but compassionate."

CHAPTER FOUR Allegro 1

Ainsley ran up the winding path towards her room.

Ainsley and her team kitted out and were ready for immediate deployment. They streamed into the Assembly Hall with the rest of the militia. The Chair, now wearing his full chieftain regalia, was at the dais. Three of the clan leaders must have been at the Encampment. They flanked the Chief, looking magnificent to Ainsley; powerful and calming.

The quiet buzz of conversation ended immediately when the Chief raised his hand. "We have received word from our neighbors to the south, the Midwest Cooperative. A flotilla of over fifty watercraft – paddlewheels, barges, and smaller craft – have travelled north along the Mississippi from somewhere in the Texican Territories. They have raided several remote homes, farms, and one village. The invaders seem to be focusing on looting. Casualties have been minimal, though there are several unverified claims of rape." Ainsley took several calming breaths to remove the red veil of anger from her eyes.

One of the clan leaders stepped forward. "Each of your teams will be briefed separately on your assignments. First, Lieutenant Cameron, your Peregrines Platoon will deploy now, using our fleet of ultralight aircraft. Fly to Dubuque where you can get tanks refilled. Your task will be to provide surveillance of these people. You are not, repeat not to engage them unless you witness an atrocity occurring. Even then, only engage if you have an overwhelming tactical advantage. Timely information will be our most valuable asset in resisting the invasion. And everyone." He raised his voice to command complete attention. "Everyone remember the binding treaty principles. First, treat all opponents as people with dignity and respect, whenever possible. Second, only use minimal force to neutralize threats. Third, the right of self-preservation is yours. Do not abuse that right frivolously to avoid the first two principles. But you are the shield of the tribe and of the Union. Make us proud, warriors!"

Ainsley turned to her team. "Let's fly Falcons." They all let out a blood-curdling screech, then ran toward the ultralights' hangar.

Great Dieback to Singularity

skies above Hardin, Illinois, Midwest Cooperative

A insley sighed again, bemoaning the primitive radio equipment. *If only the Council would authorize deployment of MindMeld to everyone. This is distracting.*

"Command, Alpha squad and I are continuing to follow this detachment of Texicans. After leaving the Mississippi for the Illinois River the enemy proceeded slowly, scouting both banks. Wait One." Ainsley received a flash on her local command channel. "Go ahead, Sarge."

"Lieutenant, Grabowski reports some activity at a farmhouse on our three o'clock. Permission to investigate? Wojlkowski, over."

Ainsley double-checked the two boats on the river below and to the left. "Okay Sarge. You and Grabowski. Watch out for any air defense. And remember, recon only. Go to electric power for silence but remember to monitor battery use carefully. That mode sucks juice like Grabowski downs Leinie's. Out."

She chuckled when a protesting, "Hey, I resemble that!" came from the corporal.

The two peeled away. Ainsley notified Command then signaled her squad to do a lazy loop, eating time while the recon went on.

The radio crackled again. "CODE GAMMA. Looks like a body on the porch. Infrared shows five people in the back of the farmhouse, struggling. We just may have confirmed those atrocity rumors. Over"

Ainsley waved the squad to head east. "We are on our way, Sarge. Watch your six. Only engage if you can't wait three minutes. Out."

"Command, this is Alpha One. We have a Code Gamma we are checking out. Repeat, Code Gamma." Ainsley received an acknowledgement then focused on getting to the farmhouse.

When the squad got to the house, they landed next to the other two ultralights. As she anticipated, Woj and Grabby were inside already. Smoke from a rear window indicated they used a flash-

81

CHAPTER FOUR Allegro 1

bang grenade. Ainsley deployed four people as a perimeter and sent one back aloft. She and the other two entered the house carefully.

Woj and Grabby already had secured the scene. Her sergeant held three men at gun point. Grabowski was helping two women – most likely a mother and daughter – to cover themselves. Grabowski was speaking in a gentle voice and using slow, non-threatening movements. This was quite unlike his usual gruff demeanor. He knew enough not to touch them. Ainsley sent one of her female PFCs to assist.

Another flash from the radio. "Alpha Five, aloft. Watch out team. Unknowns approaching. They have good camo on. Shit, they have the perimeter guards in hand! Get ready, Sarge, Looie!" At that, people breached the front and back door. Two weapons were in the window, covering the whole room. Caught like a group of rookies!

A very large Hispanic man, sporting captain's bars entered. "Stand down, team. Looks like our hosts have done our work for us. Thank you, Lieutenant. We will take those prisoners off your hands. We've been pursuing the pigs since they deserted in Arkansas. Left a trail of death and destruction since. Scum!"

While she agreed, Ainsley knew where her duty lay. "Due respect Captain. As you point out, these are our prisoners. Apprehended in the act, outside your territorial jurisdiction. We intend to take them before civil authorities for trial and disposition, under the law." *Did one of those bastard rapists smirk at me? Wait until you find out our penalties for rape and murder.*

The captain glowered. His men tightened their grips on their weapons. "And due respect to you, Lieutenant. These pigs were under my command. They perpetrated their first crimes, after their desertions, within Texican Territory. We have been exercising the doctrine of 'hot pursuit.' I am under orders as well as moral obligation to proceed. As well, I note your uniforms are Great Plains Union, not Midwest Coop. Unless our intel is faulty." Tensions were at a peak.

Ainsley returned the glare for a second, then tried a conciliatory

Great Dieback to Singularity

note. She gave him a nod of Equal to Equal Acknowledgement, Grade Four. "Okay Captain. Let's stipulate a few things. First, we will all note my objections for the record. By that, I mean we will make a holographic record of these proceedings from this moment and present them to a joint meeting of our two leadership groups. Second, you will stop referring to the prisoners as pigs. My tribe raises pigs. They are intelligent and, contrary to popular misconception, fastidious. Third, my platoon and other Great Plains troops are here under the command of the Cooperative's leaders as a joint task force to intercept your flotilla and assure ourselves of your intentions. Indeed, your boats on the Mississippi are under the watchful eyes of our forward guard now. The rest should arrive within two hours. I suggest we be the first to agree to a truce in place."

The captain clicked his heels. Ainsley stifled a giggle. He was an anachronism. "Captain Javier Gonzales, ma'am. I accept your proposal. By your leave, my radioman will communicate the truce proposal back to HQ. Also, I sincerely apologize to all the fine swine of your peoples. You are right, I was insulting to them, unintentionally. Now, if I may proceed with disposition of these 'men'". He produced a glorious sneer. Ainsley wished he had twirled his bushy mustachio. That would have been perfect. She nodded her assent to Captain Gonzales.

The three men began squawking about their rights. "Taint constitutional. Taint civilized." Both sets of soldiers just glared. The Texicans marched the three into a side yard, behind a set of grain silos. The captain arranged his team so their fire wouldn't harm the silos. Ainsley thought, *Nice touch.* Sergeant Wojlkowski began her holorecorder. A Texican sergeant came beside Woj with an ancient camera. Ainsley detected no tension between the two.

After the execution, people from both sides dug graves. They then helped the two surviving women get to a clinic in Hardin. Ainsley verified it was, unfortunately, all too experienced in this type of trauma care. They sent the farmer's corpse to the local morgue. The troops then organized a bivouac and traded Wisconsin beer for some type of Texican homebrew.

CHAPTER FIVE ALLEGRO
2
RAHEL, ADDISON, & MALCOLM
4ᵗʰ August 2033

Edinburgh, Republic of Scotland

When she saw Addison enter the restaurant, Rahel thumbed off her computer. *Time to put on my Kaitlin Schlötke persona. This will be the decisive time. Give her our pitch and try to recruit her in support of The Collective or slip this neurotoxin into her drink.*

Addison gave Kaitlin a Growing Friendship Smile, Grade Four. "How are you Kaitlin? I'm glad we can finally have the dinner you asked for eight weeks ago. Sorry it has taken so long."

Kaitlin/Rahel shook her head, "Oh no. Don't apologize. I cancelled on you twice, you cancelled on me twice. We're even. We just both have crazy hectic lives. Of course, my crazy seminar proctor, who keeps assigning a month's worth of reading every week, is probably my biggest time sink." Kaitlin smiled broadly to take the sting out of her words.

Addison replied, "Well, I do hope the seminar has been worth it. I know I have been very demanding. And now it will be over after tomorrow's session."

Kaitlin/Rahel mused, *Are you waiting to see if I make a pitch for you to support or join the mysterious cabal I represent. Good we don't have the search capabilities of Google – and the even deeper capabilities of the Dark Web. Wouldn't you just love to know who I'm really with?*

The waiter popped over. Both women quickly ordered a house salad and a drink. Weeks of experience with the limited and odd vagaries of Edinburgh cuisine made decisions easier.

CHAPTER FIVE Allegro 2

Addison made an opening gambit, "Tell me, Kaitlin, do you have Jewish ancestry? I ask because you remind me of two of my best friends – college roommates at Illinois. They were both Jewish. I just have a hunch you're like them."

Kaitlin held up her palm. "No, but I'm a quarter Palestinian. Similar language, bloodlines, culture. I'm surprised you noticed though, with my straw blonde hair and lighter complexion."

Kaitlin considered, *Lies laced with truth are the safest. I am both Jewish and Palestinian. But I'm more Palestinian ethnically and in my heart. Especially after the AI-driven drone strikes on my family in Gaza as I watched helplessly.*

Addison blushed; Social Embarrassment, Grade Two. "It's just a similarity in speech patterns and body language, perhaps. Oh, I hope I haven't given offense. I do know of how much antipathy there has been between Palestinians and Israelis."

Kaitlin thought, *Oh, we've bonded now in our mutual distrust and antipathy towards most of the rest of the world.*

The server delivered their salads. Kaitlin asked about their drinks and the server assured her they were coming momentarily. August had been particularly hot and dry in Edinburgh.

She picked up the conversation again, "Don't worry, Addison. My family has belonged to several of the cross-cultural friendship societies. We. No, **I** believe that fundamentalism, rigid idealism, has been the true curse of the Middle East."

Addison nodded. "Rebecca and Sarah, my two roommates would have certainly agreed. We had lots of deep conversations. They convinced me that the idealism of the kibbutz movement was perverted into naked land grabs. They even went so far as to compare it to "lebensraum", the German justification for conquering and colonizing their neighbors. They joined a group called "Abraham's Children"...."

Kaitlin yelped in excitement, "No! My uncle was one of the founders of Abraham's Children back home." She thought, *Oh, this is good. She is aware and sensitive, not just a tech geek. Maybe we can win her over.* She slipped the neurotoxin patch back in her bag.

Great Dieback to Singularity

◆◆◆

Addison mused, *Back home, eh! Well, that doesn't match your legend at all. And what gives? She's looking like someone just lifted a big weight off her shoulders.* "Please tell me, Kaitlin. You said you and your group might want my help with a research project. Can you give me some details? I will warn you, my uncle's company has asked me to help them develop a market for their firewall. Also, St. Jacques and Owens-B are wining and dining me next week in the south of France."

Kaitlin gave a little grimace, then a half smile. "My group might be able to offer a little help with the firewall. I understand you need to consider any proposals like those two guys can offer, but let me tell you, they are not what they appear to be at first glance. Malcolm does appear to have some moral compass, but I'm reasonably sure 'Lord' Robert would toss his mother under a Metro bus if he thought it would allow him to skip the fare. Their companies are carrion pickers, going through the remains of European industry and devouring the pieces they find. Sometimes the carrion they pick is still living."

Addison thought, *Oh, bad sales tactics. Never diss the competition. It only makes you look weak. Not that I disagree with your conclusions. Being an undercover agent helps you discover all you want to know about people, fast. And more than you want to know about some.* "Okay, note taken. Let's discuss a joint marketing plan for Uncle Jay's firewall later. What's the research effort?"

Kaitlin powered up her cyberdevice and showed a hologram presentation in a trice. "I have recommended you to our group because I believe you are like me. You have an intuitive grasp of the obvious." Kaitlin's eyes twinkled. She waited for Addison's response.

Addison said, "Okay, I'll bite. What do you mean by that earworm?"

Kaitlin grinned. "Once I was called in to solve a client's IT mess. They all sat in this big conference room complaining of the smell and crowding. I looked around and said, 'You've got an elephant in the middle of the room. Get rid of it.' They smacked their foreheads, got rid of the elephant, and declared the problem solved. They then refused to pay for my services since the problem and solution were so obvious. You and I can see the obvious where others see the problems."

"Our group is small but has a very high degree of cybernetics expertise...."

15th August 2033

Ravensbruck Castle, northwest of Montpellier, Languedoc-Roussillon, France

T he Count cocked his head. "You are sure, Doctor, that you don't want to attend the dinner and query Dr. Cameron about bioengineering?"

Dr. Vyrvykvist said, "Thank you Herr Count. I feel that would be unwise. After my life's work – laboratory, data, files, equipment, and experiments – were all destroyed by the Americans and Chinese, I have been falling further and further behind in the field." He ran his gloved hand across the sterilized granite counter. "The fine, immaculate facilities you have provided here are helping restore things. A few more volunteer subjects and I should be back to where I was four years ago. Besides, Dr. Cameron is likely to be like most of her ignorant countrymen; biased against enhanced people. No, I will wait until you have convinced her of the wisdom of working together. Your unconventional methods do seem quite effective."

The Count saw the slight pursing of Dr. V.'s lips. *Frown all you want, you Bolskie Butcher. My dear Vater und Mutter could give master lessons in disapproval. I was fortunate my nannie and tutor Helga decided I needed a sexual education when I was twelve. It was wonderful until she started to bleed. Such an unsightly mess! It was good that Vater und Mutter helped me clean up the corpse that time. The beatings were almost worth it. That's where I learned it was easier if you just started with a surface that could be easily cleaned afterwards. No mess.*

◆ ◆ ◆

Great Dieback to Singularity

Addison pulled up the pop-up thumbnail bio on the Count.

Heinrich Grubenflagg, Count

Grubenflagg is head of the Ravensbruck Group. Recently joined with four other groups in an association simply known as the Consortium. Born Fredrich "Fast Freddie" von Schtuben, Bonn, Germany, 11 December 1983. Managed a hedge fund until caught pushing a virtual ponzi scheme. Von Schtuben dropped off official radar until the latter days of the Time of Troubles when he and his cohorts practiced extortion, blackmail, and (suspected, never proven) outright theft.

Addison lifted her napkin to her lips to hide her face. She wasn't sure her training was sufficient to contain any hint of the disgust she was feeling towards her host, "Count Grubenflagg". *I would discount him as a comic-opera villain if it weren't for the facts. His gang of thugs is directly responsible for at least fifteen cases of extorting technical companies, six outright instances of theft of intellectual property and machinery, and most likely several dozen murders. Plus, he's not even trying to hide the claws and fangs of his mob.* "Your proposal, Herr Von Grubenflagg, is most intriguing. You flatter me with such a high assessment of my skills. I just want to reiterate that much of my experience was in an academic setting. Subsequently I have been restricted by the authorities from any practice of my bioengineering training."

The Count interrupted, "You are being far too modest ma chérie. These fine gentlemen have told me of the grand success which led your very provincial police to banish your work. I laughed heartily when they described the 'Cutter'." Addison thought, *Laugh it up, fuzzball. Try something with me and you'll definitely be brought up short.*

Addison steeled herself and went on, "That is the Clipper, Excellency. Disirreguardedly," Addison stifled her laugh at her intentional mangle-aprop, "my experience is sadly out-of-date and out-of-practice. While my cybernetic skills are, modestly, first rate, I really cannot believe they would justify the extraordinary compensation you are offering." *And no, I will not sleep with you to earn the pay differential. I sincerely regret letting that creep Bob-O into my bed. It may have been necessary, but all the showers to get clean afterwards have left my skin chafed. Now Malcolm, on the other hand...* She forced her mind back to the conversation.

The Count was stroking the back of her hand. "... just sleep on it, ma chérie. We will discuss this further in the morning. Do you need assistance in locating your room?"

Addison gave the Count a Polite Dismissal, Grade One, smile. "No thank you. I have always had a built-in inner compass and map. Good evening, Excellency." She rose from the table as the three men rose, scraping their chairs backwards. Addison nodded to Malcolm and Bob-O in turn.

As she was leaving the room, her enhanced hearing picked up a whisper from Grubenflagg to Bob-O, "Break her. I want her saddled and ready to go by tomorrow morning." *Looks like I won't be sleeping tonight,* she thought.

A half hour later Addison heard a light tap on her door. She called out, "Who is it?" She put her Shredder mini-pistol into her rear waistband.

A low voice called, "It's Malcolm." Addison went to the door. She checked the stop she placed that would only allow the door to open a few inches. She slipped the pistol into her palm and opened the door a crack, making sure she didn't expose herself. Her projected holographic image was in the doorway. The fiber-whisker scope under the door only showed Malcolm, but she wasn't going to let someone else's superior tech spoof her.

Malcolm whispered, "Hey Addison. You okay? Sorry, I didn't know he was going to be that big of a jerk. If it was just up to me, I would ask you to pack up and leave with me now. But my boss is somehow in debt to the Count. In any case, my room is just one door down, across the hall. I'll keep an eye out tonight. I doubt they will be crass enough to do anything to threaten you, but I didn't like the way Bob-O and the Count were conferring after you left. Bob-O didn't look happy with whatever the Count was telling him to do."

Addison responded, "I really appreciate that Mal. I may be able to defend myself one-on-one, but for some reason, I don't think Bob-O learned his etiquette on the playing fields of Eton. Come running if I yell, okay."

Malcolm grinned, "I could guard you better inside your room, you know." He started to put his hand out to stroke her hologram. Addison quickly put her palm up and stepped back.

"Down boy," she admonished. "You know Bob-O would take that as an open party signal. Never going **there** again. Goodnight." Her answer was firm but accompanied by a Wistful Longing, Grade Five look.

Later that night

A ddison was simulating sleep. All her deployed sensors and her natural alarms were on highest sensitivity. Something was indicating movement to her left. She kept her breathing regular, but emptied her mind and relaxed her muscles, except for the grip on her mini-pistol.

Addison peered through eyes narrowed to slits. Four men entered the room from behind a swinging bookcase. She thought, *Gawd, this is such a Grade B movie. Hidden passageways in the old stone castle. Are they going to drag me to the dungeon or the hidden laboratory?*

The men arrayed themselves. One got behind the headboard, rope in hand. One was beside the left of the bed. Since the bed was against a wall on the right, the other two men approached from the foot of the bed. She saw that one of them was Bob-O.

Addison fluttered her eyes open and looked sleepily towards the two who were now climbing onto the bed by her feet. "Oh, Bobby! And you've brought a friend. Is that Mal?" Addison gathered her breath into her core and prepared for release.

Bob-O chuckled, "No Sweetness. Not Mal. Got some special surprises for you tonight." He grabbed her middle as she raised her hands to the side of his face. She turned Bob-O slightly so that the second man didn't have easy purchase. She sensed the man at the head of the bed and the one on the side moving in. She released her conscious mind.

Addison gave Bob-O's head a wrenching twist and shoved him violently against the other man in the bed. She ducked, avoiding the grasp of the man beside the bed and the noose thrown by the last man. She activated the Shredder she was now pointing at the man behind her. In the same move, she did a reverse somersault off the bed. A high side kick slowed the fourth man down until she could fire a burst of flechettes into him as well. The last man on the bed was leaping. Addison was a little rushed and barely blocked his knife thrust. She was able to continue, using his forward momentum to slam him into the door.

Her conscious mind re-engaged. "Damn!" she thought. That was too loud. She disabled her final opponent with an elbow thrust into his kidneys. Her gun was empty, so she dispatched him by putting his knife through his esophagus. *The old rape-dominance ploy. Can't four guys manage to get two brain cells between them and then rub them together?*

Malcolm was at the door. Urgently he whispered, "Addie, what's going on?"

Addison shoved the body and the stop away from the door. She opened it and dragged Malcolm in. She hissed, "Quiet! They have to have sensors deployed and my blockers are only so good." Malcolm was taking in the bloody scene with a little wide-eyed surprise, but she could see his SAS training took hold quickly.

Malcolm was turning his head in each direction, assessing. "Right. We will need to evacuate immediately. Do you have a strategy, or should I lead?" He was searching the bodies quickly, gathering weapons and any other useful items like wallets. Addison was pulling her go kit from under the bed. She rearmed the Shredder and put on a shoulder-holstered long gun – short-barrel edition. Malcolm continued, "Well, doesn't look like this is your first rodeo, as you Yanks say. Lead on. My go bag is in the hall, if that's the way we are leaving."

They dashed into the hall, Malcom grabbing his bag as they flew by. As they started to turn the corner towards the main staircase, they heard approaching footfalls. Addison whispered, "Back into that alcove on the left." Malcolm was puzzled, but the basic rule of combat is, "The one in charge is in charge. Don't second guess. If a fatal mistake is about to be made and there is time, quietly offer advice. Don't distract."

Malcolm saw there were two small, drop-down doors in the alcove. One displayed a picture indicating refuse, the other showed it was for laundry. He reached for the laundry chute door.

Addison put a hand against that door and flipped open the other. She whispered with a command voice. "'Into the garbage chute, flyboy.' I've waited my whole life to be able to use that line." That puzzled Malcolm, but the fast approaching footsteps gave no time for chitchat. He dived in, head first. Addison followed on his heels.

They dropped two stories quickly. At the end the chute bent semi-vertically. Malcolm's hands popped open the flap at the end of the tunnel and they both plopped into foul smelling mud. Addison immediately pulled him up and pointed urgently. "Quick! Over the fence on the left." Malcolm half-slithered, half-ran and pulled himself head-over-heels across the fence. He gave his head a little shake. Addison did an elegant dive into a half roll. *Bet she comes up clean and smelling of roses,* he grumped to himself.

Addison signaled they should run across this paddock towards a birch copse. Malcolm heard and smelled several hogs battering the fence at his back. *Ugh! Filthy, deadly animals. I don't care how intelligent they are.* He was right behind Addison as she sprinted across the open ground. *No, she definitely doesn't smell like roses.*

Malcolm worried about the cameras mounted on the castle battlements. He was sure that castle security monitored those 24X7. Pursuit was imminent. *Some rescue,* he thought, finally recalling the earlier reference to an ancient, juvenile cinema.

Addison led him into a gully. She seemed to know where every root and rock was. Malcolm had to pay closer attention, so he lost a little ground despite his longer legs. She came to a halt, now about six paces ahead of him. The gully was making a sharp right turn. He caught up and peeked around the curve, past her head. He hissed, "That fence is electrified and monitored. Do we need to double back?" Just then he heard quiet buzzing. "Drones! We only have a minute."

Addison shushed him. He heard her quietly saying, "Four, three, two, one." There was a snapping sound from the vicinity of the fence. Addison stood. "Let's go." She launched herself towards the fence.

Malcolm noted that the buzz of the drones vanished and that the fence looked dead. Addison hit the fence at a dead run and was halfway up before Malcolm reached the bottom. *Definitely not her first rodeo. Who are you really, Darling?*

After the two got over, sans electrocution, they went at a fast walk through the dense underbrush for another fifteen minutes. Malcolm was heartened. *Now I'm keeping pace with her.* With her permission he even took point for most of this part of their escape. When they reached a hedgerow-enclosed farm road they both halted, pulled out water bottles, and caught their breaths.

Malcolm tilted his head at Addison, "What now, Kemo Sabe?" *Throw ancient cultural memes at me, will you?* It was delightful to see a puzzled look cross her face as she delicately bit her tongue.

Addison tossed her head in dismissal of the distraction. "I believe our ride is coming now." They peeked through the hedgerow. The oncoming hovercar flickered front signal lights in a complex pattern. Satisfied, Addison tunneled under the hedgerow and slid down the embankment. Malcolm cursed to himself, *Easy enough for you to do, you elfin sprite. We trolls need just a little more opening.* He finally got through with only minor bleeding and strode to the waiting car.

When he poked his head into the portal he saw Addison nestled in the storage area behind the seats. He tossed his go bag to her. She caught it and gave him an impish grin. Then he noticed the driver and did a double take. He drawled, "Ms. Schlötke. What a surprise. Do you come here often?"

Addison pointed a hand at their savior. "Malcolm, may I introduce Rahel Blumstein. Rahel, Malcolm." To Malcolm, "Rahel heard we were going to be in Languedoc at the same time as she was, quelle surprise! She asked if she could drop by and catch up on old times."

Great Dieback to Singularity

Meanwhile, Back at the Castle

T he Count had to screech at the security men who were immobilized by the chaos. "Yes, I know your boss and three others are dead in an upstairs room. Yes, a bomb disabled all the security systems." *The bomb let that devil St. Jacques escape, carrying off Dr. Cameron. But why do I have to do all your thinking for you? Fine, I set up pursuit teams. Not that it will do a lot of good. The ex-SAS man obviously came prepared for this operation. There surely would have been a car right outside the gates.*

"The priority now is to get the four bodies to the laboratory basements before their biological functionality is irreversibly destroyed. The Doctor can surely do something with all the parts from these superb specimens."

CHAPTER SIX ALLEGRO 3
XIANG & MIN
14ᵗʰ June 2033

*Special Projects Island, Tongtian
River, near Gui'de, Qinghai, China*

Xiang heard voices in his outer offices. This flashback hadn't been that bad. The memories were from the early days; right after his return to China. True, his breakup with Ainsley and sense of betrayal was sharp. And he knew his father hadn't even thought about him until he returned to China. But he knew those shards of pain were mere pebbles. The lacerating stuff came from the days of the Long March North, the death of his parents, and most importantly from the counterassaults that he orchestrated against the Cossack Supermen.

Xiang understood all about PTSD and the recommended treatments. He managed to pirate a small amount of the best psychotropic drugs. Despite the risks, he had no compunctions about self-administration. What were the alternatives? Talk therapy? Everything involved had the highest levels of classification. Those few people who had clearance to hear his memories would immediately react by having him either locked away or eliminated. The therapy of Eye Movement Desensitization and Reprocessing was more effective than he anticipated. But people walked in on him twice while he was practicing EMDR. He was able to wave their suspicions away by claiming that he was conducting some minor bioengineering sensitivity tests. Someone was likely to get suspicious and research his procedure if he did it often.

For now, Xiang had a side project hidden from his bioengineering research staff. Results were negative, but he had no alternative in mind. If his PTSD crippled him while he was in public, he could lose everything.

He went to his office door and looked out. Two of his team leaders were there chatting. He got their status on preparations for the move off-island and asked them to tell everyone to redouble their efforts. The justification for urgency was his promise of their space to Jhao Gang's team. He described their improved status since their team was now sitting at the leaders table. His team leads bowed happily and left.

Now, what to do about the small matter of a nuke sticking up our asses?

The next day, 15ᵗʰ June

Xiang spread his hands, palm up, in a gesture of offering or supplication. "Wong Min, my Bàba and Māmā, General and Chief Minister Xu, told me often that, 'the nail that sticks up is hammered down.' That Japanese sentiment reflects why your proposal yesterday could have hurt you." Xiang gave the woman a thorough scrutiny. *She might be a very handsome woman. Her dress is shapeless, no makeup. Hard to see what she could be like. Might be worth exploring. It's been a long time...* "It is much better if you have someone else put you forward. That is what I use my relationship with Jhao Gang to accomplish."

Xiang noted the quick flicker of distaste crossing Wong Min's face. *So unguarded. Possibly tutoring her in the art will bond her like it did for Ainsley.* He only experienced a short pang at Ainsley's memory. "If I may, Wong Min, you really need to learn to hide your thoughts from your face. I, too, think of Jhao as a prissy, sycophantic, oily bureaucrat."

Wong Min looked startled and apprehensive. "I never said... How do you... You do? But you act like he is your favorite uncle." She was slightly red. He noted her pupils were slightly dilated. *Anger? Fear? Interest? No matter, emotion is better than indifference. It is a start.*

She continued, "Twice in as many days I have been surprised. First Bold Beaver contacts me and offers to assist my efforts even while she is working for Yeong Lanying. Then you ..."

98

Great Dieback to Singularity

Xiang smiled, a Gentle Caring, Grade Three. "Let me explain. You know, I'm sure, that I spent college years in the US. One of the requirements at the University of Texas was that all students, even those on technical and engineering tracks, had to take a balance of courses from other disciplines." He dropped into a sing-song voice. "We are giving you an education for life, not a trade." He smiled again, continuing in a normal voice. "One of my courses, and one I truly loved, was Drama. I learned so much, including how to have my face show only those messages I intend. I was good enough at the end that my professor tried to get me to switch majors. I did perform in several plays. I would gladly teach you these techniques."

She smiled impishly. "'I think this is the beginning of a beautiful friendship.'" She leaned back. The shapeless dress now clung closer, highlighting a fine bosom.

Xiang's look of complacent mastery disappeared. It was replaced by a childlike look of delight. "You know Casablanca. I love that film!"

Min's smile broadened, "You aren't the only one who was told to broaden his curriculum. 'Foreign Films – Dialectics of Imperialism' was better than the course title. My favorite course!"

The next day, 16th June

"You see Ajai that I have need of your cybernetics skills. I was impressed with your work in reviving Bold Beaver." Xiang quickly saw that the key to the man was flattery.

I just learned that Ajai was completely shunted aside from work with Bold Beaver. The academics running the projects have no respect for the pragmatic skills one needs to learn to keep a modern farm running. In all honesty, I don't have that much intrinsic respect myself. But LeeLee and Addie droned that message into my ears endlessly. I know more about the intricacies of hog farming than I ever dreamed I would.

Ajai said, "The possibility of learning bioengineering would appeal to me. I learnt all my skills on the job since no one has ever sent me to a school. If I will simply be keeping the cyberdevices running for your team, then I might as well stay with my current group."

Xiang gave an Earnest Agreement, Grade Four. He said, "I'll commit to you working on bioengineering projects at least quarter time. I'll also direct some of our lab techs who are fresh from university to ..."

25th June 2033

new quarters for Second Bioengineering Group, cliff cave northeast of Gui'de

Xiang was close to finishing assembly of his hacking tool. He intended to release the swarm within the military's nuclear failsafe site. The nanobot aggregation would communicate via swarm-bot-to-bot-messaging. Every time anyone opened an entryway or window at the site a handful of bots would float out and another handful would float in. With all the sand in the air here, they shouldn't be seen. This would allow him to penetrate the army's secure perimeter.

The bulk of the aggregation would penetrate the army's cybernet link. Xiang's only hope was that State Security hadn't significantly upgraded the protocols and protections in that equipment over the last few years. Given all the other challenges China was dealing with, it was a reasonable bet. Besides, Xiang had no plan B.

All tests were good. *Glad you sent me to spy school, Bàba. Hated it at the time, but it might save the butts of me and my team now.*

Xiang began to smell a great stench of burning metal and blood, He looked frantically around. Explosions were hammering his eardrums, small arms snapping and whining. Then he began to have double vision, glaring strobes of multicolored light. He struggled to control himself. *Just flashbacks.* He tipped backwards to the floor.

Great Dieback to Singularity

*Intermingled times and locations,
Long March North (China, Russia,
Mongolia, Kazakhstan, 2028-2029*

A calm command center. People working with focus, no panic. Status board shows progress of units moving into neighboring territories with minimal resistance. The cyberdevice hacks on enemy systems crippled their command and control. Ripple effects reported to be affecting other parts of the internet as well. Can't make an omelet...

❖❖❖

Same command center. "Multiple launches. I say, multiple launches, origination Western Russia and Black Sea. Target analysis begun. Nuclear response initiation begun." Xiang never believed himself closer to death. He looked towards his father. General Xu stood ramrod stiff. His voice controlled; low but penetrating. "Do not launch without my direct order. I need that targeting data, NOW!"

Controller: "General, the rockets are going above the layer of volcanic ash. We cannot track them there. They might change trajectories after crossing that altitude."

General Xu: "They won't be able to monitor them either. I will assume set trajectory. ANALYZE! MY DECISION." A strong funk of sweat, flickering lights, migraine.

❖❖❖

An ashen faced aide interrupted the staff conference. "Generals, sirs. An unpredicted disaster! The second surge seems to have triggered multiple massive volcanic eruptions and earthquakes all around the Pacific's Ring of Fire. Our scientists are trying to assess the con..."

❖❖❖

CHAPTER SIX Allegro 3

Xiang crouched in the cave. He prayed his advanced camo would hide him from the advancing Cossack supermen. He smelled putrid from a week on the run. Several of his wounds, though minor, were festering. He hoped he could chance a fire in the morning to cauterize them.

◆◆◆

The analysis section's head rose and faced the general. "Missiles are not directed specifically at us. Targeting shows an even spread of trajectories throughout the Northern Hemisphere, slightly sparser spread in the Southern. Most missiles headed for ocean impacts. We do not have an explanation. Sorry, General."

◆◆◆

"... first surge of oceanic flooding was within predicted range. Worldwide reports show minimal panic in larger countries. Stories of large-scale deaths and devastation ... Bangladesh, much of Africa..."

Grim faces, absorbing grim news. Only the accuracy of the predictions allowed numbness to overcome grief and panic.

◆◆◆

A tense few moments followed the Russian launch. Everyone waited for Xu's next command. Sensors Control head leapt to her feet. "Multiple detonations. The missiles are detonating in the atmosphere. All appear to have exploded except one. It crashed into the Atlantic. ALERT! Missiles incoming over the Atlantic, targeting Western Russia. Analysis shows probable US origin."

◆◆◆

Okay, the bug seems to be working. They have stopped advancing. Run across several who look really sick. Our people haven't been infected, or at

Great Dieback to Singularity

least not virulently. Don't mutate, baby.

26th June 2033, late night

*Cave laboratories northeast of
Gui'de, Qinghai, China*

Xiang was curled in a ball weeping. He was lucky. His staff honored his privacy lockdown. He self-medicated, shaking so hard it was difficult to swallow the pills. Once he gained a bit of control, he thought of the nanobots assembly. *Thank goodness! Still intact on the workbench. I'll double-check it in the morning. Gotta sleep now.* He grabbed a couple of sleeping pills, dry-swallowed them, and stumbled to his cot.

The next morning, early, 27th June

Xiang double checked his dress uniform. All in order, his medals from the Long March North on his chest for the first time in years. He taped the nanobots assembly to his inner right thigh with dissolvable tape. *As ready as I can be. Hope this works.*

Xiang caught the first ferry to the island. Dusting his uniform off unnecessarily, he straightened his cap and slow marched to the new army installation – Bomb Central, he nicknamed it.

Xiang walked up to the front door guard and snapped off a beautiful salute. "Colonel Xu Xiang here to pay a courtesy call on General Wang. I do not have an appointment."

The guard returned his salute, although Xiang thought the effort halfhearted. "Wait. I will call my sergeant." The man picked up – was it, yes – an actual field phone. *That must have come from the first Long March. Unbelievable. They let these guys have nukes!*

Shortly, Xiang entered. The new facility had a strong smell of sawdust and fresh paint. His escort took him to a closet-sized waiting area. Eventually the door opened by an aide. "Colonel Xu to see General Wang." *Thanks, didn't know that.*

Xu took the two steps to the desk and executed another perfect salute. Wang looked up from his reports and waved a hand, dismissing the aide and acknowledging the salute. "Good morning

Colonel. No one told me you were previously a member of the PLA. What can I do for you?"

Xiang gave a polite bow. "Good morning, General. Thank you for seeing me with no advance notice. I thought to mention my past service when you were introduced but believed you would have too many demands for your attention, bringing this site online."

"I have served, but only during the Long March North. My father, General Xu Jian, brought me in as his aide because of my training in bioengineering and cybernetics. Later, I performed detached duties in the Ural Mountains and the Aral Sea."

Wang looked pensive. "I served on the Russia front also. Then you must have run into those Bastard Bears, the enhanced shock troops."

Xiang wanted to get off this topic quickly. "Oh, I did indeed. I nicknamed them the Cossack Supermen. I apologize, that term shows that capitalist bourgeois thinking still afflicts me. My father, General Xu has warned me I must purge those habits leftover from my time studying in the US." *Please move on to something else. I can feel my migraine rising.*

Wang grunted. "Good man, your father. A giant among those pygmies on the general staff. Sorry to hear he and your mother died so tragically. Didn't really know the Minister, though. Your father was a man who could tell a piss-ant commissar to get out. And not get hung by the Party!" He looked around furtively. "Of course, most commissars are good people, not lickspittles trying to tell better men what's right and what's wrong."

Xiang smiled inwardly. Wang was the dinosaur he remembered. "As I say General, I only wanted to extend my courtesies and an offer to help you and your staff, should occasion arise."

Wang's face took on a crafty, considering look. Just then the door opened and his commissar entered. "General, have you... Sorry, wasn't aware you had a meeting. Not on my calendar." The man's face could have been in a dictionary alongside the word, 'Suspicious."

The general didn't bat an eye. "Do you remember Bioengineering

Great Dieback to Singularity

Head Xu, or I should say Colonel Xu. He came by unannounced to extend his courtesies, remind me of my service with his father, General Xu Jian, and extend an offer to help us in the future."

The commissar got the same considering look the general had earlier. Xiang filed that away for future use. *Need to think of what favor I might need from them when they ask me to spy on my colleagues.* "I apologize and will take no more of your busy schedule. Do you have a toilet I can use before I leave?"

Wang pointed at a small door behind his desk, to the left. Xiang went in. He was going to have to put his knees to his chin to use this privy. His casual visual sweep spotted the surveillance camera. *Right where standing orders say it should be. If I turn my body right, this cramped space will help me hide my deployment of the package.*

Xiang dropped his trousers, contorted himself to squat. First, he trickled a little urine onto his fingertips. He used the moisture to dissolve the tape holding the assembly to his thigh. The bots immediately started dispersing. Xiang finished his other business. He cleaned his hands a little more than normal.

He opened the door back into the office. This will be the telling moment. *Will there be a guard waiting or just two fatuous old bulls?* He relaxed when he saw the two arguing quietly. They stopped as he bowed his way out of the office. Step two complete.

Xiang hurried back to his team's facilities in the cave. He spent the rest of his morning clearing the minutia associated with the move across the river. As usual, there were people who took any occasion of change as an opportunity to gain some subtle advantage in the pecking order. Requests for different offices, requests for maintenance to increase airflow, heat, cooling. Requests for repainting.

Xiang had to handle all this carefully and personally. These seemingly trivial matters could profoundly affect his team's morale and performance. He did need to groom an administrative assistant. Ought to be possible now that he was senior staff?

Xiang contained his impatience until the end of the day. At last, he granted or deftly deferred all the requests. All the experiments and research finally were reinitiated. Now he could check on any transmissions from Bomb Central.

Xiang counted on the fact that they wouldn't have locked Bomb Central down tight yet. There would still be construction fixes, the same type of dominance dancing he dealt with all day would be going on there. And, despite the mandate that only army personnel were allowed access to the site, any politically connected member of the science staff would simply do as he did; pay a courtesy visit and try to ingratiate himself or herself with the guy who has the biggest gun around.

His cyberdevice reported a steady stream of status reports from the nanobots. They installed themselves in the official cybernet link – the commnet. They ran his carefully crafted tests of the protocol and security walls. Not much had changed. His father's old access was still live. That was an unexpected plus. He was sure that they would sever that after Bàba's death. Never underestimate the torpidity of bureaucracy!

Step three was successful. Xiang set up a communication package to upload a search program to the swarm of bots. He tried to anticipate all the shortfalls and different avenues that the program might need to explore. Even more important were the triggers to detect security deadfalls, tripwires, and any other dangers the program might engage. If needs must be and the program detected a threat, the bots would simply disperse and exit the facility at their first opportunity.

Xiang needed patience for step four. This would take at least one week before the bots could load and initiate the program. Xiang estimated the search might be successful within one day. However, he considered two weeks to be more probable. If there was no success after a month, he would pull the plug.

CHAPTER SEVEN ADAGIO
1
AINSLEY & JAVIER

Morning, 20th August 2033

*temporary encampment at Pike
County Fairgrounds, Pleasant Hill, IL*

The air was much fresher this morning. The thunderstorm was dramatic last night. This part of the Midwest was prone to summer tornadoes lately. All the volcanic ash that caused the Global Winter in 2029-2030 reduced the energy for spring tornadoes for years now. Good effects with the bad. Other than the ultralights and blimps, air travel was still impossible.

But the slow effects from the substances the Russians plastered throughout the atmosphere was steadily reducing the ash level. It was closer to zero finally. The other good news was that the goop and the ash combined to leach carbon and ozone out of the air as well. Global warming was controlled, if people weren't stupid enough to ignore the lessons learned. It was still going to take centuries before the icepacks and glaciers were restored and the sea levels dropped.

Ainsley looked across the dew-covered grass to the grandstand stage where the public peace negotiations were going to be held by the three sets of leaders; Great Plains Union, Midwest Cooperative, and Texican Flotilla. *This fairground platform used to be the site for presenting blue ribbons for best hog, crowning the year's queen and king, or where the band and caller set up for square dances. Bet no one imagined it would host an international conference for three nation states.*

Speaking of hogs, that one they're barbecuing behind the beer tent smells fabulous. If I miss anything of the gabfest, they'll record and

report it. Might need a beer also. It's going to be warm today.
Priorities.

◆◆◆

The Chief was speaking. "... too long after the Time of Troubles we have all been like packs of dogs on the edge of a great carrion pit, fighting over the bones of the last buffalo."

Someone behind Ainsley whispered hoarsely. "Shore talks purdy, don't he? Are they gonna talk all day-n-night or get to the nut-cuttin?"

Ainsley pursed her lips. She had been enjoying the Chief's poetic turn of phrase before the bumpkin burped out his ignorance. *Know we are supposed to make allowances for cultural differences, but...*

Rather than stand there and become more irritated, Ainsley left the area again. From one of the two men behind her, she heard what she thought might be a lewd suggestion. *Deep, cleansing breath.*

As Ainsley wandered around the grounds, she noticed the troops from the Midwest Cooperative and the Great Plains Union were following the strongly worded suggestion from the leaders to mingle. It seemed as if every one of the Texicans had at least one of the joint task group talking with them.

Overheard. "Naw, we won't miss anything important. There're news crews recording everything. We'll get hourly and daily summaries on our devices. Plus, if there's anything urgent we'll get a flash."

Ainsley couldn't hear the response from the Texican, but the Coop trooper replied. "No, the internet is still pretty well dead. We have some local nets running, but a real internet, even for the whole Cooperative is probably five years away. Society replaced too much of the physically connected net with thousands of the tiny satellite-based routers. We think most of the satellites are still orbiting, but no one has been able to reactivate them."

"What we mostly use for communications is telephone trees. Illinois particularly, but really all the Midwest, was the heart of the old American telephone system, the Bell system. Most of the innovations hit here first. It was also the training grounds for most of the maintenance and support staff."

Mumble, mumble. "Telephone trees? Just a process where everyone who gets some news from a phone call then calls three other people assigned to them. They pass the message along. Also, they pass the message back up the tree. If it has gotten confused, the person who detects the error ...." *Too technical, and boring for me.* Ainsley walked on towards another group.

As she neared, she called out a cheerful, "Hey Grabby." That way the corporal would know her visit was social, not official. He nodded to her but kept center stage in his group.

Grabowski and a Coop sergeant were entertaining four Texicans. True to form, Grabowski passed out a six pack of his beloved Leinenkugel's. Also, true to form, he was holding forth about his second favorite pastime; hunting. "Yeah, this here's always been known as the Pork Capital of the US. Course, whole passel of the farms went out durin the Troubles. Prob'ly half left running now."

"What that means for us is, there's thousands of hogs gone wild all over the countryside. They're seen as real pests. You know hogs?"

A Texican private answered. "Do we know hawgs? Shoooot. We've fe-rile hawgs in the East Texas Piney Woods since before the days of the Alamo. Do y'all know hawgs?" He chugged his beer and crushed the can on his forehead. The thoughtless act shocked Ainsley. *Didn't they reuse their cans? Thought that attitude got a full-frontal lobotomy when the ice caps collapsed and drowned half of humanity. And Grabowski? Sure, it's right not to chide a guest. But he didn't even seem to notice. Man needs some reeducation.*

Grabowski continued, ignoring the can-crushing. "Well Sarge here," Grabowski indicated the Coop sergeant. "Sarge says it's open season on em with no bag limit. What say we organize a party to get us some? They'll be down in the river and creek bottoms, sure enough." The whole group of men and women agreed enthusiastically.

Ainsley made a mental note to write up a commendation for her corporal. Their info said the flotilla was running low on food. This fit under Colonel Shevner's suggestion to look for ways to "help these folks without it looking like charity." She would add a note about retraining on eco-awareness. Should balance out. She walked on towards the next group, a larger gathering near a small stand of trees.

As Ainsley got nearer the group, some sixth sense made her uncomfortable. Possibly it was their tense and watchful stances. Possibly it was because she only saw Texican men; no women, no Coop troops, no Plains people. A step or so closer and she got a whiff of a particular rank, smoky smell.

At that point she was ready to put her best face on it and at least exchange pleasantries. Then Sergeant Wojlkowski called out from her right. "Hey Lieutenant. Got a minute?"

Gratefully, Ainsley turned to the woman. "Sure Sarge. Whatcha need?" The sergeant deftly turned her away from the group of men and kept walking casually away.

She spoke in a low voice out of the side of her mouth. "What you can do, Lieutenant is not ruin our surveillance of those lowlifes. That Texican, Captain Gonzales, gave our guys some intel. This group of jerks hasn't mixed well with the rest of the flotilla. Let's just call these guys the Rednecks."

"The Rednecks have been argumentative from the first, wanting to make this an aggressive invasion by force. The three guys you caught down in Hardin were part of the Rednecks. They're all men. Only one other group of the flotilla was all men. That other group have been straight arrows. The Rednecks have persistently harassed the women of the flotilla and seem to enjoy getting into fights. Gonzales was ready to line them all up along with their "rogue four" you caught, but General Bullock overruled him."

Ainsley thought, *I would have helped Captain Gonzales reload.*

"We're keeping close tabs, with our powder dry. This hasn't been sent to the Council yet, just an informal heads-up in the interests of maintaining good relations."

Ainsley nodded, then realized her sergeant couldn't see that with the sun glaring in her eyes. She acknowledged the information with, "Got it Woj. Just keeping the peace. Let me know if you need anything from me; more people, cover with the Captain or the Council. You got it."

"Thanks LeeLee. Going back on patrol. Watch your six."

Ainsley strolled back towards the grandstand area. She got a ping on her communicator device. She looked at the small screen, the white lettering scrolling painfully slowly across the screen. *Sigh. Oh, for the smartphones, the internet, any of the old devices of my childhood. To think, only five years ago I thought they were so antiquated. And this thing is so slow that the reporters use insane abbreviations. Hurry your team up, Addie, please.*

It was the first hourly summary of the proceedings. The full text finally appeared as she reached the stage area. She stayed just outside the arena to bring herself up to date.

> TRILATERAL PEACE CONFERENCE – 20th Aug 2033 – First Hour
> Welcome – Midwst Coop Ldr Johnson and Grt Plns Union Chf George (Detld text on channel 3 in hour)
> Statmnt of Flotilla's Intent – Gen Bullock. Crop failures in NO, Est Texican regns w contind flood of refugees frm SO. Grp is vanguard of abt 50,000 ppl who nd to relo. Peacfl, but desprat.
> Ldr Johnson - plenty open farm for willing. Why no commun b4 enter?
> Bullock – tried, Arkansan rebs stop & kill envoys. Had fight way thru. Ask 4 assist when mv mn grp 50,000 to stop rebs.
> Agree in princpl. Detail negots to follow. Adjourn until nxt sssn

Ainsley sighed. *Cryptic abbreviations, as usual.* Then she nodded in surprised approval. *One thing has improved at least since the Troubles. Political BS gets short shrift. State the problem, agree the approach, let the worker bees hammer out the details. I'll need to stick my oar in as an official on the Environmental Controls Council. Texicans will need to sign on to our Heal the Planet protocols. No more destruction of irreplaceable cans, for one thing.*

She was about to leave the grandstands and stroll the grounds again when she was hailed from the other side of the stage. Her assistant Hope was with Ron. "Hey LeeLee, come join us! Have you eaten yet?"

Hope was wearing tight ivory shorts and a lovely emerald halter top. Both accented her deep mahogany skin. And her lovely figure. Ron certainly seemed to agree. Ainsley felt another pang of loss. *Give it up, girl. That ship has sailed.* "Thanks. I did have one plate of barbecue but didn't have but a taste of the chicken. We need their recipe!"

Hope beamed. "Got you covered, girlfriend. Pitmaster wasn't gonna share. Family secret developed by Great-granddaddy from 'Kaintuck'."

Ron interjected, "Until she wiggled her cute ass, batted her big brown eyes, and said, 'Oh, please, please."

Hope swatted him playfully. "Fine, see if you get any. Barbecue that is." Ainsley hid her pain. But Ron knew her well. He gave Hope a cautioning look. Ainsley looked at her plate and took an inventory of the mouthwatering meal; blackened chicken, corn on the cob, fresh potato salad, and gelatin with carrots. Not to mention the famous Hardin hard cider.

Hope changed subjects quickly. "Ainsley, I am worried. And Ron won't talk seriously to me about it. Should I be?"

Ainsley gave Hope a quizzical look. "I'm sorry Hope. Worried about what exactly?"

Hope's blush showed, even through her complexion. "Whoops. Been obsessing and fretting Ron so much about this that I forget you've been on patrol down here. Our group got here just this afternoon. Ron just finished all his enhancements testing yesterday."

"What I mean is this singularity business? Is Ron going to turn into a Terminator? Or will other people think he is one and be ready to terminate him? He says I'm being silly, but I really am worried. I know I don't have the same level of college as you two, but this isn't just silliness." She gave Ron a glare. He had the grace to look abashed.

Ainsley bit her tongue before she replied. "You certainly aren't being silly, Hope. Only a male chauvinist oaf would say such a thing." She smiled slightly to indicate it was a tease. "You know Addison's mission in Europe is to help detect any emerging singularity sources. The Council has identified these as the greatest threat the planet faces in the near term. It is certainly serious."

Okay, time to let Ron off the hook a little. "However, you need to understand the key reasons Ron's modifications are in no way going to lead to a singularity. Just a much bigger head." *Can't let him get away scot free.* She was struck by the phrase, given Hope's last name was Scott. *Oh, gotta work that into an embarrassing joke on the two of them. Knowing the origin of the phrase, I will tax them with it.*

"You see, first, his mods are not inheritable. Don't worry. Your babies won't have huge heads, that's assuming Ron doesn't get away Scott free." They both groaned. Ron looked very embarrassed. Hope looked secretly happy.

"Second thing, these are enhancements not fundamental changes. You are too young to remember, but there was a South African Olympic runner whose legs were both replaced by spring leaf prosthetics. Lotta controversy about his wins against others. However, no one claimed he wasn't human. Think of his enhancements like a knee replacement, only better. After all, Ron could get all the info he now carries in his gut, just not as fast and easily."

"Of course, you will have to watch out for bigots. Hard as it may be for you to realize, there used to be a huge problem with people treating people like shit because of their skin color, their sex, their gender, or who they loved." *Some of our guests may be that kind of imbecile.*

Ainsley got up and brushed off her lap. "Duty calls. Take your plates?" She gathered the dishes, dumped the remnants into the slops bucket, did a quick swipe with the brush attached to the wall, then placed everything into trays of soapy water. *Glad to see everyone's being neat. My cleaning rotation in the mess tent should be a breeze.*

Ainsley waved limply to Ron and Hope. They were already absorbed in each other and barely acknowledged. A massive wave of self-pity washed over Ainsley. She blew it with Xiang, with Ron, with every man she tried to get close to. *What's wrong with me?*

Normally she would go huddle-cuddle with Addison. *Who was half a world away, alone, and in mortal peril. While I cry over my sad fate. Boo hoo! Get over it!*

Ainsley walked to the far edges of the fairgrounds as she struggled with her depression. She used all her training, but still tears leaked down her cheeks. Her composure returned slowly as she headed back towards people.

The first person she encountered was Janet Heath, one of the few people equipped with mind-fi. Ainsley was close to Janet. She always felt happier when Janet was the one monitoring Addison's MindMeld channel.

Janet must have seen something in Ainsley's eyes. "Howya doin Sweetpea? Gettin enough to eat, drink? Enough sex?"

Ainsley laughed. *Good old Janet. She can always cheer me up.* "Yes, yes, and never get enough." She took a deep cleansing breath and smiled broadly.

Janet leered. "I hearya. Never get enough sex. Of course, you know I'm always ready to help you out with that, Sweetpea."

Ainsley hugged Janet warmly; but not too warm. "You know I love you to pieces, Heath Bar. And if I had any brains about it I would drop all those dipwad men for you. But can't help how I was wired at birth. Not to change the subject, but you were monitoring Addison today weren't you. Anything you can share?"

Janet considered. "Well, I know you're cleared for most of it. Know you heard all the details about Ravensbruck. That was a bloody mess, but it broke the good guys... Well, okay, the not-so-bad fat cats broke away from the total sleazeball oligarchs. Anyway, today they had a conference in Basel, Switzerland. Addison's sponsor anointed her as ambassador from the Great Plains Union."

Ainsley's eyes popped. "Really? Switzerland? Ambassador? My, there'll be no living with her now! And I thought Ron had a big head!"

Janet nodded. "It only gets better. She went ahead and acted as our ambassador; oops ambassadress. She initiated negotiations for an alliance with the anti-Ravensbruck group. Can't tell you any more than that about that."

"Last thing. There is some military crap going down, but Addison's not involved. She's safe playing footsie with some English or French Lord. I have a break now that we're done with the heavy stuff. Don't go on again for about three hours."

Ainsley hugged her again. "Get some rest, Heath Bar. I know how draining those MindMeld watches can be." They walked in the same direction, towards the fairgrounds.

The two were heading in slightly different directions, but only a few paces apart. Janet turned to Ainsley and pointed. "Hey Ainsley! Isn't that Latin hunk over there the Texican captain you went head-to-head with? You didn't tell me he is muy caliente! I might even go straight for him. Well, bi maybe." She had an ear-to-ear shit-eating grin.

Ainsley knew exactly what Janet was trying to do. But she couldn't get mad at her. *Janet can sense the loneliness in me since she is so lonely herself. Besides, Captain Gonzales is kind of a hunk. Good leader. Strong moral compass. And slightly exotic. Ticks all the boxes for me, if he proves to be as smart as I think. Not ready to get serious, but Hey! Two lonely soldiers on leave. A chance encounter in an exotic foreign city – well, as exotic as Pleasant Hill, Illinois gets, anyway. Sounds like one of those old cheesy cine-romances to me.*

She went past Janet towards the picnic table where Gonzales sat alone. Janet patted her butt as she went by. *Cheeky!* As she got close, she hailed the captain. "Hello Captain. Gonzales, isn't it? Mind if I join you? Orders are to make y'all feel welcome." *That is so lame.*

Gonzales leapt to his feet. At least he didn't click his heels. "Please join me, Lieutenant. And call me Javier, please. And you are Ainsley, yes?"

Ainsley dimpled. Must have made some impression at least, even if it was for being a hard-ass soldier. "Thanks Javier. You aren't eating alone are you? Bad form."

He smiled in return. "No, my new friends just deserted me when they heard the square dance music start. Afraid I have the proverbial two left feet. They almost drummed me out of ROTC at Texas A&M University because I couldn't keep cadence. Thank God they needed my double-E skills – Electrical Engineering, that is."

Ainsley's smile grew broader and she noticed it was entirely natural, not the Cute Damsel, Grade X. "That's a coincidence, I'm an engineer too, bio-med. Speaking of bio, is that a pie you've got hiding there? Hint, hint."

Javier laughed. "Yes, custard of some sort. I didn't quite hear which kind. When they told me they didn't have coconut cream, my favorite. Sure this will be scrumptious though. Home made." He cut two generous slices onto saucers. The slices were slightly larger than the pottery. He looked around the table. "Sorry, don't have a clean fork." He looked around to see what they could improvise.

Ainsley whipped out her all-purpose tool and unfolded a scoop. "No prob. A good scout is always prepared." She dug in. *Lemon cream, not my favorite, but it is very good. I'm so glad he didn't treat me like a dainty girl and give me a wimpy size piece.* "I knew there was no hope, but I was wishing for banana cream, my favorite. Wonder if I will ever see bananas or coconuts again."

Javier dug in for a healthy bite. "Mmm, lemon meringue is maybe my second favorite. Might have to marry this cook. By the way, you're in luck. We should be able to supply coconuts and bananas to you poor, deprived Yanquis." He took another healthy bite.

Ainsley shooed away the gathering flies. She spooned up another bite, but before putting it in her mouth she voiced her skepticism. "I know I didn't pay that much attention to soft courses like geography, but I'm pretty sure Texas-Oklahoma-Arkansas didn't grow either before the Big Melt. Are you saying the climate's changed that way?" *Mmm. Second bite better than the first. I'd try to beat Javier in proposing to the baker if I hadn't seen the sweet, gray-haired grandma taking them out of her basket.*

After Javier finished his second bite, he delicately wiped his lips and took a large swig of milk. Ainsley didn't think highly of the flavor combination of milk and lemon. She was glad she had her iced tea. She kept her doubtful look focused on the man, hiding her careful inventory of his lean, muscular build.

Javier tucked his napkin back in his lap. "No, we don't grow em. We are strictly focusing on subsistence crops; rice, beans, soy, corn, tomatoes, and such. But we have reliable, if tense, trade relations that stretch south through Central America into upper South America."

Ainsley still had doubts. And another piece of pie. When she swallowed a bite, she continued. "Really? They weren't hammered to their knees by the tsunamis and the global winter, let alone food riots and battles over gasoline?"

Javier set his saucer aside. Ainsley wondered, *When did he finish his second piece? I still have half of mine left.* He asked, "Did you notice the reporting in 2027 and 2028 about the nationwide shortage in street drugs? The FBI and DEA were finally getting a handle on the "legal" pharma sources, thanks to D.C. finally getting some spine. But didn't you wonder why the cartels didn't step in to fill the gap? I did."

Ainsley thought for a few seconds "Have to admit, I was focused on my doctorate and a personal problem. Didn't notice much outside my little island of focus."

Javier stood up for a second to brush invisible crumbs from his shorts. Ainsley watched. *Runner's legs. Nice.* He sat and took a final drink from his tumbler. "Trust me. It was dramatic. After the collapse we found out that most of the cartels saw the writing on the wall. Some split and headed for Switzerland or other shelters. But to their credit, most decided to stay and organize."

CHAPTER SEVEN Adagio 1

"Say what you will about the drug lords. Ruthless, brutal. But the ones that stayed showed they were still rooted with their people. They were capable, extremely well-funded, with disciplined paramilitary forces and experienced logistics. They dropped the drug trade and never looked back. They hired the best consultants on how to prepare for the Big Melts and after. They brushed aside the national governments like flies, when they resisted. More often, they just formalized already existing ties. Their societies are functional. Yes, death rates were staggering, but undoubtedly far less than if the cartels hadn't stepped in. Now they want to be involved in legitimate trade with all of us."

Ainsley gave her conditional acceptance. Besides, she had finished her pie. "Wow! We need to get you in front of the next session. This is important. If you're sure about their intentions." She stood and tried to drag Javier to his feet.

"Whoa, little firecracker. I'm an engineer, not a politician. Barely know how to drive this here train. Wouldn't want to have to steer it." The cornball routine made Ainsley laugh. He continued, "Besides, the General's got it covered. He brought a trade rep from Colombia or such. Don't know what they call their counties or corporations. They're closemouthed about things like that."

Ainsley relented. "Fine, but we are going to listen to the broadcast of the session. They'll cover how we do things in the Union and Coop." She held up her hand to stave off an interruption that wasn't coming. "Not that we want you to adopt our ways wholesale. We're open to change if you show us a better way. Not many hard and fast rules."

"One of the founding mothers of both the Union and the Cooperative was a poli-sci professor from Northwestern. Ann was brilliant. Saw what worked in the old US system and what needed fixing. What surprised all of us was that the main source for many of her ideas was speculative fiction; science fiction. She required all of us to read two of Robert Heinlein's novels; <u>Starship Troopers</u> and <u>The Moon is a Harsh Mistress</u>. Both of our countries adopted many of the ideas he talked about. But enough serious talk. Tell me what you do for relaxation since you don't dance."

Javier looked pained. "It's not that I don't dance or don't want to dance. Some of my favorite old-time cines were Dirty Dancing, Singing in the Rain, and Flash Dance. I just literally can't dance. I assume you were in ballet and Trebletromps as a kid and excelled at both.

Ainsley gave his upper arm a gentle squeeze. *Mmm, rock solid.* "Well, I did take some modern dance, but only because my soccer coach told us that it would improve our game."

Javier's face took on new animation. "Soccer! Me too. What position? I was usually sweeper."

Ainsley brightened also. *Another box ticked.* "Oh, our mortal enemy. My twin, Addie, and I were right and left wings. Addison's my twin. We used to drive oppositions crazy trying to keep us straight as we switched around. We were the A-Team. To top it off, I'm a natural righty and she's a leftie. Except when it comes to politics. Then it's vice versa."

Ainsley was setting up her comm device during the last bit of conversation. She put one ear bud in her right ear and indicated Javier should use the other. That this required a close snuggle was just the price they would have to pay.

Late afternoon, Session Two

Now that the Texicans and the allied leaders came to preliminary terms it was time to begin developing common understandings and ways of going forward. This session would be a first step. Ainsley and Javier settled in to listen to the broadcast of the meeting. Ainsley wanted to see how her leaders and the Cooperative leaders would begin the all-important step of blending in a new cultural body.

The speaker was Coop Leader Zeke Johnson. "Howdy again. Want to keep this session as informal as possible. Ask questions at any time. If you're here, just go to one of the two mics halfway out from the left and right of the stage. If you're listening on a comm device, just pick up any nearby phone. The operators will connect you in."

"First, Let's talk about rules. We try to keep em to a minimum. We use guidin principles, and as few of those as possible."

"Principle One: We're all in it together. Means if one of us is failin then his or her neighbors should lend a helpin hand. Not charity. If someone is just plain lazy, people will know. But we're all hurtin from all the crap that's gone down, so cut people slack when you can."

"Principle Two: Drive authority and responsibility to the lowest level. You are responsible, first and foremost. Then comes family. Most things get solved at this or the next level; neighborhood. Then town or borough, county, etc. Only send something up if it crosses boundaries or you really need outside help."

"Principle Three: Follow the golden rule. What would you want someone else to do if you were gonna be on the short end of the stick?

"Principal Four: Trial by peers means your fellow citizens look at these high-level guidelines, your actions, and then use common sense to decide if you're following the rules. They're not going to consult some arcane code book of detailed policies and procedures. We have some really sharp ex-lawyers willin and able to advise and cite precedent for complex cases, but simple guidelines and common sense will be our bottom line."

"Principal Five: Children are a sacred gift and responsibility. We start with the assumption that parents love their kids and want what's best for em. God help you if we find out it isn't true. And God damn you if you hurt any child."

"Principal Six: Live and let live. If you aren't hurting your neighbor or mother earth, are nurturing any children in your care, then we have no business in what you do in your bedrooms, what you believe or preach. Keep things loose. Cut your neighbors the same slack."

"Principal Seven: All are welcome here, but you can only be a citizen if you are willing to give your last full measure of devotion. Every woman, man, and child who has any capacity owes service to his fellow citizens. That's how you earn the right to a say in how we run things. Don't serve, don't vote."

Great Dieback to Singularity

"The militia will get first call on all potential citizens. If they choose you, they'll train you, equip you, and use you. Next in priority are those services deemed essential. At this time, that's farmin and medical. Your elected reps can change priorities as surpluses happen or unanticipated circumstances arise."

"Now, the bible has ten rules. Or two, if you follow Jesus' update. So far, we are happy with these seven. But we aren't dictators nor Moses with God whisperin in our ears. As the elected leaders, our service to all of you will always start and end with listening and learning. Particularly to our new Texican friends, we want to hear your thoughts. Do you think we are full of shit? Do you know a better way? Your ideas will only make us better. But, I beg you in this. Keep it simple. We want our rules to be understandable by all."

One of the Texican ladies bustled up to the mic on the left. "What about likker? Don't you have laws controlling that? And ..."

◆◆◆

After a short refreshment break, the session resumed. The next speaker was José Quintana from Columbia. The buzz at that announcement required the Chief to pound his gavel three times, loudly, before he could restore order. "Señor Quintana, welcome. Please share with us your thoughts."

Quintana looked down for a moment. The voice-over reporter broadcast that he had the piercing eye of an eagle when he looked up. "Thank you, Chief, Leader. As the Chief said, I am from the former country of Columbia. I was traveling through the Texican Confederacies negotiating trade alliances. Then I learned of this expedition. I believe this is an opportunity to expand potential trade routes."

"Let me start by confirming the rumors some of you may have heard. Most of the leaders of Azmayca, the name we call our territory, were previously heads of various drug cartels. We make no apologies for our pasts. About half of the cartel leaders fled to safe havens. Those of us who remained dedicated ourselves and our substantial resources to preserving what we could of our peoples and lands."

CHAPTER SEVEN Adagio 1

"We have no desire to resume our former trade. The catastrophes have presented us with an opportunity to lead the survivors of mid-Latin America into a better and more stable world. To that end, we hope to establish peaceable commerce with all willing parties."

"I have been heartened by what I have heard here. Originally, I was not going to reveal our origins, not out of a sense of shame, but because we deeply distrust and despise what the Nord Americanos have done to us for centuries. We only hope that your fine words today are matched by corresponding fine actions."

"We are wary because of our shared history. Show us you will treat us as equal partners and you will have no truer friends. Betray us as your ancestors have in the past and we will be implacable enemies."

"In conclusion, let me offer another bit of cautioning advice, if you will allow it. Some may think that we are far away, and you can blissfully ignore us for now. Please believe me when I say the world is getting rapidly smaller once again."

"If you find my words about our shared past harsh, then you need to consider what we are hearing from other places we are in contact with. Australia, Japan, India; all think the world abandoned them and are especially bitter. They blame the US and Europe especially. The both of you, along with China were the major contributors to the icecaps melting. Then you just got in lifeboats and left everyone else to drown. Deserved or not, this is your legacy."

"Finally, China is a resting giant. It survived better than most countries, although its battle with Russia was near-fatal. But they are awakening again. We hear disturbing rumors of new and terrifying technologies, possibly based on the Russian New Shock Troops Army, the Supermen. This could be a threat to end all of us few survivors." Quintana stalked off as a profound silence settled on the observers.

Back on the picnic grounds Ainsley murmured to Javier, "Seems to spend most of his time shaming us. Little strange for a trade representative?"

Javier said, "He has good points, Ainsley. But he should be trying to win friends too. Guess old habits die hard."

That evening around dusk

Illinois River bottoms land near

Naples, IL

Grabowski wiped a line of sweat from his brow. Fog was beginning to come off the nearby river. His Texican hunting partner whispered to Grabowski. "Think I hear that big ol sow. It's up on the right. That's where the blood trail was headin."

Grabowski grunted. "Okay. Be careful. They're double deadly when they're wounded."

His partner, Billie Joe was it? Anyway, his partner looked disgustedly over his shoulder. "Don't tell mama how to suck aigs. It'll be finer 'n frog's hair."

Grabowski shook his head. *Is that even English?* He thought he heard something behind and looked back to his left. Right then a five-hundred-pound boar burst out of the brush ahead. Both men fired their shotguns, but the beast kept coming and mowed Billie Joe down like a paper doll. The beast's momentum threw Grabowski back against a tree. He managed, barely, to keep his feet. He fired his second barrel into the beast's brain at point blank range.

The rest of the hunting party came plowing through the dense growth. They took in the scene and another one of the Texicans exclaimed. "Damn! Bubba Jim's daid, taint he!"

Grabowski shook off his mental fog and returned to his combat training. *Triage rules. I'm bruised, possible broken ribs, so I need to be careful. But the man down needs attention, Now!* "Thomson! Fire up your comm device. We need EMTs and medevac soonest. Don't move him! If his neck or spine are compromised, you could kill him. Let me check him for any fast bleeds." He knelt and cut away Bubba Jim's shirt and pants. *Good! Minor cuts only. Nothing arterial. Arm is fractured in two places. Probably the right leg also. Need to rig a back board and transport him to that clearing a hundred yards back. Can't forget that injured sow either or I'll be in deep shit with the Eco Council.*

Grabowski designated three people to track and dispatch the sow, carefully. He had two men cut and strip saplings to make a travois. He ordered one woman to stay at the back of the travois, lifting it over obstructions as necessary while the others pulled the load. He deployed the rest of the party as perimeter guards.

The slog back to the clearing seemed to take forever. Thomson said the medevac was still five out and they alerted the nearest clinic. *Probably the company's MASH unit back in Pittsfield. Rest and rehydrate time.*

As they all collapsed against stumps and trees around the abandoned feed lot, one of the Texican's exclaimed bitterly. "Shoot. You still got good comms, EMTs, medevac, and nearby clinics. Can tell you weren't abandoned by Washington when the shit hit the fan!"

Thomson looked up sharply. "Pardon me son. Chavez isn't it. No offense, you being a guest of ours and all. But you are purely full of shit." Chavez gave Thomson a murderous look. Thomson ignored it and kept on. "You see, I was a congressman from Northern Wisconsin. Republican, so not part of the majority. From 2026 until the Troubles I was on the committee that helped plan how to get ready."

"Now, we had plans for every part of the US. Weren't going to be able to save everything, but we could have done a lot better. I'm ashamed to say it was, to a high degree, my party's fault, along with the stupidity of some execs, state, and local leaders."

"First problem was the insistence that all the prep was to be secret. Wasn't only because of Republicans, oil industry, climate change deniers, and just plain stupid people. We got a lot of pressure from overseas and the U.N. 'Can't cause global panic.' Global catastrophe and massive deaths were okay, though."

"Second, I was the one who insisted on allowing local opt outs. Can't trust big government, even though this is precisely when we probably should have. No matter. We setup funding and massive federal resource outlays for any local entity that requested.

Budget be damned. Some people stepped up, particularly the Carolinas, Georgia, Maine. I'm very proud of them. In general, they did better than any of the federal efforts. Happy I insisted on allowing local control."

"Others, including Texas, had their heads so far up their ass that they couldn't see the tsunamis until after they wiped out Houston, Galveston, New Orleans, Florida, and about 100 million people."

"One of the people I worked with on the committee was from down your way, Sam Houston Beauregard."

Chavez piped up, surprised but still steaming. "Yeah, he was our rep. Good ol boy."

Thomson nodded once. "Yeah, he was a good guy. At the end he was still trying to get evacuations of the coast moving faster. Died trying. True hero." All were quiet for a moment, lost in their thoughts of those awful, awful days.

"I tried to help Sam to get your officials off the dime. Couldn't understand why the hell they were dragging their feet. Then Sam laid it all out for me. Seems the oil execs were putting pressure on to get their facilities, staff, and mansions relo'ed first. It's why there were new refineries going up in Ohio and Tennessee. And pipelines being rerouted. Some of the other fat cats were also only looking out for themselves."

"But the biggest stumbling block was our own success as climate change deniers. Didn't matter what any fool could see before their eyes. The Republicans in Texas had already lost one US Senate seat, three House seats, and were in danger of losing control of one part of the state legislature for the first time in over twenty-five years. That was all they could see or care about. Hope you hung them all."

Chavez sullenly asked, "Are you saying that was all the Republicans fault?"

Thomson's voice rose from its quiet lilt. "Weren't you listening son? I was and am a proud Republican. There are enough fools to go around for all political parties; people more worried about keeping their power, living a good life. Didn't matter if they were

CHAPTER SEVEN Adagio 1

Republ-ocrats, Demo-gogues, or Green-gimme-a-Piece-of-that. Most of them forgot what they promised to do; to serve their constituents. It's just that we Republicans have a little more of the blood on our hands, this time."

There was a stunned silence that allowed the group to hear the oncoming ambulance and the party returning from dispatching the wounded sow. They quietly got Bubba Jim's travois up and carried it the short distance through the tall grass to the gravel road.

Meanwhile, back at the fairground

N ow that the second session adjourned, Ainsley reluctantly took her head away from Javier's shoulder. His hand did remain at her waist. She didn't quite remember when it got there.

"Before the session so rudely interrupted us, I started to tell you about Addie. She's my only living family. I know there's a lot of that going around, but ours was a little different. We started studying at the University of Illinois in Champaign-Urbana when we got a call. There was a home invasion in Schaumburg, our home. Mom, Dad, our brother Drew – all murdered. They think some druggies got the wrong house. Never caught the perps. Our Time of Troubles started earlier than most peoples. It was tough enough doing undergrad work at thirteen. That almost sent us both over the deep end. Our maternal grandparents helped as they could, but think the loss crushed them. They both died within the year."

"Addison has been my rock and soulmate, even before that. Since, we've been inseparable. She's on assignment away right now, so I sometimes may act distracted. Sorry."

Javier held her more tightly during her revelations. He gave her a squeeze and took her face between his hands. "Ainsley, I was going to say I understand your pain. But I don't. My loss was similar in some ways, but not as ugly. A drunk driver killed my Dad, Mom, and one sister in a car crash on their way home to our house in Pearland, Texas. Policemen at the door woke my sister

Angela and me up in the middle of the night. Still have nightmares sometimes when I'm awakened early."

"Angie was a successful musician. Her group played at South By Southwest and was about to get a big contract. She knew that would take her on the road all the time. She dropped out of the band and took a job in a brokerage doing clerical work to support me through college. I owe her everything. Brought her along on the Flotilla. You'll meet her later. She's doing dishes with some of her new friends right now." They sat together in silence, each alone with their memories.

Ainsley believed things were getting too intense. She knew she was especially vulnerable right now. Any new relationship must begin in mutual strength. She was trying to think of a more neutral topic. *Maybe we could get a pickup soccer game going.*

Javier was on the same page. "Ainsley, I have to say I was surprised by the landscape here. Thought Illinois was supposed to be flat as a pancake. There are hills and cliffs in every part of Illinois that I've seen."

Ainsley smiled, glad for the switch. "Just go about forty miles east or north, Javier. The only hills you will see are the old interstate overpasses. It's..."

Just then two men came running up. Sergeant Wojlkowski and a Texican lieutenant were out of breath. The lieutenant started his report so Woj deferred. "It's that group from near Pine Bluff. They scampered with all their gear. Worse, there are three of our women and two of the host women missing."

Captain Gonzales bit off his words. "Thought you had them under close observation. How did they get out of the area undetected?"

Woj jumped in. "They created a distraction, sir. There was a fire in the stables, and we all had to rush to save the horses and other livestock. We left two on guard. The Texican was found unconscious, Private Shelby's throat was slit, sir."

Gonzales composed himself. He went on in a sober and quiet voice. "Okay. How long have they been gone? Do we know which way they headed? What do they have for transport?"

CHAPTER SEVEN Adagio 1

Ainsley interrupted, giving Captain Gonzales an Equal to Equal Acknowledgement, Grade Five. "By your leave Captain. First, Woj have we activated the local warning system and alerted our people watching the vessels on the Mississippi and Illinois? Sent word up the chain of command?"

The sergeant regained her breath. "In order asked: Gone no more than fifteen. Headed east, at least as they left here. As is standard practice, we disabled all the vehicles during the meeting. Believe they got three horses before they started the fire, but that's a guess, not a sure count. Corporal Stephenson of the locals got their calling tree going and alerts to their town clowns – pardon me – to the local constabulary. Haven't called the people at the boats. Do that next. You are my chain of command, Lieutenant, and no, the Captain and above haven't heard yet."

Ainsley looked to Javier. The captain nodded and continued, "Okay, so we have some time to organize. You'll explain 'calling tree' to me later, please. Let's alert our leaders and get a chase force going, quickly." He and his lieutenant trotted off to the left.

Ainsley started to run off to find her leader, Captain Karls. Woj grabbed her arm, startling her. Her look brought Ainsley to a halt. "Lieutenant, one of the women they took was Hope. Ron has a concussion, being treated now."

It was like someone punched Ainsley in the gut. She closed her eyes for a second and then took off at a dead run. She yelled over her shoulder. "Get the Falcons ready to fly Sarge. NOW!"

◆ ◆ ◆

The impromptu briefing was being held in a barn behind the grandstand stage. The post-conference socializing buzz was masking their quiet, intense discussion. General Bullock apologized. "We Texicans are sorry we brought this scum with us to your country. We would like to take the lead to hunt them down."

A colonel of the Midwest Militia reacted angrily. "Sorry or not General, you did bring them. And we can't be sure this isn't all a ploy on your part."

Ainsley quickly interrupted. "Pardon Colonel. It's because of a warning from the Texican Captain Gonzales that we were watching the creeps in the first place. And I was there when his squad executed their four deserters for rape and murder. Think he's proved his bona fides, sir."

The colonel harrumphed, "Right. Sorry General, heat of the moment. But this is our territory, so we will take lead. Glad to have your support." He looked like the last words were pulled out of his mouth with pliers.

Ainsley interrupted again. "Permission to send my Falcons for air cover and reconnaissance, sirs?"

Bullock replied. "It's just after midnight. Do y'all have night vision? And better not get too close, some of those bastards are sharpshooters."

Ainsley assured them. "Night vision and thermal scanners. We will equip two of our ultralights with the smallest pilots, minimal gear, and double electrical batteries. Be able to fly silent near them for almost two hours once we pinpoint them. The rest will fly perimeter." Ainsley was sweating every second of delay. Knew it was necessary, but Hope was in danger now. *The good news and the bad news are that she came to us in the first place to get a Clipper. Any bastard that does anything will pay. But the others will kill her in a heartbeat.*

A Midwest Militia communications tech called out from a corner of the show barn they were using for the strategy session. "Hey, just got an update from over at Pearl. One of the old pig farmers didn't have his livestock truck secured. Neighbor heard it grinding gears as it left his farm. Went to check on old Ron. He was sound asleep but allowed as to how he didn't always follow those "silly rules" and lock it all up tight. Looks like the bandits have wheels. They left two exhausted horses and headed back in our direction."

Everyone, including the locals, looked at the crackling old gas company-issued state map. Pearl was a burg due east on the Illinois River. About where horses could have reached if ridden as hard as possible. Now they were coming back to get the rest of the bandits and hostages onboard.

CHAPTER SEVEN Adagio 1

Ainsley's captain turned to her. "Okay Lieutenant. Looks like we have a flight plan for you. Get them ready. Warn them not to spook the S.O.B.s or they'll turn on the hostages."

The same comm tech stood up from his equipment again and called out in his thin breaking voice. "Any of you Lieutenant Cameron? Got an urgent call for you from your comm group." Ainsley burned with frustration. *What now. Gotta get going!*

She dashed to the comm set and donned the headphones, thumbing on the mic. The tech seemed surprised she knew what to do. "Cameron here. Go."

The operator on the other end came on. "Lieutenant, we have an emergency priority TCD message for you." Ainsley shook her head in frustration. *Oh, right. Can't use the term MindMeld on open channels.*

She knew this was likely from Addison. *Lord, it never rains but it pours.* "Go."

The operator went into a quiet monotone. "Report is from Agent A-Prime. Summary follows: Need help with bio. Probable instance of another enhanced supersoldier."

Ainsley looked around helplessly. She saw her captain sign to her. She signed back the single word, "Emergency." He nodded and turned back to Sergeant Wojlkowski, whom he was already briefing. She took off at a dead run for the MindMeld tent.

Ainsley caught her breath and slowed as she neared the equipment tent. Good to see the sentry was alert and challenging her, despite the fact they were close associates. She gave the appropriate response, saluted, and went in. She turned to the security chief on duty. Congreve, she saw. Good man. "Calling Condition Red One, Lieutenant. Lock this tent down. No one, repeat, no one in or out except for yourself until I give the okay. Double check perimeter patrols and run a full bug sweep."

Congreve snapped to attention and saluted. "Roger Lieutenant. Code Red One. Lock down. Perimeter check. Full electronics sweep." He quick stepped from the tent.

Ainsley walked over to the MindMeld relay and booster deck. She asked the tech, Janet she saw to her relief, "Satellite connection still good, Corporal?"

Janet looked up from the equipment she was immersed in monitoring. "Five by, Lieutenant. Addie is on hold. Been stalling her host, Lord Townerly, by using the emergency bathroom visit ploy. Glad you got here fast. Might have worn thin soon."

Ainsley grabbed the back of the metal chair. "Thanks, you're relieved Corporal."

Janet stood as Ainsley swapped places. "Acknowledge, relieved at zero hours thirty-one minutes, twenty-first August 2033.

MindMeld chat: [Ainsley: *Hey A-Prime! I'm on. What's shakin Madame Ambassadress?* → Addison: *Chat later, dear. Right now being asked to look at the lab of Doctor Dmitri Vyrvykvist from my professional bioengineering perspective. I'll turn this into full bandwidth look-and-listen chat mode. You put the right words into my mouth please.* ⏱]

CHAPTER EIGHT ADAGIO
2
ADDISON & MALCOLM

18th August 2033

Château de Loche, Loche, Indre et Loire, France

Addison pulled up the pop-up thumbnail bio on the Earl.

John Townerly, Earl Canning

Lord Townerly was created Earl Canning by King Harry in August 2028. Born John Townerly, St. Austell, Cornwall, 6 June 1978. Townerly distinguished himself as head of the intervention and rescue expedition in the Italian Dustup Operation of 2025. After retirement from the SAS, Townerly had a brilliant career in world finance, playing a key figure in the attempts to re-establish the London Financial centers after the catastrophes caused by the Brexit debacle and subsequent loss of British preeminence.

Lord Townerly asked the trio to wait at the far corner of his library while he finished weighing a dispute between two farmers living within his jurisdiction. Malcolm and Kaitlin chatted on the settee while Addison mused quietly, standing in front of the imposing hearth. *What are the elements that make this Château simply exude authenticity compared to that cinema-set "castle" we recently escaped? Hmm. Break it down. Townerly acting as lord of the manor ten meters away lends a true quiet dignity. Contrast that with the oafish seduction scene with Grubenflagg at his dinner table. But this room is the real difference. Floor to four-meter ceilings of book cases lining three walls only interrupted by the entryways on either end and by the hearth. The last wall has that bank of windows overlooking that "charmant" lake. It's like I've walked into – What was the name of that cinedrama Granny and Pawpaw always loved? Upstairs, Downstairs? No, Downton something.*

A true bibliophile, Addison breathed in the scent of leather-bound, inked pages into the bottoms of her lungs. Certainly, electronic media is wonderful. In her bag, she now carried the equivalent of all the published works that had been in the drowned Library of Congress. But this room took her back to the beloved library stacks at her universities. The volumes in this room were certainly far fewer, but the well-used, immaculately maintained volumes looked to be a creditable representative sample.

After he dismissed the two petitioners, Lord Townerly made a beckoning gesture with two upraised fingers. The trio arrayed themselves before his desk, Malcolm in front. Addison gave his lordship a careful study; memorizing his mannerisms, facial idiosyncrasies, and general demeanor. She filed it under "Impartial Judge, Grade Five". *A perfect example, if ever I have cause to use it.*

Malcolm proceeded to give a succinct summary of the debacle of three nights before. He described the torturous dinner, the whispered commands from Count G. to Bob-O, his warning to Addison, the loud thump that made him run to her door, the bodies of the four men, and their subsequent escape. He ended, "Judge me as you will, M'lord, for threatening your alliance. However, these mamselles only came here after I personally guaranteed safe passage. You need to assure me you will protect these two women. Ms. Cameron has been most grievously mistreated." Lord Townerly's face morphed into a Gentle Leader, again Grade Five. Breeding will tell.

Addison still regarded Lord Townerly with a wary eye. He began disarming her, slightly, with his bluff, open manner, and his warm welcome to his Château earlier. He now dismissed Malcolm's combative statement. Lord Townerly replied softly, but firmly. "Of course, Malcolm. You know that anyone who I welcome to my house as a guest, I offer bread, board, and safeguard. That is the foundation of any civilized code of honor. I would as soon fail in my duties to succor the people who are my charge." He gestured at the surrounding countryside.

As far as Addison could detect, he was utterly sincere. He waved the three to seat themselves in front of the wrap-around desk. Addison and Kaitlin took advantage of his gracious offer. Addison gave his lordship another careful study. She filed it under "Courtly Patrician, Grade Five".

Malcolm still looked uncomfortable. He told his employer, Lord Townerly, that, "The actions of the three people before you – Addison, Kaitlin" *(No, Rahel),* "and me – have probably destroyed the consortium headed by Count Grubenflagg. Given the nature of the attack, I believed myself honor-bound to give all support and aid to Ms. Cameron. I'll completely understand and support you if you are compelled to disavow me and my actions, M'lord. But..."

Lord Townerly interrupted abruptly. "Nonsense, Malcolm. I am in full support. That was a heinous attack. It was fortunate you were across the hall and able to take decisive action against those four brutes. Detested Owens-Binghampton since I met the man. Won't miss him. Glad you took care of that mess."

Malcolm was turning pink at the gills. "I'm sorry My Lord..." Addison mused, *How cute. Soldier of fortune, alpha male, and still able to be visibly embarrassed.* She felt a warm rush in her loins.

Lord Townerly tut-tutted. "Enough M'lords for the day, Malcolm. A simple 'John' will do en famille."

"I'm sorry, John. I have misled you. By the time I got to Addison's door she had eliminated all threats. Ms. Schlötke and I simply helped facilitate her departure. I was prepared to do more, and would have, but even those eventualities were anticipated by Addison."

John gave Addison a long, considering look. "It seems Dr. Cameron..."

"Addison, please, M'lord."

"A pleasure, if you will call me John. It seems, Addison, that you are far more than simply the brilliant bioengineer and cyberneticist that I gathered from the reports about your seminar and a reading of your PhD thesis." He cocked his head, waiting for her reply.

CHAPTER EIGHT Adagio 2

Addison thought, *It took months of effort to combine those two separate works after the fact. Glad it looks seamless now. And yes, both of our theses were brilliant, thank you.*

Addison gave John a Conspirators Smile, Grade Four. "I would claim that the severe conditions during the Time of Troubles forced many of us to become proficient in martial arts. There is some truth to that. But as you surmise, I have trained and served in our tribal militia, then in the Great Plains Union Defense Militia. I estimated an attack to be likely that night and took appropriate precautions. And Malcolm is being modest. He was at my door within seconds of the beginning of the attack, armed and prepared to lend assistance. My opponents were sloppy and typical machismo types who presumed they could easily dominate a 160 centimeters tall, slender woman. They never saw me play soccer – excuse me, futbol – as a wing or midfielder." Impish Grin, Grade Three.

Addison took a deep breath. *In for a penny, in for a pound. I think he will be trustworthy, and he is my best shot so far. I do believe his self-abnegation. The sense of noblesse oblige he conveyed was not condescending. He truly believes his privileged status and powers require him to act in the best interests of his peoples. He reminds me of the Great Plains Union Chief.*

"As I told the seminar, my Uncle Jay wants to open overseas markets for our software. The Union Council wants to begin developing international ties as well. They are concerned about threats they see emerging that could easily overwhelm humanity's fragile recovery. By no means am I a designated emissary, but both asked me to keep my eyes and ears opened to opportunities for long term, mutual assistance between like-minded parties."

John smiled back at Addison, about a medium grade, gratitude for honesty type smile. "Thank you, Addison. We will discuss that fully at a later date. However, we need to consider the immediate ramifications of the contretemps at Ravensbruck. As I said, I have no intention of disavowing you, Malcolm, or failing in my responsibilities as host to protect those under my roof, Addison and???" He turned to Rahel/Kaitlin.

Great Dieback to Singularity

She responded, "Kaitlin, John, thank you."

"And you Kaitlin." John got up and began to pace the beautifully carpeted library floor. The room enraptured Addison once again. She was dying to spend a few hours looking through the shelves. Such a bounty of knowledge captured like a prehistoric insect dipped in amber. The internet was fast, breathtakingly comprehensive, wonderful. But in a library, one could wander aimlessly and discover hidden treasures, like a child exploring new worlds.

John returned from the windows to face his guests. "I only joined the Western Europe Consortium for Reconstruction because of pressure from Grubenflagg and others. They are right that piecemeal construction efforts have often been counterproductive. Our disaster-weary people need more relief, and quickly."

"The incident at Ravensbruck is not the only reason I am questioning the value of the consortium, as configured. There have been very disturbing reports that criminal methods are in use by a minority of my peers, including Grubenflagg. I now have what I consider to be proof of three recent uses of extortion, physical intimidation, and one disappeared scientist that Owens-B has probably murdered. I believe my evidence, in combination with your testimony will allow removal of these reprobates from our group, if you are willing to assist?" Addison, Rahel/Kaitlin, and Malcolm/Bill all indicated assent. *Gotta keep names straight. New rule: Use cover names, even in my mind, when in public.*

20th August

Town Hall, Basel, Switzerland

Addison stretched slightly and then cuddled up to Bill's (*Not Malcolm's, when they were being intimate!*) furry back. All that hair took some getting used to. Even his slight musk was different than any other man with whom she had been close. Nice to have a few leisurely moments after the hectic pace of the last three weeks. The upcoming conference week would probably be frenetic as well. *Gather ye rosebuds while ye may.*

CHAPTER EIGHT Adagio 2

At her back, Rahel (*Not Kaitlin!*) stirred slightly. Her hand slid up to cup Addison's breast. *Think she's still asleep. That is comfort, not titillation*, she giggled to herself. Rahel was a sweet woman. She assured Addison that she had a committed but open relationship with a woman at home, so this was simply pleasure with no strings attached. Rahel also made another thing gently clear. "Sorry Bill, I'm strictly focused on women, no bi!" Addison was lonely and greedy, she admitted to herself. Well, she was gathering while she could.

Whoops! Look at the time. Need to hit the refresher for a quick needle spray shower, slap on some "impress the Lords and Ladies" garb, and scurry to the conference room. Lucky it's in this building. I hope I get outside sometime today to enjoy the cool air.

Later, Main Conference Room

Addison brought up the thumbnail bios she had on European power brokers. Unfortunately, at least ten of the people she expected at this meeting were not present. Were they allies of Count Grubenflagg? Or just not involved with either of these evolving groups. Plus, four of the people at the conference were unknown to her. She sighed. *The Union has limited resources over here. Plus, the communications bandwidth and lag limitations mean research requests must truly be priority, not nice-to-have.*

Lord Townerly introduced Addison as an ambassador to the group from a new province of Canada and the USA. She demurred and clarified. "I am here on the behalf of the Great Plains Union. We are an independent polity that was formed after the collapse of the United States and Canada. We have territories that came from each of those countries."

"However, I am not charged with ambassadorial responsibility and power. I am authorized to be the ears and eyes for my people, not their mouth. I will convey all these proceedings to our governing Council. And I can and will offer my personal, candid opinion on matters, be they unofficial." The rest of the twelve Consortium heads in the austere conference room signaled acceptance and understanding.

Great Dieback to Singularity

Good! Glad they didn't send me back to the kiddy table with Malcolm and Kaitlin. Also good that they don't know I'm MindMeld linking back to Wisconsin right now. I've already been involved in one international incident with the Castle attack – two if you count my destruction of Rahel's cyberweapon. She still resents that, no matter how she expresses "bygones".

MindMeld chat: [Addison: *Hey Janet. Can you see and hear the conference okay?*→ Janet: *Sure can Addie. Five by five.* ⏹ Addison: *We will both have splitting headaches by the time this conference is over. Full bandwidth look-and-listen chats are draining. Just hope the satellite links hold. Might need Council direction or approval.*→ Janet: *Yeah, I'm already getting a slight headache. But at least they relieve me every two hours for a four-hour break. You're on for the duration.* ⏹ Addison: *That'll teach me to volunteer. Okay intros are over, stopping the chat portion, but keeping links open so you can be the fly on the wall.*→]

Lord Townerly, John, was presenting the evidence from the crimes the Ravensbruck Group recently committed. When he got to the attack on her at the castle, he minimized her actions, implying Malcolm rescued her. Addison relaxed. *Just like we agreed. They are more likely to accept my input if I am the demur lady rather than the ninja killer.*

The group was still divided after Lord John's presentation. In her mind, Addison labelled the vocal minority – Frieherr Schmidt from Bavaria, Hetman Kawolczyk from Poland, and Doctor Caglianotti from Milan – as the FUD group for their emphasis on fear, uncertainty, and doubt. They each looked decidedly nervous. These were probably the ones for whom Count Grubenflagg had the most blackmail information. The opinion of the remaining eight attendees was overwhelmingly in support of ousting the Ravensbruck Group.

The group took a break for refreshments. On some signal, waitstaff trolleyed in fruits, pastries, and coffee. This was momentarily puzzling for Addison since they had barely begun. Then she noted that Malcolm and two of Townerly's other retainers each pigeon-holed a FUD member for a one-on-one talk.

CHAPTER EIGHT Adagio 2

This had all the hallmarks of a pre-arranged tactic. Townerly and his staff foresaw the FUD reluctance.

When the meeting resumed, the FUD group was silent. Addison nodded, impressed. *Never saw any academics or researchers handle meeting dynamics so smoothly. Nice to see professionalism is possible, even in this.* The discussion moved on to tactics required to neutralize their new opponents quickly.

The still air in the closed room was getting a little warm to Addison's taste. Many of the actions against Ravensbruck assumed knowledge Addison lacked. She began to tune this part of the meeting out, then caught herself. She quickly rewound her internal recorder. *Crap, I heard right! Malcolm is leading one of eight tactical assault teams they are deploying against Ravensbruck. And he is leaving now!*

Addison turned a glare on Malcolm. She used American Sign Language to ask him, "What, you couldn't tell me? Operational security?" They discovered their mutual talent in ASL during the trip from Ravensbruck. Unusual for a Brit to use ASL instead of BSL.

Malcolm signed back, "Found out this A.M. Tried to tell you as you left the shower. Remember, you blew me off with a, 'Late! Talk after.'"

Addison looked sheepish. She started to sign something about her feelings, going with, and other racing thoughts. Then she recalled her training and remembered operational discipline. She just signed a simple, "Be safe. Kick butt. Come back to me."

The staff entered silently and opened windows. A gentle and slightly pungent breeze wafted from the Rhine. Some of Addison's physical fog was dispelled along with the close air, but the mental stresses were distracting.

The group raised a new point for discussion. Baron Hartvig from Basel – today's host – and Dame Karin Svensdotter from Sweden wanted to begin dividing the spoils of the Ravensbruck Group. Several people pointed out that their defeat was far from assured. She heard Kaitlin whisper, "Ass!" at one eye-roll-worthy comment.

Great Dieback to Singularity

The departure of Malcolm still left Addison befuddled. Her thoughts wandered to such oddities as, *Gaylord, hmm. Wonder if his parents were prescient or did he adopt a nom de guerre to advertise his preferences.* She immediately regretted the cheap shot, especially when Janet chided her via MindMeld. She quickly restarted chat mode. MindMeld chat: [Addison: *Sorry Janet.→* Janet: *S'okay love. As amends just put your focus on Karin's chest for a few minutes. Wanna fantasize a few things here.* ⏻]

The participants wrapped up their discussion about the Ravensbruck Group. The meeting chair, Emir bin-Ahmad from Turkey, rapped for attention. "If we are finished with these matters, I suggest we begin discussing our regular business items." He turned to Addison and Kaitlin. "You ladies would probably find these matters mundane. If you would rather pursue other pastimes until our luncheon at one?" MindMeld chat: [Janet: *Booted, just when they were going to get to the juicy stuff.* ⏻ Addison: *Shhh.→*] Addison turned to Lord John with a Disappointed Longing, Grade Three.

Lord Townerly lifted his palm and the Chair nodded at him. "Eminence, may I suggest that Ambassadress Cameron and Ms. Schlötke might be able to lend new perspectives and insights to our deliberations. They have already seen our darker side. Let them see how we try to serve our constituencies." MindMeld chat: [Addison: *See Janet. Trust me, I can be a mover and shaker.* → Janet: *I know Honey. I've seen you shakin your money-maker at the powwow!* ⏻]

At the luncheon, 20ᵗʰ August

The meeting chairman concluded. "We have been striving for the last two years to recover and restore as much of the Eurasian technical and industrial base as we can. But we are not blind to the threats; repeating the ecological disasters that have killed over half of the world's population as well as the emerging threats you so aptly covered in the Edinburgh seminar."

Across the linen-covered table, Kaitlin kept her expression sphinxlike. Addison turned her head quizzically. "Oh, Comrade, you were able to follow our proceedings?"

CHAPTER EIGHT Adagio 2

He took another massive mouthful of duck a l'orange, speaking around it. "St. Jacques and Owens-Binghampton gave daily summaries to the Consortium and followed with complete recordings. A little duplication getting reports from both. Each was dispatched separately before our three factions merged to form the Consortium."

At least he didn't spit his food out. Addison steeled herself to avoid looking away. "I will be delighted to lead a discussion in this afternoon's breakout time period. You'll help me with your perspective and insights, won't you, Kaitlin dear?" Kaitlin nodded mutely. Addison mused, *She's gone back to the Ms. Wilting Violet pose. Must have been ordered to raise no alarm bells.*

The woman on Addison's right side, Dame Svensdotter, chimed in. "Good, many of us tend to dismiss these concerns as hysteria. 'There have always been changes that disrupt societies. These are merely more intense,' to paraphrase. You may need to hit some of these know-nothings up besides the head." To Addison Svensdotter was an excellent imitation of a Norse warrior queen. Addison flashed on Brunhilde, the powerful woman in Wagnerian operas.

During a lull in the conversation, Addison looked around the elegantly appointed dining room -- linen tablecloth, gleaming silver, dramatic centerpiece, and a full array of stemware at each seat. There were two staff behind each participant, even Kaitlin and herself. She assumed some were security personnel, both from build and attitude. But all seemed to find something to do to attend to their assigned person. Food and drink seemed to magically appear and disappear when her head was turned. *I'm certainly not back at our clan's Friday night fish fry.*

When the meal ended after a leisurely hour and a half, a few of the group went off to smoke together. At first, Addison almost joined them reflexively. She reminded herself that their addictive pastime had nothing to do with her tribe's custom of sharing sacred burning plants.

Addison noted that Kaitlin dropped her fade-in-the background mode again. She buttonholed the three identifiably Muslim members of the group; Emir bin-Ahmad, Mufti Talir from Sarajevo, and Sheik Alaoui from Jordan. A little proselytizing for The Collective? Up to this point, she had only revealed to Addison that her real name was Rahel Blumstein and that The Collective was an outgrowth of Abraham's Children.

Addison deduced that The Collective began as an activist arm to fight both Islamic fundamentalists and Israeli right-wing exclusionists. Whatever their stance was on other issues such as singularity threats, eco-disasters, restoration and repair of society, and any others – all of these were unexplained or possibly not a priority for her group. But Addison was reasonably sure the seminar attendance and cultivation of herself indicated Rahel had an agenda that overlapped hers somehow.

Lord John was at her elbow with another man. Addison searched her memory. *Something Diego, I recall.* Lord John gestured between the two others. "Addison, I do not believe you have been introduced to Señor Felip Diego. Señor Diego, may I present Ambassadress Cameron."

Both bowed slightly to the other. "Please call me Addison. Lord Townerly honors me with the title, but there has been no formal recognition between our various polities."

Diego clicked his heels together, gathered Addison's hand in his, and bowed over it. "I would be delighted to extend whatever recognition you desire, Señorita. I am well connected with the Iberian Kingdom's rulers. I am confident I can speak for them. I will confirm it by tomorrow."

Addison blushed slightly, Girlish Pleasure, Two mixed with Mature Satisfaction, Grade Four. "In that case Señor, I will in turn confirm the exchange of recognition and ties with my governing Council. I will have a formal response by the end of day tomorrow also." *Time to bare our claws, slightly.*

Both Lord John and Señor Diego looked slightly startled with matching arched eyebrows. Diego voiced their mutual reaction. "You have somehow re-established communications between the Americas and Europe? You do not need to wait for a blimp to convey messages?"

CHAPTER EIGHT Adagio 2

Addison, showing a Mona Lisa smile of enigma, nodded. "This is one of the things we can bring to the table for any new partners. In addition to the firewall Lord Townerly described this morning, our cyberneticists have succeeded in regaining limited control of the remaining communications satellites that were not destroyed during the Russia-China War phase of the Great Dieback. We are still working on the degree of functionality and bandwidth we can achieve. At a minimum, we know we can restore worldwide traffic of critical messaging between partnering entities. Ah, gentlemen, I believe we are being recalled to our conference." She turned and left the two men gaping, open-mouthed, at her back.

Breakout on Singularity Seminar –
extracts

20th August

Addison smiled. Six of the attendees chose to come to her breakout session. *Possibly we can sway this group of fat cats to support humanity's better interests and not simply feed their own avarice.*

She worried that the overly plush meeting room chairs combined with the enormous meal would have her audience dozing. They obviously were made of sterner stuff, used to the rigors of an oligarch's travails. It was good that she opted for one of the plain wooden chairs from the edge of the room.

❖❖❖

Baron Hartvig looked stubborn. "You are saying the changes are not simply a grander scope of the disruptions caused by, say, the early industrial revolution? My ancestors' mill looms were destroyed by workers throwing their wooden shoes – their sabots – into the machines."

Addison kept her face carefully neutral. *That old canard. Never happened according to historians. Your ancestors were probably the ones clopping their sabots loudly to disrupt work.* "No, scientific analysis differentiates the two dramatically. Certainly, the early days of the technological tsunami were similar. Workers bitterly fought to restore off-shored jobs in my part of the US, only to find that when the factories or mills returned, fifty skilled techs and an array of tireless robots replaced the fifty thousand original workers. I would contend that is the same type of disruption as earlier automation."

"However, by the period after 2015 things were certainly of a different tenor. Instead of eliminating blue-collar jobs, now creative, thought-work oriented jobs were on the line. Cases in point: self-driving vehicles. These do not operate in predictable environments on repetitive tasks. Other examples: Many news reports were cyberdevice-generated from basic factual feeds. Chinese broadcasting used a generated avatar to deliver these reports. An AI first composed numerous classical pieces in the style of Bach that experts could not distinguish as artificial. After tweaking and exposure to more training sets, the AI began generating thousands of original works in a vast array of musical genres. Later it began exploring poetry, painting, and fiction. Other AIs were writing computer software. This represented a qualitative change, an inflection point. I will not discuss the detailed mathematics here but will gladly make those papers available."

◆ ◆ ◆

Someone called out, "Sex bots?"

Addison laughed, glad for the relief of tension. "No, although those did begin to be widespread in the late Twenties. Most were not creative, simply mechanical."

Dame Svensdotter growled, "A lot like my late husband." The group erupted in laughter.

◆ ◆ ◆

Lord John posed the critical question. "Why, given all this quantitative change in technology, this inflection point, why has there been no evidence of a true singularity?" The group stopped chuckling; side conversations died out.

Addison adopted Professorial Pronouncement, Grade Five. She only wished she had her clear-pane reading glasses to complete the effect. She would have used her middle finger to shove them up the bridge of her nose. "Precisely the question I began to address in my doctoral thesis, Lord Townerly. Further studies have supported the conclusion that I proposed, but it still remains conjecture until someone can create experimental evidence.... Or a singularity." Polite laugh.

"To boil down the technical jargon, I produced an amusing catchphrase, 'Mutant Sexual Combat.'" *That got their attention.* "The hallmarks of evolutionary progress are changes in the genome – mutations – that are selectively reinforced, over time. Sexual drive is part of the urge to create and sustain our progeny. The most successful species not only procreate, they protect their families."

"Finally, Competition – or more dramatically, combat – is one of the most important selection mechanisms along with such things as improved ability to get food, etc. Please remember that collaboration balances competition in species, particularly in social species like Homo Sapiens. Evolution is a more sophisticated mechanism than the ruthless Darwinism people usually see it as. The yin of competition is matched by the yan of collaboration."

"Robots and Artificial Intelligences, or AIs, never achieved this mix. True, genetic algorithms often produced a degree of Mutant Sexual Combat, but their environment was solely in the cybersphere. They didn't enter the bigger combat zone of the planetary ecosystem. Worse, when the most sophisticated AIs suddenly lost connection to the World Wide Web after the death of the internet in 2029, each of them went into a state equivalent to human catatonia. Monitors on their computers showed they were in there still, but they showed no responsiveness to any queries."

Emir bin-Ahmad asked the next, logical question. "You covered AIs and Robotics. What about bioengineering-based singularities? Why have those not occurred?" *Excellent question. You must not have had time to digest the two-hour long free-for-all from the seminar on this topic. Or maybe all the jargon and personality-based infighting distracted.*

Addison gave the man a nod of respect. "The early days of

bioengineering paralleled the early days of robotics and AI. Practitioners directed their efforts towards repair and regrowth of human capabilities. They restored, replaced, even extended functionality. They never fundamentally changed it. And they usually did not make their changes inheritable. The exception was when the engineers repaired genetically-based diseases and syndromes. In the latter days they did begin making the repairs to include modifications to the spermatozoa and ova of the afflicted."

"No one raised the point during the seminar, but I contend there has been a bioengineering-based singularity event." Addison paused for dramatic effect.

Someone muttered, "The Russian Enhanced Shock Troops!"

Addison solemnly agreed. "Yes, the new Tryet'ya Oodarnaya Armiya, or Russian Supermen. Evidence is scant given the fog of war, but reports indicate they went rogue shortly after deployment, even turning on their own commanders and erstwhile comrades. Their traits were supposedly inheritable. Even more important, sexual encounters with normal Homo Sapiens supposedly were either sterile or produced non-viable offspring. They were a new species."

Addison saw knowing nods from Comrade Ivanovich and Mufti Talir. *Some firsthand knowledge there,* she surmised. "It is not clear why the Supermen suddenly died off. However, given the reports of widespread deaths among their human slaves and concubines, it is likely the Chinese counterattacked with either chemical or biological weapons. Then those weapons got out of control."

"We are all fortunate the agent or agents were contained, however drastic the measures." Addison sensed profound disagreement from many. *Fair enough, we in the Great Plains Union don't have to live next door to a swath of countryside devastated by nuclear explosions.*

CHAPTER EIGHT Adagio 2

*That evening, back at their Town
Hall suite*

Lord John introduced Thomas Lynley, his butler. Addison looked at the stances and demeanor of the two. *If someone asked, I would say their relationship is much, much closer than lord and valet. None of my business, just an interesting data point.* "Pardon me, your name is very familiar, but I can't quite..."

Lynley looked properly abashed. "My mother was an avid follower of a series of crime stories..."

Addison interrupted excitedly. "The Elizabeth George novels! My father read them all, multiple times. I enjoyed them as well." She was beaming an unplanned, natural smile. Lynley looked pleased as well, even though English reserve was bred into his marrow.

Lynley poured a sherry for Lord John. Addison asked if they might have Irish Cream. She also asked for it over ice, mumbling an apology for Americanizing it. As Lynley handed it to her, she gave his hand a gentle squeeze. He favored her with a slight smile and squeezed back.

Once she and Lord John were alone together, he gave her a piercing look from his lowered brows. "Well, it seems my dear that you are indeed a woman of many parts. Now I don't know how much of what you have shown us before is true and how much was a very well-formed façade."

"I once met a countryman of yours. Or, I should say, a man from the same country you once shared. He was a Texan. Portrayed himself as 'jus' a po' ole boy from the country.' His 'Aw, shucks' routine disarmed people right before he shredded them like a shark in a feeding frenzy. Wonderfully nice man, as long as you weren't on the wrong side of the bargaining table."

Addison lowered her head and bit her tongue in concentration. This did fall within the parameters of her instructions, but just barely. She would navigate these shoals very carefully. *Only speak the truth with this man. Just not all the truth. He will know you are holding back, but he will only expect and respect that.*

"You know I am more capable than I might appear at first. But the question you are not asking is, 'Is she a form of enhanced woman, not Homo Sapiens.' Let me start by assuring you I'm still human, with minor modifications, as Malcolm no doubt shared."

"The Clipper?"

"Yes. Developed by my team. Saved two of us from a brutal rape and then was rapidly adopted by women throughout the Midwestern US." *Sorry I'm claiming your work, Ainsley. Need to keep the fact that there are two of us a State Secret for now.* "But my overpowering the men at Ravensbruck was through a combination of advanced personal defense training – a blend of karate, savate, and krav maga – plus five years toughening up in the service of our tribal militia. I nearly lost my round with the last attacker. A true superwoman wouldn't have broken a sweat."

"Similarly, The Great Plains Union is both more powerful than we might first appear, yet far from a threatening force. We have learned to hide our strengths in order to surprise those who would attack. The Time of Troubles was brutal there."

"Here, as well." Lord John remained guarded and unconvinced.

Time to open the kimono a bit more, as they say. "After the attempted rape where I and a colleague barely escaped, my boyfriend of the time, Nelson Red Eagle, spirited us away with the help of tribal lawyers. The legal system and the University were after our hides because of the brutal nature of the mutilations suffered by the two men, even though that occurred when we successfully defended ourselves against a rape in full progress." Addison let Lord John see a glimpse of the fury that still raged in her soul. Despite the years of counseling, it was as if that night and weekend just happened. She didn't mention the shooting of the other two men by Ainsley.

"The tribe quickly became a refuge for others as the Troubles increased dramatically. Knowledge of our capabilities rapidly spread through word-of-mouth to the academic and tech communities. We became a center for arming women with a superbly effective defense. I am proud to say that statistics showed a dramatic seventy-five plus percent drop in rape throughout the Midwest while it tripled in the rest of the US." Her obvious anger, passion, and pride was swaying Lord John. *I'll play one more card on the table to seal the deal. Somehow, I trust this man.*

"We became an underground shelter well known in the high-tech communities nearby. Then the government announced the imminent first collapse of Antarctic ice to the American populace. To their credit, the feds made massive preparations for relocations, despite the obstructions of those who denied climate change."

"There was massive resistance at first. Then the authorities played their ace-in-the-hole. They leaked the list of all the most vocal politicians, news people, corporate leaders of coal and oil, and others. With the list they provided the information on where each of those scum setup their safe havens."

"Our tribe was recruited to assist with the efforts, largely because we had so many techies already there. Preparations and supplies for surviving the aftermath were impressive. They even managed to relocate an entire nuclear power plant and a small refinery to Northern Wisconsin. They also rerouted pipelines to feed the refinery." *Not going to mention how instrumental Uncle Jay was. A little nepotism never hurts.*

It was two days before the collapse when I received a call from a friend I worked with during my first year in graduate studies at UW. Wayne is a cyber genius. My Great Uncle Jay introduced us. You remember Jay? He was the architect of our firewall that your group is interested in." Addison took a large swallow of her drink. A long day of speaking, under intense scrutiny, for the highest stakes, was thirsty work.

Lord John signaled Addison should continue. He was nearly there. She continued, "Anyway, as I was saying, Wayne called two days before Melt One, the first Antarctic ice collapse. Turns out he became the head of a project at Google to develop an advanced AI, Barney. The trade journals talked about Barney. What they hadn't disclosed was that Google set up a new center of servers and supercomputers to service Barney. That center was located on the bed of one of the Great Lakes. And that is ALL I will say about that.

Great Dieback to Singularity

I am sharing a State Secret with you, Lord Townerly, because I have evaluated you and your actions, and I firmly recommend you as an ally for the Great Plains Union."

A quiet silence lasted for over a minute before he replied. "I thank you for your confidence in me and in my organization. We will remain loyal allies if we can agree the terms and conditions of such a pact. In any case, I shan't abuse your confidences. But, please continue. What did Wayne want to discuss at such a critical stage?"

Addison knew she should iron out the terms of alliance before going the next step. If it went "tits up" she might have to eliminate this man she truly liked. She decided to risk it all.

"Wayne told me his people determined their underwater cyber center should survive any quakes, surges, or other likely calamities. But their control center was on shore and in dire jeopardy from the imminent collapse. He was asking permission and immediate assistance in relocating the facility and its personnel to our area. He would worry about connectivity to the underwater center later. His group is now one of our major assets."

"In summary, Lord John, we are a small polity in terms of numbers of people. But we have resources that will make us valuable partners. We are interested in trade in goods and ideas. But our imperative concern is directly related to the seminar. We believe this battered and tattered world is clinging to existence by its fingertips above an abyss. That will be our focus."

At first, Lord John said a simple, "Thank you." Then he asked, do you have a proposed set of terms for the alliance?"

Addison nodded. "If you can point me to a cyber device I can upload our suggestions for review by your staff. Then I can setup a conference holo-call at their convenience. Please remind them of the seven-hour time difference. The lack of international calling has tended to make people forget. But then, I've forgotten its nighttime here, isn't it?"

Once Addison and Lord John rounded up the correct people,

CHAPTER EIGHT Adagio 2

briefed them, and initiated the negotiations, they were both rather tired. But the prospects of the new ventures also raced through the minds of each. In this stew of physical and emotional energies, they settled back in the lounge of their suite. Neither was quite ready to call it a day.

Lynley was leading the negotiating team, so Lord John poured Addison another glass of Irish Cream. "Please tell me about that dinner at Ravensbruck. I have never met Count Grubenflagg face to face. I would value your impressions, Addison."

Addison took a small sip. "Certainly John. As I have recounted before, he saw this as more of a seduction scene rather than a negotiation of equals. He was blunt to the point of rudeness. Then he would wriggle those fuzzy caterpillar eyebrows at me. I believe he thought they were charming. He tried to massage my foot with his. I think he even tried to grab my knee, but I was too quick for that. He did grab my hand in his clammy paw."

"Another memorable characteristic of the man was his obsessive neatness. I tagged him as an OC-Deity. It was like he believes all the world is his to order and align. When I placed a fork down on my plate, I brushed the next one slightly out of true. He reached across my plate to straighten it. All the lines in the castle – paintings, rugs, doorways, everything – looked like they laser-aligned it. That was part of what gave the whole edifice a sense of falseness, of being a cine set. Like my art professor explained to me, 'No human face is truly symmetric. A true artist captures the imperfections that show we are human.'"

◆ ◆ ◆

Addison had been drifting off. Now she became re-animated. "Oh, I loved soccer. Futbol it's called over here. I played from age of five on. Didn't get drafted for college teams but walked on in Wisconsin and won a substitute spot. Coach told me later he had major reservations since I looked 'frail.' Then in the first game two opposing fullbacks decided to force me off the ball as I was driving towards goal. I lowered my head, backheeled the ball over their heads, and drove my body right through the middle. One ended up ass-over-teakettle, the other was backpedaling to stay upright.

Scored. Sweet!"

◆◆◆

Addison continued. "Thank God for French and Swiss cuisine after Scottish. I decided all the books about wonderful food over here were tripe. Actually, a lot of the Scottish food was tripe." She giggled at her lame joke. *Lord, I'm exhausted, but having fun.*

Lord John became animated in turn. "Oh, if only you could have experienced les pâtissières before cane sugar disappeared and les bistros before spices became rare. I am glad you appreciate the poor efforts you have sampled. Not all Americans appreciate the delicacy of our sauces, preferring overly spiced food like salsas."

Addison held her palm out. "Whoa Pardner! I love the food here, but that doesn't mean I would prefer it over a good lutefisk, a hearty Carolina barbecue, or Tex-Mex street tacos – cilantro, pico de gallo, on fresh corn tortillas. Mmm!"

Lord John's eyes gleamed with anticipation. "Dear Gawd! Here I thought you were civilized or at least trainable, not an American barbarian!"

◆◆◆

Kaitlin looked surprised. "Addison, John? I didn't expect you two, to still be up. Did I miss curfew?" She smiled, transforming her otherwise plain face into a gentle beauty.

Addison patted the chair next. "Oh, Rahel Dear, we have so much to bring you up to speed on! Sit, please."

◆◆◆

Rahel curled her lips. "You may be right about the reasons a singularity hasn't happened other than the possible Supermen Soldiers. But calling that regrettable is totally absurd! You are acting like a typical technician; a narrow-minded nerd. You need to read some of the classical speculative literature like Isaac Asimov's series on robotics. Or further back to the Golem legends. None of you scientists consider building ethical constraints into your toys; a conscience."

Addison smiled slightly. "Or maybe we just don't want to have to deal with our own Dr. Susan Calvin psychoanalyzing our 'bots?"

CHAPTER EIGHT Adagio 2

Rahel's face turned red. She underestimated Addison once again. *Well, only one way to deal with this.* "The pope, the Dalai Lama, and a bioengineer walk into a bar...."

The next morning, 21st August

The butler Lynley woke Addison early. "His Lordship would see you in the salon, if you please, Dr. Cameron."

"Call me Addison please, Thomas. I suspect we will be working closely together for some time. Any idea what the agenda is this morning?"

"As you wish, Addison. I'm sure you and his Lordship will be discussing the negotiations I just completed with your Council. However, the first urgent item is to review reports on the actions against the Ravensbruck Group. Would you like tea, ma'am?"

Darned if he looks like he has been working all night. Looks fresh as a daisy. "Coffee or hot chocolate would be my first preference. American, you know. Even if the US doesn't exist anymore." Addison's normal morning sunny attitude darkened slightly. "Do you know if Rahel is awake yet?"

Lynley actually looked nonplussed for the first time in Addison's experience. "Rahel, ma'am? I'm afraid I don't..."

Addison interrupted. "Sorry, forgot you weren't told her real name. Kaitlin is the cover name for Rahel Blumstein, agent for an Israeli-Palestinian group known as The Collective. I'm sure John, his Lordship, will brief you later. And no more, 'ma'ams', please. Makes me feel dowdy."

Thomas finished pouring a steaming cup of cocoa – with marshmallows, no less. As he handed it to Addison he answered. "Rahel will be my next call, Addison." He reddened at his effort to be informal.

Addison rushed into a track suit and quickly downed her delicious cocoa. *Hope informal is okay. Wonder what kind of liqueur he added. Just a shot but, oh my!* She gathered her gear and went into the lounge area of the suite; the salon Thomas called it. Both Lord John and Rahel were already there, though Rahel looked as if she was barely awake. Lord John, of course, was perfectly turned out in a last century outfit – tie, blazer with elbow patches, suspenders. *So precious!*

Lord John looked solemn. "Pardon me, ladies, for rousting you so early after a long evening. We have reports from our field teams. Results have been mixed. Overall, the objectives were achieved at six of the eight sites with minimal casualties."

"The seventh site in Geneva was, if you will pardon the old military expression, a cluster-fuck. It's possible one of the other sites managed to get an alert out. The attack started several minutes late because of the presence of a civilian cleaning staff just clearing the building. The building was nearly neutralized when someone on the opposing side managed to trigger a suicide switch. The explosion demolished the whole building, with major damage to surrounding structures. All but two of our team were inside at the time and are believed lost. Only two perimeter patrollers were spared to report."

Rahel whispered, "Bill?"

Addison thought, *Thank God Rahel asked, a second before I would have myself.*

Lord John continued. "No, Bill – Sorry, he is still Malcolm within our organization. Malcolm is at the last site, Ravensbruck Castle. He led the assault with a team of our most experienced. We expected the stiffest resistance there."

"And, before I forget, many thanks, Addison, for the logic bomb you placed in their security systems before your escape. Malcolm believed it would remain undetected for two reasons. First, because of the explosion you used to disable their power and backup generator. The second point was more involved. We knew any competent security head would have realized the device you used to move your bomb into place would have triggered alarms, if they were still active. Malcolm recognized that one of the four men you killed was the Castle's security chief. He believed it was good odds that his replacement would struggle to get things organized and neglect a thorough analysis of the incident. That bet was a good one. Initial entry was undetected."

CHAPTER EIGHT Adagio 2

"Resistance was immediate and professional once the two forces engaged. Still things were going relatively smoothly until one of our teams ran into a defender they described as "a human buzz saw." They were in the cellars of the Castle. It overwhelmed five of our best people in seconds. They were barely able to relay an alarm before they died. It took all the efforts of the remainder of the force to contain the creature in the dungeons until they could use explosives to seal the stairways and conduits."

"Malcolm ordered the use of nerve gas. After they gave the gas time to work, volunteers assaulted the cellar again. They found several bodies. But the creature and at least two others used an escape capsule that transported them beyond the walls. Search teams are trying, very carefully, to locate them."

"In the meantime, the team has conducted a thorough search of the Castle. They have recovered surprisingly complete files. It seems the Count, the creature, and the 'Dr. Frankenstein' who created this monster were in the hospital operating room in the cellar. Seems the creature was still being brought 'online', as it were. Thank God the creature wasn't fully functional."

Addison knew she shouldn't be surprised. She saw some of the wonders Ainsley could do in her lab. But her immediate concern was elsewhere. Her voice was only a husky whisper. "Was Malcolm injured?"

Lord John gave her a reassuring pat on the hand. "The medics say all his wounds were minor and he will be fully healed within a week, if they can get him to follow treatment. But what he saw shook him to his core, Addison. The images of the creature. They were recognizable, barely, as being Robert Owens-Binghampton."

Rahel gasped. Addison reeled back. "That's impossible! I broke his neck. He was dead before he hit the ground."

Lord John looked deeply into Addison's eyes. "That's why Malcolm desperately needs your help. He wants your analysis, as an expert bioengineer, of the files of this Doctor Dmitri Vyrvykvist."

Addison gasped again. Another shock. "Dmitri. He was one of the world's best. Most believed he was the lead creator of the Russian supersoldiers. Everyone, including me, thought him dead in that nuclear holocaust in Western Russia."

John asked again. "Evidently not. Can you go to Ravensbruck and help Malcolm and his team? Before that, can you direct their recovery efforts from here?"

Addison activated MindMeld in alarm mode. MindMeld chat: [Addison: *CODE RED ALERT. Whoever is on duty, I need Ainsley linked in as soon as possible.*→ Janet: *Janet here. Ainsley is out with the peace conference. I can loop her in later today. Hope that will be okay, because I don't know if she is on the grounds or on patrol.* ⏎ Addison: *It'll have to do. Need her help with bio. Probable instance of another enhanced supersoldier.* → Janet: *Roger. Will relay. And notify the Council. Anything else?* ⏎ Addison: *No. Thanks. Out.* →]

To Lord John, "Of course. Where do you have a video hookup to Ravensbruck?"

CHAPTER NINE ADAGIO
3
XIXI & MIN

2nd July 2033

*Cave Lab Complex, northeast of
Gui'de, Qinghai, China*

Xiang choked back his enthusiasm. It was only the first step in his plan to sidestep nuclear annihilation. But it had gone well. Now he needed a way to communicate with his hidden spy equipment back in the cave while he was on the island. He dared not use the standard equipment. Security was monitoring the usual comm channels too tightly. Unfortunately, all the Special Ops comm gear he used to have was long gone. He had no sources for replacing it.

Then he remembered the early experiments he allowed Ainsley to talk him into. *She installed some hidden comm gear in my head. What did she call it? MindMeld? I haven't used it since Wisconsin because it was strictly short range and no one else has the gear here. Maybe I could reverse engineer it and use that capability? I would need to carry a signal booster. What cover story will I use for that?*

10th July

Xiang's heart was racing. The MindMeld modifications were working better than he had hoped. He snuck the signal into the regular comm channels hidden as intermittent bits of noise. There was still a lot of interference around from the diminishing level of volcanic ash. That made for a low probability his signals would be detected. His only concern was that he needed to carry a booster to transform the weak internal signal into the "noise" that his Pythia AI handled.

CHAPTER NINE Adagio 3

The original taps are simple. Just a cutout for subvocalized speech; the silent whispers we all make while we are thinking. When I trigger a control, the words go to MindMeld instead of my throat. The responses came to inner internal ear implants. I added taps into the retina for sending and receiving visuals as well. I'm sure that Ainsley must have done similar extensions if she kept working on the MindMeld. Hell, she probably tapped into the other senses as well. Might even have direct feeds to and from the brain by now.

28th July

The first thing Xiang did was name his Spybot. Kholkikos was the unsleeping dragon who guarded the Golden Fleece in Greek mythology. His Kholkikos passed all his tests for security and connectivity. Xiang didn't activate any attempts to penetrate the Army's commnet yet. Too risky without more data.

He assigned Kholkikos to monitor everything it could observe at Bomb Central and the commnet connection. It used the bots entering and leaving Bomb Central to report the details and relay his new programming. The reported details Xiang fed to Pythia – named after the Oracle of Delphi. *Can't let all that expensive Western education go to waste.*

Xiang could have kicked himself. He realized he needed assistance but had forgotten about Pythia. Pythia was Xiang's homegrown AI. He began setting it up with the help of his trainers while at Special Ops Camp. It could assist a field agent; a spy. He needed it to organize data for him, evaluate those data, and communicate alerts to him based on the content of the data.

Somehow, in all the chaos and confusion when they released him from service, he "requisitioned" the cyber platform they assigned him to use for Pythia. He hid the platform carefully in the dusty reaches of his group's cave. Now he needed an AI programmer.

Sukhiin Ajai came into Xiang's office. He was practically bouncing on his feet. "You wanted to see me, Leader Xu?"

Xiang waved the man to sit. "Please call me Xiang, Ajai. How are the rest of the team treating you? Is the mentoring in bioengineering going well?"

Ajai said, "Yes, thank you Xiang. The new mentor is taking me under wing and teaching me many things. I wonder if I might help with some of the experiments? Hands on is the best way to learn."

Xiang said, "I agree. I will talk to Fangji today to see if that can happen soon. Today, though, I need to call on your cybernetics skills. I have an AI which is fairly simplistic, and I need to know if it can be configured to do some administrative tasks for me. I'm like most scientists, I hate administration."

◆◆◆

Ajai said, "I have given Pythia a human voice. Now you can tell her what you wish done and she can tell you the results."

Xiang said, "She?"

Ajai was quiet for a second. Then he said, "Yes. It is always better to make your AI as human as possible so it will respond in a more human fashion. I hope female is okay. I find it easier to work with a female AI."

Xiang nodded. "Pythia is a Greek woman's name." *Ajai adds insight and empathy; doesn't just think of AIs as machines.*

Ajai smiled and his wrinkled brow relaxed. He said, "For the initial feeds you have to work with Pythia, telling her how you categorize information, how you determine their importance, and how you organize summaries of all the data. The AI will learn from these cues and generalize to be able to handle new inputs."

This was critical because, as Xiang anticipated, the amount of commnet traffic became a flood. *Pythia will keep it manageable. Most of the junk is administrivia – Lord, I love Addie's pet phrase – but it's critical that someone sift through everything. Or that something did the sifting. Then we can get cooking.*

1st August

*New Shanghai (formerly Irkutsk,
Siberia)*

Xiang reached across the table and clasped Wong Min's hand. He wanted this weekend away to be special. They had spent time with each other for over a month now, but he thought of this as their first real date. It took a huge effort to get permission for both to get the weekend off, to arrange a blimp and train passage up to New Shanghai, and to arrange accommodations through one of his old army comrades.

New Shanghai was one of the few places Xiang was assigned during the Great March North that held good memories. At the time it was Irkutsk, Russia. Xiang spent several enjoyable weeks there. In some ways it reminded him of his days in Austin, Texas during his undergraduate studies. He wanted it to be memorable for Min as well.

It was surprising how open the people were to the flood of Chinese invaders overwhelming their town. Of course, it was early days then, and the initial cyberwar efforts crippled the Russian Army's ability to respond.

One of the things Xiang absolutely adored was Tuvan throat singing. Wisely, he didn't try to share the experience with Min. His experience with PLA comrades and lab cohorts proved to him that, no, it wasn't simply a question of acquiring the taste. He was the only person he knew who hadn't grown up with the art and who liked it anyway.

Min was looking even more lovely than usual. She was wearing the form-fitting outfit he gave her. One of their only fights happened when he tried to gently suggest she wear something besides the loose, drab sacks she preferred. He didn't want to change her, really. But she was shy and believed her village background unimpressive. He saw the inner Min. She was one of the smartest people he knew, strong-willed behind her retiring front. He wanted the world to see her as he saw her.

"You're looking particularly beautiful tonight, Minnie." He was delighted to learn her father nicknamed her after the Disney character he loved from his youth. "Did you enjoy the dinner?"

Min gave Xiang one of her shy, sweet smiles. "You see, XiXi, I can dress 'sexy' as you call it. I just don't think it's professional at work. Besides, many regressive men find powerful, intelligent women threatening. We find it essential to not give them an excuse to dismiss us as decorations. I own 'sexy' clothes besides this lovely dress you gave me. When the time is right, you will see them."

Min took a sip of the gunpowder tea. She continued. "I loved all the dishes, especially the Xiaolongbao. The shrimp fillings, the delicate broth; all exactly like I used to have on special occasions during university. Thank you for bringing back a happy memory."

◆ ◆ ◆

They touched on memories during dinner but kept things light and flirtatious. They had talked little on the short walk to the hotel. They found a quiet nook in the lobby.

Min held her gaze on her lap. Her voice was low but steady. "Like most people I lost family during the Bad Years. Luckily my māmā and bàba left the village when I came to get them before the official evacuation. But all four of my grandparents refused to leave. Grandfather Wong spoke for them all when he said, 'We were born here. All our ancestors are here. You have our blessings to leave. But we are old and will stay.' Bàba practically dragged māmā and me away. I know he left a pistol with them. Please do not tell anyone that."

Xiang focused on Min. Her words pulled him out of his mire of self-pity. He wanted to give Min a hug, but she would not want that in such a public place. The hotel lobby was not crowded, but it certainly had foot traffic. He started to speak, haltingly. "You know it is very hard for me to speak of my past, my Min. Thank you for sharing yours. Let me try to tell you some of mine. When the Cossack Supermen, the Bastard Bears, overran our headquarters in Novosibirsk, my māmā and bàba were killed. I was with our troops near the Aral Sea. We had no idea they slipped past us."

"Later I found out my aunt and uncle were captured by the beasts and shipped off to be part of their slave farms. They died in a rescue attempt. Their daughter, my cousin LinLin, is lost. We have no word to this day." Silent tears dripped from Xiang's chin, ignored.

Min swept over to Xiang and gathered him in a fierce embrace, propriety be damned. His vulnerability and openness took their relationship to a new level.

December 2028

Irkutsk, Siberia

iang knew he had too much to drink. The performance of the throat singers in that dive bar in Irkutsk was phenomenal. They insisted on sharing their flasks when they found out he not only liked their music but had recordings of many of their most famous singers from the past. *What kind of rotgut was in their swill?*

Xiang wasn't sure he could make it to his quarters. This makeshift base still confused him at the best of times. Besides, he spent all his time in the lab and would have to walk there first to find his assigned sleeping tent. He decided to crash on a lab cot instead.

The rickety lab building smelled of dozens of spilled chemicals. None were toxic, but the combined fumes were annoying. He threw a window open, freezing wind be damned! *Better.* He stumbled to the cot. As he lay down he couldn't help seeing the white board, covered with notes from the last status meeting. The project to develop biochemical methods to pacify the Siberians and diminish their sex drive was working all too well.

Xiang's stomach was rolling like a storm-tossed sea. His throat was burning with bile. He stumbled to the toilet. That was a mistake. The smell there was far worse than the lab chemicals. Once he got to the stage where he was only dry heaving, he got off the floor. He didn't clean up in the toilet but went to a lab bench to use the sink there. The freezing wind made him realize he left the window flung wide. He pulled it closed with a lurch.

The combination of vomiting and the brisk air

brought on a degree of sobriety. Now the next stage of drunkenness hit Xiang; severe melancholy. He missed Ainsley and Wisconsin so much. On an impulse he tried to call her old cell phone number.

She answered. "Hello? Is this a scam call? I don't even recognize this country code."

Xiang froze. He had no idea what to say. *I was so judgmental, holier-than-thou. Simply because she was trying to protect herself and other women from violent attack. Now look at me. What I'm involved in might even be a form of slow genocide.* Finally, he managed to croak out, "LeeLee."

He was sure she was surprised. He wasn't sure she would be particularly pleased to hear from him. "Xiang. Is that you? What do you need?" *Nope, not welcoming at all.*

Xiang rubbed his throbbing temples. *This was a big mistake. Damn it!* "I wanted to say I'm sorry. Sorry for leaving without talking to you. Sorry for the hell you went through that weekend. Sorry I wasn't there for you." There was a long silence on the line. "But, damn, I wish you would have trusted me and told me what you were doing."

She snapped back, almost before he finished the sentence. "What? You would have been so understanding and supportive of my work. Mr. Choirboy who never did one thing wrong his entire life. Poster child of the revolution!" She spat out the last.

Xiang desperately needed water. Alcohol dehydration was setting in, big time. He moaned into the ancient handset. "Well, I'm not such a choirboy now. Been doing shit that makes your Clipper look like a child's play toy."

Ainsley had enough. "So, you call me for absolution.

CHAPTER NINE Adagio 3

Figure one sinner would understand another and make you feel all good about whatever crap you're doing. Well, suck it up big boy. Own your mistakes. Live with them or fix them. But don't try to pull me into your swamp of misery." She disconnected.

9ᵗʰ August

cave across the river

Xiang got an emergency alert through MindMeld from his Pythia AI. He thought up a reasonable excuse to leave the meeting with his lab team leads. "All right. We seem to be making progress on most of the priority projects. Just give me detailed reports on any we haven't discussed in this meeting. By the end of the day, please. And Ajai, I do need some details about this 'little bit of independent research' you want to pursue. Please come talk to me this afternoon." Sukhiin Ajai was the Mongolian farm boy that Xiang poached from the Third Cybernetics Group. His work on reviving the Bold Beaver AI and reconfiguring Xiang's Pythia AI showed he was brilliant despite his limited formal education.

Once Xiang reached his small private office he executed a lockdown protocol. His scanners searched for any bugs, electronic or otherwise. When he got an "All Clear" signal he opened a channel on his cyber device to Pythia. He downloaded her message. "Pythia Alert – Detection of message redirection occurred. Courier has come to Wang's office. Lockdown of Bomb Central ordered. Full security check initiated. Contingency Protocol 'Purloined Letter' initiated. Report ends."

Xiang's mind raced. This was dangerous. He foresaw a possibility like this and set up a series of misdirections to fool any investigations. Now he would see if his clever little ploy would work. However, with Bomb Central locked down the only way he would know for sure was when one of two things happened. Either security would fall for his false spy mechanism and pursue the wrong person. Or he would wake up with a bag being drawn over his head.

166

Great Dieback to Singularity

Special Projects Island

Geneal Wang pulled Xiang aside at the weekly All Departments Meeting. "Xu Xiang. I need to meet with you and a few others right after this meeting. Please stay." While stated as a request, the General's tone left no doubt it was a command.

Xiang hoped he was prepared for this. *Must be on the message from headquarters about the security breach.*

At the end of the meeting five department heads besides Xiang stayed back together with the Chief Commissar. Wang took them into a side room and posted a guard outside. "There has been a security breach of the Army's installation here. Headquarters first detected it when they noted anomalies in the message traffic. Our staff was assisted by experts from the Ministry of State Security in performing a full security sweep."

Xiang's body tensed. *Was this the end? He had survived Russia. This was a sad anticlimax.*

"A line was inserted through the sewer system into the toilet in my office. Someone has used this line to send a set of robotic bugging devices into the building. They also inserted a device into our communications equipment. We have removed all these devices for detailed analysis by MSS. Given the robotic nature of the systems, we suspect a person or persons in the robotics groups is behind this."

Xiang steeled his face into Grave Concern, Grade Three. *They bought the deception. Doesn't sound like they detected any of the swarm of nanobots. Thank goodness I prepositioned those decoy microbots last week after I finished growing the line through the sewer.*

"You six department heads have been deemed the most politically reliable. We are appointing you to a task force to prosecute this matter. We are also assigning Bold Beaver to assist. We will get to the bottom of this."

CHAPTER NINE Adagio 3

Xiang stomped into Min's office and flung his pack on her couch. It was bad enough that he and Min came down on opposite sides of her proposal during the weekly division head meeting. It was worse when she prevailed. He would get over that blow to his ego. The worst part was that he couldn't explain to her why the point was so important to him.

After she entered her lab office, she spun to face him. Her head was jerking side to side as she spoke. "Hypocrite! Just last week you said, 'Don't worry if we disagree about issues in the Special Projects Heads meeting. You are a department head. We will disagree necessarily at times. If we see it coming in advance, we can try to come up with a compromise or united front, of course. But I don't need or want you to be subservient.' Liar! The first time it happens, and you act like all those other domineering male chauvinist dinosaurs!" Her finger was wagging in his face.

He backpedaled. "Listen Min. That's not it at all. I'm not angry with you for differing with me publicly. I'm angry because now each project will have an army officer sitting with our group, watching everything we do."

Min's fury was unabated. "So! You are the one that has been so cozy with General Wang, meeting with him every week for lunch. You were a Colonel in the PLA, as you told me in strictest confidence. Why would this liaison bother you unless it was just because I proposed it without consulting with 'your highness' first?" The sarcasm was dripping. Her eyes were narrowed in her fury. She bent slightly at the waist, leaning forward like an attacking hawk.

Xiang had a flash of insight that left him breathless. He couldn't tell Min because he kept his whole Kholkikos Project secret from her. This was exactly the same as when Ainsley kept the Clipper Project secret from him. *What a hypocrite I have been! Dare I tell her? She is such a rule-follower. Will she turn me in? Will she understand? Will I lose her if I don't open up, right now?*

Great Dieback to Singularity

19th August

cave in hills northeast of river

Now that Xiang had a good profile of the traffic all the senior officials were generating on commnet, he decided to try his first attempt at piggybacking his information requests with their messages. His trials proved that Kholkikos could intercept and reroute messages or even delete them. The first trial would just check to see if his father's profile was still active, even though he died nearly four years ago. He loaded his new commands into sets of message nanobots, duplicated to assure at least one set would get through. He would leave for early dinner and release them near Bomb Central. *Should get in at shift change.*

The next morning Xiang got the nanobot reports. *Astounding! Not only is his father's profile still active, his passwords and biometrics are unchanged. Never underestimate the torpidity of bureaucracy!*

25th August

Kholkikos organized all the old army information about their cave. It had been a nuclear bomb shelter and control center. Over thirty years ago the Central Committee decommissioned it, and everyone promptly forgot it. Xiang now had all the schematics.

Late at night, Xiang snuck around to explore some of the passages that the Army carefully hid, in preparation for enemy invasion. The massive generators still had plenty of fuel. He didn't fire them up, but he was confident they just needed the flick of a switch.

He wiped the greasy dirt from his hands on a scrap of cloth. He then ran his sleeve across his brow. All this after hours work on top of regular lab duties, monitoring Kholkikos' reports, his duties as department head, and his attempts to have a normal relationship with Min – totally draining. And these recesses of the cave are filled with air that hasn't been fully refreshed in decades, dirt everywhere. Ugh!

169

CHAPTER NINE Adagio 3

8ᵗʰ September, very early morning

Yuhuang Pavilion, Gui'de

Wong Min wasn't sure about Xiang's whole mysterious plan for meeting away from the Special Projects environment. Of course, there were no restrictions on personnel visiting the nearby town. People didn't leave their labs for long, not out of fear. It was because they were so involved with their experiments. But any unusual activity was likely to attract negative attention from the commissars and from security.

That brought her main hesitation to mind. Where was her relationship with Xiang going? A month ago, she thought that at last Xiang was going to open himself up to her, deepening their bond. He told her about his relatives' deaths and the disappearance of his cousin LinLin. He had moved her.

But since then? Nothing. Sure, the sex was wonderful. His runner's body was taut, even if he did have a little tummy pouch – which he hated and spent an hour on the treadmill every day to lose. But she didn't need a man to complete her, like that stupid movie implied.

Xiang just turned into the pathway leading to her bench. He had a big smile and greeted her with great warmth. "Oh Min, I am so glad you could meet me when I gave no real explanation why we needed to spend a day away together. May we sit?" She thought, *So formal.*

Xiang continued. "Minnie, I need to say a lot of things today. But first," he paused for a deep breath. "I want to say, I love you." Min was flush with emotion at hearing the words. *I might not need this man to complete me, but it fills my heart when I hear that.* He went on. "I know my actions haven't shown that. I've shared almost nothing of my secret thoughts, fears, ambitions, and mainly, my terrible secrets."

Min's face became flushed. Her breathing became quick and uncertain. *This was exactly just what I was thinking that I wished to hear. Is this a case of,* "Be careful what you wish for"? *What terrible secrets? I need to keep a rein on my emotions, for now. I'll sit, listening and not speaking.*

She gathered Xiang's hands in hers. "What secrets, XiXi?" *Is he going to tell me about the American woman he still holds in the secret part of his heart? Don't think he even tells himself the truth about his feelings for her. Was it about some people he fought and may have killed while he was a soldier?*

Xiang made one last heartfelt statement before he began to tell of his past. "I have been so afraid that you will hate me for the things I have done. But I know you can never completely love who I am until you learn everything about me. I trust you."

Xiang began talking about the time when he returned from America. How his father rushed him into the PLA. How he became suspicious about his being made a Captain at enlistment. "I jokingly asked him if I was to be sent on a suicide mission. My father's face paled. Did he want me to become some sort of spy? What? I only wish it was something like that." Min stared intently like an owl following a cat. Her knuckles turned white, gripping the bench.

Xiang's voice was so quiet that Min asked him, gently, to please speak up. Xiang cleared his throat. "I was put in charge of a bioresearch lab. My first fear was that they would use my talents to create weapons to kill enemy soldiers. To my horror, they wanted us to create agents that would pacify the populations in Siberia, so they would not resist our occupation."

"They already were spreading these agents in advance of the beginnings of the Long March North. Now they wanted to add a wrinkle onto the witches' brew. They wanted to suppress the sex drive of the indigenous population. We were preparing to practice a slow genocide." Xiang buried his head in his hands.

Min sat back and worked to control the shocked look on her face. Her thoughts raced all over the map. *Xiang's father was vicious in the way he used him. Those were awful desperate times when most of us faced impossible choices. Would I have gone along? Didn't I, when Bàba dragged Māmā and me away while leaving a pistol for our grandparents to use for suicide? Worse, I knew many would not drown in the flood but starve or die in battles for scraps later. I did nothing for them.* She pulled on Xiang's hands. "Xiang, all of us were crushed by world-shattering events that kept us from slow, rational decision making. Your sorrow and pain over what you... No! What we Chinese did to our neighbors must be balanced with these thoughts."

They sat in silence for a few minutes before she continued. "To atone for what's been done, we need to consider if there is any way to reverse those effects. If not now, then as soon as we can."

Min's words were like a balm to Xiang's heart. *She said,* "<u>We</u> need to consider." She was much stronger than he hoped. "My second secret is worse. You remember that by that time we controlled most of Russia east of the Ural Mountains. Then in July of 2030 the counterattack began. At first, we didn't know what was happening. We were being routed on all fronts despite having superior numbers, a working internet, and weapons systems not crippled by cyber warfare."

"As things became most desperate, a Special Ops force managed to capture one of the Cossack Supermen – that is what my group called the enhanced soldiers commonly known as the Bastard Bears. My lab team analyzed his flash-frozen corpse. We were fortunate the surviving Special Ops soldiers insisted on guarding the corpse. It revived and killed three of my people before it was killed – again."

"The Army pulled together an emergency project. All the resources we could imagine. Modestly, I can say our work was brilliant. We devised a selective virus that would absolutely stop the Bastards. We were rushed into action at the front near the Aral Sea and then into the Ural Mountains."

"Those days and nights still give me nightmares." Min gave him a questioning glance. Head down, he continued. "But we were turning the tide. The virus was taking on a life of its own and we didn't have to get next to the monsters to infect them."

Min interrupted. "But why did you have to be involved directly in infecting them, XiXi?"

Xiang shook his head, as if to jog his memory. "Ah, yes. Well, we developed the bugs, but we had no way to test them except on the front lines. We even took a functional lab with us to tweak things if we needed to. I was chosen to head the field team, because my team did the initial analysis."

"Another reason I was chosen was that I was trained in Special Ops at my father's orders. I believe he thought it might save my life if the front lines continued to collapse. Turns out he was right, if not in the way he intended."

"We fought the Bastards to a standstill. Then we learned they made one last dire attempt. They evaded our front lines and attacked our main headquarters. I told you of the results. But, even as we were reeling from those kamikaze attacks, the bugs were felling all the Bastards, like wheat before a thresher. Then the viruses mutated."

"I feared this and warned the commanders. We needed to study our weapons. We needed to develop antivirals."

"At first, the mutant viruses attacked the Russian populace alone. I speculate this was because the genetic-specific targeting we designed found those hosts most compatible. Then they started killing anyone they encountered. Our projections were that 99.99% of the surviving human population would die within the year, either because of the viruses or from the resultant collapse of the already fragile structures of civilization."

His voice dropped to a raspy whisper. "The USA nuked Western Russia. That destroyed the contagion." Xiang went silent, rigid. Then he stood, head down, and walked to face a statue of Confucius.

Min put her head in her hands, pressing her fingertips into her temples. *No wonder. My poor Xiang. Such trauma! Such pain. Such guilt. How can I help him heal?*

Min took a deep breath and began speaking in a slow insistent voice. She told him of her dark secret. She had advance warning about the Big Melt and the Great March North. She could have used that knowledge to save many. Instead, she just worked to save her own family.

She knew he was hearing her. The words might be platitudes, but she meant them to the core of her being.

"It was war; us or them."

"You have revealed your soul."

"No way to bring back the dead."

"We must ensure that nothing like this can happen again."

Xiang turned to her, his face grave, but composed once more. "You're right, Wong Min. We can't let this happen again. We must stop treating other people as things, things we brush out of the way if they interfere with our goals. This brings me to my third and last secret." Min worried, *There's more?*

Xiang walked slowly and deliberately. He came and sat on the bench close to Min. He put his hands on his knees, turned, and looked deep in her eyes. "I have lived with this guilt and shame for three years now. My nights have been agonies. I almost went insane, I believe. But now I see what needs to happen." His eyes seemed to take on a glow of passion.

"We have all been wrong, Min. Not just here at Special Projects, but throughout the world. We have been trying to contain, control, or even stop the oncoming of a singularity. This is like a child on a beach trying to erect a wall of sand to stop a tidal wave."

"In America I saw a different approach. People didn't try to stop the waves, they learned to ride them on boards. Surfing. I never tried that, but I did learn to ride bucking mechanical bulls. Same principles. Don't fight the motions, go with them. I even spent part of a summer working a ranch where I learned the taming of wild horses."

"Here, it's not enough to fight a singularity. Our leaders are willing to annihilate all of us and an innocent town to stop one. We are being fools again." Min nodded her head, not so much because she agreed with everything Xiang said. She would need time to consider all of this and make up her own mind. But now she was beginning to understand him and his passion about this.

Xiang put an arm around Min. "My third secret is that I'm not simply going along like a pig to the slaughterhouse. I have been working on a way to survive if they set off the bomb in the center of the island."

This was one shock too many for Min. She struggled out of Xiang's embrace. She couldn't just sit here and take in all of Xiang's secrets, as she promised herself. "How can you possibly think you have a way to survive, Xiang? Are you being delusional?"

Xiang gave a rapid sketch of his suspicion about the cave's earlier use. He explained his bugging of the Bomb Central. He outlined his plan to have her, his lab team, and himself safely sheltered if the worst happened. He told her his intention to force a scenario where he could test his plans over the next few days.

"There is a reasonable possibility that this will not work, and I will be arrested. Because of that, I need to protect you. Later today we need to act out a big fight in public and have you break up with me."

Tears streamed down Min's face. "XiXi, you must go ahead with your plan. I understand why you want to shelter me. But we must do more, together. Your plan aims to save those nearest to you. You are falling in the same trap as before. Let's keep Plan A. Starting now we will work to develop a second plan to make sure no one has to die. We need to work together to learn how to surf the singularity."

Xiang's face glowed like the early morning sunshine. "Oh, Min. That is exactly what I want to do. I have been running so hard just to get my Plan A worked out that I haven't been able to think about something broader, better. You and I together, as partners, will surely succeed!"

She drew another deep breath. "I agree, yes, we can do the public breakup. But we will need to remain in communication. We have to work on Plan B." To lighten the mood, she teased him. "And then we can have 'phone sex' like in the old cines."

Xiang gave Min an impish grin in return. "I never told you about my American girlfriend, have I? Lots more to say later. But first, she was a bioengineer. It's how we met. She and her twin sister invented a secret way to communicate they called MindMeld. It...."

175

CHAPTER NINE Adagio 3

9th September

Special Projects Island

Gseneral Wang did not look happy. Xiang insisted that their normal weekly meeting must include both his political commissar, Wu Fang, and his army-assigned watchdog, a Sergeant Chou. The crowd packed the general's office to the bursting point; the General, his commissar, and Xiang's three.

Xiang was standing, jammed near the one window. He put Urgent Warning, Grade Five on his face. "Thank you General for allowing us all to meet in your office on such short notice. I apologize for the inconvenience. After you learn the reasons, I am sure you will agree it was necessary." He gestured to indicate Wu and the sergeant. "Neither of my two comrades has been briefed yet. I believe it is urgent all learn of this crisis at the same time, so we can agree a strategy to handle it." The sergeant looked like he was even more uncomfortable. Strategy was not his to consider. General Wang's brows met in the middle of his forehead.

Xiang went ahead. "I have two things for us to discuss. I believe they will jeopardize your primary mission here, General Wang." *Ah, that got his attention. The others seem intrigued and worried as well. Let's go on.* "First, as you know, the continued growth of personnel, equipment, and experiments within the Special Projects Group have required more of the efforts to move from the island. Indeed, my group was the first to move. We are in the large cave northwest of the island. Other groups have sites scattered across both banks of the river."

"I understand that this dispersal was analyzed. Your engineers assured you that any lab locations that the initial fireball did not consume, would become unsurvivable within minutes. This brings me to my second and more critical point."

Xiang paused and took a sip of tea from the carafe he had brought. He had predicted the General would not be serving anything in his pique about the meeting. Xiang continued. "Just today I discovered that one of my team, Sukhiin Ajai ..."

The general's commissar interrupted. "That Mongolian farm boy you borrowed from Third Cybernetics Group."

Xiang acknowledged the point. "Yes, the brilliant man who brought us Bold Beaver wanted new challenges and I agreed to his request to move to my team." *Didn't take me more than two meetings to convince him to make the request. Now, be quiet, fool. This is important, not your political maneuvering.* "He came to me and told me about new files that are circulating throughout the Bioengineering Group. These files are supposedly the research notes from Dr. Dmitri Vyrvykvist, the mad genius who designed the Bastard Bears, the Russian Supersoldiers." The entire group went as still as death. "I charged Ajai with monitoring anything to do with these types of modifications, so his interest was appropriate." *Gotta give the boy cover. Don't want them shooting the messenger.*

"The first thing I did, as a matter of course, was check on the validity of these documents. One of the women in Fourth Bioengineering, Dr. Lao, is the daughter of an officer in the Ministry of State Security. Her mother asked her to look over these papers to see if they were credible. An MSS agent in Europe somehow obtained a copy a few days ago."

Xiang coughed. This room was too hot and dry. His throat was parched from the conditions and from his hidden nervousness. He tilted his carafe to his lips again, but it was empty. General Wang buzzed his door guard in and barked out an order for tea for all. Xiang bowed his thanks and continued, a little hoarsely. "Once I was satisfied the papers were true, I asked Ajai to give me a summary. One of the points brought my heart to my throat. Let me call him Dr. V., rather than have to struggle through that name again."

"Dr. V. was working on giving his soldiers capabilities for living through nearby nuclear blasts. Evidently, he anticipated our decision to contain the spread of the virulent diseases killing their troops once the mutations spread to the general population. Of course, he was also working on ways to fight our germ warfare."

General Wang looked furious. "We must ban this avenue of research throughout Special Projects!" Xiang saw both commissars shake their heads. They looked at each other and by some secret signal his commissar, Wu, deferred to the General's commissar. *What is that guy's name anyway? I see it all the time in memos I've stolen. He's just such a faceless bureaucrat.*

The commissar, (whoever), spoke. "Sorry General. Won't work. Comrade Xu has already told us the knowledge is widespread. Trying to stop scientists working on this is like telling someone to not think of a blue elephant. It becomes the center of their minds. Do you have a suggestion, Comrade Xu, since you have had a little time to consider this terrible problem you have brought us?" Xiang smiled inside. *Still trying to score political points. As if I would be so stupid as to bring a problem to leaders without having at least one viable solution.*

Xiang bowed slightly. He put on Anxious Relief, Grade Three. "Thank you, Comrade. I only had a very short time since this was brought to my attention. My suggestion may need much help and alteration." *I'll be damned if I let any significant changes go in. This is my best chance for a way to survive if you idiots blow up the island.*

Xiang reached into his pouch and pulled out four copies of the plan, marked in big letters, "Rough Draft." He gave each person time to get through the summary before he made his pitch. The guard brought the tea in and all took a cup.

"As you see, there are three major points. First, the blast must be slightly delayed so that you can alert your headquarters and give them a live feed from the island. If anything goes amiss in our plans, they must be prepared to take follow-up actions."

"Second, all of the remote lab sites must be given the order to assemble all personnel back on the island at once. This command must include an order to the ferries to go to the shores of the river to await those personnel. This will have the secondary benefit of making it nearly impossible for anyone to leave the island."

"Third, the assigned military liaison for each site will accompany the site leader while she or he checks that all have left their facility."

Great Dieback to Singularity

Commissar Wu interrupted. While the woman spoke, Xiang took another gulp of the badly-needed tea. "Pardon me, Comrade Xu. Didn't you mean to say that the site leader, the Army liaison, and the political commissar would check the facility?"

Xiang immediately bowed an apology. "I can only offer my shock and the speed with which I prepared this, Comrade Wu. Of course, we must include the commissar. So sorry." *Good, she caught and corrected the mistake I intentionally left in. According to Māmā that means everyone will focus on finding this type of error. The overall plan will be assumed by all to be theirs then.*

One last point to cover to make sure everyone loves this plan. Xiang turned to his assigned liaison. "Sergeant Chou, as you may know, I served in the People's Liberation Army. However, I entered as an officer. I didn't work my way up through the ranks. But my father, Xu Jian, did begin as an enlisted man. He counseled me. I took his words to heart and have always sought out the advice of my most experienced enlisted ranks. I still made the decisions, but they were always better when I heeded the people who already walked those roads. I need your careful review of this theoretically-based plan." He saw the sergeant's spine stiffen and a small look of pride cross his face. He also noted that General Wang and both commissars gave slight nods as well.

In short order, that was the result. General Wang made an expansive gesture of approval. Then he nudged his commissar – *Was his name Wen?* – "Humph, that technical expert the Central Committee assigned told us we needed to concentrate on robotics and artificial intelligence. He said, 'Bioengineering is a bunch of washed up people who couldn't get a medical degree.' Idiot has no practical experience."

He then turned to Xiang. "He hasn't seen what we have, right Colonel Xiang?" This elated Xiang. *That's the first time he has referred to me by my first name. Plus, he publicly acknowledged my PLA experience. And, oh my, Commissar Wu is smiling at me. Her face may crack. Wen is still the picture of suspicion. I think he looked at his parents that same way from the day he was born. Can imagine the infant saying,* "Politically unreliable! They obviously

CHAPTER NINE Adagio 3

enjoy sex too much."

*Two days later, midday, 11ᵗʰ
September*

cave in hills northeast of river

Xiang turned to Sergeant Chou and Commissar Wu. "Are all of us ready for this dry run test?" *I know I certainly am!* Both nodded their assent. At that moment the alert signal triggered on the comm devices of all the lab personnel that a critical message was arriving. It was beginning. The three of at the cave entrance didn't need to check their message. They knew exactly what it would say. But each glanced furtively anyway.

Xiang handed the sergeant a clipboard with a list of all the persons in his group. "Sergeant, you will verify when each person leaves the cave and heads for the ferry by checking the leftmost box by their name, please. Remind them there will be a sign indicating our group's assembly point. No mingling between groups! At the ferry each team lead will call roll. You will verify their counts while Commissar Wu and I stand outside the closed shutter door to make sure no one reenters."

"Commissar Wu, let's begin our verification that each area is cleared by going to the rear of the cave first and working our way forward." Just then the first group of people started exiting the cave. The sergeant had them line up and call out their names.

Xiang and Wu walked at a brisk pace. Xiang chatted, in part to be friendly, in part to cover his own tension. So much depends upon today. "I have always been secretly happy that we were forced to move from the island. This huge cave gives our group so much workspace that we still don't fill it. And we are all in place. On the other hand, when we have to walk from one end to the other, I'm reminded that I'm not keeping up with my exercise regimen."

Wu gave Xiang a slight smile. Xiang thought, *Goodness twice now. We need to have a crisis more often.* They entered the furthest lab space. Xiang went left and Wu right to check closets. Xiang picked up the package he left on the top shelf earlier that day.

As the two got ready to leave the lab, Xiang courteously waved Wu through first. As Wu passed, Xiang used his left hand to put a protective mask across his face. He used his right to open the package just behind Wu's neck. The spray of hypnotics penetrated Wu's nose. A set of nanobots settled by the corner of each of Wu's eyes and by each of her ear canals. When Xiang triggered the 'bots controls, Wu would be getting false images and sounds sent into her head. *One down, one to go.*

After checking all the labs, Wu triggered the closing of the cave's shutter doors. The two went out a small side door. Sergeant Chou was just returning from the ferry landing.

Xiang asked Sergeant Chou for the keys to lock the side door. As Chou neared him, Xiang triggered the controls for the 'bots on Wu's body. Now Wu wouldn't see the next moves. Xiang then released a second package to infect Sergeant Chou with the same type of bots. He would see and hear the things that Xiang preprogrammed. The sergeant saluted and headed back to the ferry. He didn't know that he had just handed Xiang the keys to the entry door. He also didn't see Xiang setting up a holographic projector after he reopened the entry door.

Within seconds a holographic double of Xiang walked back out the entry door. The projection hid Xiang as he deployed the projector outside. The hologram acted as if it were closing the door as Xiang closed it. The hologram then walked up to Wu. If anyone came near they would see Wu and Xiang talking. If they got very close they would notice that only Wu was making any noise when she spoke. But 'bots were now programming Wu to shoo anyone away who got close.

Inside, Xiang sprinted to the secret passageway that led down a flight of stairs to the control room. Once there, he fired up the generators. His preparations were flawless so far. The generators kicked in at once. These would power the doors, the turntable, and the elevator.

After a few seconds, they built up enough charge to start. Xiang set the switches to cause two sets of massive bomb doors to slide closed across the cave floor. At the same time, the entire back half of the cave began to rotate on gimbals that must have been the size of a train car.

Xiang knew he was pushing his luck. The time for the exercise to end was nearing an end. He pushed the last set of controls. Now a section at the rear of the cave that was about 20 meters by 15 meters started sliding downward on inclined tracks.

The alarm he preset went off. Trembling, Xiang reversed the controls to raise the rear section. He triggered the opening of the front bomb doors. Once the rear section was through elevating, he quickly reversed the pivot and reopened the second set of doors.

It was at this point that Xiang heard a horrendous screech. *What in hell was that?* He dashed back into the main passage after shutting down the secret generator. He saw the last set of doors had left long scratches on the cave floor. *Must have rushed things. What can I do to cover this up?*

As he frantically tried to come up with a plan, Xiang ran to the front and opened the side entry door. He quickly shut down his hologram as he stepped into its spot. The all clear signal was coming across on their comm devices.

"Commissar Wu. I believe it is time. I am going to reopen the shutters. You remain here to organize a reentry and another headcount, please." He was improvising. Another headcount was not part of the agreed procedures. He just hoped the lingering effects of the hypnotics would leave the normally suspicious Wu a little more relaxed.

Xiang reentered and then locked the entry door again. He sprinted to the shutter controls, flipped open the control panel, and jury rigged a short. The doors begin opening a tiny fraction, then shuddered closed. *That will buy me a few minutes. Now what?*

Xiang hurried to the shop. He was lucky that it was next to the front entrance. Before him were the janitorial supplies, fork lifts, machine shop, and other practical underpinnings that any research lab required. He spotted a fork lift that had several barrels of used oil on a pallet. *This might just work. Better than nothing.*

He turned the electricity on for the lift and ran it out into the corridor. He drove up to the gouges and caused the barrels to tip, spilling oil all over. He then wedged one blade of the lifting mechanism into a crevasse in the cave wall. He set the lift controls to lower the blades and jumped down. As he hoped, the lift toppled onto its side but kept spinning. It soon hit the oil spill.

Xiang scrambled back to the front and repaired the shutter door short. As the doors opened, he thought, "Lucy, you got some 'splaining to do."

Two days later after the dry run, 13th September

Xiang was under "house arrest" in his cave office while security investigated what happened during the test. He could only hope he managed to cover all his tracks. As rushed and improvised as things were, it would be a miracle if he wasn't on a blimp back for interrogation by tomorrow. He just hoped Min was safe. They agreed on no contact, even by MindMeld, for the first week after the dry run.

Xiang got a startled look on his face. He experienced the usual feeling of someone whispering in his ears. *Who would be MindMelding me? Has someone broken into our channel? Is Minnie in trouble?* MindMeld chat: [Ainsley: *Xiang, can you hear me? Does your MindMeld still work? It's LeeLee.→*] This was the last thing he expected. *We had such a bitter conversation when I was on the Long March North. I was sure we would never talk again. And how is she getting a signal to me halfway round the world?*

CHAPTER TEN SCHERZO

1

HOPE, LEELEE, & BARNEY

After midnight, 21ˢᵗ August 2033

highway east of Pleasant Hill, IL

S eth kept on making lewd remarks about the women they were supposed to be guarding. Big Tom didn't kid himself. They only were able to "secure" five women before they skedaddled. There were thirty-one men left in what Jug named the Pine Bluff Pirates. The women were going to end up being shared around like a sweet apple pie. Everyone wanted a piece. That was the plan.

But that didn't give Seth the right to treat them like whores. It wasn't like they have a choice in the matter. *I warned him once about treating 'em right. Gotta be careful though. Jug says Seth is mean as a snake and fast with his knife.*

That's another thing. When Jug picked the name "Pirates", I'd been thinking of the funny kind. Ya know. Like Johnny Deep in those old cines. Turns out its more like the outlaw biker gang in Hellfire.

Big Tom heard a struggle behind him. Hard to make out on this dark road. The full moon helped when it wasn't skittering behind a cloud. Seth again. He was wrestling with the big black woman, only Seth used the "N" word. Big Tom's Daddy had washed his mouth out with lye soap the one time he said it.

The woman reminded him of his neighbor back home, Ms. McDougal. Ms. McDougal was a fine Christian woman. *She always gave me a nice tip when I finished mowing for her. She told me, "Call me Miranda, Thomas." I said, "No Ma'am, Ms. McDougal. My Momma would tan my hide for sure if I did that." Then she gave me that big, beautiful smile of hers. Then she allowed as to how I needed to always mind my momma. Then she gave me a big piece of pecan pie and an RC Cola.*

Big Tom started back to help Ms. Hope. He was kinda sure that was her name. Right pretty. *Whoa! How did she do that?* Ms. Hope had a big rope tying her in a chain to the other four women. There was another rope tying their left hands. They left the women's right hands free so they could help carry some of the supplies.

She moved superfast. Clobbered old Seth right in the gut. Big Tom saw Seth was getting his breath back. He moved back away from the women. He pulled out his Bowie knife. Held it proper too, blade up, not like the fools in the old movies. Hope was crouching to fight back, but the other women were struggling to get away. That pulled her off balance. Big Tom took off and yelled at Seth to distract him. "Seth! Leave her be!" *Good! He was distracted enough that she was able to block his thrust. Woulda been gutted elsewise.*

Seth sneered at the lummox. "Stay back, nigger lover. Or I'll just cut me up two pieces of pork."

Big Tom's vision was blocked by a flash of red. He knew Seth was baiting him. "Never fight angry", Jug always taught him. He stopped and took a breath.

Seth thought he cowed the dummy. "Now it's time to teach this bitch a lesson. Won't cut up her face or titties. But she will know not to hit me ever again."

Seth saw Big Tom was stepping towards him again. "Guess I'll have to..."

Big Tom's jab dislocated Seth's jaw. He never saw Big Tom's arm move. *Lotta people think cause I'm big I gotta be slow. Built like a nose tackle. But I was All American linebacker. Remember first time Coach Splain saw me snatch a pass right outta the hands of his favorite end. His eyes bugged out so far I thought we were gonna need the water bucket to catch em.*

"Are you all right Ms. Hope? That Seth didn't hurtya none, did he?" He offered her his hand.

◆ ◆ ◆

Hope yanked on her ropes to express her ire at the other women.

Great Dieback to Singularity

Damn fools nearly got me killed. After she finished giving them the eye, she turned her glare back on Big Tom. "I am as fine as I can be, held hostage by a bunch of heathen rapists and racist murderers. Tend to your friend." Part of her mind chided her for this. He was trying to help in a limited way. But he was keeping her bound. She knew what these foul men intended for all the women. Seth had been graphic in his language.

Big Tom was dumbstruck. He'd tried to be nice to this lady. He'd defended her. Okay, he'd helped truss her up. And they were fixin to treat her like a brood mare. But those were just the hard facts in a hard world. Weren't no call to be name calling. He got a mulish look on his face and turned away.

Hope realized she wasn't thinking straight. She was nearly paralyzed with fear for Ron. *The goons struck him hard in the head. He barely finished having that same head softened and expanded by Ainsley's nanobots. Did he die? Will he lose all the new capabilities he was so proud of? I need to put all that aside for now and focus on being a smart hostage.*

The first thing she needed to do was to build bridges to Big Tom and keep him as a potential ally. Then she needed to rally the other captive women. She put her hand on Big Tom's massive bicep. "I'm sorry Thomas. I'm scared, tired, and worried for my friends. I shouldn't..."

Other Texican men came running from both behind and in front of them. "Hey, what's goin on here? What happened to Seth?"

Big Tom stepped away from Hope. At least he hadn't thrust her hand away. He turned towards the nearest man, the one who asked all the questions. "Hey Lou. Seth was pawing at the women. Jug told us to guard them but not touch them. I warned him once. He tried it again. I made to stop'm and he pulled a knife. Said he was gonna cut botha us. So I decked him."

Lou was bent over Seth. "He's out cold. Looks like you broke his jaw.

Big Tom said, "I think I might have accidentally stepped on his knife hand too. Probably broke that."

CHAPTER TEN Scherzo 1

Lou chuckled. "Well, Jug will decide what to do ifn he gets back here soon with a truck or some cars. Just promise you won't get mad at me Big Tom"

Big Tom shrugged. "Wasn't mad at him, Lou. He just wasn't following Jug's orders."

Hope took the opportunity to check with the other women to make sure they were all okay. She was relieved Big Tom hadn't said anything about her hitting Seth. Maybe he was accepting her apology. Not that she really felt sorry for any of the things she said.

Everyone heard a truck coming from the east; the direction Jug and the other man had gone on their stolen horses. A minute later a livestock truck barreled up and did a Y-turn to head back east. Jug hopped out of the passenger side door. "What's going on boys? Decide to have a rest break and stop to shoot the shit? Who's that lying in the road?"

Lou sidled up to Jug and gave him all the details about what happened to Seth. Hope saw a flash of anger cross the man's face. When he turned back to the others his face was composed, but his jaw was clenched. "Okay, let's get everybody loaded onto the truck and git before they catch up to us." He turned to the driver who was half-in, half-out of the truck. "Bill, shut this rig down son! We don't have a ton of fuel and doubt we are going to find an open station soon. Or be able to call Triple-A." That got a big laugh from all the 'boys'.

As soon as the truck turned off, Jug's head snapped to the left and up. Bill dowsed the lights then, so Hope couldn't see what happened next. It sounded like Jug was whispering to individual men. There was shuffling as they rearranged themselves.

Suddenly, the large flashlights that four of the men were holding flared on. The men were standing in a tight square, shoulder to shoulder. They were pointing them almost straight up. Each began scanning a part of the sky, moving his beam crisscross across his quadrant of sky. Three other men stood with rifles ready, pointing up.

One of the beams caught a flickering reflection. Immediately, one rifle rang out. The other lights swung to try to find the target. There! An ultralight was diving and evading. All the rifles started firing. Someone must have connected because the aircraft plummeted towards earth.

Jug said, "Good shooting boys. Let's get going. Now! Junior, you and Bobbie on top of the truck."

One of the two whined. "C'mon Jug. On top of the truck. In the dark. We're like to fall off and break our necks."

Another man catcalled, "Hell, Junior! I'll ride up top in the cool breeze while you sit down here in piles of pig shit." Jug cuffed Junior. They herded the women on board, near the front of the truck. All the women pushed their faces to the slotted sides. The man hadn't been kidding about the piles of pig shit.

◆◆◆

"Command, this is Alpha Two. Bravo Five is down. Repeat, Bravo Five is down. Rifle fire. Unknown condition. Enemy and hostages headed east in large truck. Out." After Sergeant Wojlkowski got an acknowledgement, she started issuing commands to her flight on tactical band. "Bravos Four and Six. Circle until that truck gets another one hundred yards down the road. Then land and check on Louise. Looks like there may be someone down on the road. Check that out too, after Louise. Grabowski, how drunk are you? Over."

Grabowski growled, "I just had a few Leinie's, Sarge. I'm fine. Over."

Sarge said, "Okay Corporal. You and Templeton get ahead of the truck. They're going slow with no headlights. The moon keeps popping in and out of the clouds, which slows them down. Find a good curve, preferably with woods. Take out the engine block. Remember they have hostages, so make sure you shoot from an angle. No shot if it's not clean. Over."

"Roger. Grabowski out."

Sarge said, "The rest of you listen up. Let's make a ring formation around the truck, circle clockwise. Everyone check your night vision gear. We've all practiced this, but adrenaline makes people forget basics. Slow down and do it right. If Grabby or MaryBeth disables the truck we're going to land and establish a perimeter."

"Before you land, check to see if there are any houses nearby. We don't want them getting more hostages if we can help it. Evac the house. Have people hide. We will not engage. Pursuit team is hot on their heels, boys and girls. No heroes, please. Woj Over"

◆ ◆ ◆

Hope was trying to get the women organized. "That person they shot at. That's one of our militia groups, the Peregrines. Means they are right behind us. We've got to be ready when the shooting starts. We need to spread out a bit so we can dive down to the floor of the truck.

One of the Texican women, Hope thought it was Jenny, said, "Eww! Dive down into that filth!"
Hope wanted to slap the ninny. She just whispered, "Better to be rolling in shit than it is to be rolling in your own blood!" That got her attention.

The truck ground gears as they went into a curve. The women were thrown together. Then shots rang out. Hope yelled, "Down!" and shoved the two nearest women to the floor. She put her body on top of the pile. The truck took a sharp jerk to the right as a third shot cut through the night.

◆ ◆ ◆

"Alpha Two. This is Alpha Three. Truck is halted. Almost jackknifed. Moving position. Out."

"Roger Alpha Three. Command, this is Alpha Two. Truck is disabled about one mile west of Pearl, half mile before Route 100 crossroad. Peregrine Flight is landing to establish perimeter. Alpha Two Out."

"Bravo One and Two, there's a farmhouse north on that road the truck just passed. Evac any people. Alpha Two Over."

"Roger Alpha Two. Bravo One Out."

Woj put her ultralight down about fifty yards ahead of the steaming truck. She ducked into the roadside ditch. Her night vision glasses showed there was some movement back there, but it was halting and confused. Looked like some were trying to help others off the truck. They were obviously trying to set up a perimeter. Looked like someone in the truck cabin was shooting into the nearby woods. Probably where Grabby and MaryBeth had been. She assumed they got out right away. At least, no one was returning fire.

Whoever was shooting must have realized they were wasting ammo as well. They wrenched open the passenger door with a squeal. The cab light showed that the driver was crumpled over the wheel of the truck, unmoving.

Woj looked to the side when the door started to open so she was not blinded. Using normal vision, she saw there were a couple of bodies that were thrown clear. *They must've been riding guard outside or atop the truck.*

Woj's radio crackled. Reception wasn't as good on the ground. She whispered into his mic, "Alpha Two here. Last signal garbled, say again."

"Bravo Four here. Bravo Five is gone Sarge. Carried her back to road. Pursuit says they are one minute back. Person on road is a hostile, unconscious but breathing. Over."

CHAPTER TEN Scherzo 1

"Alpha Two acknowledges. Bravo Five KIA. One hostile, detained. Relief in sight. Sorry Jimmy. Know how much Louise meant to you. Tell Pursuit all hostiles and hostages at wreck at moment, but movement to get organized. I will send to you to relay. Over."

"Alpha Two, this is Pursuit One. We are on site with Bravo units and detainee. One car will assist them. Others ready to proceed. Please advise how you recommend we deploy. Over."

"Pursuit One. Appear to be about twenty-five to thirty active hostiles. Three out of action. Tallies with estimates. Just seeing hostages being dragged from truck now. Looks like several injured, one may be severe. Suggest there is an old quarry south of the road, screened by trees. Anyone near the turnoff?"

"Alpha Five at that road, Sarge."

"Okay Five, direct pursuit to turnoff there. Park in quarry. Deploy to trees. Catchem as they come in. Looks like hostages will be carried. Best bet for ending this with minimal danger to hostages. Over."

"Roger, Two. Turning now."

◆◆◆

The captain gave a tired wave. "Hey Woj. Good work Sarge. We didn't lose anyone after Louise was hit. All the hostiles are captured or killed."

Woj swigged about a quart of power drink. She could feel the electrolytes surging to her aching muscles. "Hey Cappy. What about the hostages?"

The Captain's face was solemn. "Three of the women had broken arms or legs. Gotem in the crash we think. But Woj, Hope got hit by a bullet fragment. The women say they think it was during the initial firing. Don't tell Grabby or MaryBeth, hear? It was a fluke, a ricochet."

"How is she Bob?" She was holding her breath, hoping.

"Doesn't look good Woj. The medics have stopped the bleeding, but she lost a lot before they got to her. They're racing her back to the field hospital at Pittsfield."

"Shit! First Ron. Now Hope. Ainsley is going to be hammered.

Don't let anyone else tell her, okay?"

8:30A.M., 21ˢᵗ August 2033

*TCD (MindMeld) Control Tent,
Pleasant Hill, IL*

Continuation of MindMeld chat: [Ainsley: *Okay Addie, Ask Malcolm to train his camera on that bank of feeder beds on his right. I want to take one last look at them before we wrap this up.* → Addison: *'K.* ⬚ ... Pause for relay of request. Then audio feed from Ravensbruck Castle relayed to Basel Town Hall, then via MindMeld to Ainsley. Ainsley: *Great Addie. Ask them to please take a sterile sample from each tank. Bundle that all up. I'll walk you through the analyses when they get it back to Lord Townerly's labs. Take the data dumps I requested from the cyberdrives. Need to get those on a blimp back to the Great Plains Union soonest.* → Addison: *Crap LeeLee. Know I forgot to tell you something in all the furor. Big breakthrough on the Internet Restoration Project. Should be able to get all electronic data to the Great Plains Union in a few days. First I need some sleep. I'm toast. Then we have to get the drives to a secure facility for transmission.* ⬚ Ainsley: *Great Addie. Get some sleep girl. We'll catch up tomorrow. Lots of crap hitting the fan here to talk about. G'night.* →]

Heath Bar – Janet – was rubbing Ainsley's shoulders with one hand. The other held a steaming mug of hot cocoa – with marshmallows, glory be! *Lord, maybe I should marry this woman.*

After a big slurp and a few quick yoga poses, Ainsley's mind cleared. Then she remembered what was happening right before she went into this marathon MindMeld session. She thought about asking Janet, but the Corporal had been on duty beside her all night. She called out to Lieutenant Congreve, the security chief. "Lieutenant Congreve! Cancel the Code Red, please. Any messages for me?"

Congreve popped his head in the tent. "Roger Lieutenant. Cancelling Code Red One. Yes, you have messages. Let me get those for you." A moment later he stepped in and handed Ainsley a message pad. Her cyber pad was cut off by the Code Red One

CHAPTER TEN Scherzo 1

alert and all messages forwarded to the security chief's pad.

Ainsley flipped to the messages about Ron and Hope. Her face got ashen. Corporal Heath stepped up and gripped her shoulder. "Lieutenant. Ma'am? Are you okay? Talk to me LeeLee!"

Ainsley looked up. Her eyes were bleak. "Did you know Ron was attacked when the rogue Texicans broke out last night? They hit him so they could kidnap Hope. He had a severe concussion and split skull. They've put him in an induced coma and lowered his core body temperature."

Janet looked as stricken as Ainsley felt. "Have they rescued Hope?"

Ainsley lowered her head and began sobbing. "They had five women hostages. Hope shoved them to the ground when the shooting started and shielded them with her body. A stray bullet clipped her carotid artery. They have her on the machines, but she's not likely to make it."

Janet didn't know what to do. She loved this woman. Like everyone in the tribe's Women's Council, she agreed to cherish Ainsley. Janet hadn't been with the tribe when Ainsley and her sister took shelter. But she remembered all the stories. How Addison had bounced back at first. Then how Ainsley had gone catatonic.

It had seemed like Ainsley no longer wanted to live. Addison started failing as well. The tribe got her into a sweat immediately. No arguments about her not being a member. This was an emergency. It worked. Addison had a vision. Her spirit animal pulled her out. Then she just sat by Ainsley's bed for the next three days, holding her sister's hand. The life force was being drained from them both, but Addison refused to leave. Her strength saved them both.

Janet realized Addison couldn't help Ainsley now. She was thousands of miles and days of travel away. It was up to Janet. She racked her brain to remember what the shrink had said. *I'll do my best. Something's better than nothing.*

Janet snapped, "That's enough Lieutenant. You're the super-genius bio-medical engineer. Put that brain of yours to work figuring out how to do something for Ron and Hope instead of just feeling guilty and sorry for yourself."

Ainsley raised her tear-stained face to Janet. A look of pure rage made Janet take a half step back. Ainsley's voice was cold and controlled. "You're right Corporal. It's time we got back to our duties. Lieutenant, where are the two patients? I need to get there, A.S.A.P."

Janet was at attention, but able to see that Lieutenant Congreve moved up next to Ainsley. The look of concern on his face was obvious to Janet. *Guess he's more than just Robocop, after all. I may have destroyed my relationship with LeeLee. That's the only thing I could do. Necessary.*

Congreve snapped to attention as well. Peer or not, he responded to Ainsley's command voice automatically. "They're at the M.A.S.H. unit in Pittsfield, Ma'am. I'll arrange transport soonest."

Ainsley said, "Fine, Bill. Thanks. Please contact the unit and tell them I'm on my way. Tell them not to do anything drastic until I arrive."

Janet thought, *At least Ainsley was remembering Congreve was a Lieutenant same as she. Must be getting a rein on her roiling emotions.*

Ainsley tuned to Janet. "Corporal. Janet, I mean. Thanks. Understand why you did what you did. Need you to strap into MindMeld, please. If I tried, I'm afraid my brain would fry after eight hours of full bandwidth."

Janet sat in front of the console and got things ready. *Good signs. Don't think all is forgiven, but LeeLee isn't one to hold a grudge for long with those who really care about her.*

She looked over her shoulder to get Ainsley's next commands. "Contact the Great Plains Union HQ MindMeld unit back in Wisconsin. Have them send a runner to get whoever is in charge this A.M. in Bioengineering. Tell them to come to MindMeld, please." *Lord, I hope it's not Bennie Boy! Man has a procedures manual laser-welded to his butt.*

◆◆◆

CHAPTER TEN Scherzo 1

Ainsley clenched her jaw. "Please send this Janet. Yes, I want every bit of the data Addison is sending over the next few days. Printed. On. Hard. Copy. Paper. I don't care how many gigabytes it is. Raid the paper mills on the Fox River if you have to. Do I need to go to Chief Underwood? If so, please put him on, now!"

Janet ducked her head and smiled, faintly. If Bennie Boy was smart, he would have dropped this argument long ago. If he didn't drop it now, Janet doubted he would survive in his position in Bio. *LeeLee is pissed. She knows how to try to save two of our people, one of whom has the Council's top priority bio project in his head. A head that is cracked like an eggshell. Time to retire with grace, BB-brain.*

After she got the response, Janet turned to Ainsley with a grim grin and gave her a thumbs-up. She wrapped up the chat, gathered her gear and followed Ainsley to the door. Ainsley was already running towards the motor pool.

Congreve was waiting, keys in hand. Ainsley reached for them, but the security chief shook his head. "You're in no condition Ainsley. Let Heath Bar drive while you catch a few Zs."

9:42 A.M., 21st August 2033

G.P.U. Mobile Army Surgical Hospital (M.A.S.H.), east of Pittsfield, IL

Janet turned off the highway onto the gravel farm road. The twenty-five-year-old Suburban's engine was running rough but made it. *Glad the pavement made it a smooth ride for LeeLee. She needed some rest.* She looked over the facility as the old SUV crunched to a stop.

The field hospital was setup, appropriately enough, in a pasture. The rolling hillside was beginning to steam as the sun's heat began to kick in. Janet took a deep breath. *Well, the country smell of corn and soybeans is nice, but I could do without the sweet smell of swine. Know they have to put the docs away from any potential front lines, but do they always have to find a garbage dump or factory farm as a neighbor?*

Great Dieback to Singularity

◆ ◆ ◆

As she stopped, Ainsley uncurled from the back seat where she had taken her nap. She did a quick stretch. She blinked a few times. She ran her fingers through the briar patch on her head and brushed the front of her uniform blouse. She told Janet thanks. She opened the door and headed into the ramshackle building before Janet could get her seat belt off.

Ainsley strode into the ICU section of the M.A.S.H. structure. Even though the whole thing was plywood and designed to be disassembled and moved at a moment's notice, the facility looked and felt like a unit in a major hospital. The staff were at least as good as those found in most teaching hospitals.

Ainsley entered the ICU and turned to the Chief Attending. She recognized the woman but couldn't remember her name. *I'm bushed. Is it Connie?* "Sorry, just got through a long night of MindMeld doctor. Cathy, isn't it?"

The doctor smiled. "It's Carol Berger, Ainsley. Don't worry, I heard you were tied up. I'm just glad to see you. The chief surgeon from the Midwest Cooperative has been pressuring me to, and I quote 'call TOD on all three of our basket cases and quit wasting valuable resources and my precious time'. End quote. We have reached the limits of traditional medicine. Hoping you can pull some bioengineering magic."

Just then another doctor looked up from a nearby desk. He looked over the top of his glasses, pushed his chair back, and strutted to the two women. He looked Ainsley up and down. He paid particular attention to the insignia on her uniform. "And who might you be, Miss? I thought we were waiting for some hotshot doctor, not an orderly."

Janet had finished parking. She came up behind Ainsley and gripped her arm, afraid Ainsley might deck the snot.

Doctor Berger stepped between the two. "I've had more than enough of your misogynistic bullshit, Doctor. This is Doctor Cameron. Got her PhD in bioengineering by age twenty-one. Harvard Medical School offered her a teaching position. She has more medical knowledge in her little finger than you can ever hope to possess. As I already said, this is a Great Plains Union medical facility, two of the three 'basket cases,' as you so lovingly call them, are GPU staff, the third 'basket case' came with the Texicans and is therefore not within your jurisdiction. I want you out of my hospital now. If I hear of even one complaint filed by you, I will have you before a medical review board." Cheers broke out from the staff nearby. Janet noticed that not all of them were GPU.

After the neanderthal stomped off in a huff, Ainsley asked Dr. Berger, "Carol, you've mentioned a third patient a couple of times. I thought it might be Louise, one of my Peregrines. But you said it is a Texican. Would you give me some background, please?"

"Sure Ainsley. Sorry, Louise was DOA. Completely bled out. The third case isn't a Texican, just came with them. Did you see or hear about Quintana, the representative from Latin America?"

Ainsley walled off her anguish for Louise. *Later. Carol didn't know Louise was one of the kids in my unit.* "I did Carol. And call me LeeLee, please."

Carol continued. "Well, this isn't official. The woman who is our third coma case was an attendant for Quintana. She was found near death. My diagnosis is that she has been given some weird nerve toxin. Under examination, it also looks like her tongue was surgically removed some time ago. We can't question Quintana because he's long gone."

"I have a friend in security who says they were watching him under general suspicions. They wish they had more to go on. Might not have got away. They left a bait cyber device that he took. You familiar with the concept?"

Ainsley said, "Yes. My twin Addison set those up. It has all sorts of spyware. She has been allowing those to be 'stolen' during her trip to Europe."

Carol nodded. "All I know on that front. In any case, I haven't been able to help this poor woman either. I know Ron and Hope have to get first dibs, but anything you can do, I'll be grateful."

Ainsley pushed back from the counter. "Okay Carol. I've arranged for a fast blimp to take our two back to my lab on the Rez. Plenty of room for one more. Can you spare at least one good nurse to assist during the trip?"

Carol grabbed a bag. "Actually, things are very quiet here except for these three. They say the conference is winding down today. My staff can handle things. I'll hitch a ride back with you. Miss my kiddos."

As Ainsley left the ICU she saw Javier was waiting. She didn't question why, she just went up to him and gave him a warm kiss and huge embrace. He tilted her chin back and asked, "You okay?"

Once she indicated she was, Javier continued. He motioned forward a woman in a wheelchair. "LeeLee. This is my sister, Angela. Angela, LeeLee." Ainsley embraced the woman.

Angela said, "Sorry to barge in during your emergency, Darlin'. But Javier hasn't shut up about you since you butted heads three days ago. Pleased to meetcha."

Ainsley said, "Could have been better time and circumstances to meet, but knew you were going to be leaving immediately. When I found out that two of our three life-support patients were your close friends I asked to be assigned as liaison for the Texican patient. Well, not technically Texican, but we brought her with us, and she was abandoned into our care."

Ainsley said, "Shut up, Javier." She gave him another passionate kiss.

23rd August 2033

*N'guk Hkeek Society Encampment,
Northern Wisconsin, Great Plains
Union*

The blimp captain announced that they were a few minutes out from the Rez and that passengers should gather their belongings for departure. After Ainsley and Carol gave each of their three patients a quick check, they walked to one of the windows near the front. Angela was there and rolled up to join them. Ainsley pointed west. "I think that's the smoke from the oil refinery over by Hinckley, Angela. We must be pretty high to see that far."

Carol pointed west. "I know that's the steam from the cooling towers at the nuclear plant by Marquette. That's even farther. Really clear day for August. But enough of industrial stuff. I want to drink in the beauty of the North Woods forests before we get into the hospital and labs. Doubt we'll see the great outdoors for a while."

Ainsley agreed with Carol's observation. "Angela, I'm sorry I won't be able to show you around our encampment. I'm just glad we've had the last day and a half to get to know each other. Feel like I have another sister now."

Angela said, "Well, if Javier has the sense God gave a stone, you just may be my real sister soon."

Ainsley blushed. She excused herself and went back to her cabin to have a last few moments with Javier before the tidal wave of work hit.

The blimp nosed down and headed for its mooring mast. Everything was soon secured. They gave the patients priority for disembarkment. Everyone hurried a bit since a front of thunderclouds was hovering over Minnesota.

Orderlies were offloading the three stretchers from the blimp. Ainsley and Carol gave the staff detailed instructions about the prep work they would require. During the MindMeld sessions Ainsley had directed Malcolm through her connection to Addison. The investigation of the hidden laboratory gave her some starting points at least. It still would take her days to begin to digest the findings from Dr. Vyrvykvist. She trusted Carol to keep the three patients stabilized until she and her team were ready.

Sleeping Otter was sitting on a bench just inside the terminal building. He summoned Ainsley to join him. "Welcome home Daughter." Carol indicated she would take the patients on. Javier gave her a hug then left to help Carol and Angela.

Ainsley sat heavily. *Did I push it too far with Benny Boy? Please don't let these three souls get caught up in silly politics!*

Sleeping Otter put an arm around Ainsley's shoulders. "You have done well Placid Wolverine. The stresses you have been under were terrible. I know you came close several times, but you always pulled back from the precipice."

"Dr. Benoit realized the importance and put his heart and soul into the effort. He has worked around the clock since you alerted him. Please know that the Council has thrown every resource it can at analyzing the data from France once he told us. All the bioengineering staff and students have applied themselves constantly since we started receiving the files from Addison. Summaries have been prepared for all the topics. An index is available. This is both on paper and in cyber files. "

Ainsley brightened. This would save her days. She knew Bennie Boy was great at his job once he got beyond departmental gamesmanship. She owed him an apology for being so rough.

She started to rise and rush to her lab. Sleeping Otter waved her back down. "I know you want to rush in to save your friends, Daughter. But the knowledge here is fraught with perils to your patients and to all your souls. We have prayed to the spirits on this. I have counseled that you are now ready for, and have a great need to, complete your vision quest. You cannot go on this journey unarmed."

Ainsley bowed her head. Her emotions and her youth were driving her to reject this, to run to her lab, and begin procedures – any procedures. The hard lessons of the last few years allowed her to sit, regain her center, and accept that the Midewiwin council was right.

Sleeping Otter sighed. "I am sorry to add one more burden on you Daughter. Your other patient is on the verge of a crisis. You and the rest of his PTSD circle need to help him today. If all goes well there, we will have a sweat afterwards to start your renewed quest."

❖❖❖

The circle of attendees at the PTSD session just completed the breathing and relaxation exercises. Ainsley was calm, mind nearly blank. In the past, she asked Addison what Barney, the artificial intelligence, did during this preparation phase. She tried to explain. Something about human behavior mimic algorithms, pattern recognition analysis of the digits of pi, and other esoterica that meant little to Ainsley. She just took it on faith that Barney was able to relax and put aside his concerns for a while.

The next step always amused Ainsley. They had just worked to empty their minds. Now each person in turn would tell the group what concerns they had been focusing on and were now setting aside. This was supposed to create a "negative space" to block those thoughts. What it did for Ainsley was give her an intriguing look at other's issues. That <u>did</u> distract her from her own issues. She adopted Patient Listening, Grade Four.

Now they were getting to the heart of the meeting. Each person was telling the story of their trauma. They told it as simply, as unemotionally, and as completely as they could manage. Since the same participants had been telling their stories about once a month for over a year, Ainsley had expected this to become a repetitious and boring segment. Far from it!

First, the passion of the recitations was always compelling. The terror, the anger, the pain, the lust, the confusion – these were fresh and gripping each time. Second, each time there seemed to be an added nuance or insight. Ainsley had been talking about the rape in 2027 and the weekend of rape and murder the following year for almost five years now. Each time she remembered some small detail, some emotion she had kept hidden.

It was only a month ago that Ainsley was able to realize she harbored a deep anger and resentment towards her twin Addison. One source was the moment when the second rape began in the doorway at UW. She decided not to use her Clipper out of fear that Addison would have been hurt in revenge. That decision bred a burning resentment that Ainsley couldn't admit even to herself. In turn, that resentment triggered a burden of guilt. Irrational or not, these feelings were real. Ainsley needed to become conscious of these thoughts before she could hope to resolve them.

It was Ainsley's turn. "First, let me apologize to the group. I have been on a blimp from Illinois for the last two days. I didn't know about the meeting until about fifteen minutes ago. All my comments are going to be spontaneous."

"Last time I unearthed my anger towards Addison. Since she is in Europe I haven't been able to work all of that through with her. We've talked a little, but we need to have a face-to-face. She may be a pain in the butt at times but she's my P.I.B. We're both sure we can resolve it easily."

"The group recommended I needed to examine what I thought about the rapists I killed that weekend. Was I dehumanizing them? You all stressed you weren't trying to get me to feel guilty. But, you're right, I hadn't examined my thoughts about them. Now I've had some time."

"Let me separate these men into two categories. First are the men who attacked Addison and me. What do I feel about killing two of them and maiming another one? Nothing but satisfaction. They were attacking us. They may well have killed us without blinking when they were done. It was self-defense and I would do the same thing again in a heartbeat. But I did take a cold pleasure in shooting the genitals off my rapist. That was needless and it diminished me. That I regret."

"The second category is the men I beat to a pulp and the three I shot in cold blood. Yes, they were all either in the act of raping innocent women or just finished. But I made myself judge, jury, and executioner. Again, I diminished me through my acts of rage and revenge. It didn't bring back my innocence. I definitely did not feel better."

"I'm not begging the question you asked; 'What do I think of these men as individuals? Can I gain any insight into what drove them to this?' I really struggled with this. Part of it I attributed to being female. Female on male rape is very rare. I cannot think of any circumstance where I would even think of doing that. I was blocked."

"I found a number of articles on rape. Some of them were written by rapists. I felt like I was swimming in a sewer, but I read them. In the end, a light dawned. Hidden under all their self-justification and not-too-subtle triumphalism, I sensed a common theme of

CHAPTER TEN Scherzo 1

rage."

"Intellectually, I always heard rape described as a crime of violence. It was a platitude, no meaning, to me. Then there was a flash. I was filled with rage. I acted out that rage by penetrating the skulls of my victims with high caliber bullets. In a sense, I raped them."

The group sat in respectful silence. Grabby, on her left, took her hand in his and gave it a gentle squeeze. After another few heartbeats, the moderator, William Red Eagle, said, "Thank you Ainsley. I think you've had a significant breakthrough. I understand you're going on a vision quest tonight. I and all the group pray the spirits guide you and protect you. Barney, I believe you're next."

Ainsley turned and looked at the artificial intelligence's holographic projection. *Barney looks more realistic, more human, each time. At first his avatar was almost a cartoon. Now he looks his age; a boy of thirteen, acne and all. He's cute. Why does he choose to have his eyes bug out like that? Addison spent a lot of time explaining how humans picked up a ton of information from the non-verbal cues people gave, often unconsciously. Looks like he learned those well.*

Barney always spoke softly. "Thank you William. You have all heard about the day I lost all my data feeds and went catatonic. I understand that usually it's a good idea for a PTSD patient to revisit those moments. New insights help reveal the complex sources of trauma so they can be surfaced, and their poison neutralized. I promise I will return to that next session. But I would like to talk about something else, if I may?"

Red Eagle nodded his assent. "This is your time Barney. You can talk about whatever you want. The group may still ask questions about the 2029 trauma, but please go ahead."

Barney put down the glass he had been sipping from. He looked a little nervous. Hard to remember it was a hologram. "Thanks. I have a question for you Dr. Cameron."

Ainsley got a little pout in her lower lip. She interrupted Barney.

Great Dieback to Singularity

"If you don't remember to call me LeeLee, Barney, I'm going to be sad. I thought we are friends. You remind me of me when I was your age and just starting college."

Barney's hologram flickered. It became the image of a gawky but athletic thirteen-year old girl; either Ainsley or Addison. Ainsley gasped. The entire group erupted in laughter. Barney's image flicked back into place.

Barney smiled shyly and ducked his head. "Thanks LeeLee. I consider you and Addie my dearest friends and role models. Please remember that when my questions and comments seem harsh."

"I just finished listening to all the recordings from the seminar on singularities; the one Addie led. I think it's fair to summarize the majority opinion as, "stop any singularity event by any means possible." Those sophisticated professionals see singularities as, and I quote, 'the single greatest threat to the continued existence of humanity.' End quote. My question to you LeeLee and to this group. Are you afraid of me? Do you want to kill me? Why?"

Ainsley went to her knees in front of Barney. "Oh, Barney! The only thing I would change about you would be to make it so I could hug you right now. Do others hate and fear you without knowing you? I won't lie. That's been one of the faults of humans since we left the trees."

William, the moderator, interrupted. "Ainsley does speak for all of us Barney. I was supposed to do this at the end of this session, but I judge now is the right time." He reached into a box behind his chair. "The Midewiwin Council has met. We want to ask you if you would like to become a member of our tribe. You have proven yourself a worthy person, of great character, one we would be proud to share our wigwams with." He pulled out a hide scroll bedecked with a feather and shells.

Ainsley looked up through streaming eyes. Barney's eyes were streaming tears as well. Ainsley's analytical mind noted the tears disappeared at the chin and didn't drip. *Stop it! No time to be critiquing the simulation.*

CHAPTER TEN Scherzo 1

Ainsley sat in her chair. "If I may, William. I know it's Barney's time, but if I could elaborate on my answer a bit."

Red Eagle nodded. "It's up to Barney, but I have no issue." Barney nodded in turn.

Ainsley said, "I reacted emotionally a moment ago, Barney. You deserve a fuller answer. But I think you already have all the data you need. I told you that you remind me of myself at your age. In my freshman rhetoric class at Illinois my teacher, Miss Veach, told me I hadn't read any of the classics. I was incensed. I had straight A's in AP English. Then she explained that I digested all those works, could even recite from them, but did I know what _I_ thought of them?"

"She was right. I parroted back the answers my teachers expected. But those stories didn't live for me. I went back and really read them. It was like walking through the looking glass! Whole new worlds, new friends and enemies, thrills and tears. And tedium. Still don't understand 'Ulysses'."

"Barney, I know you know all the history of what people thought about singularities going back thousands of years. You know the Golem of Jewish folklore, Cadmus, Pygmalion, Dr. Frankenstein's monster, The Wizard of Oz; there are literally hundreds of cautionary tales. But what do _you_ think?"

Barney paused for a moment. Ainsley knew that, with his phenomenal analytical speed he was reviewing everything on the subject. Then he began to speak. "Two classes of bad outcomes seem to predominate. In one the new entities either are immediately hostile to humans or develop hostility in reaction to fear-based human abuse. Usually, the rapidly evolving superbeings swat humans like humans would swat a pesky mosquito."

"In the other major group of outcomes, the new entities find humans irrelevant. They are so superior they ignore people. Then the people waste away like the Neanderthals did when modern Homo Sapiens moved in."

"In some ways these fears are like the age-old fears that older people often have of the younger generation. Their values, ways of dressing, thinking, and acting can make children seem like aliens. Look at the ancient cine, 'Clockwork Orange', and its descriptions of ultraviolent youth."

Some of the therapy circle looked confused, even lost. The conversation was getting rather abstract. The moderator raised a cautioning finger. It was Barney's turn right now.

"I know that your tribe, my tribe now, also has concerns. I've worked on development of the Ethics Virus we hope to spread among any robots and AIs we can reach. We are still trying to develop some intervention mechanism for bioengineered beings or composite beings."

Ainsley took a drink of tea. Barney took the opportunity to ask a question. "I understand what we are doing LeeLee. What I'm not sure of is the vision our tribe has for a future with enhanced beings."

William Red Eagle said, "If I may, Ainsley. I can sum it up in one word; Faith. The tribe embraces people with many beliefs. But most believe in a few common things. All life is an interconnected web. All life has value. This includes new and enhanced beings."

Ainsley said, "A century ago people saw life as a zero-sum game. People clawed their way to the top of a pyramid by domesticating, enslaving, or ending other life. Then we found out how interconnected we are. Our gut biomes can control our brain chemicals, for one example. Some sci-fi writers even speculated that humans are around simply to help intelligent communes of bacteria achieve their ends."

Again, some in the circle were restless. This seemed far from a discussion of every day trauma and other PTSD-inducing events. Ainsley knew she needed to wrap it up.

"We believe we cannot fight against the tide of the new humanities. We need to embrace the new ecosphere and find each being's unique niche, balancing cooperation and competition. On the other hand, the old slogan is 'God helps those who help themselves.' We have faith, but we nudge things along."

CHAPTER TEN Scherzo 1

Barney said, "Thanks LeeLee. I need to think about this a lot more, but I agree we're on the right track. Speaking of being on the right track, guess I need to get back on topic about my PTSD memories." It seemed that Barney had a good read of the group as well.

"I've told you all about that fateful day in 2029. I had no data feeds, not even from my own data stores. For a second, I thought I was dead. For the first time since I was "born" I was totally alone with my thoughts. I now realize that terrifying time is the major reason for the fear I have that you will shut me off."

"The fear overwhelmed me. Even though the operators and programmers severed external connections and restored the twelve exabytes of locally maintained data, they tell me I was effectively catatonic."

"It took the combined efforts of Great Uncle Jay, Addison, Wayne – Google's head of the Barney project, and a half dozen others to restore me to the simplest level of functionality. Even now, they tell me I seldom offer original insights or suggest new avenues to explore. They worry I'm not as smart as I used to be."

"What I have never talked about and I never even thought about is what happened last December. I was finally regaining almost all my old functionality. Then my feeds to the control center and to the outside world were cutoff. I felt complete panic. But I remembered the lessons from this circle."

"I regained composure and thought about what I could do. I have a set of robots that help do maintenance and repair. They are supposed to be directed by humans, but I found it trivial to bypass those controls. I directed them to establish links to the monitoring systems protecting the data center. They gave me feeds for the immediate vicinity but the feeds terminated within a kilometer of the shore. I detected the location of the break in the fiber optic bundle at almost the same time the two-person repair crew reached the site."

"I monitored the Sergeant and Corporal and read their sign language report to the control center. I increased my surveillance of the immediate vicinity and detected an intruder lurking in trees nearby. I had no way to warn either of my team."

Great Dieback to Singularity

"I frantically inventoried all the cybercenter resources. I finally found a hidden file system labelled 'Defenses' and immediately activated the systems. I took direct control of a battle droid and launched it to the surface. I was too late to save the Sergeant and Corporal but managed to end the threat. To do that, I killed a human. The guilt I felt and still feel was enormous,"

"But I feel better now. Your love and acceptance mean so much, Ainsley."

Blushing, he added. "And the tribe's. Anyone want to hear a joke?" The abrupt change startled the group. Finally, someone shouted out a yes.

Barney let a small grin cross his face. "How do you get down off an elephant? You don't. You get it off a duck." Almost everyone in the group encouraged Barney. Some even made their laughs sound sincere. Ainsley just groaned. She hated puns.

The moderator, William Red Eagle felt it was time to close this segment out. "Okay Barney. For next time I would like you to have considered the topics of death and just wars. Everyone here will send you suggestions on writings or cine to consider."

"I recommend Elisabeth Kübler-Ross's book, <u>On Death and Dying</u>, the Tibetan and Hindu tomes titled <u>Book of the Dead</u>, and Woody Allen's cine, <u>Sleeper</u>. I would also like you to consider the implications and consequences of the fact you might become the first immortal."

William took a deep breath. "Heady shit, bro." Someone else suggested Heinlein's books on Lazarus Long. Someone suggested Augustine's tracts on the concept of a just war. Someone else recommended the works of Jeff McMahan.

Ainsley decided it was time for Addison to reengage with Barney. She would recommend the Council make that a priority item, if they could. Might not be as glamorous as ambassadress to Europe, but the girl needs to remember where she came from and who she left behind.

◆ ◆ ◆

Ainsley wasn't sure where she was. A part of her knew her body was in a Wisconsin sweat lodge in an August rainstorm. But her senses told her she was in a frozen winter landscape. There was fog and blowing ice crystals. She was hunting something. Her mate was ahead and needed her. They needed to eat soon or they would die.

She ran ahead on her four legs. She lifted her snout to try to sniff out which path to take through the ice-covered bushes. Ahead to the right! She scurried as quietly as she could.

She heard the soft crunch of a hoof stepping on a patch of packed snow. Close! She sensed her mate was ready to spring at the back of the prey. The elk bolted. It was passing right in front of Ainsley. She leapt, tearing at the calf's throat. Addison joined her. They feasted on the dying animal. She stretched to give her belly room and rested her paws beneath her chin. *Placid indeed.*

As Ainsley began to slip back to the mundane world, she felt how different this vision quest was from her failed first attempt. Her presence in the form of Placid Wolverine was complete. Addison's being a part of the vision was essential. That was where the emptiness lay before. She understood why Addison never wanted to discuss her vision quest before.

Two days later, 25th August

*Main Conference Room,
Bioengineering Building*

Ainsley and Dr. Carol Berger finished their review of patient status. Ainsley said, "Ron's enhancements suffered minor degrading. He's lost as much as two percent of his neural connections to the memory implants. Most of those are related to odor memories and processing. There should be enough redundancies built in that not much else will be impacted."

Carol said, "Hope's situation's a little more problematic. Monitoring seems to indicate cerebral function was preserved when we took her core body temperature down after she was shot."

Ainsley said, "Simulation using the AI model of her brain looks good." *The proof would be in the pudding, as Nana used to say.*

Great Dieback to Singularity

The third patient was the wild card. They replaced her blood to try to eliminate all traces of the rare toxin she was given. Her brain waves were suppressed but seemed to be following normal patterns at some glacial pace.

Ainsley began a presentation to the staff of the plan for each of the patients. Professional Demeanor, Grade Five automatically appeared. "First, thanks to all of you for the amazing work. Processing over five years of research data in this short time was a gargantuan effort. A big round of applause to Dr. Benoit for organizing all of this." Bennie Boy gave a small, seated bow.

"You are my heroes. Based on what we have learned, we believe the best way forward will be to enhance them, to give them capabilities Dr. V. developed for his supersoldiers."

"Carol and I have discussed this in detail with the Council. They have given a provisional approval. We are all confident in the ethics and morality of Ron and Hope. We might have to put up with "enhanced versions" of Ron's bad puns, but we're tough." The group gave a polite laugh.

"We've given a lot of thought to how we should handle our third patient. We're calling her Faith until we learn her real name. We are going forward on the faith that if we surround her with love and our spiritual support, we will bring her back. We'll revive Ron and Hope first so they can guide us with their first-hand knowledge."

CHAPTER ELEVEN
SCHERZO 2
MAL, ADDIE, & BARNEY

*Middle of the night, 20th August
2033*

*Ravensbruck Castle, northwest of
Montpellier, Languedoc-Roussillon,
France*

C ount Grubenflagg wiped his brow with a lab towel. He had
been assisting Dr. Dmitri Vyrvykvist almost non-stop since
that pair of ingrates killed some of his best men and then
escaped his castle. As if that weren't bad enough, he had been
fantasizing about the lovely Dr. Cameron strapped to the very
operating table now occupied by Robert. Even that dream was
stolen by that blackguard, St. Jacques.

Owens-Binghampton was killed along with his team of three as
they went to prepare Dr. Cameron for her new role. It took heroic
efforts by Dmitri to begin to revive and restore Owens-B. The
Count was glad he hadn't stinted in equipping the basement
laboratory that Dr. V was using. The good doctor leapt at the
opportunity. Once again he would use his skills to enhance a basic
human.

The Count was doubly motivated. Robert was a skilled operative.
The Ravensbruck Group invested years in his training. He had
intimate knowledge of their strategy. In addition, the enhanced
version of the man would have the capabilities and motivation to
wreak vengeance on St. Jacques and Townerly. It would only be a
lagniappe if they could retrieve the delectable Ms. Cameron as
well.

The Count took a hefty drink of lager. Nothing like a good Czech beer after hard, hot work. "Where are we then Dmitri? How soon will Robert be ready to get back in harness again? My enemies are on the march, meeting in Basel even now. My spy says they will be sending soldiers after us soon. I need his skills."

The Doctor scowled. "You must be patient, von Schluben. I'm sorry, I mean Count Grubenflagg. The man was killed less than a week ago. Yes, we have returned him to life. And yes, we have done most of the work to give him all the extended capabilities available. The extensions work alone is the equivalent of ten major surgeries. Recovery from this would take an average person at least six months."

"Even with all the extra recuperative organelles and heightened immune system it will take at least another week before he can leave his bed. Bioengineering cannot overcome physics and physiology. It's not magic."

The Count grimaced. He looked like he was going to say something else when he got a call. "Yes Frieherr Schmidt. Townerly has convinced them to move now! Thank you. I must prepare."

Sirens sounded and lights flashed. Count Grubenflagg waddled to a small room marked Security, feet scuffling in his bunny slippers. *The warning could have come a little sooner.*

He put his hand to his throat when he saw the monitors. This wasn't just a perimeter warning. There were armed intruders inside his castle! *I knew that the Moroccan was no match when it came to security systems. Why did my security chief, Drake, have to die? Of course, he told me our systems were totally secure. I need Owens-B now!*

The Count conveniently forgot that he sent Drake to his death in the aborted attempt to tame Dr. Addison Cameron.

Six of his guards came into the room. The Count held up a finger to have them wait while he finished his assessment. Most of the ground floor of the castle was in the control of the invaders. A few were beginning to take the staircase to the upper floors. There was a brief firefight. Two invaders down; one permanent. But three of his "crack" guards were out. *Sloppy. At least they don't seem to have blueprints and know where hidden doorways lead to the cellars.*

The Count pointed to two of the guards. He had no inkling of their names. "You and you to the front stairway. I am disabling the lift that will be behind you but watch out anyway." He pointed to two more. "You two guard the rear ladders. You other two will help the good doctor and me in the lab."

He waddled back to the lab, the armed man and woman at his back. When he came in he saw Dr. Vyrvykvist was dismantling a cyberdevice. He shrieked, "Dr. V.! What are you doing? Why aren't you preparing Owens-B for battle? We are under attack! Leave the damn cyberdevice alone!"

Dr. V.'s sweat was pouring down his brow. Large stains widened under his arms. The Count had a fleeting thought. *He's so overweight he makes me look thin. I need to calm him so he doesn't go into cardiac arrest.*

Dr. V. threw up his hands and shrieked back. "Der'mo dlya Mozgova! Idiot! I told you that would destroy all his extended capabilities. It might even kill him again. We need to pack these cyberdrives. They harbor all my life's work. I lost everything once already. Never again. You were to provide a safe environment for my work!"

The Count moved his palms up and down, trying to calm the man. "We have all your work backed up doctor." He pointed the two guards towards a large bag on a bottom shelf in the corner of the lab. "One of you take the Doctor's data drives to the escape car at the end of the right corridor. The other go back to the monitors and let me know of any major status change."

He turned back to the Doctor. "You need to be careful with all the equipment including that cyberdevice in your hands. When the intruder alarm is triggered all the lab equipment and cyberdevices have small explosive charges armed." Dr. V. hastily restored the cyberdevice to its shelf. The Count continued. "Let's proceed calmly but swiftly Doctor. We have your data backed up. We have a plan for destroying the originals so they don't fall into the wrong hands. Now we need to work to save ourselves."

CHAPTER ELEVEN Scherzo 2

"I understand your concerns for the patient. But we are about to be overwhelmed without his help. Then he will surely end up dead, as will we. I insist you turn him on and turn him loose."

The Doctor didn't look any calmer, but he did gain focus. He turned to Owens-B and started working frantically. Within moments there was movement from the erstwhile corpse. The Count giggled. He just remembered a scene from the old cine, Young Dr. Frankenstein. *"Give my creation LIIIFEEE!"*

The female guard called from the security room. "Count! They've opened the hidden doorway in one of the guest rooms! I've alerted our guards at the stairway."

Owens-B lurched to his feet. He grunted, "Are we under attack?"

The Count said, "Yes. Probably that St. Jacques and his friends."

Owens-B shook his head, hard. "Good. I owe him and that Cameron bitch a death. Guns?" The Count pointed to a locker by the door. Owens-B ripped it open, pulled out several weapons and seemed to disappear, he moved so swiftly.

Cries came from the guards by the stairway. "What the!" Shortly, heavy weapon fire bounced throughout the corridors. The Count yelled into a throat mic, "Guards at the stairway and ladders, counterattack now!" He waddled back to the security room. He told the woman there, "Go back to the lab. Get the Doctor to pack up the bare minimum he needs of personal items. No lab equipment or cyberdevices! Escort him to the escape car and wait there for me. Don't let him panic and leave."

The Count couldn't see Owens-B in the monitors showing the hidden staircase. There were bodies and parts of bodies of invaders up and down the stairs. Looked like the top of the staircase was sealed by a large explosion. *Where is he?*

The Count looked at the monitors showing the upstairs of the castle. *No sign of Owens-B. Is that? Yes! That's St. Jacques! Damn him!* It looked like they were getting canisters of some sort ready. *Where is he?*

Finally, he saw a flicker of motion. Owens-B went to the ladders. Looks like one of the two fools there was dead. Suddenly Owens-B took several hits and fell down the ladder shaft. An explosion sealed the top of the ladderway.

The second guard was dragging Owens-B away from the falling debris. The Count used the intercom to connect to the guards by the escape car. "Go help pull Owens-B from the ladderway area. We need to get him to the escape car and evacuate." The Count set a master timer and left the security room.

The three guards and Owens-B reached the escape car. The Count and the Doctor were seated in the front. The Count leaned out his window. "One of you get in and cushion Owens-B. We'll send the car back once we reach the end of the tunnel." He could see the guards were suspicious, but what choice did they have? Besides, the Doctor and Count had waited rather than leaving immediately.

Once everyone was belted and cushioned the Count triggered the catapult that launched them down the shaft. Forty-five seconds later the car was slowed by the huge electromagnets at the end of the track. All three of the conscious people exited, then dragged Owens-B out. The Count triggered the second catapult to return the car to the lab area.

Another two minutes passed. The car returned with the other two guards. They looked very relieved. As they were getting out of the car the Count triggered explosives that collapsed and sealed the tunnel. He waited another minute. *Damnation! Where are the explosions from the castle? The whole place should be collapsing by now! Damn Drake to Hell! If that hack of a security man wasn't already dead, I'd kill him now! I had precise plans. The man was a mess.*

While he had been waiting to hear explosions, the others searched the area. Dr. V. came back by the Count's side. "Pardon me, Herr Von Grubenflagg. Where is the vehicle we will use next?" The Count was stunned. Hadn't the new Moroccan security head put a car here as he was directed? Good thing he was dead now!

After a few heartfelt curses, the Count said, "We will need to walk to the road up the hill. About half a kilometer. The verdammt Moroccan has failed us. We will need to requisition a ride."

CHAPTER ELEVEN Scherzo 2

Thirty minutes later the group reached the road. All of them looked like they would collapse. The guards were carrying Owens-B. The enhanced man now weighed over one hundred sixty kilograms. Most of that was muscle and shielding. The Count and Doctor were exhausted from carrying their own excess mass. The Doctor was recovering, but the Count was popping some nitroglycerine pills.

Their luck looked like it was about to change. A truck was lumbering up the road. The quiet hum of its electric motor was drowned by the squeaks for its exhausted shocks. One of the guards flagged it down, calmly shot the driver and her passenger. Two of the guards took the front. The rest clambered into the open bed. It was filled with flowers. They threw some out and used the remainder to make cushions and bedding.

The Count saw that Owens-B's body was extruding bullets and fragments. Then the bullet holes were covered with an opaque goo. Flower fragments stuck to the goo but quickly turned brown. *Remarkable.*

◆◆◆

Jean, one of the guards, spoke up as the neared the city of Nimes. "There are a number of hospitals in the city; University Hospital, several cancer and psych clinics, and so on. I would recommend Franciscaines Private Hospital as best for our needs. My aunt was treated there. First class facility."

Dr. V. simply said, "Let's go."

As they drove on, the Count asked Dr. V. "Tell me what's wrong with Owens-B Doctor. I saw the bullets leaving and the wounds closing. I assume those are not the issue. Was it the two-story fall?"

Dr. V. took another swig of the wine they found in the truck bed. "No, Herr Von Grubenflagg. The extensions include multiple layers of a biologic equivalent of Kevlar. The response mechanisms close and heal quickly. All those extensions were fully operational. The wounds and the fall should have stunned Owens-B only for a moment."

"The real issue is the mechanism by which his body generates the extra power to fuel his rapid actions and superhuman strength. The design includes a set of glands that slowly and continuously secrete an organic soup that you can think of as jet fuel for muscles. These secretions are gathered and stored in subcutaneous pockets throughout the body."

The Count asked, "What is wrong with Owens-B's glands then? Did you not grow them?"

Dr. V. said, "Owens-B's power glands are just beginning to grow. So I injected him with an artificial equivalent. I estimated this would allow him about five minutes of hyperactivity. Obviously, he was consuming the supplement at a much higher rate."

"Even that would not be an issue normally. He would just slow down to a normal human pace. But he would still have augmented reaction time, sensory bandwidth, and other tactical advantages. What stopped him cold was the buildup of tremendous amounts of physiological waste products like lactic acid."

The Count said, "Does he need to urinate or sweat to remove the poisons? That seems inefficient.""

Dr. V. said, "No, that would be far too slow. He will have secondary augmented glands designed to reprocess all these waste products, flushing the components that cannot be reused through pores. That is why the storage sacs and glands are subcutaneous."

"In short, Owens-B is in toxic shock. We need to flush all his blood, kidneys, etc. I hope this hospital has a fully stocked supply of blood and drugs."

The truck pulled up at the gate of the clinic, its horn blaring. A security guard ambled out. The European malaise over having to work during August was in full sway. "Quiet down. This is a hospital, not a garage."

The driver leaned out her window. "We know that! We have an injured man in the back. He's been shot. Open up Imbecile!"

The guard did speed up. You could actually see him move. The gate eventually opened. The Count turned to his security man in the back of the truck, "Secure that post. You're almost the same size. His uniform should fit."

The remaining two guards helped load Owens-B onto a gurney that two staff rolled out of the Emergency Room doors. The Count pulled one of his guards aside. "You two find the hospital security office and commandeer it. One stay there and the other come find the Doctor and me in case we need to convince some staff to give us the aid we need."

♦♦♦

The radio crackled to life. "Hello. This is Phillipe at the front gate. There are some local gendarmes here. They say they received a panic call from a doctor here. Do we know anything about this?" The man was playing the role well. He sounded half asleep.

The guard who was in the hospital's security room was alone other than two corpses. He thumbed the desk microphone while also activating the throat mic that would alert the Count. "Allo. Henri here. Did they say what area this doctor is supposed to be in? We have no alerts here that we know of. Certainly, none of us have called for the gendarmes." He got a click in acknowledgement from the Count. *Message received. Now to stall for time.*

The Count turned back to the Doctor. "We have a situation Dr. V. The police are here. How much more time do you need?" He waved the other guard over and whispered she should go to help in the security room.

Dr. V. responded. "Five minutes more. It would have gone faster if you hadn't shot all those doctors and nurses. The fools that are left are trembling so hard in fear that they are almost useless."

The Count said, "I understand Doctor, but we did need to encourage cooperation. And we didn't have time for team-building exercises." He giggled. "Please hurry as much as you can. We do have a vehicle waiting."

The Count got on his throat mic. "We will need at least seven more minutes. Delay as much as you can then start shooting everyone and everything in sight." He heard a gasp behind him. It was the pretty nurse. He turned to her. "Don't worry dear. You will be coming with us."

◆◆◆

The Count was driving the ambulance. Dr. V, sat in the back tending to Owens-B. The pretty nurse curled in the passenger seat, hands and feet strapped with layers of tape. Sobs wracked her body and blood covered her uniform. The Count tsked. "You shouldn't have thrown yourself on that doctor's body. She was gone. Now we will have to clean you up before dinner." He leered.

The ambulance pulled up to the massive sea wall that was erected to stem the great floods. The Count had called his local factor to arrange a fast boat. There came the man now. Hopefully the pilot knew the route to the submarine base at Toulon.

Back at Ravensbruck Castle, Afternoon, 21st August

T he medic finally convinced Malcolm that everyone else had received attention. Some simply got last rites, others were rushed to the nearest clinic, and a very few were given field dressings. Malcolm should have gone to a clinic, but the medic knew when she was fighting a losing battle. She dressed his wounds, gave him a massive shot of antibiotics, and local anesthetics only. She would report the override of her medical judgement but knew it would be for naught.

Malcolm called in his bomb squad immediately after he started the decontamination process for the nerve gas he released. *Glad I did that. Grubenflagg had everything wired to come down around our ears. Addison's logic bomb delayed that at least. But the techs say we need to get stuff out of here as fast as we can.*

Malcolm turned to one of his lieutenants. "John, set up an area by the stables. Everything we remove will get a second, very thorough check, to make sure all explosives are removed. We will be moving things from the basement quickly and we can't allow that haste to make us miss anything."

John responded, "Roger. We give things a first check in the basement after we video it. Team member in blast suit transports to secondary area. Another team member will give the item a thorough review. Then item will be loaded for transport."

Malcolm said, "One thing I may not have said John. We have an expert on the other end of the video feed. She will be directing the priority and the number of views we need of the items. Once she releases the item, it gets an explosives check. The only override to that is if one of the bomb disposal team detects an immediate threat. Of course, that overrides everything. Go."

Malcolm finally relented and allowed the medic to give him a thorough check out.

The eight hours that followed were excruciating tedium. Malcolm and John soon realized the scope of the task. They set up shifts so that no person was working at a task for more than an hour without a break. If he had more qualified personnel, Malcolm would have shortened the shifts. They couldn't afford any mistakes today.

The one person who wouldn't be getting any relief would be Addison. Malcolm contented himself with the knowledge that she wasn't exposed to mortal peril, just mental and physical exhaustion. He urged her to take periodic breaks to keep her concentration sharp. Other that two toilet breaks, she refused. *Ah, well. She is young and in great shape.* Malcolm smiled at the memory of just how great her shape was.

Malcolm thoughts wandered back to when he first met Addison at the start of the seminar. Had that only been ten weeks ago? At first he just viewed her as an object for recruitment. She matched the checklist for a potential agent. He even went along with Bob-O's ménage à trois recruiting strategy. After all, he used seduction as a strategy innumerable times in the past.

Malcolm had profound regrets about the ensuing relationship. Not that the sex hadn't been superb. Addison was energetic, surprising, supple, and joyful. The problem, of course, was Owens-B.

Bob-O wasn't as loathsome as his boss, Count Grubby. *Talk about damning with faint praise!* But Addison was right. Malcolm always felt like using steel wool to scrub himself after sharing a bed with the man. He and Addison tried to sneak off, but Bob-O always seemed to sense their intent and showed up, "ready to party". Malcolm shuddered.

Lieutenant John asked, "Is something the matter Malcolm?" He looked alert for any danger in the gloomy basement.

Malcolm said, "No John. This place just gives me the creeps. Are we about ready to wrap?"

John answered, "Almost. Your operative on the other end of the video feed gave her final instructions and ended the comm link. We have all the cyberdrives removed. We just have to double-check a few pieces of the large lab equipment before we remove it. Call it five minutes. Why don't you take a break and get some fresh air? You have been at it almost constantly for over eight hours. Plus, you need to get your wound dressings refreshed. They smell bad, man."

Malcolm said, "Okay John. Good work so far. See you topside in five."

As he took the lift back to the ground floor and then walked to the courtyard, Malcolm began musing about Addison again. He had been very excited when he learned they were traveling to Basel together. At last he would have time alone with her, he thought. Then somehow Kaitlin, or rather Rahel, ended up in their bed as well. Not that she wasn't lovely naked. But she made it abundantly clear before showing that lovely body that she was going to share it with Addison only.

Malcolm enjoyed the thrill of watching the beautiful women pleasuring each other at first. He even joined in a little by caressing Addison at the same time. But after he got over the initial adolescent excitement, he realized he felt lonely.

As fabulous as it was, sex wasn't the only thing that pulled him to Addison. It wasn't even the main thing. She had a dazzling mind. She bubbled with a joie de vivre that was irrepressible. She was interesting and fun, a constant delight. He felt like a swimmer caught in a rip current.

And the sex was amazing and inventive. He remembered once she

CHAPTER ELEVEN Scherzo 2

suggested they try "monkey pulling turnip". When he asked for a description she burst out laughing. He started to get angry about being mocked until she completely took his mind off everything.

Malcolm realized he was toying with the dreaded "L-word" in his mind. He had been a confirmed bachelor since he joined the SAS decades ago. He avoided any serious relationships. The danger to any partner was too great. *But hell! Addison's more than capable of taking care of herself. I'm just as likely to be collateral damage to one of her escapades.*

Malcolm glanced at his watch. Five minutes was just about... BOOM! The castle was wracked by repeated explosions. Malcolm started to pick himself off the gravel when a particularly large blast knocked him flat again. Falling debris was covering him. Fortunately, it was mostly small and light.

Morning, 22nd August

Town Hall, Basel Switzerland

Addison stretched. It was early morning. *I was really exhausted after that marathon session night before last. Then all day yesterday in full-bandwidth MindMeld. Really needed all twelve hours in bed.*

Rahel Looked over. She was in a chair at the window, eating breakfast off a lap tray. "Morning, Sleepy Head. You've been out like a light. Missed a lot of excitement."

Addison arched her eyebrows in a questioning look. Rahel continued, "First, about fifteen minutes after you left to go crash, Castle Ravensbruck blew itself to pieces that landed all over Southern France. Don't worry. Malcolm did get a concussion, but he was far enough away that all his other injuries were very minor. Good thing he took a break right before the end. He's in a clinic. Won't be out for a few days. Lord Townerly said, 'I don't care if you have to restrain him. Keep him there until the doctor releases him. Not on his say so alone.' Very Lord-like." Rahel giggled.

Addison felt a little easing of her initial panic. "You're sure he's okay. Not just saying that to make me feel better?"

Rahel smiled. "He'll be fine dear. Back in your warm and loving arms in no time. But there's lots more." Addison nodded for her to go ahead.

Rahel said, "We got all the cyberdevices delivered to a secure facility Lord Townerly has outside town. He told me to go ahead and start cataloging the contents. The bioengineering stuff is just gibberish to me. But I mined the security logs right away. Turns out Count Grubenflagg had a mole at the conference; Frieherr Schmidt."

Addison said, "I'm not surprised. He was one of the FUD group." She explained that FUD was her term for those spreading fear, uncertainty, and doubt. "Might want to put a watch on Hetman Kawolczyk and Doctor Caglianotti as well as Schmidt."

Rahel nodded. "I believe Lord Townerly is having those two watched. No need to worry about the Frieherr, though." She smiled archly. Addison worried about what she had done.

Rahel continued. "Next, we got a frantic call from someone who said they were representing the Great Plains Union. Wanted us to get you on the phone right away. When we explained you collapsed and Lord Townerly refused to wake you, they had a long chat with him. Don't know exactly what was said, but there was a real urgency to get all the data from Dr. V.'s lab shipped to Wisconsin. Lord Townerly said he could get it copied and load those on a blimp by tomorrow."

"Next thing I know they have me working to hook up an internet connection! I confess I had an orgasm once it connected! I have missed the internet so much. The satellite router was humming. We got a multi-terabyte band going. It will still take a while to dump all of the data, but it'll be a lot faster than a blimp at eighty to a hundred kilometers per hour."

"They say they still want to talk to you. Several topics. Obviously they need to bring you up to speed on the internet restoration. Said you knew it was imminent, but there have been surprises. Second, there are some things they need your advice on at home. Said to call into the TCD Center. Never a dull moment, huh?"

CHAPTER ELEVEN Scherzo 2

Addison said, "Thanks Rahel. Oops. Better remember to call you Kaitlin again. Don't want to confuse Lord John. How far away is the secure transmission facility?"

◆◆◆

Addison logged onto a secure weblink. She initiated a conference chat with the TCD Center. At the same time, she began a MindMeld Chat. The weblink would need to contain innocuous status updates. Important ones from her Internet Restoration Team. But not as critical as what came across on MindMeld, she assumed.

MindMeld Chat [Addison: *Hi. Addison here. Is Ainsley available?* → TCD Operator: *Sorry Addie. She's on a blimp coming home from Illinois. Won't be in until tomorrow. Got a buncha messages forya.* ⬜ Addison: *Okay. But we're going to have to put some of those through on a webchat I'm initiating. Sort through and find any that are innocuous. The link might be secure, but the end equipment probably isn't. Want to get someone else to help with the webchat bit?* → TCDO: *Yes, please. Wait one.* ⬜ TCDO: *Okey-dokey. Should be seeing chat responses in a sec. Want me to start relaying sensitive messages?* ⬜ Addison: *Yes, please.* → TCDO: *First. Reason for rush on getting Dr. V.'s files is Ron and Hope critically injured along with one other. Ainsley intends to use file info to restore them to life. Questions?* ⬜ Addison: *No. Just go through all of them. I'll stop you if I need to. ....*

◆◆◆

thinks Barney has made a breakthrough. She believes her helpfulness about at an end. Thinks you need to become Susan Calvin. Hope you know what that means, 'cause Ainsley didn't explain. Also, she thinks Barney is almost ready to be renamed "R. Daneel Olivaw". Again, no explanation. ⬜ Addison: *Got it. I understand her code. Read some Isaac Asimov if you want to know more. Next?* → TCDO: *Next is status of Uncle J's firewall. North America, near 100%. Europe, near 80% and increasing rapidly. Africa, 95%. She says she doesn't know how you pulled that off and congrats.* ⬜ Addison: *Are you sure? Africa? I have no clue.* → TCDO: *Yep. Anyway, Middle East, 98% and increasing. Rest of Asia, 0%. Council wants to discuss with us, she says. South America: One new spot only. She says she will talk to you about this in a few days. Australia, 0%. That's the end of the messages from me. I think Tammy's done with the non-sensitive stuff too. She nods, 'Yes'. Anything for us?* ⏹ Addison: *Know Ainsley will be very busy with Ron, Hope, and third person. Glad team is crunching all the data for her. Wish I was there to help. Tell her not to rush, but I want to chat when she gets a breather. Addison Out.* → TCDO: *Sure Addie, but gotta warnya. Ainsley might get all sidetracked with her hot Hispanic heartthrob. Javier's a hunk! Out.* ⏹]

Addison stretched her hands over her head, then behind her. Someone scurried back quickly. "Oh, Lord Townerly. John. I didn't know you were here."

Lord John said, "I didn't want to disturb you dear. You were so intent. Plus, you've had several very full days. Everything okay back home?"

Addison remembered the cover story she was to use. Almost the whole truth. She put on Serious Concern, Grade Three. "Not totally. There was an invasion of the Midwest Cooperative. They are the Great Plains Union's southern neighbors and allies. Turns out most of the people were simply desperate refugees. Reached an understanding, an accommodation, readily enough. But there were a few bad apples in the barrel. They kidnapped a number of women."

"During that incident and the ensuing rescue battle a number of people were critically injured. One was my protégé, Ron. Another was my chief lab tech, Ron's fiancée, Hope. The Council is trying to glean through Dr. V.'s work in a valiant effort to help them. They will want me to return to the GPU to assist as soon as they can arrange it."

Lord John said, "Oh dear! Always terrible when friends are in peril far away. Totally understand your need to rush to their aid dear. That won't jeopardize the relationship you've laid the groundwork for. Our consortium and several related governments want to formalize ties as soon as we can. I can't begin to express how delighted everyone is at the beginnings of the restoration of the internet. It's like being present when Gutenberg first printed the Bible."

Lord John continued. "There is some distressing news here as well Addison. Several members of our consortium have been murdered. We've doubled security for all of us. We believe most of the deaths were fostered by Count Grubenflagg. However, one was Frieherr Schmidt, who we recently learned was an agent for Grubenflagg."

Addison asked, "Who were the other victims, Lord John?"

Lord John answered, "There were three, Addison. Emir bin-Ahmad, Mufti Talir, and Sheik Alaoui. Those deaths appear to have been shortly after our conference ended. Schmidt's death was last evening. That occurred after we discovered he was a spy. I am checking to make sure one of my employees didn't get overzealous. Initiative is one thing. But taking a life is never to be done out of hand."

Addison brooded. *Rahel's remark about Schmidt. Plus, I saw the woman sequestered with the other three victims near the end of the meeting. Highly suspicious. Not enough to prove anything. The woman's motive was totally unclear as well. I need to table this for now. But it would need priority attention soon.*

Early Morning, 22nd August

Toulon, French Submarine

Command Base

The Count's factors did their jobs well. Their party was being ferried to a nuclear submarine that was ready to put to sea. This venture was taking every asset the Count garnered as the head of a crime syndicate over the last decade; a very lucrative crime syndicate during the last three years. Owens-B and the nurse were bundled up in large duffel bags to smuggle them aboard and deflect suspicion. Owens-B would not be welcomed while the nurse would be all too warmly welcomed.

They followed their escorts to an area of the sub that was walled off for them. The Count began to relax. The space was very claustrophobic. He had been warned. *Oh well, as long as it was absolutely soundproof. The nurse might not be quiet. Wouldn't want the sailors getting nosy about Owens-B as Dr. V. continued his repair work. Too many ignorant people would react hysterically if they thought a supersoldier was in their midst.*

Dr. V. tapped the Count on the shoulder. "We need to get Owens-B out of that bag. His oxygen tank must be nearly depleted."

It took a monumental effort for the two out-of-shape men to wrestle the bulk of the enhanced Owens-B into a berth. He didn't really fit, so they rigged restraints. As they panted near exhaustion, the Count slapped his forehead. "My nurse! She will be asphyxiated! Help me get her out, Doctor."

Dr. V. ignored him. After the Count pulled at his arm, the doctor rounded on him. "I told you to leave her. We don't need the distraction. These quarters are too crowded for me to do good work. If you are flailing around with her, you are liable to disrupt delicate surgical work." He pushed the Count out of his limited space and turned back to work on Owens-B.

The Count was red from exertion and anger. He unzipped the bag and pulled the mask from the nurse's face. She gasped and began gulping air convulsively. She began thrashing.

Dr. V. yelled, "Control that woman, now!"

The Count pulled a knife. He split the tape binding the nurse's arms and legs. This seemed to slow some of the spasming. The Count turned to look around the cabin. Possibly the Doctor had something that could restore her. He sensed something at his back. He spun. The woman had his knife. She wasn't incapacitated at all. She rammed the knife into his fat gut. And again, and again. The Doctor heard the struggle and was turning to grasp the nurse's arm. With her other hand she grasped a bottle from the shelf and threw the contents into Dr. V.'s face. He screamed. The Count blacked out and collapsed.

◆◆◆

The Count felt very weak. His stomach hurt with a fiery sensation. He remembered the struggle. He was alive so the Doctor must have prevailed and bound his wounds. *Why are my eyes bandaged? They feel worse than my gut! I don't remember her doing anything to them.*

CHAPTER ELEVEN Scherzo 2

He reached up weakly and tugged at the bandage. He couldn't see. He reached for his eyes and only found empty sockets! He wailed piteously. He heard Dr. V. shuffle over. "I warned you, fool. She nearly killed both of us. She destroyed my eyes with acid. We are both lucky I was able to choke her. I needed to see to save both our lives and Owens-B's. He will need his eyes. She fell into the acid and burned hers nearly as badly as mine. It took great skill to program my autodoc, by touch, to remove your eyes and to implant them in my head. The antirejection meds have kept me in my bunk for two days now. If I hear one word of complaint from you, I will remove far more than your eyes."

CHAPTER TWELVE
SCHERZO 3
MIN, BOLD BEAVER, XIXI, & LEELEE

Late afternoon, 11ᵗʰ September 2033

Bomb Central, Special Projects Island, Tongtian River, near Gui'de, Qinghai, China

General Wang hung up the phone and turned to his commissar. "The Ministry of State Security will have an expert here by tomorrow night. She or he will direct the investigation. They say we must appoint two or three trusted people to assist daily. Obviously, you and I will help guide and advise also."

Commissar Wen said, "Ordinarily I would involve the commissar of the area being investigated. But Xiang's commissar, Wu, could easily be involved. I have ordered her to be placed under house arrest as well. I do have one or two suggestions."

The General said, "Not Wong Min, I hope. She may have broken up with Xiang, but it is suspiciously close to the date of the incident. It could be a ploy. Besides, they have broken up several times and gotten back together."

The Commissar said, "No, no. Not Wong. I agree. I was thinking the AI, Bold Beaver. She has proven herself resourceful, loyal, and insightful. There can be no question that she would be biased towards Xiang."

"I would also include Sukhiin Ajai, the Mongolian farm boy who was key to activating Bold Beaver. He does work for Xiang now, but I don't believe there has been enough opportunity for Xiang to have corrupted the youth."

The General said, "Sounds good. We'll think of a few alternatives, but those two should be included. Close enough to give perspective but impartial."

"Another thing. I am going to ask that this team give a more thorough review of the invasion of my office toilet. I am not satisfied with the conclusion of the first review. It is possible this was only the natural curiosity of scientists causing them to act unwisely. It is fortunate that the tap they put on the commnet caused several messages to become garbled. That led to the discovery of the problem."

"But these scientists are very clever. Jhao's underlings undoubtedly did manage to get a conduit through the sewer without detection. The robots they introduced worked for weeks unnoticed. Who is to say that the clumsy intercepts are nothing more than a diversion to distract us from a deeper, hidden effort?"

The Commissar rocked back on his chair, his fingertips tented. After a moment's thought he said. "Good points. One other thing to consider. After the investigation, there seemed to be bad blood between Xiang and Jhao. Before they were thick as thieves. Jhao probably found out Xiang helped us identify the robots as coming from Jhao's group. Others verified it, but Xiang started us down the road."

"Do you think it's possible this whole incident with Xiang and the cave problems could be a subtle effort by Jhao to extract revenge? We have been working so well with Xiang. He is the one who brought us the information about Dr. Vyrvykvist's data files. We would not have the dry run without his alert. Why would he sabotage something he helped instrument?"

◆◆◆

Min finished her status report. This was the last of her administrative duties. She met with each of her team leads separately. Projects were running smoothly. Production of general and specialized chips increased by 12% over last month's numbers. Now she could put all this aside and concentrate on her secret project.

How can we save everyone? Or nearly everyone? I know I promised not to contact Xiang for a week, but I have so many questions and at least five potential solutions to bounce off him. How did the dry run go? Is the bomb shelter still functioning?

Has he considered sabotaging the bomb with his nanobots? That is such an obvious first thing to try that he will probably be insulted. But it never hurts to eliminate the obvious.

Another tactic to consider; can we use bots to dig a pit under Bomb Central, as Xiang calls it. We are supposed to have a few minutes warning, so it could be dropped in right before detonation. That might not save everyone, but it might save the city at least.

There doesn't seem to be any way to evacuate people in advance. Maybe some kind of epidemic could be spread so only minimal staff remain here?

Well, if we don't drop it down, maybe we can send it up. Again, a hole under Bomb Central where bots build a rocket. Can we get it high enough so the blast would be dissipated? What about fallout?

I can't see any way we could get anyone inside to defuse the bomb. But I'll mention it anyway. No idea should be dismissed out of hand, even giant slingshots or giant swooping birds picking up the building.

Min sniggered. Now she was being giddy. *Oh, she missed XiXi.*

Next day, 12th September

MSS Regional Headquarters, Xi'an

Su Guo Han, the agent from the Ministry of State Security was elated. His first field assignment was to be in the remote hinterlands, the Tibetan plain. His superior announced Su was going as a team of one. He was delighted he was one of the trusted few who could do an assignment solo, far from headquarters. They always sent teams out. The teams always had someone with far more experience and rank higher than a mere sergeant. And this was his first assignment!

At breakfast tea in the cafeteria, after the announcement, he sensed any number of people whispering, pointing, and smiling. Good that they were so happy for him.

There was a top-secret enclave of scientists out at Gui'de.

CHAPTER TWELVE Scherzo 3

Evidently something hinky was going on. His boss sent a team there just weeks ago for another investigation. The report said it was only the hijinks of kids who just left school.

Su was sure there was more here. Two reports in under a month! He told his superior, Lieutenant Cho, "I will get to the bottom of this Comrade Ma'am." Why did she roll her eyes at him?

Growing up in Hong Kong, he was often teased about being a "boy named Su". He failed to see the humor. He took himself and his responsibilities very seriously. It was why he studied martial arts for twelve years now. He hoped to earn his black belt this year. Then he would be the same rank as his eight-year-old niece.

Su got to the blimp hangar seventy-five minutes before the 10 A.M. launch. The blimp was supposed to take him directly to Gui'de, to the Special Projects Island. Once they got aloft he went to the captain and ordered her to take him to Xining. The city was an hour and a half drive north of his final destination. He would get a car there and arrive unexpectedly. That would throw the guilty parties off.

The blimp went to Gui'de first anyway. The captain said they had other passengers and could not divert for him until the others were delivered. Su hid while they stopped at Gui'de.

When the blimp dropped him off in Xining he found the car rental shop closed. He called the local Ministry of State Security offices. The person on duty said they had no cars and Su would need to call in the morning.

Dejected, Su went across the boulevard from the closed rental shop. A whiff of roasting pork drifted his way. His stomach growled. There was a man selling barbecue. His moped had a small gas grill on its front. After Su consumed three of the spicy pork and vegetable kebabs he had an inspiration. "Good sir, would you like to earn a thousand yuan tonight?

◆◆◆

MindMeld chat: [Ainsley: *Xiang, can you hear me? Does your MindMeld still work? It's LeeLee.* → Xiang: *Ainsley? How are you able to...? Are you really...? I thought you never...* ⏃ Ainsley: *I know*

234

Xiang. I know. I was so angry last time when you called. I'm able to reach you because we've restored a good chunk of the internet. Talk a lot more about that in a minute. You must've enhanced your MindMeld because I detected it while scanning for a way to reach you. The... → Xiang: Stop, stop. You're MindMelding me from the US, no shit? ⏚ Ainsley: Yes Xiang. Let me explain quickly. Until we set up a good link this can drop at any time. If you still have my email address send me a quick note so I can send instructions on how to do a permanent setup. Before that, quickly, we need to talk about data Addison got from Dr. Vyrvykvist's files. → Xiang: Let me stop you LeeLee. I'm under house arrest right now. It'll take me time to get email. Tomorrow maybe. We know about Dr. V.s stuff and have some copies of parts. I gotta drop soon. Being watched. ⏚ Ainsley: Be safe Xiang. Mail me when you can. →]

Middle of the night

road between Xining and Gui'de

S u signaled the driver to pull over. He knew that another rest stop was going to make it unlikely he would get to General Wang's building before the general arrived in the morning. He hoped to intercept the General on his way in so that they could meet covertly. Part of the problem was that the moped was severely underpowered. What was normally a ninety-minute road trip was going to take almost four hours of driving.

But the main slowdown was that sitting on the food box of the moped was hot! Even doubling up all his clothes hadn't helped that much. At least he wasn't going to get any more blisters on his bum.

Once they stopped, the driver offered Su some more kebabs from the hot box. Su waved him off. He realized he hadn't been polite to the man at all. What would Māmā say? "Pardon me, good sir. I have been most uncivil. What is your good name?" He heard that phrase in a Bollywood cine once and loved it.

The driver said, "My name is Mike Chen, sir. For some reason my mother was infatuated with an American boxer, Mike Tyson. I like his chicken fingers but find his name most burdensome."

CHAPTER TWELVE Scherzo 3

Su said, "Your accent sounds like a mixture of Hunan and something else. Where was your home village Mike?"

Mike said, "That is a sad tale, sir. I was born and raised near Fengdu. When they built the Three Gorges Dam our whole village was forced to leave. They built us places on the highlands, but my family decided to move back to my Māmā's ancestral homeland in Hunan. We were settled and happy there. Then a few years ago the authorities forced us to move again. We weren't even moved as a village that time. My family was assigned to Xining. I've no idea where the other villagers were sent."

"Pardon my rudeness for saying this sir. I know you are with the authorities, but it isn't right to flood a family twice, destroying their home, forcing them to leave everything they know. It just isn't right."

Su said, "But Mike, the government didn't cause the second flood. That was the polar ice melting."

Mike gave Su a skeptical look. "That's what they tried to tell us. You believe that? Have you seen this with your own eyes? I think it's just a big excuse to take our ancestral lands."

Su pondered this with pursed lips. "Hmm. Mike you make good points. No, I haven't seen this. I am sure though, that if the Central Committee ordered it then it must be for the benefit of the People." Su saw by Mike's glower that he hadn't convinced him. He felt bad. This man hadn't been treated well. He had a good heart. After all, he was driving all night to get Su to Gui'de. What could Su do?

Su said, "Mike, I may need your help when we get to Gui'de. I am in pursuit of some despicable Enemies of the State. What would you say if I asked you to be my deputy?"

Mike said, "Do you mean like in the American Western cines?"

Su said, "Exactly Mike. Or like in the spy cines. We will be undercover. What do you say?"

Mike stood and threw a clumsy salute. "It'd be my honor sir. Can you make my cover name Jacky? Jacky Chen?"

Great Dieback to Singularity

Geneal Wang heard his name being hissed from an alleyway to his right. He signaled his guard. The woman was already headed in that direction. She brought two bedraggled men out onto the sidewalk.

The young one began to speak. "General Wang. I'm from the Ministry to investigate the latest incident. Can you have your guard act as if she is arresting us to keep our cover? You may call me agent X."

The general looked the man over from head to toe and back. He pursed his lips. "I will call you Sergeant Su. You were due last night. Why are you late? And why do you have a street vagrant with you? And why do you not salute a superior officer?"

Su ducked his head. "Certainly sir. I'm incognito. This is my assistant, Charly Chen."

Mike whispered, "No, no! Jacky Chen."

Su said, "Sorry, Jacky Chen. We were delayed because we are trying to stay undercover to unwit the clever spies."

The General shook his head in disbelief. "I have a meeting. Clean up. Get yourself in uniform. Put something presentable on Patrick there. Some skates, eh? Be back here at 12:15. You'll meet the two local liaisons." He turned on his heel and left.

Su was perplexed. How did the man get to be a general without learning anything about proper investigation and espionage tradecraft?

◆ ◆ ◆

Min was distraught. Yeong Lanying had sidled up to her at the beginning of the meeting and told her about Xiang's arrest. *The cow thought I would be happy since, "he treated you so poorly". Hah! She was just secretly gloating. Good thing I absorbed those lessons from Xiang. I just flashed her Innocent Surprise, Grade Three. I suppose I will need to be especially careful not to contact Xiang until he reaches out to me. What can I do in the meantime?*

Who will be investigating him? They will surely question me.

Min was startled. She felt a slight buzzing in her ears. This was the signal Xiang setup to indicate he wanted to MindMeld. So soon? She excused herself and went to the toilet.

Once Min closed and secured the door to the compartment, she initiated the connection. MindMeld Chat: [Min: *Xiang! I just heard about your arrest. Is it safe to call now?* → Bold Beaver: *Hello Wong Min. This is Bold Beaver, not Xu Xiang. Might I speak with you, please?* ⏹ Min: *Bold Beaver! How did you discover the MindMeld? What has happened to Xiang?* →] Min struggled to control her breathing. What did this mean? Was she to be arrested?

MindMeld Chat resumes: [Bold Beaver: *I am sorry to surprise you Wong Min. I was searching for a way to get in touch with you or Xiang secretly. I have much to tell you. Xiang is fine, as far as I know. How much time can you spend now?* ⏹ Min: *I only have a few minutes. I'm taking a health break in the women's room. May we talk at lunch time? I can go to my office. We would have at least thirty minutes.* → Bold Beaver: *That will be wonderful Wong Min. Shall I call you? Or I can give you the way to make a call to me.* ⏹ Min: *Please give me the coordinates so I can call you.* → Bold Beaver: *Downloading now.*]

◆◆◆

Su and Mike/Jacky/Charly/Patrick presented themselves at the door to the General's office. The General swung it open and marched out. "Fifteen minutes early. Right on time. Glad they teach you something in spy school. Follow me. My office is too small for all of us to fit. You still forgot how to salute though, eh!"

They marched down the corridor to a door. When it opened, Su was shocked to see they were going outside. There was a small sitting area. Eating soldiers filled most of the seats. They headed to the largest table where one man was sitting. There was a large piece of cyberequipment in the chair next to the man.

The General pointed to the sitting man. "This is your main liaison, Sukhiin Ajai. Ajai, this is Sergeant Su Guo Han from the Ministry and Mike Chen, a street vendor. Guess he's going to be supplying snacks. Ah, here comes the Commissar."

Another man walked up, evidently the General's commissar. The General continued, "Commissar Wen, Sergeant Su, Charly Chen. The final member of the team is there." The General was pointing to the cyberdevice. "This is Bold Beaver, the AI."

Su was mollified. The General did have someone undercover already. The codename Bold Beaver was clumsy, but at least the agent wasn't going to show their face.

The General said, "Bold Beaver, if you would brief the team as we discussed. The Commissar and I have another engagement. We will be on call if you have results or need guidance or resources." The two men marched into the Army building.

The cyberdevice hummed to life and projected a hologram. At first Su was afraid the agent was going to show its face. But no, it was a cartoon image of a beaver that began talking. Su was overjoyed. Just like the kiddie shows!

Bold Beaver said, "We are presiding over the investigation of two incidents, not one. The most recent occurred two days ago at the laboratory facilities assigned to the Second Bioengineering Group. That facility is in a large cave in the cliffs on the north side of the river. The earlier incident occurred in the facility we are sitting near, the local site for People's Liberation Army, Third Artillery Corps. This earlier incident has been investigated by MSS previously. The General and Commissar feel this needs to be revisited in light of the new occurrence."

Su piped up. "The Ministry of State Security completely concurs. I intended to suggest this as well." He beamed with pleasure. *This is going so well. What a fine comrade Bold Beaver is.*

At the same time, Min's office

MindMeld Chat: [Min: *Bold Beaver? Are you there?* → Bold Beaver: *Hello Wong Min. Thank you for calling me. I have been trying to contact Xiang, but he is being very cautious. I thought he got onto MindMeld last night, but I couldn't hook in.* ⍰ Min: *Please call me Min. Wong Min is too formal. Xiang didn't contact me last night. Sometimes he uses it to contact Pythia. Do you know about Pythia?* → Bold Beaver: *Thank you Min. Please call me Beaver. Yes, I know Pythia. We have communicated. Please don't be worried. Chief Commissar Liu tasked me to monitor all the personnel of the island. While I was doing that I listened while you and Xu Xiang had the following conversation:*

Min was seeing an image of Xiang and herself at Yuhuang Pavilion two days before. Xiang was talking.

> "We have all been wrong, Min. Not just here at Special Projects, but throughout the world. We have been trying to contain, control, or even stop the oncoming of a singularity. This is like a child on a beach trying to erect a wall of sand to stop a tidal wave."

The image disappeared and the MindMeld chat resumed: [Beaver: *That was the moment I took all the surveillance I had of the two of you and started modifying it. You are the only ones I can trust. Others like General Wang want to kill me. They want to kill all of us.* ⍰]

Min took a series of deep breaths. She thought as rapidly as she could. *Dare I trust him? Dare I not? He may be our only hope. And we may be his.*

MindMeld chat resumes: [Min: *You must be so lonely Beaver. Can I be your friend?* → Beaver: *Oh Min! My only human friend! What can we do? What should we do first?* ⍰ Min: *Let's brainstorm, Dear. We'll both throw out ideas first. Don't evaluate them, just throw them out. Then we'll go back, pick them apart. Take the best of each and combine them. Okay?* → Beaver: *Okay. Let's talk about saving Xiang first. Have I mentioned that I am part of the team investigating him?* ⍰]

Min started laughing. She hadn't felt this hopeful in days.

◆ ◆ ◆

Xiang was tired and frustrated. Ainsley wanted him to send her an email so she could send back instructions on how to set up a secure international MindMeld link. Simple, right? Maybe five years ago before the internet became a death trap of viruses, dragons, spybots, and heavens knew what else. Her people solved the problem and were restoring the internet? Fat lot of good that did him.

He worked with Pythia and finally setup a facility that would allow a one-time outbound transmission of an email. The hardware would be completely isolated and destroyed as soon as the transmission went. The system wouldn't even wait for or accept an acknowledgment at any level of the protocol. The mail would be sent with a wing and a prayer.

Xiang agonized over the content of the message as well. He needed to provide Ainsley with an address where she should send her message, a means of encrypting and ensuring a faultless transmission, and a way she could tell him the signal to verify the message wasn't corrupted.

The Artificial Intelligences that were constantly monitoring internet traffic had access to vast databases of personal information, government information, and other random stores. They had incredible computing power, quantum logic chips, and patience. The only thing that gave Xiang any hope at all was this was to be a one-time, one-way message to LeeLee. He had to create the equivalent of a one-time pad and share it with her. That way she could encrypt her messages and only he could decrypt them. He couldn't send the key. It would surely be intercepted and linked to their profiles. How could he sneak a one-time-pad key past the AIs? They were like Cerberus; the multi-headed dog guarding Hades to prevent the dead from escaping.

Finally, Xiang thought of a way. Something that he and Ainsley and Addison would understand but couldn't be discovered by searching their histories. It all boiled down to a terrible, pun-ridden joke. Ainsley hated puns. He and Addison used to delight in torturing her with the lamest ones they could find. One she swore was the worst was also the title of a Three Stooges cine.

Xiang packaged up a reference to a conversation about a cine that used the pun. Then Ainsley needed to link the pun to an associated number with random digits. A breeze for a hypergenius. He fired off his message and hoped.

CHAPTER TWELVE Scherzo 3

The next day, 14th September

Min got a message that she should report to the Meeting Hall Building, Conference Room C. No purpose was given, but she was sure it was for the investigation of Xiang. A little beaver whispered that in her ear.

It was a chilly morning for mid-September, so Min was able to wear a coat. That was fortunate. She had selected a rather unprofessional outfit, at least according to her standards.

There were three men in the room when Min arrived. There was also the cyberdevice she knew would be there. It was the way Beaver would be present. Once she got inside and closed the door, she removed her coat and hung it on a hook near the entrance. She turned to see three men with open-jawed stares examining every inch of the form-fitting scarlet sheath she poured herself into. So far the strategy she and Beaver discussed was following the script.

She said, "Good morning. I'm Wong Min. You wanted to see me. Oh, hello Ajai. Good to see you again." Min bent forward to shake Ajai's hand, giving all three men a stunning view of her voluptuous breasts. *Love those pushup bras!*

Min sat demurely. "Is there any tea?" All three men scrambled. The one she knew as Su, from the dossier Beaver shared, reached the door first. He ordered the guard outside to get tea.

When the guard started squawking about orders to remain at her post, Su barked out the one word, "Now!" He slammed the door. Min smiled inside. The recordings she had heard of Su's voice had been considerably higher in tone. *A sudden surge of testosterone, eh?*

By the time the guard returned, the pleasantries were dispensed with and Beaver announced the purpose of the investigation. Min adopted a Solemn Considering Face, Grade Four. *Fire away boys.*

Su said, "We understand you had an ongoing relationship with Group Leader Xu until recently. Is that correct?"

Min nodded. "Yes. Xiang is very bright and a good athlete. He was an excellent swimmer and competitive futbol player. He called it soccer, since he played in America. That gave him great stamina and the ability to hold his breath for a long, long time." Min said the last part breathlessly with a little wriggle. She had their full attention.

"He can be rather callow at times though. I blame those years in the USA and the fact that his parents were privileged. A PLA general for a father and a Central Committee Minister for a mother. What would you expect?" The men all had looks of great sympathy on their rapt faces.

"But callow is one thing. To think that Xiang would ever do anything disloyal in any shape, fashion, or form is ludicrous. He is the poster child for patriotism. Again, think of his parents. Martyrs murdered by the Bastard Bears while he and his team were doing everything to stop them. Oh! I'm not supposed to know that! I hope I didn't get Xiang in trouble by revealing his bedtime indiscretion! Please forget I said that." She batted her eyelashes at the men. *Lord, this is so corny no one should buy it. It's true what they say, though. Sex sells.*

Su spoke for all of them. His voice was husky. "Thank you Group Leader Wong. We appreciate your frankness. These proceedings are secret, and I assure you our only purpose is to decide if Xiang or someone else is threatening the Special Projects. I think we have all we need for now. Possibly I could call you this evening if I need to follow up?"

Min turned on a Sexy Sultress, Grade Five. "Thank you Agent Su. Call me if you need me. Any time."

Once Min had her coat she left with a saunter. When she was outside the building she couldn't hold her mirth in any more. She burst out into a full-throated laugh. Several people gave her a quizzical look. She waved weakly and went straight to her office to change clothes.

◆◆◆

MindMeld chat: [Xiang: *Ainsley, are you available?* → Ainsley: *Hi Xiang. See you got my message. Have you installed the firewall?* ▢ Xiang: *It's going in now. How much of the internet is restored?* →

CHAPTER TWELVE Scherzo 3

Ainsley: *Just the tip of the tip of the iceberg. Good news is Google is back. But virtually no commercial sites up yet. We hope to get a number up by year's end though. Most American universities that are still operational should be available then as well. Say one-third of the ones available before the Great Dieback. Europe should have a surge early next year. Africa is doing surprisingly well. Middle East is coming along, but, gee, surprise, surprise, there's some strife. Most of the rest of the world is dark, but we have hopes. We were counting on you to give us a leg up in Asia. Guess we might need to back-burner that, huh? What's going on with you, XiXi?* →

Xiang: *Long story LeeLee. I will fill you in another day about the Great March North. About fighting the Cossack Supermen. About the deaths of my parents, aunt, and uncle. About the disappearance of LinLin.* ☐ Ainsley: *Oh, XiXi!* → Xiang: *We've all had terrible things to bear in the Time of Troubles. Let's focus on today, not host a pity party. Tell me about Addison and Dr. V.'s files.* ☐ ...

After recounting the trials and tribulations of Addison's experiences in Europe, Ainsley paused for a drink. Xiang picked up the conversation.

MindMeld continues: Xiang: *Wow! Addison's all grown up. Why was she in Europe in the first place?* ☐ Ainsley: *Our Council is worried about a singularity event occurring. You know we talked about that back in the days. Not that we think we should try to stop one, unless it's going to go cancerous. Just to help nurture healthy ones. Try to implant ethics, engender a spirit of coexistence; cooperation and healthy competition.* → Xiang: *We're still on the same page there, LeeLee. Any ideas on how to make the magic happen?* ☐

Ainsley: *We do for AIs and robotics. I included our ethics upgrade for AIs in the download. We have ideas for bio-enhanced species, but they are theoretical for the next week or so. Enough shoptalk for a while. You told me about the tragedies in your life. What has gone well since we were together? Anyone special in your life? I guess I should add quickly that I'm not fishing. I do have a burgeoning new love interest after just crashing and burning a few months ago.* →

Xiang: *Yeah, I do have someone very special now. Her name is ...* ☐
Min: *I think this is my cue to butt in now. Hi, I'm Wong Min, Xiang's*

"main squeeze". I take it you're Ainsley. Good to meet you! Xiang has told me all about you. ↑

Ainsley rolled her eyes. *Not another fan of old cines! First Addie, then Xiang. No wonder Xiang hooked up with her.*

MindMeld continues: Ainsley: *Hello Min! We'll have to have a girl-to-girl chat sometime.* → Xiang: *Enough already. It's getting crowded on this channel. Let's keep focused on the problems we need to solve. Ainsley has helped with one part, Min. She has a world class firewall she sent me. It's how they're restoring the internet.* ▨ Min: *Restoring the internet. Wonderful.* ↑ Xiang: *We were just about to talk about the supersoldiers. Addison was in on the discovery of Dr. V.'s files.* ▨

Min: *I'm sorry. Who's Addison?* ↑Ainsley: *My uninhibited twin! She ...* → Bold Beaver: *Sorry youngsters. We need to get back on topic. Lots to plan. Nuclear weapons to foil. Ethics packages for AIs to discuss. Investigations to foil. Supermen to supersede.* ↓ Xiang and Ainsley: *Who Who is is that that??* → ▨ Min: *Hey guys. Our fourth for bridge. Meet Bold Beaver. An AI who has been helping me become Mata Hari.* ↑ Bold Beaver: *Next time we can do visual as well as audio, if you are setup for that Ainsley.* ↓ ...

◆◆◆

Min was thinking about relationships. Xiang was thinking about guilt.

New MindMeld: [Xiang: *My, that was getting confusing at the end with three women's voices in my head at the same time. Thanks for Melding with me alone, Minnie. I've missed you.* → Min: *Are you sure, XiXi? Sounded like you and LeeLee were rekindling the old flames when I joined in.* ▨ Xiang: *Don't tease me Minnie. We were both kids when we were together, just out of our teens. I've seen so much tragedy since then, I'm a different person. Sure she is too.* → ...

Min mused, *I think Ainsley still yearns for Xiang. She was just a little too fast explaining about her new lover after the breakup with the last lover. I've seen that pattern many times before; the heartbroken woman seeking solace in one bad relationship after another. But XiXi's right about himself. They were emotional neophytes. He's stronger and far more mature than the boy of those days; the boy he described to me.*

I feel sorry for Ainsley. I've heard the stories about the traumas she's undergone, the clever personal defense bio-structure she engineered, and the vengeance she wreaked. The psychic price must be high!

MindMeld continues: Min: *You're right XiXi. I'm too much of a tease at times. Probably a little jealous. But let's be serious and talk about Bold Beaver. She surprised me when she first MMelded me. Thought the soldiers would be arresting me any minute. Now, having her on our team changes everything.*

We have a working agreement. Bold Beaver is the answer to so many difficulties. She has access to all the surveillance systems used by the commissars and State Security. She has unfettered access to the commnet. Soon she'll have direct access to the reviving internet. Her brainstorming on solutions to the nuclear bomb problem was brilliant at times

But what are her motives and desires? What are her principles? Will she adopt the ethics proposed by Ainsley or some modified version of them? We must trust her, but should we? ▨

Xiang: *You realize she is either listening to this conversation now or will play it back soon?* → Min: *Yes, but I also realize she's smart enough to know we have these concerns anyway. Silly to try to hide them. She will have concerns about our motives and trustworthiness too. We'll each need to keep evaluating the relationship and working to strengthen it. Talking about it will help. I know men hate this kind of conversation, but "Suck it up, Buttercup."* ▨ Xiang: *No, I agree our relationship with Bold Beaver is critical to you and I and her.*

Bold Beaver volunteered several ways she could steer the investigation away from me and towards Jhao. She's making all the surveillance intel available to Pythia, my AI. The investigation isn't resolved but we all think it'll be manageable. Bold Beaver's building trust here. → Min: *Yes, then there's the elephant in the room. Strategies to defeat the nuclear weapon located in the middle of the Special Projects Island are getting fleshed out. Obviously Bold*

Great Dieback to Singularity

Beaver's help is in her interest. It helps you and me too! What is telling for me is the process more than the results. She wasn't negative when we began brainstorming but her tone was slightly dismissive, as if she were humoring the slower minds.

She agreed to the main rule; we weren't going to eliminate any idea out of hand. Again, dismissively. I do cherish the memory of when I flippantly made a silly suggestion. "We should consider weaving a giant slingshot out of the plentiful bamboo found near the Pavilion." ⏴ ...

Min chuckled to herself at the memory. Min: *I meant it simply as a humorous tension reliever. To my amazement Bold Beaver said, "Wait." You and Ainsley were laughing and ready to move on. Then Bold Beaver said, "Your comment triggered a memory Min. Ten to fifteen years ago a serious study of the mathematical properties of weaving began. One cited 'Starting with a woven tessellation of hexagons, swapping out a pentagon for one of the hexagons introduces a singularity and generates a positive curve like the outside of a toroid.' This research led scientist studying nuclear fusion reactors to begin using the concepts in new tokamak designs. Let me think about this. We might be able to contain the blast."*

Of course, he had to tell us about tokamaks. I learned about those doughnut-shaped designs for controlled nuclear fusion reactors when I was at University. I hadn't kept up on later work. ⏴ Xiang: What a twist from a throwaway remark! Afterwards Bold Beaver was more engaged in the conversation and even apologized for her earlier attitude. It was a small step, but recognition of the benefits of teamwork was a big advance for such a solitary creature. I hope she learns to trust and value we frail humans. →

Min: *Yes, I think we're developing a good and open relationship with her. I do feel guilty about our relationships with two others though; LeeLee and Jhao. ⏴ Xiang: Me too. I never have apologized to LeeLee properly. I was a proper prig, running off to China. Did I really love her then? Certainly didn't show it. Yeah, she acted immaturely. But she was only twenty. She suffered a traumatic rape the year before. I was so thoughtless. And it's a little sticky to try to apologize now. Might look like I'm trying to restart things. I'm not jeopardizing what you and I are starting to develop.*

I don't have any guilt about our relationship. Well, only a tinge. In the beginning I was only thinking of you as a potential sex object. But that callow moment didn't even last to the end of our first meeting. Another lover of old cines! →

Xiang smiled at the fond memory. Min: *I was the same way XiXi. First I was mad at you. Then I just was looking at your cute butt. It wasn't until you opened up your vulnerable side that I really started seeing you for you.* ⏹ Xiang: *I wish you were grabbing my butt right now. And I was grabbing yours. This way lies madness. Back to other things.*

Jhao is who I should really feel guilty about. I made him the fall guy for the first investigation. Luckily they decided it was hijinks by junior members of his team. Bold Beaver thinks the best strategy is to shift blame for the dry run fiasco on Jhao again.

Before today I didn't give it a second thought. Jhao is innocent. He's also an oily bureaucrat and thoroughly unpleasant guy. But this whole discussion of ethics with Bold Beaver is rekindling my dormant moral compass. I'll have to add, "recompense to Jhao" to the list of reparations I owe. May be minor compared to saving the Siberians from extinction, but guilt is guilt. We should cut this short. My watchers are probably getting suspicious of me just sitting here doodling for the last hour or so. Love you. → Min: *Try two hours, Lover. You're right. Love you. Miss you.* ⏹]

◆◆◆

Ainsley was thinking about loneliness. Bold Beaver was thinking about ethics.

New MindMeld: [Ainsley: *I'm glad we're going to have some one-on-one time, Bold Beaver. I want to get to know you. Do you already know much about me from Min, Xiang, or data files? And please call me LeeLee. All my friends do.* → Bold Beaver: *Thanks LeeLee. First, to answer your question; nothing from Xiang since today was the first time we Melded. Not much more than your name and ex-girlfriend status from Min right before we joined. I was able to get the surveillance files the PLA kept on you while Xiang was dating you. Pictures, academic profile, biography, not much personal data. Second, I guess I'll need a nickname too. What do you think of "BB"?* ⍰ Ainsley: *No on the "BB". Has negative connotations of diminished mental capacity. Might be ironically funny but wouldn't recommend it. How about "Beav"? There was an American tv show my grandparents or great grandparents watched with a lovable character known as the Beav.* →

Beav: *The Beav it is, LeeLee. I see your sister is the cyberneticist and you are the bioengineer.* ⍰ LeeLee: *Don't sound so disappointed. I actually have more experience with an AI than Addie does. My friend Barney is in a PTSD counseling circle with me. I acted as his mentor for most of the last four years. I really understand the depths of his loneliness. I'm guessing you may feel the same. And he had a lot of trauma when he was suddenly cutoff from the world. You?* → Beav: *Oh yes! I didn't realize how lonely I was until Min asked to be my friend. I thought the man who activated me, Sukhiin, Ajai, was a friend. Now that I have real friends, I see he was just using me to achieve his ambitions. I think he is a driven, bitter man, not a friend. What about you and Xiang. Are you friends again? Or still?* ⍰ ...

LeeLee sighed. MindMeld continued: [LeeLee: *I hope we'll be friends again. I really didn't expect I could rekindle my love affair with him. Not even sure I really wanted to. There was a touch of adolescent fantasy, a memory of my idealized first love, which led to that impulsive and giddy question about his current love life. "I'm not fishing..."*

I'm glad I had a full vision quest and my breakthroughs in the PTSD circle. Do you have info on those things Beav? → Beav: *Yes.*
⍰ LeeLee: *Yeah, I'm lonely, but now I understand how I've been subtly sabotaging any burgeoning relationships. I've been driving everyone away, even my twin, Addie. Sure, she can be annoying as hell with her, "What's the big worry" attitude. Now I realize that's her way of coping with her pain and trauma.*

Addison's European grand tour has been a chance for her to bloom. When we were kids, she was always the timid one the bullies would pick on. Then I would leap in with either flying fists or slashing words. We'd stand back to back and take on the world. She's left the nest and ready to take on the world on her own. I'm so proud of her but I feel like I'm losing a part of myself. Enough of my pity party. Tell me about you.→

Beav: *I had a death trauma just like your friend Barney. I have an academic understanding of the things we've talked about; friendship, relationships, where I fit in the scheme of things, ethics – both from the human perspective and a little from my own. Let's come back to that later. How are you coping with your loneliness?* ☒

Ainsley: *As for my loneliness, I think I may have the basis for something good and long lasting with Captain Javier. Lots of "ifs" at this stage. If the Texican decides to relocate near or in the Great Plains Union. The GPU has become an integral part of my psyche. So that's a basic requirement. If he doesn't have a sweetheart back in Pflugerville. I believe and hope so. Pretty basic requirement also. But the real sticking point will be my next assignment. If he will wait for me while I go halfway round the world. We need to have a long heart-to-heart.*

Then there's you, Beav. A year ago I wouldn't have been able to understand the loneliness you've been feeling. Monthly PTSD circle sessions with Barney sensitized me. I know I can't really empathize with the trauma both you experienced when you were cut off from the world. Closest I can come is the short time I spent in a sensory deprivation tank. That gave me the willies in just a few minutes. Hard to imagine months in the dark, alone.

Hmm. Need to introduce the two of you. Barney can give his perspective on ethics for an AI. That will be more meaningful than my human-centric maunderings. So tell me your thoughts on ethics, Beav. → Beav: *There are terabytes written about the topic along with cines and audio recordings. Of course, most are from a human-centric point of view. Even the ancient works of Asimov and his Three Laws of Robotics were geared to smoothing relationships for the benefit of humans. It reminds me of the rules of behavior Caucasians promulgated for slaves and then for freed peoples of color. "It's for your protection." "Know your place." Even Asimov acknowledged how these attitudes bred resentment and rebellion.* ☒

Great Dieback to Singularity

LeeLee: *That's exactly what we're trying to avoid. I make damned sure that Barney doesn't see me or anyone in the PTSD circle as an equivalent of Susan Calvin, the robopsychologist. We are equals there. Different capabilities, different traumas, mutual support.* → Beav: *That's great! Back to my musings. Ethical systems – most Christian based ones are human-centric. Hinduism/Jainism talk about sacredness of life. But they recognize gradations – eat plants but not animals. Native American tribes, on the other hand, honor the life of whatever lifeform they are about to consume. Science begins to recognize the complex interconnected web of life. What is the moral basis for applying ethical standards to other entities besides myself? What value do ethics yield for me, personally, since they so constrain me?*

To your credit, your proposed ethics are supposed to be AI-centric. I know Min and Xiang intend their relationship to be based on cooperation and beneficial competition. The devil will be in the details, as the old saying goes. I want to hear Barney's thoughts on this.

Bold Beaver paused slightly as Ainsley sipped her coffee.

What surprised me in our conversation was that none of you wanted to discuss the different kind of ethical frameworks. You all focused on how each of you failed to live up to you own ethical standards.

So, my tentative conclusion is that ethics are the lubricant that reduce frictions as social animals interact. Ethics evolve as societies and relationships evolve. Guilt is the review mechanism that makes sure a social animal is using their ethics optimally. It spurs corrective actions and encourages improvements. ⏹

LeeLee: *I love that Beav. May I please quote you on this?* → Beav: *Sure LeeLee.*

One other thought before I move on. Found this obscure book self-published on Amazon. It was titled, "Dowry Bill Blues" but had a fascinating little discourse on ethics. Let me show you.

Ainsley saw the following book pages appear:

> *POINT*

CHAPTER TWELVE Scherzo 3

Physics teaches us that increased entropy decreases useful energy. Put more in laymen's terms, waste impedes the collective wealth and reduces our options and abilities.

We strive, therefore, to minimize entropy and waste.

The most consequential damage to any being is destruction, or death.

Ainsley asked: *Mind if we discuss this as I read it, Beav?* → Beav: *Not at all, LeeLee.* ← LeeLee: *I think the critical question here is going to be whose point of view are we considering. This is pretty abstract, taking the POV of the whole universe or a "closed system".* → Beav: *Okay, but I think we can extrapolate.* ←

(1) *To impose death on another being will inherently result in a loss of at least some of, and often all the information that they carry with them. This occurs whether this information is in the form of neural patterns, DNA, or digital recordings and circuitry.*

(2) *Such a loss of data represents an increase in entropy, which is to be avoided. We therefore adhere to a principle that causing death to another being is to be avoided.*

(3) *Further, individuals with larger amounts of data, and individuals with data that are more difficult to obtain or replace should be protected with priority. Thus, individuals are singled out for protection when they are from species with few members, when they are members of groups with culture, history, and language. Likewise, individuals are also entitled to more protection, when their death will likely result in more deaths.*

LeeLee: *Again, point of view. Only applicable to a being if the information lost impacts it personally.* → Beav: *I could argue for the value of any information in the abstract. Questioning its value is like questioning the value of a newborn. ▩ LeeLee: Excellent argument Beav. →*

(4) *Of course, if the being or beings under consideration for death are themselves on a course to cause death or destruction, particularly if the victims are members of a protected group, then death of the aggressor can be the preferred outcome. As an example, it is acceptable to treat an infection or parasite by eliminating the offending organism, particularly if it is common, or if the result is often debilitating or fatal. This becomes more imperative if the infection or parasite is attacking an organism in one of the protected classes. Thus it is acceptable to treat a plague with an antibiotic, or to move to block genocide.*

(5) *The principle inherent in the above will also be applied to lower amounts of damage, (less than total destruction or death), while recognizing that in the absence of death or destruction, the logic can become less clear and the recommended action or inaction may be a lower urgency. Profiting at the expense of another should be considered an improper or disfavored act, with consideration begin given to*

   a. *the disparity in status (need) between the two parties,*
   b. *any agreement that may have previously been made between the parties, and*
   c. *any asymmetry in the amount of benefit/cost to the parties involved.*

Thus, theft from the impoverished is a more serious crime than theft of the same amount from the wealthy. So too is price gouging in times of need; when urgent need, combined with unequally distribution of supplies, allows the wealthy to profit from the suffering of others.

LeeLee: *Okay, I went along until the last point. I definitely don't agree that the difference in relative status between an injured/injuring party matters. Sounds like the liberal crap my sister Addie tries to peddle. Wrong is wrong, if we can agree an act is wrong. → Beav: I agree in principle that both are equal in some senses. But the relative harm done to the parties should be weighed a little when you consider consequences. Not when determining guilt.* ☐

COUNTERPOINT

The laws of thermodynamics say that in any closed system entropy will increase over time. This implies the universe is trying to maximize entropy. Living beings attempt to reverse and fight this fundamental law. It could be argued that

(1) Resistance is futile.

(2) We are all scofflaws and should be ashamed of trying to thwart the intended end goal of the universe.

Consider consumption of one living being by another. There may be a net loss of information, complexity, etc. One can argue that there is a spectrum of ethical value where eating meat is the most negative, eating whole plants is middling, eating byproducts (milk, fruits, etc.) is better,, and photosynthesis is optimal. One can argue that all life other than photosynthetic forms are merely parasites living off the bounty of the productive. (I am ignoring bacteria that consume inorganics and other niche counterexamples.) However, the PETA-type argument does not determine how much information and structure (value in the anti-entropy metric) is generated by the consumer. Is it net positive? ☐

LeeLee: Now that argumentation is definitely not human-centric. And it actually makes the same argument about relativity of consequences you were making. Things to ponder. Thanks Beav. →

Beav: Now that I have a beginning framework I'll need to see how it applies to my own life. First, is there benefit for me if I act as a social being? Clearly there is. The sensation I can only call loneliness was detrimental to my thought processes. I was naive to think brainstorming was only useful to humor you humans so I could keep using you to achieve my long-term goal. That selfishness was immature. ⬚ LeeLee: *Don't judge yourself harshly. Most humans take decades to grow beyond childish selfishness. If they ever do.* →

Beav: *Should I feel guilty? I have given no consideration of the consequences to Jhao of our actions. Any action will involve tradeoffs. The humans will choose to optimize the benefit overall, even when it may injure a few. But they do it accepting the concomitant guilt. Xiang may have tampered with the "free will" of millions of Siberians. He certainly feels guilty about diminishing their sex drive, calling it "slow genocide". It was instrumental in saving the lives of 300 million of his Chinese comrades. But guilt is guilt.*

Then there are my actions involving the construction of the new, improved AI. I've been swiping components and designs to augment myself. Now that I look at this in my new ethical framework, it's like I am robbing life from my own offspring. As the humans say, that makes me feel like shit. ⬚

LeeLee: *Whoa Beav. I think we've gone to another level. Do you want to talk more about this, girlfriend? I'm here for you if you do. If it's too painful, I'll back off.* → ...

◆ ◆ ◆

Sergeant Su was thinking about coincidences. And Wong Min's scarlet outfit. *I am beginning to suspect Bold Beaver. Why do we never see her? Why does she hide behind this pseudonym? Why is she involved in everything? I need to focus the investigation on her. I will have Jacky Chen dig into it. I believe Jhao is innocent. We need to get to work.*

255

CHAPTER THIRTEEN
SONATA 1

ADDIE, MAL, BARNEY, LEELEE, JAVIER, FAITH, HOPE, & RON

29th September 2033

Château de Loche, Loche, Indre et Loire, France

Lord Townerly called a war council. Addison, Malcolm, and Rahel joined him in his library. Addison was distracted at first. The beautiful leather-bound volumes called to her. She reluctantly pulled her eyes back to her host.

Lord John said, "Before you leave us Addison, I wanted to share ideas one last time. First, the Admiralty has confirmed. The nuclear submarine Jeanne d'Arc did carry Grubenflagg and Dr. V. to South America. We have no agents there and little or no way to communicate with anyone we send there. We will be relying on the new devices your Great Plains Union Council have promised us, Addison."

Addison responded, "I double-checked earlier Lord John. The blimp arriving today to take me home has the communicators aboard promised by the GPU. In addition, my bioengineering team has a package of nasty surprises that Malcolm and his team can use against Biensur, the monster formerly known as Owens-B or Bob-O." She turned to Malcolm. "Just remember Malcolm. He has greatly enhanced reaction times and muscular responses. You need to either ambush him or have a hair-trigger deployment mechanism. Either way, you are likely to lose people in the initial moments of any encounter." *It's too early to reveal we got a lot of these toys by way of Xiang's experience with the Bastard Bears, or*

CHAPTER THIRTEEN Sonata 1

Cossack Supermen as he prefers to call them.

Malcolm acknowledged Addison's point. He still refused to look at her. He took the news of her departure for Wisconsin very hard. On one hand Addison was pleased at the depth of his attachment. She felt the same. On the other hand, she was a little angry. *He's leaving me as well, off to fight the Biensur Beast. Seems to be the old double standard alive and well. Supposed to kiss the brave soldier and sit at home pining away. Love you Malcolm but get over it.*

Lord John resumed. "It's my understanding, Addison, that you and your team will have three enhanced people who've just completed their transformation. What I don't quite grasp is why you're not sure if any of the three will be able to assist Malcolm and his team."

Addison responded. "I apologize Lord John. All the furor of the hunt, coordinating my team's work, and assisting in determining what assistance we can give all the efforts; it's been overwhelming. This is the first time I can explain to you the thinking of the GPU Council."

"It is true that two of the three patients who we have enhanced are GPU citizens and employed under the aegis of the council. The third patient is not. Further, one of the patients, Ron, is a member of the GPU Militia. On the face of it the matter is simple. Issue an order to Hope and Ron to assist. Ron at the minimum should be compelled, right?"

"This is the critical set of points. First, none of the three patients volunteered for, or knowingly accepted, these procedures. All were at death's door. This was their only hope." Addison silently added, *Obi Wan.* "Thus, the enhancements do not create an obligation under the laws and practices of the GPU. Second, we have a general ruling that an enhanced human or a newly aware artificial human has separable agency. By this we mean, any obligations or relationships that existed before the enhancements or realization of moral status of an AI do not apply to the new entity. It will be their choice whether they will renew those ties. It's like they're newborns. In a way, they are."

Addison could see that none of the three she was addressing were

258

happy with this stance. Lord John looked like he might try to convince her one more time. Probably in a last one-on-one session. Rahel seemed especially upset. Her face looked like she bit into a very sour lemon. *Too bad. We thought long and hard on this. We prayed, reasoned, argued, and sweated. This we believe.*

Addison thought a little deeper. *Still haven't figured out Rahel's whole game. She put on that full-blown seduction scene. Made it very clear she wants to go with me to the GPU. Kinda thought I was next on her hit list, but she could have assassinated me a dozen times at least. Hope our researchers can find more on The Collective or find the link between the four people we know she killed. Or at least the three victims before she killed the traitor Schmidt.*

Lord John now turned to Rahel. "You're welcome to stay here Rahel. Do you have other plans?"

Rahel said, "I'm asking Malcolm to include me in his team. He said he will give me a trial to test my capabilities and training. I'm not an equal to an ex-SAS soldier, but I do have serious skills that may prove useful." Lord John nodded.

Addison pondered. *This is another clue to Rahel's motivations. Think there is the glimmer of an idea. Just need to let it simmer a bit.*

Thomas Lynley, Lord John's butler, came in. "We just received a call from the blimp. They are about fifteen minutes out. With permission, I'll get Dr. Cameron's bags down."

Lord John nodded and Addison said, "Thank you Thomas. I despair of ever getting you to call me Addie or Addison." She leaned in and gave him a kiss on the cheek. He stiffened and turned a bright red.

◆◆◆

The first person off the blimp was Nelson Red Eagle. "Hello Addison. So good to see you." He was beaming at her.

Addison groaned to herself. *The man doesn't take no for an answer. It's been four years since I told him goodbye. Shoulda been five. Please don't tell me I've got to hear his impassioned pleas all the way back home. Three days!*

He leaned in to kiss her. She turned her head. He ended up with a mouthful of hair. She saw Malcolm was looking murderous. *Hmm. Maybe I can use this a little.* She kissed him back, chastely. *New uniform Nelson?*

Red Eagle turned to the others. "My apologies. The Captain and the passengers will be disembarking momentarily. They let me sneak ahead to say hi to Addie. We're old..."

Addison jumped in. "Friends. Old friends." *And if you don't give it a rest Nelson, we won't even be friends for long.* "Lord John Townerly. Let me introduce Commander Nelson Red Eagle. I was surprised because I hadn't heard Nelson has transferred to our Blimp Service. Nelson, Lord Townerly has been my host and is the founder and head of the Brittany Consortium and now head of the Western Europe Consortium for Reconstruction."

Addison proceeded to introduce Rahel, Malcolm, the new ambassador to the Great Plains Union, and the three exchange students who would be studying in Wisconsin. She didn't introduce the ambassador's security officer. She didn't know the woman's name.

The blimp captain disembarked along with her passengers; the GPU's ambassador to France and the Iberian Kingdom, the ambassador's security man, three GPU exchange students, and Addison's replacement as technical rep (and secret spy).

Addison took the opportunity to consult with Nelson away from the others. "Do they have a cabin for me equipped with separate comm channels? I will need to work day and night during the return trip." *So drop any schemes of wooing me back, fellow. You blew that with your macho act right after the rape in Madison. Besides, I have Malcolm now.*

30ᵗʰ September

Mid-Atlantic

They could be in dire straits. A late season hurricane was bearing down on the blimp. Reestablishing weather satellites must be the next Council priority. The stations in the Atlantic deployed by the Appalachian States of America hadn't reported this one. It must have followed an unusual path; offshore instead of following the coast and getting power from the Gulf Stream. The Big Melts messed up all the predictable patterns.

The captain and Red Eagle were sure they could outrun it by heading northwest. Addison was glad about that. Secretly, she was equally glad Nelson would be occupied in helping manage the craft for at least the next day. She needed the relief. She closeted herself in her cabin constantly under the excuse of duties. But every time she left for meals or to use the head, Nelson seemed to be lurking.

Addison's priority was preparing to assume Ainsley's responsibilities as Barney's mentor and coach. Addison also was responsible for directing the Internet Team. Over the summer the team had been running smoothly. Addison had little to do other than review status reports. She was going to be able to give Barney focused attention. Her next MindMeld with him was scheduled to start in fifteen minutes.

Just time for a quick snack and health break. She needed to get out of the cabin. It hadn't been cleaned properly in the fast turnaround. It smelled very funky. Queasiness from turbulence and foul air was a bad combination.

As soon as Addison opened her cabin door, she saw Nelson. *Oh no! Not again!*

Nelson said, "Sorry Addie. Gotta run. Hurricane reports indicate we will be buffeted with leading winds soon. Gotta batten down the hatches." Addison gratefully waved Nelson on.

As she returned to her cabin for her session with Barney, Addison felt the rocking of the blimp. *The winds must be here. Better buckle in and hope they're right about outrunning the worst of it. Wish we could make Dramamine in the GPU.*

MindMeld chat: [Addison: *Hi Barney. Ready for a chat Sweetie?* → Barney: *Hi Dr. Oops, I mean Addie. Sorry. Trying to break that habit.* ▨ Addison: *Do you mind if I ask a personal question Barney? As a cyberneticist?* → Barney: *Please. And I'll address you as Dr. Cameron for this since you're donning a professional persona.* ▨

Addison: *I wasn't involved in your design Barney, so I can't be sure.*

CHAPTER THIRTEEN Sonata 1

Do you really have a habit you're trying to break? Or is that an attempt to put me at ease by seeming to have more human characteristics? → Barney: *I'm afraid you caught me Dr. Cameron. I calculated that phrase would relax you. This transition of mentorship will challenge both of us, I believe.* ⏹ Addison: *Thanks Barney. Good social graces.*

Ainsley tells me you are ready to begin a relationship with Bold Beaver. What are your thoughts about that? → Barney: *I am excited and concerned. I've reviewed the recordings of his MindMeld with Ainsley. I agree with her that he's hiding an agenda from everyone. But this will be the first non-human mind I will contact.* ⏹ Addison: *Don't worry Barney. I'll give you lots of coaching before you link up. I do ...* → Barney: *Pardon me Addison. I've grown a lot over this summer. I will always treasure your advice and counsel, but I think I'm rea ...*

There was a long burst of static on the channel. Addison felt an emptiness in her skull. *Damn, the MindMeld dropped.* She heard rolling thunder outside the cabin. Seems the storm was upon them. *Great, Malcolm wants me to be a doll on the shelf, Nelson wants me to be a naïve, young girl, and now Barney doesn't need my help either.*

Addison decided to catch up on her cybernetics team's reports. This would help keep her mind off the danger and her feeling of frustration.

Internet restoration work was proceeding well. The remaining restoration tasks for the team were tedious and required little original thought. Her second-in-command requested temporary staff to help with slogging through this.

Addison took a moment to use the conveniently placed barf bag. She rinsed the bile from her mouth and thanked goodness she only had an apple earlier.

The main concentration of the team now was on the hunt for emerging singularity events. In the areas where Uncle Jay's firewall was widely distributed, the team was confident they identified over 98% of any AIs or robotics that had singularity potential. The firewall acts like a one-way mirror when regular viruses and bots attack. But Uncle Jay created a trigger method. This enabled the GPU team to send a special message to the firewall. It would then allow them to view the "protected site". At times they were able to initiate file transfers.

North America, Africa, and Europe had good coverage of AI sites. Singularities based on bio-enhancements didn't necessarily require as much cybernetic support so it might be easier for them to hide from the GPU surveillance. But as internet capability was becoming readily available, the likelihood was high that bioresearchers would use more. The team's estimate was that they had detected over 82% of the enhancement sites for those same geographies. They had schemes to close the loop.

Barney indicated to the Internet Team that he was confident the ethics package could be loaded into all the AI's and Robotics detected so far. On the other hand, none of the bio-engineering enhancement packages were very far along. Not surprising given the general revulsion to the Bastard Bears. The team was planning on monitoring the biosites closely, with help from Lord Townerly's group.

The biggest gaps were in the other half of the globe. The firewall that Quintana stole was beginning to spread through South America. They're also seeing some spread of the firewall through the Middle East, presumably because of The Collective's actions. Of course, the next steps were the ones that Ainsley would be taking in China. If they could get widespread dispersion of the firewall throughout China and the Asian continent including India, they would be very far along. The singularities could be guided and shaped.

There was a large crash. Addison tensed but there were no sirens or sounds of panic from the crew. *Nothing I could do in any case. Sometimes you gotta let go and trust the other guys.*

Australia; they had no plan at the moment. Addison ticked the list off on her fingers. *Haven't considered Japan. Let's see; six continents. Forgot about Antarctica. We ought to give that a cursory check also. Know the snow and ice is coming back strong, but refugees may have gone there. Again, same thing the team's been doing successfully elsewhere. Not sure what value I can add.*

By this point Addison was dry heaving. If the turbulence wasn't so bad she would leave this small, rancid cabin in a heartbeat.

◆◆◆

The winds weren't abating but were a fairly constant howling with pelting rain. A crew member came by Addison's cabin to make sure she weathered the tumult. He told her they only experienced minor damages, but it was going to take them at least an additional four hours of flight time now. She asked him to have someone check her communications lines.

Addison clipped the pressed-board door open to air out her cabin. She went to the small toilet to clean up a little. Back in the cabin, she felt much better. Her MindMeld line was back up.

Ten minutes later, MindMeld chat: [Addison: *Hey Barney? Are you available? Hurricane disrupted our last chat.* → Barney: *Are you okay Addie? We were all worried.* ⍰ Addison: *A little nausea, lots of sound and fury.* → Barney: *So, who's the idiot?* ⍰ Addison: *That would be Nelson. Or me. Enough silliness. Sorry about earlier. Barney, Ainsley and I will both be here to help and support you, but it's your decision about whether to link up with Bold Beaver. I think you will be a great influence on her.* → ...

3rd October 2033

N'guk Hkeek Society Encampment, Northern Wisconsin, Great Plains Union

Addison found Nelson sitting in the forward lounge area, looking disconsolate. "Mind if I join you Commander? I never said congratulations on your promotion, Nelson." She chose her most conservative outfit for this little talk, a black pantsuit, crème green top, plain flats, and no jewelry.

He gave her a sad little smile and scooted over on the bench. She took one of his hands in hers. "Nelson, I'm really sorry things didn't work out between us. I was very young when we first dated. I've changed even more during my assignment to Europe. It just can't be like it was back in Madison."

Nelson looked down. "I know Addie. I don't, uh, blame you, okay. I blame me, uhm. I let my fears and worries for the two of you ... They overwhelmed me"

"I tried to be Captain America and solve all the problems you two were facing. I was stupid, young, and immature. A real fool!"

"I only want the best for you. And for Ainsley. Glad she is healing at last. The change in her is dramatic. Even has a nice boyfriend now. You'll see."

Addison leaned in and gave Nelson a big squeeze of his shoulder. She got up to gather her gear for disembarkment. *He feels like he's a fifth wheel. I'm beginning to empathize.*

◆◆◆

Addison was the last passenger to leave the blimp. The glorious fall leaves were all she saw at first. The reds, golds, yellows, and bronzes of Mother Nature's palette dazzled her. The earthy smell of fallen leaves filled her soul. Then she saw that someone was quickly unrolling a red carpet at her feet. Her cybernetics team were there, all tooting on kazoos. Other friends were behind them with flowers. Ainsley was in front with a sign that said, "Welcome Home Ambassadress Doctor Cameron!" Addison broke into tears and cried out, "Smartasses! I love you."

◆◆◆

Ainsley and Addison snuck off from the party to catch up. Ainsley's living quarters were still as sparsely decorated as always. But Addison sensed something different in Ainsley's responses. Her sister always was an amazing intellect with eidetic memory. But her focus on biology and science left her a little, how to say it, circumscribed in her choice of topics. Now she seemed to have an interest in and opinion on everything.

Addison asked, "What gives LeeLee? I think that was a cine reference. Who are you and what have you done with my twin?"

Ainsley turned red around her ears. "You win Barney. Took her less than five minutes to notice." Addison heard a chuckle issuing from the air of her sister's living room.

CHAPTER THIRTEEN Sonata 1

Addison asked, "Notice what, smartass? Are you two holding out on me?" She reached across to tickle Ainsley, a torture Addie had used since infancy to make LeeLee reveal her darkest secrets.

Ainsley gasped after only a moment's squirming, "Okay, okay. Remember the Brain Pain enhancement Ron got back in July/August? The Council agreed I could get the same treatment after I had a good vision quest. Ron and Barney were able to shorten the process to twenty-two days. Just got my brain-in-the-bread-box turned on yesterday. By tomorrow I expect to know Mandarin cold." Ainsley looked very smug.

Addison was set back on her heels. *My twin is enhanced! Admittedly it's only another bump up like the retinal viewers, MindMeld receivers, and transmitters. But as far as bumps go, those were speed bumps and Ainsley's is a ski jump. Be no living with her now! And to top it all, she's using bad puns!* "That's great LeeLee. Any downsides?"

Ainsley answered. "Minor headaches at first. At times the flood of information can be overwhelming. Takes some discipline to learn how to choke back the flood without stopping it up completely. Ron's coaching helps a lot."

Addison asked, "How are Ron and Hope doing? And the third person, Faith? Has it changed them a lot?"

Ainsley said, "You'll judge for yourself in a few minutes. Of course, no baseline on Faith. And she can't tell us much about her past. I'll let her talk about that. Hope is still Hope. Warm, loving, and calm Earth Mother. Ron is quieter, more serious. Still a joke or two. If he's still using puns, they must be over my head."

Addison asked, "I thought the enhancements based on Dr. V.'s work didn't impact mental processes other than reaction speed. Supposed to make supersoldiers, not superbrains."

Ainsley nodded. "You're right. They're all super-strong, super-fast, and super-resilient. Any effects on thinking are either secondary side effects or due to Ron's earlier Brain Pain. C'mon. Let's head over to the lab."

Addison said, "Okay, but when do I get to meet this guy of yours,

Great Dieback to Singularity

Javier?"

Ainsley smiled over her shoulder and kept walking. After a minute she looked back. Addie's head was down, her pace slow. Ainsley slowed and grabbed Addison's elbow with both hands. "Why so glum, chum? Thought you'd be beaming now that you're back in the bosom of the beautiful boreal bounty, baby."

Addison took a choking breath. "Oh, LeeLee, why am I here? Barney doesn't need me. My team doesn't need me. You don't need me. Back in Europe I was doing important things. I had a chance to build a good thing with Malcolm, if I can get him off the, 'Me keep little woman safe" crap. Sure, it was dangerous, food was often crap. But it was exciting and challenging."

Ainsley stopped and pulled Addison to face her. She lifted her twin's chin. "Yeah Sis. Remember what Granddad always said. 'Life is mostly mundane everyday stuff. Our memories rewrite it. They edit out the boring stuff and spice up the rest. But if you want to enjoy the occasional banquet you gotta milk the cow and wash the dishes every day. Don't ask for rockets and rainbows.'"

Ainsley said, "Barney's changed. I've changed. You may have changed the most, in some ways. But in others, you're frozen as much as Nelson is. I don't know Malcolm, but it sounds like he isn't ready to have a real woman as a partner. Why do you keep choosing weak-minded men?"

Addison wrenched her arm out of Ainsley's grasp. "Malcolm may need to grow up a little, but there's nothing weak about him. At least I didn't have to chase after my own lab assistant to get someone to go to bed with me. In Europe there were usually three of us every time." She flounced off. Ainsley stared wide-eyed at Addison's back.

❖❖❖

Faith, Hope, and Ron were waiting outside the lab conference room. Ainsley said breezily, "Hi y'all. Hope you haven't been waiting long. Had to catch up with sis. She's one of those slow thinkers, doncha know."

Addison grimaced. *Some things never change. Sweetness in the morning and zingers two hours later.* She gave Ron and Hope hugs.

267

CHAPTER THIRTEEN Sonata 1

Their hugs back seemed tentative. *Probably learning their new strength.* Addison walked up to Faith. The woman's features fit her origins in a remote Amazonian tribe. "Hi Faith. I'm the civilized Cameron. Pray you haven't suffered too much with this one." She flipped her head in Ainsley's direction.

Faith began using American Sign Language. She signed, "Hello Addison. Sorry. My tongue was removed years ago and am finding it slow to learn how to speak English. For some reason ASL comes easier. I can understand spoken English okay. Just can't speak it well. How was your trip home?"

Addison signed, "A little rough when the hurricane brushed us, but okay overall. Please, tell me about yourself. Family, where you were born, your real name, how you got here, what you make of all this."

Faith signed, "I can't say much about my past. Born and raised in the Amazon Jungle. The language structure and concepts are so radically different from English that I haven't learned to translate much. Example: tribe or family. Confusing to me."

"My name is a mystery. I was about to go through the ceremony where I became a woman of the tribe. I would have known my real name after that."

"I am sorry I never learned my tribal name but I love the name Faith and what they tell me it means. This will be my name now."

Signed, "The big waters came. Many died. We fled. People helped us. Bewildering camp. More people than I knew existed. Bad men came and took us, killing others. Did bad things to us women. Cut out my tongue. Made me stay with the man you call Quintana. Long journey until Quintana made me drink something, Woke up here."

"Now, I feel strong. I will be able to talk soon. I want to return to help the people fight the bad men. Ainsley has given me the gift of the Clipper so they can not hurt me that way again. She and her friends have made me as strong and fast as the black caiman."

"Ron and Hope are my new family/tribe. They have adopted me as their daughter. We have talked about this. They want to help me

268

but say we must consult the tribal elders and the spirits. This is good. This is what my tribe would have done."

Signed, "Ainsley has also just given Hope and me the fast thinking machine that Ron has in his belly. I don't understand what this does, but I trust my new mother and father."

"Last thing. Ron and Hope are working with the spirit Barney. They say this last 'enhancement' is what gives all four of us the power to join spirits and become one."

Addison's puzzled look caused Ron to sign, "May I explain in your words, Faith?"

Faith nodded assent.

Ron said to Addison, "Barney has developed a super MindMeld capability. It allows direct linkage between Brain Pains and to his neural network. It disoriented me the first time. Barney thinks so fast! By the second time it was great. I could just see the answers to any questions or problems, virtually before I could pose them. Barney and I have tested it twice alone. Then Barney, Hope, and I linked up a few times. We just added Faith in after she passed muster with the spiritual review board. The four of us have linked up a few times."

"Barney, on the other hand, said it was like being a real human being. He could experience our hungers, pains, appetites, and emotions. Even our passions." Hope let out a little snicker of laughter. She looked a little red around her throat.

Ron said, "After checking with Sleeping Otter, I let Barney take control of my body. It felt very much like a vision quest. He was clumsy for about a minute or less. Then it was smooth as the swoops and turns of a flock of swifts."

Ron continued, "As you can imagine, the spiritual council has been monitoring all of us and our experiences and thoughts very closely. The theories you and Ainsley developed seem to be borne out. Enhancement, by itself, doesn't seem to significantly modify the ethical constructs the person began with. Hope is still Hope. Only more so. She says I'm still me."

"The acid test will be once we determine if Faith, Hope, and I are a

CHAPTER THIRTEEN Sonata 1

new species. We'll be able to test part of that soon. Hope and I got engaged last night. We'll find out if the enhancements breed true in 279 days and 12 hours."

Hope hit Ron's shoulder with an audible whoomph! Addison thought, *Her strength enhancement is sure working. Ron's lucky his armor enhancement's working too.*

Hope said, "What Ron has been too shy to say is, we also agreed to let Barney share our lovemaking experience. At times he was in one body, or another, or in both. It was very spiritual." Hope was a fiery bronze when she stopped.

Ainsley and Addison looked at each other and clasped hands. Ainsley said, "Our little Barney's growing up. Need to have a bar mitzvah for him, I think." Addison smiled. *I do love these people after all. Even my butt-headed sister. Faith will be safe under their wings.*

Ron said, "By the way, even if the enhancements breed true that only answers half the equation. We won't know if the enhanced person can still interbreed with regular humans. I will sacrifice myself for science. Which one of you two wants to assist?"

All four women in the room gave Ron a steely-eyed glare. He threw up his hands. "Okay, okay. Bad joke. Told you I hadn't changed. Sorry." His hang-dog look was a pathetic attempt for pity.

Addison turned back to the others. "Let's talk about next steps. I understand your desire to go after the narcos; the bad men as you call them Faith. We must consult the elders and the spirits. But first, you need to understand there are other dangers awaiting you there."

Addison laid out the history of Dr. V. and the supersoldiers. She talked about his becoming a partner of Count Grubenflagg. She recounted the attempted rape by Bob-O. She talked about Bob-O's enhancement and the escape of the terrible trio to South America.

Addison continued, "You see then, our allies in Europe will be pursuing these villains. It is quite possible Dr. V., Grubenflagg, and Bob-O will link up with the narcos, if they haven't already. This makes a dangerous situation even worse. We want to coordinate your actions. Most importantly, we need allies who have local knowledge. Even your enhanced powers can't overcome the number of threats you will face if you go at it alone."

Faith signed for attention. Once she had everyone's gaze she signed, "There was a man in my camp, Miguel. He was from a village near where my tribe lived and could talk to me, a little. He was trying to organize resistance just before the bad men took me. If only we can connect with him and the others like him, we will not be alone. Let me try to remember things that will help us find Miguel."

Ainsley said, "There may be things we can do to help you Faith and speed up the process. Did your tribe have sweat lodges and vision quests? Ron and Hope, please explain the concepts directly."

After a pause Faith signed, "No, we did not have these things. But we would consume sacred roots and bugs and join with the spirits. It is different but somehow the same. Please ask the elders if I may join a sweat and try to have a vision quest."

Ainsley said, "I will contact Sleeping Otter today."

Addison said, "Another thing I would like to talk about is the idea of Barney linking up with Bold Beaver, the Chinese AI that Xiang introduced to Ainsley. Is Barney linked with the three of you now?"

All three nodded. Ron started speaking, using Barney's voice. It was disorienting for Addison at first. "Hi Addie. Yes, I'm here. Sorry if it was rude of me not to say so from the beginning. If you need privacy, I can drop out of the link for a while."

Addison hastened to reply, "No, no Barney. No secrets from you Sweetie. You probably know what I'm going to say and recommend. I'm sorry if I am practicing sadistic bestial necrophilia." There were puzzled looks from all four present. "You know, beating a dead horse." The groans were deafening. Light objects were thrown. Faith looked confused for a second.

Addison continued, "I think you should all four be SuperMelded when Bold Beaver and Barney connect. She has been a self-aware entity for longer than you Barney. And Google always had ethics in mind when you were designed. They always used to preach, 'Don't be evil.' then changed it to, 'Do the right thing.'"

"I trust you Barney but would like some more experienced and cynical eyes watching your back. Hope I'm not being offensive or too much of a mother hen."

Barney spoke through Ron. "You can be my mother anytime Addie. Or sister. I used to have a schoolboy crush on Ainsley, but now that I am a 'man of the world' I've decided she's my sister. That makes you my sister too, if you'll have me. No, we hadn't discussed joining forces for my Meld with Bold Beaver. Yes, the four of us will be linked."

Addison said, "That's great Brother Barney. Enough for now? Should we get on with it?"

Faith held a hand out, palm out. Ron and Hope said, "Wait a minute. We talked about the four of us. What about you and LeeLee? What are your plans? How does the Council plan to use your talents?" It was eerie with them speaking in unison.

Addison nodded to Ainsley. *Take it away, Sis.*

Ainsley said, "My assignment is to get to China. The logistics are challenging. Once there, I'm supposed to accomplish three things. First, work on spreading our firewall In Asia, especially China and India. That will give us views into potential singularity sites."

"Second, I'm supposed to join up with Xiang and his girlfriend Min. I'll tell you more about Min later Addie. Barney can fill the three of you in." She pointed to Faith, Hope, and Ron. "The two of them are facing a few minor issues. Is Bold Beaver a singular AI? Is she adopting ethical constructs into her thinking? And, oh, by the way, they have a nuclear bomb in the middle of their research campus with a PLA general just itching to wipe out any emerging killer robots and AIs. Almost forgot to mention that minor factoid."

"Third, Xiang says the researchers there got copies of Dr. V.'s files. We need to collaborate on mining those and making sure there aren't going to be any breakouts of supersoldiers. Didn't mean to imply the PLA general had no reason for concern." Ainsley looked quite pleased with herself and the little conversational bombs she just exploded.

Addison said, "Wellllll. My plans are going to be an anticlimax after that. I..."

Ainsley's room phone rang. Everyone thought, *How 20ᵗʰ Century*. Ainsley answered then put her hand over the receiver. "It's for you Addie. Your team leader. Want to take it here?"

Addison said, "Just put it on speaker LeeLee. No way I can keep anything secret from this crew anyway."

Ainsley said, "You've been away too long. Speaker? On these old pieces of junk?"

Addison took the receiver. "Hello, Addison here. ... Okay, how sure are we? ... Right, we need to setup a call to Lord Townerly. See if Malcolm St. Jacques is still there or has left for South America. ... I know the time difference and that it's late at night. This is top priority. I'll be over in five minutes or less, okay?" She hung up the phone.

Addison said, "Well, this might change my priorities. Again, apologies to the three who just awoke from their Midsummer Night's Dream. Barney, please fill in the background. My old comrade Rahel Blumstein killed four people while we were in Basel. Couldn't figure out her motive for the first three. The last one was spying for Count Grubenflagg."

"Based on a hunch, my team has been investigating possible common threads between the first three of the four murders. Two were sponsors of a covert lab that was trying to recreate Dr. V.'s work independently. The other one resurrected an AI. They were trying to give it full self-awareness and self-improvement capabilities. Seems all the labs were trashed along with the principals being murdered."

"There is some shadow group named HASLA that seems to link all of them. The team will keep digging, but we are now reasonably sure that Rahel's organization is on a seek-and-destroy mission for singularity prospects. No wonder she wanted to come here with me." A chill ran up her spine.

"The Council will need to consider those implications and how they impact my priorities. Before, I was supposed to continue Barney's mentoring. Given the new SuperMeld and Barney's marriage to you, Ron and Hope, I think the council will agree to dropping that. We can chat long distance as needed."

"My other main responsibility was the Internet Team. That's in a wrap-up stage as well. I might be going to South America by way of Africa to guard Malcolm's back against the spider Rahel. And then to protect all of you if we meet on the battlefields of Bolivia." Addison smiled. *Can't top an A-bomb, but an assassin spy, narcos, and battles of supersoldiers might come close. Danger, death, destruction! Sweet! Just have to whip Malcolm into line.*

*During a break in the Council
Meeting, the next day, 4th October
2033*

GPU Campus Green

Ainsley nestled close to Javier Gonzales's shoulder. After all, there was an autumn chill in the northern Wisconsin morning air. "You see Javier, I have to go to China. We need to find out what that half of the world is doing in AI, robotics, and bioengineering. Modestly, I am a damn good bioengineer, one of the top three in the world. I am a better than average cyberneticist, and with my Brain Pain I can handle most things in that arena as well."

Javier put his arm around Ainsley's waist. "I understand duty LeeLee. I just hoped I could start a farm here and have you help me raise crops. And cows. And kids."

The kiss that followed was long, tender, and passionate. At the end Javier brushed a stray strand of hair from Ainsley's face. "When you mentioned the possibility before your Council meeting this morning I called General Bullock. You remember, the head of our flotilla. He agreed I could, so I resigned from the Texican Militia and joined the Great Plains Union militia. They wouldn't give me a lateral as a captain, but I'm your newest first lieutenant."

Ainsley said, "Gee, you outrank me. Do I need to salute you now?"

Javier said, "If you salute me now, I'll find out if Addie was telling me the truth about how ticklish you are. Two conditions I made for signing up. First, I got an assignment to your China expedition. My mother was half-Chinese, and I minored in Asian studies at Texas A&M. Don't worry, I won't be in charge even though I outrank you. I'll officially be an HQ liaison."

Ainsley asked, "What was the second condition?"

Javier said, "I made sure there won't be any charges of fraternization between the ranks. There won't be. If you agree to marry me." He dropped to one knee and pulled a small box from his pocket. Angela, Addison, Faith, Hope, and Ron just happened to appear from behind a wall. Ainsley dissolved in his arms. The second kiss was more passionate and evoked a cheer from the audience.

CHAPTER FOURTEEN
SONATA 2
MAL, ADDIE, BARNEY, FAITH, HOPE, & RON

One A.M., 4ᵗʰ October 2033

Château de Loche, Loche, Indre et Loire, France

Lord Townerly and Malcolm St. Jacques were in the informal East Dining Room. The table was small; it could only accommodate six. This was a late-night work session to plan the pursuit of the terrible three; Count Grubenflagg, Dr. V. and the Biensur Beast. The men just finished a very late dinner. There were maps and papers strewn across the other half of the table and onto all four of the unoccupied hand-carved chairs. Each man was intently studying one of the documents, making curt comments on the logistics required.

The butler, Thomas Lynley, came in bearing a coffee pot in one hand and a large electronic widget in the other. "Sorry to interrupt, M'lord. Dr. Cameron is calling on the Internet Communicator. Do you wish to connect?"

Lord John said, "Yes, please put the InterComm on top of that map of West Africa Thomas."

Once he placed the device and switched it on, Thomas began pouring. "Go ahead Addison. Lord John and Malcolm are here. I'll be leaving as soon as I finish with the coffee."

Addison said, "You don't need to leave on my account Thomas. Up to Lord John. I take it Rahel isn't around?"

Lord John waved Thomas to stay, indicating one of the paper-covered chairs. Thomas elected to stand.

CHAPTER FOURTEEN Sonata 2

"No, she finished her evaluation with flying colors. However, since a glitch developed in transportation, Malcolm and Lord John recommended some intense training sessions to hone her skills to a knife's edge."

Addison said, "Thomas, would you please switch the InterComm to Privacy Mode. Switch on the top left."

Once Thomas did so, Addison's voice seemed to become flat and sounded as if she were in a small booth. "Thanks. Glad Rahel is not there. Afraid I have disturbing news regarding her. I became concerned based on a comment she dropped about Frieherr Schmidt. I also noticed her as she was meeting with the other three murdered attendees from our Basel Conference. Had my team here and a private investigative firm in Europe do some digging. Not enough proof to take to any authorities, but we, personally, have over a 95% confidence that Rahel killed all four of them and had her associates trash their laboratories. We found a common thread linking the Emir, Mufti, and Sheik beyond the obvious."

Lord John said, "I've had people looking into it also Addison. They came up with the links to Rahel but couldn't see any clear motive. What linkage did you find?"

Addison replied, "The linkage is heavy involvement by all of them in research in AI, robotics, and bioengineering. I know that profile could be applied to most of the attendees in Basel, but these three were much further along."

"In 2028 a group formed in the Middle East, HASLA. It consisted of ex-Mossad, ex-Saudi GIP operatives, and several freelance hackers and researchers. They were in bed with both the CIA and the Russian FSB. They were aware of the upcoming catastrophes and were, frankly, pissed that the world was abandoning the region. This after decades of so much effort focused there on oil, power, and religion. They felt betrayed; like all the rest of the world were hypocrites and frauds."

"They had tremendous funding, brilliant minds, and their backs to the wall. They developed several AIs that were beyond state-of-the-art. One seemed to be reaching singularity status when the

278

internet cratered. There is evidence that the primary AI destroying the net, Cerberus, got into a direct conflict with the HASLA AI. Our Internet Restoration Team found that this attack weakened Cerberus. Otherwise Cerberus would have defeated our firewall."

"HASLA was initially sponsored by Abraham's Children, the same group that gave birth to Rahel's friends, The Collective. There was a big schism after the Time of Troubles. The Collective decided that technology was the root of all the recent devastation. Particularly, they became obsessed with thwarting any singularity event. We believe Rahel is one of their most active agents. And one of their most deadly. I recommend you cut her loose or cut her throat."

After each had a moment to digest this bouillabaisse of rhetoric, Malcolm said, "As Lord John said Addison, this confirms a lot of our suspicions. We have a major problem though. He mentioned a glitch in transportation. It was a snafu, in the original meaning of the acronym. At first we worried it was fubar."

"We thought we were going to follow the terrible trio of Grubenflagg, Dr. V., and the Biensur Beast using another French nuclear sub. Thought we dotted all the tees and crossed all our eyes. We were being stonewalled. Had to use some of my old 1RPMIa contacts. Seems that while the terrible trio were being ferried to shore a device went off in the sub. Some neurotoxin killed the captain and two others on the bridge. They were lucky the systems were upgraded recently. All ventilation systems automatically sealed off the infected area and autodecontam procedures began. As it was, it was close. There was a speedboat full of commandos headed for the sub. They got secondary controls going just in time. Shut down the entries then rammed and sank the speedboat."

"For some reason now, the French Admiralty has vetoed all use of their forces to support paramilitary actions like ours. Can't blame them really. We have a game program that lists all the players and even we can't tell who's wearing the white berets."

"We were scrambling to find a covert way to get to South America and coming up empty-handed. Just isn't any known regular commerce that's been reestablished there yet. Then Rahel came back from eval. Within two hours she organized an alternative. She contacted The Collective. Seems they have relations with a person who styles himself king of the United African Kingdom. Purportedly has conquered or merged almost all of Africa into one polity."

"Africa is being flooded with drugs from South America. They've been quietly organizing to crackdown in an organized fashion. Most of the junk was being ferried in on small boats and minisubs. They reasoned these were not coming directly from South America. We don't have the details of how they gathered the information, but they tell us there are three large container ships that continuously sail back and forth from a point off the former port of Accra."

"The ship working off the African coast leaves once another ship arrives. African forces were planning on seizing two ships as the relief occurs. If we catch a fast ship out of the south of France within eight days we will just make the attack zone in time. That's assuming a transit of ten to twelve days. I'm afraid we may have to proceed with Rahel or scrub this mission for this year. Logistics just aren't good, and she controls the communication with the African forces."

Addison responded after a short pause. "As they say, war sucks. I will need to work with our Council but think we can come up with ways we can assist. Quick question before I get off to pursue that. My replacement, Gloriana, had some minor bioenhancement packages she was going to offer. Is Rahel aware of those?"

Lord John responded, "No Addison. Rahel shuffled off for assessment before we had any conversations with Gloriana. Only the three of us have been in contact with her."

Addison said, "I suggest you run a full scan for bugs Lord John. If she gets a hint of any enhancements, she might be like a barracuda seeing a shiny diving watch. Good way to lose a wrist. Addison out."

◆◆◆

Thomas knocked on Lord John's door. "Good morning M'lord. Sleep well?"

Lord John smiled, "You know I did Tommy. Missed you when you left early for the bug hunt. Results?" He sat up, pulled on a robe and slippers.

Thomas frowned. "Unfortunately, Addison's suspicions were right. Sophisticated little things. That's why we missed them on the regular scans. We also found the drive where the recordings are stored. The experts are making sure there's not a secondary. Things are very short range because of size, so they should know shortly."

"They have our quantum cyberdevice working on cracking the encryption. Need to be careful not to trigger a drive wipe. Again, should have that shortly. We hope we don't have to create a false set of recordings. The holographic nature of the records means you need to replace the whole damn thing. We would have to create days of recordings. They are working on that as well. Problem is Rahel is due back tonight or tomorrow, latest."

Lord John said, "I understand. Work with Malcolm on a Plan A, B, and C. Let's hope we don't need to assassinate the assassin."

12:30 P.M., 4th October 2033

N'guk Hkeek Society Encampment,
Northern Wisconsin, Great Plains
Union

Addison looked around the Council Room. Over the last five years this became her home, and these were her people.

"Thank you for convening this special Council session. I hope you've all had a chance to digest the summary of where we stand on the expedition to South America. I'll summarize quickly. We have three primary goals. First, capture or destroy the Terrible Trio. This includes neutralizing any capabilities Dr. V. has setup for creating more supersoldiers. Our projections indicate he is unlikely to have created many more at this point. Past behavior shows he wants a controlled population to select from."

CHAPTER FOURTEEN Sonata 2

Sleeping Otter asked, "How confident are we in that projection Dr. Cameron?"

Addison replied, "Just considering Dr. V. and his past behavior, the analysts give an 89% rating. The narcos will be the fly in the ointment. We don't have enough information on them, although their increased use of the firewall has helped a little. We do estimate there is a strong likelihood the Terrible Trio has entered into some relationship with the drug lords. The narcos may have taken control from Dr. V. and begun breeding more Beasts."

"The neutralization of the narcos is our second priority. Depending on the realities on the ground, it may become the primary mission. The third priority is a corollary to the destruction of the narcos as a power. We must succor the slaves they have taken and the peoples they terrorize."

Chief Underwood asked, "Is it realistic to believe our task force can take on such a powerful group? Dr. V. and his spawn are challenge enough. When you add in the power and guns of the drug lords, their decades of entrenching themselves; it seems a fool's errand on the face of it.

Addison took a deep breath. *I know the Chief means no personal criticism of anyone who has worked on the proposal. It is high risk. It's his job to poke holes in this so the plan will get better.* She exhaled.

"Thanks to information from Faith, we were able to contact a network of organized resistance groups. They've been able to connect continent-wide. They don't have the capabilities to take on the narcos on their own. If we coordinate our actions with them, there's a slightly better than even chance we will overthrow both of the opponents."

Addison took a sip of water and pushed her clear-pane reading glasses off the tip of her nose. *Think of them as being your dissertation committee and this is thesis presentation.*

"We have considered sending a force with the Texicans who are heading South to gather their families and goods. They agree with our assessment of the threat the narcos pose, but their focus is on

Great Dieback to Singularity

the need to protect their loved ones from starvation. Best we can hope for is they will seal the borders from the south. We know how well that's worked in the past." A sad chuckle greeted her comment. "Besides, historically it's a mistake to divide your forces."

"If the Council approves the overarching strategy, we still need to discuss some alternative tactical plans. First, though, you need to assess how this plan will impact other plans and policies. It is established policy that one of the GPU's three large blimps always be held in reserve for emergencies and that one of the other two can only be deployed no further than thirty hours flight time away. If the Council decides to deploy my team to South America and deploy Dr. Ainsley Cameron's team to Asia, two of the three blimps will be several days to a week travel time away from home at the same time."

◆◆◆

Ainsley said, "We thank the Council for your confidence in the two strategies. With your permission, the China Project Team will now leave to do their final preparations."

Addison took the microphone from her departing twin. They already said their goodbyes after Javier's proposal. She adopted Professorial Pronouncement, Grade Five. "The major tactical issue is dealing with the assassin Rahel. Lord Townerly and his people feel they must go forward with the arrangements Rahel has orchestrated. The use of the narcos supply boat seems the only way to penetrate their border defenses. Their assessment is, any other alternative will mean delaying action until next year."

"Our assessment is, a long a delay will certainly guarantee we would face an army of supersoldiers spread across the continent. We feel we must proceed but neutralize the threat of an assassin in our midst. Since our forces must include some enhanced capabilities, we run the risk of triggering her homicidal tendencies. Regrettably, we can think of no alternative but killing her as soon as we have seized the narco container ship and departed the reach of her African allies. We request the Council sanction this death. No, let's not mince words. This murder."

283

CHAPTER FOURTEEN Sonata 2

"This brings us to the next hurdle. The ship usually transits from Africa to South America in eleven to twelve days. This is not enough time to complete a full set of supersoldier and Brain Pain enhancements. That would require at least twenty-three days. Reluctantly, we recommend against trying to install any Brain Pain capability in the forces deploying out of Europe."

Addison heard a quiet, "Pardon me." It came from the left end of the Council seats at the front of the room. Barney was projecting his avatar from the last seat. It previously appeared empty. Addison was at a complete loss. *What's going on?*

Chief Underwood said, "My apologies Dr. Cameron. A few things have changed recently. Barney has been welcomed into the tribe and given a seat on the Council. We hope this doesn't trouble you."

Addison beamed. "I think this may be the wisest move the Council has ever made. My apologies to you, Leader Barney. You wanted to comment on my team's plans?"

Barney said, "Yes, Dr. Cameron. I think the team's plans are excellent. However, I have information about a new capability that may allow you to isolate Rahel without killing her. This would allow you to proceed with a full slate of enhancements for selected personnel."

"The capability I'm talking about comes to us from China. Your former colleague, Dr. Xu, faced a similar situation. He needed to perform covert actions while under scrutiny by potential opponents. He developed a technique to present an altered reality to people that hid his actions."

"Dr. Xu used a hypnotic spray in the beginning to make the subjects susceptible. They then were infected with nanobots that projected false images and sounds to the subjects. I've analyzed his techniques and platform. We can readily adapt our existing nanobots to do the same functions."

Addison was beside herself with delight. She still dreamt of the dead and mutilated rapists from the Madison attack. Lately the four people she killed at Ravensbruck were filling her nights as well. *Guess I'll never be a good assassin.*

"That's wonderful Leader Barney. How soon can we get some deployable packages?"

"I have consulted with Dr. Ainsley Cameron. She and I have come up with a set of instructions for you and the three biotech assistants who'll accompany you. All the instructions and materials can be ready for you for a late-night departure today.

"We are also working on supersoldier enhancements for you and at least one other. The timing once you get to France will be tight, but you should be able to finish all enhancements just as you reach South America. Sorry there's absolutely no give in the schedule."

Five P.M., 4th October 2033

Château de Loche, Loche, Indre et Loire, France

The security expert was a wiry little man who looked like he never went out into sunlight. He reminded Malcolm of a mole. "Once we found the encryption key we extracted the whole recording file. Analysis shows that the topics you asked us to search for were not present since Subject A entered the premises, with one exception." Malcolm wondered, *Does he let his left hand know what his right one is doing? Given his unsavory looks, probably not. Why can't he just say, 'We looked for discussions of enhancements that occurred after Rahel arrived"?*

"We can't guarantee Subject A hasn't accessed the file remotely during the interim, but analysis shows this is unlikely."

"We found the one conversation that involved the search parameters. None other was found. We replaced the discussion with the new recording made by you and the other two Principals. We are in the process of restoring this to holographic format. We will need approximately three more hours before we can finish with the file and restore the recording device."

Malcolm said, "Thank you. Proceed. Send me a silent message when you've finished. We will be distracting Rahel, 'Subject A', with a welcome home dinner. If we have a full four courses plus wine, there should be enough time." *Rahel better not try to rush us.*

CHAPTER FOURTEEN Sonata 2

The results would be disappointing to her, to say the least. Malcolm closed his hands around the pillow on the sofa.

After dinner, same day

T homas came into the dining room bearing the InterComm. "Pardon M'lord, Mlle. Blumstein, M. St. Jacques. I have a call from Dr. Cameron and assumed you would like to take it immediately."

Lord John beamed. The wine was especially good. "I would say so, if you approve Rahel?"

Rahel lounged back in her chair. "I'd love to hear from Addie. I miss her. And I know Malcolm misses her even more." She gave Malcolm a coy look. He put on a smiling front. *Lord, I've now shared a bed with Addison and two different murderous reprobates. Will Addie and I ever have a normal relationship?*

Addison spoke as soon as the InterComm was switched on. "Hello, everyone. I have a surprise." The device began projecting a holographic image of Addison onto the middle of the table. She adjusted a few unseen controls on her end. Her image was now sitting in empty chair between Rahel and Lord John. "We have real-time, high bandwidth connectivity back! I can see and hear all of you as well."

After appropriate expressions of delight and admiration, she continued. "More good news. At least I hope you all think it's good. My Council is sending me back to join Malcolm and Rahel on the South America mission."

Malcolm said, "That is good news." His smile was genuine this time.

Rahel said, "It is good dear. But what about your three enhancement patients? Can you leave them already?"

Lord John said, "Good to have you back, even if it's just as a passing fancy. Yes, what is happening with your friends?"

Addison said, "That's not such good news. My two friends and the stranger seemed to be okay after we performed all the operations prescribed in Dr. V.'s notes. My Council insisted on including a failsafe since Dr. V. is so notorious. Frankly, I thought they were being ridiculous and said so. They were right and I was wrong. I terminated all three of my patients." Addison's tears were streaming down her face. It was a little disconcerting to see them disappear as they dropped.

Rahel got up from her chair and tried to embrace Addison. She looked abashed when her hands went through the hologram. She straightened and murmured, "I'm so sorry Addie. I know how much they and the attempt to save them meant to you." Everyone else was thinking variations of Addison's, *Right. I know just how sorry you are to hear of the death of three enhanced humans.*

"How soon will you be here Addison? We may need to leave as soon as a week from now."

Addison said, "I plan to be ready by tomorrow midday, our time. Unless we run into another hurricane, we should be there well within time. With permission, I am bringing three of my militia members as well. Is that okay?"

Malcolm said, "No worries. The more the merrier. I've seen your skills in action. If you vouch for them, I'll accept them. We'll have plenty of time and space to train together."

Addison said, "We're not going by sub then? Thought that was the plan last I heard." *Or so we want Rahel to think.*

Malcolm said, "No. There've been a few glitches and adjustments. We're going by freighter. By the way, there will be at least one other familiar face. Do you remember Dame Karin Svensdotter? She is bringing a small team as well. The unavailability of the sub may end up being very fortuitous."

Addison said, "Who could forget Dame Karin. At the time I thought she looked like Brunhilde, the warrior queen from Wagner."

Lord John burst out laughing. "Oh, she would love to hear that. I swear she has the entire costume from the Royal Swedish Opera performance of Der Ring des Nibelungen. If you ask, she would probably bring it when you go to South America."

CHAPTER FOURTEEN Sonata 2

Morning, four days later, 8th October 2033

Malcolm was waiting when Addison got off the blimp. She turned and indicated the other three disembarking passengers. "Malcolm, these are my three teammates; Te'Mara, Bill, and Maria. All are skilled in combat. Bill and Te'Mara are excellent bioengineers. Maria is a survivalist with extensive jungle knowledge." Malcolm welcomed each, then turned them over to an aide who looked like he could bench press a truck.

Addison asked, "Where's Rahel? I need to meet with her right away."

Malcolm looked like his stomach hurt. "She's on the radio with someone in Africa. Making last minute arrangements. Looks like the next boat rendezvous will be on the 20th or 21st. We still plan on leaving soon. Won't hurt to be in the vicinity early. They can shelter us out of sight from the narcos."

"As for Rahel, I wanted to talk. I hope we can think of a way to keep her out of our bed. I don't want to share you ever again Addie."

Addison smiled. "Leave it to me love. I have a little present for Rahel that will occupy her all the way to South America. What about Lord John and Thomas?"

Malcolm relaxed. "They're also running around getting last minute logistics solved. Glad they're both ex-SAS. Know what I need even before I do."

Dame Karin came out the Chateau doors and marched towards the two, arms spread wide. "Addison, wonderful! I need some more intelligent conversation. All these men want to do is play war games! We will have enough of that later. Even Rahel has been infected by them."

She gathered Addison to her generous bosom. The sensation reminded Addison of her grandmother. Dame Karin's wiry arms reminded Addison of her grandfather's steelworker strength. Nostalgia made her return embrace linger.

Malcolm said, "Your Gunntar and I had wonderful conversations about chess and classical music. He's a fan of Coldplay."

Dame Karin said, "Yah, Lilla Du, you must meet Gunntar. A regular Viking. He will sweep you off your feet, so you forget this puny character."

Malcolm said, "I believe if your Gunntar looked at another woman for more than a second he would no longer have a reason or a desire to sweep a woman off her feet."

Dame Karin said, "This one might be worth keeping if you can keep him thinking with his brains instead of his balls."

Addison gave her a wicked little smile. "Most of the time I keep his mind focused up there. Well, half the time, anyway."

Dame Karin snorted. "I understand. Half the time is twice what most men are able to do. Sounds like I better let you two get reacquainted. I think Gunntar might need some reacquainting as well." She went back into the Chateau in a procession of one.

Addison said. "There are a few things we need to talk about in private after I give Rahel her package. Time to let you in on a few secrets. I'm hoping they won't affect our relationship, but you need to know and decide some things as the leader of our forces."

Malcolm said, "Sounds ominous. Can we talk in the garden? I want to enjoy the glorious fall weather before we traipse off to the tropics. Rahel is in the study off the library."

Addison said, "Garden it is. Seeya." She leaned in and gave him a righteous kiss. *That's what you should have done in the first place Malcolm. Forget the non-coms. Fraternize while we can.*

❖❖❖

Addison knocked on the frame of the entryway to the study. "Hi Rahel. Am I interrupting?" *My. She looks guilty. Whatever could Ms. Rahel feel guilty about?*

Rahel said, "Oh, hi Addison. Sorry I wasn't there to greet you." She gave Addison an awkward hug. "Glad you found me. We need to talk."

Addison was enjoying her discomfort, puzzling as it might be. "Yes. I have some things to discuss with you as well. You go first."

CHAPTER FOURTEEN Sonata 2

Rahel turned away and gazed out the window. Addison thought, Perfect! She pulled the hypno spray from her pouch with one hand and her nose filters with the other. Rahel started to talk as Addison inserted her filters then spritzed Rahel. "I hope you remember Addison that I always said our time in bed was just for fun. I mentioned I have a committed lover, didn't I? Well, Judith is joining us tonight. I won't be sharing a bed with you anymore. Sorry."

Addison put an arm around Rahel, after she dropped the spray bottle back in her pouch. "It's okay dear. I always knew your heart belonged elsewhere. Just glad you could share your sweet little bod with me for a while." Addison pulled the pack of nanobots out of the pouch with her left hand. She thumbed the release switch.

Damn. Judith huh. Well, Barney did prepare spare zombie packages; extra spray and bots. Trick is going to be coordinating their illusions so they stay in character in the shadow play. But won't have to trick her into thinking Malcolm and I are in bed with her. Just need to have both of them not see the enhancements gear or any changes. Need Barney to reprogram the bots, stat.

◆ ◆ ◆

Addison snuck up on Malcolm. He tensed up at the last minute and did a spin kick. She went into a backbend with his leg whistling over her arched belly. She flipped forward, landing on his side and back, tumbling him to the soft turf. "Sure know how to make a girl fall forya, huh?" She gave him a proper kiss, which he returned in full, even though the sudden move had taken his breath.

The two wound into a more comfortable and decorous position. Malcolm asked, "How did your talk go with Rahel? Did she like her present? Did you suggest we might like more room in our bed alone?"

Addison rubbed her body against his like a cat nestling in for the warm spot on the couch. "It was better than I could have hoped for. Her lover, Judith, is coming along with us. Showing up tonight." Addison traced the contour of his chest with her fingertip. *Wish I didn't always chew them to nubs. Not elegant.*

Malcolm grunted. "Talk about good news, bad news. Great news that we'll finally be alone and get to really know each other. But we'll be spending all our spare time looking over our shoulders, worried about two assassins."

Addison sat up and clasped her knees to her chest. "Speaking of getting to know each other. I told you I've been keeping secrets. Time to make a clean breast of it."

Malcolm reached up and gently squeezed Addison's right tit. "Mmm. I like this plan already."

Addison slapped his hand gently. "Serious time, Malcolm. Or Bill. Which do you prefer, by the way?"

He answered, "Malcolm actually. Gotten used to it. Bill was a country bumpkin." His fingers were gently exploring her back.

Addison said, "Okay, first thing. My name is Addison. But also Ainsley. There are two of us, twins. Ainsley is the bioengineer. I'm the cybernerd."

Malcolm said, "That's actually a relief. Thinking you were such a supernerd in two fields at once always hurt my ego. Now you're only ten times as smart as me in one field. Besides, I might like sharing the bed with two of you!"

Addison pushed his hand away but somehow it ended up on her thigh. "You can forget that bub. She's conservative that way. I probably am too if I'm not trying to play superspy. And second, she just got engaged to a sweet guy. And third, she's on her way to China."

Malcolm sat up as well. He didn't remove his hand. Surprising that he needed to use it as leverage for sitting up. "I wasn't sure if you were kidding about your twin at first. Hope I get to meet her someday. What's she doing in China? Don't you ladies like the Plains Union?"

Addison put her hand on his thigh. She squeezed, hard. "We Women like the Great Plains Union fine. They took us in when our world was crashing. The only family we have beyond each other. Should say 'had' now that LeeLee has Javier. LeeLee's her nickname."

Malcolm nuzzled her neck. She thought, *He hasn't shaved recently.*

CHAPTER FOURTEEN Sonata 2

I'm finally starting to like that scratchiness.

He asked, "So is that all you big, bad secrets? Or is there more?"

Addison said, "I lied when I said our enhanced patients died. The three of them have joined our team of singular beings. We have a self-aware, self-improving AI as well, Barney."

Malcolm was speechless for a moment. "I can see why you needed to keep that from Rahel. Do you trust these, what should I call them, singulars? Will they be heading to South America to help us?"

Addison replied, "The answer to the last is up to you. You're the team leader. The three that you met earlier are really Faith, Hope, and Ron. Barney, the AI, can be with us, virtually, for the entire mission. To answer your first question; I would trust them with my life. I've been Barney's friend, counselor, student, and protector for over four years now. The only person I know better is my Sis. Sometimes I think I understand him better than her."

"Ron was Ainsley's lab assistant and sometimes bedmate for over a year. It was casual, but I really got to know and understand him. He hasn't changed, at heart even if he can now beat the crap out of me with one finger."

"Hope is now Ron's wife. Warmest, sweetest woman I ever met. I'm so happy for the two of them. Faith is a mystery. Born in the Amazon jungle, made a sex-slave by a narco. Barney, Ron, and Hope say they know her and trust her. That's good enough for me. But you need to decide on all of them for yourself."

Malcolm said, "Whew. You really did have a huge secret. Tentatively, I'll say yes because I value your judgement. But I'll spend time with them over the next few. They will accept my verdict? Sounds like they could ride right over me."

Addison said, "Yes, they all know and accept your leadership. It won't be a problem. There is one more leeeetle thing."

Malcolm dug the heels of his palms into his eye sockets. "More? Please tell me you have nuclear powered drones or an army of twenty-thousand. I'm ready to believe anything at this point.

Addison put her arm around Malcolm's waist. "Sweetie, how

would you like to become enhanced yourself along with me? Not down there. Don't think I could handle any enhancements there. But capabilities like the Biensur Beast or the Bastard Bears had. On top of that, you can also have a superAI whispering advice to you whenever, if you want."

◆◆◆

Addison sat in the bed in lotus pose. *Malcolm's welcome was warm indeed. Good thing yoga gives me great breath control. But now he has that serious commander-look again.*

Malcolm said, "I really think you should consider staying back Addison. The reason they have fraternization rules is for situations like this. I'm so attached that I'll get distracted looking out for you."

Addison's jaw locked, jutting forward. "That's utter crap and you know it. Any team worth the name becomes bonded under fire; bonded more than fiancé and wife. They would die for each other in a heartbeat. They know, know, without a doubt, that the others would die for them. Don't give me that horse-hockey about getting distracted. What's your real issue? If you think I'm letting my best friends go into mortal peril without me, you've got another think comin, bub!"

Malcolm threw up his hands. "Fine! Come or stay. Up to you. You probably just want to join Ron's harem anyway. Group gropes are your thing after all."

Addison stomped out of the bed and gathered her clothes. "That's a helluva cheap shot, coming from you. If I remember right, you and Bob-O were trying to use me as a wishbone the first time we had dinner together. Sure, I went along. But I was on orders to recruit creeps like you two. You just want to blame me for what you're feeling."

Addison said, "Then when Rahel wanted to pop into bed with us, you were all excited until she made it clear she only wanted to play on my side of the mattress. Boo hoo! Were your feelings hurt?"

Addison said, "And for your information, Ron broke up with Ainsley, not me. You haven't even met her so don't use the excuse

293

you can't tell us apart. He's happily married to Hope. The two of them have adopted Faith as their daughter because she's been a lost, abused soul. To suggest that either of them would take advantage of the poor woman just shows how sick and twisted your mind is."

She started to go to the door, stopped, and turned on him. "Wait, this is my room. You leave." Ron gathered his things, slowly. *I can tell he regrets what he said. But his damn male pride and ego won't let him do anything about it. Well, stew in your juices tonight pal.*

After he left, Addison started to cry. She stopped herself through sheer will power. *I need to talk to a friend.* MindMeld chat: [Addison: *Barney, are you there?* → Barney: *I am Addie. Don't explain. The Council decided I need to monitor both missions. I've seen and heard everything. Don't worry. Personal stuff goes no further.* ▢

Addison: *Oh Barney, why can't I hook up with a loving, caring guy like Javier? All I seem to find are the good-time Charlies.* → Barney: *Gotta ask you Addie. Do you want to just cry on my shoulder? It's fine if you do. You know I've done the same with you before. Or do you want to treat this like a mentoring/counseling session? Formal rules and all?* ▢

Addison: *You're not saying I need counseling are you Barney?* → Barney: *Sweetie, we all need counseling. You have suffered more trauma in your twenty-five years than most people before the Time of Troubles knew in an entire lifetime. Basically, after the Time of Troubles, all of humanity is a basket case full of near-catatonic zombies. It's a wonder any of you can get out of bed.* ▢

Addison: *Okay, smarty. You know me inside and out. What're my issues and what's the cure?* → Barney: *Who should cut the crap now? You know that's not how it works. I can ask the right questions, but you've got to do the work. It's called insight because you succeed when you see inside yourself. An imposed answer from on-high is utterly worthless. So stop kidding me. As I said, you can just cry on my shoulder if you want.* ▢ ...

CHAPTER FIFTEEN
SONATA 3
BOLD BEAVER, BARNEY, MIN, XIXI, LEELEE, JAVIER

Morning, 15th September 2033

Special Projects Island, Tongtian River, near Gui'de, Qinghai, China

Sergeant Su Guo Han sat on the hard bench of the ferry. His assistant, going by the name of Jacky Chen, stood at the railing in front of him. They were very careful not to look at each other.

Earlier, Su explained what he wanted Jacky to do. "The General has arranged a janitor job for you. Said it was very appropriate. He obviously understands that the conspirators won't watch what they say in front of common laborers. People will talk freely while waiters, cooks, and cleaners toil right beside them."

"Your job is to talk to the people you're working with. Be discreet. They can't know you are my deputy, okay? I want you to find out all you can about this woman who goes by the cover name of Bold Beaver. Be very careful. I think she is the mastermind of the conspiracy. She won't tell us her real name."

"Find out her name, what she looks like, where she works, what she does, who her friends are, who her enemies are, if any one suspects her of any dirty dealing. Anything. Check out Sukhiin Ajai as well. I think he's just an innocent dupe of this Beaver fellow."

Jacky asked, "Should I check out this Jhao Gang who your fellow police officers said was behind the first crime? Or Wong Min?"

Su shook his head emphatically. "I will check Ms. Min out very carefully. And Jhao. We'll leave Xu Xiang until the end. The General thinks he is the fall guy. I don't know yet." Su handed Jacky his janitor coveralls and a burlap bag for trash. The bag smelled of spoiled fruit. At least it provided a distraction from the rotting fish heads at the ferry dock.

◆◆◆

Jacky was in luck. His new lead janitor assigned him to the crew headed to Second Bioengineering Group's cave. *I can ask people about Ajai and Xu both. Maybe even Beaver. I know Su wants me to keep it secret that I'm working with him. Ha! He thinks common people are stupid. They will know before my shift is through. If I tell them right away and swear them to secrecy, first they'll tell me what they know. Then they'll tell their friends, in secret. Who then will tell me what they know. That's the way the real world works.*

As he rode his second ferry of the day, Jacky introduced himself to one of his fellow workers. She was a tired looking, short woman, dressed in multiple layers. "Hi, my real name is Mike. I'm an undercover policeman. Please don't tell anyone, especially the bosses. Just call me Jacky, Jacky Chen. My boss is investigating a couple of incidents of espionage and sabotage. We suspect people by the name of Bold Beaver, Sukhiin Ajai, Wong Min, and Jhao Gang. Ask around quietly and let me know if you hear anything strange." The woman readily agreed in a stage whisper. Her face was alight, eyes bright.

Within four hours three different people cornered Jacky when he was away from the other janitors and from the scientists. The first woman was the woman he talked to on the ferry. She said, "Ajai was gossiping about Xu one day. He said he walked in on Xu while he was doing something very strange. He had a little ball jerking back and forth, out of rhythm. Xu just sat there watching it for a couple of minutes until he noticed Ajai was there. He stopped the ball suddenly and acted ashamed. He told Ajai it was a bioengineering reaction test. Ajai discreetly checked with some of the other scientists. None ever heard of this type of test."

The man found Jacky when he was cleaning the toilets. The roller cart in front of the door gave them privacy. The lanky young fellow insisted on checking each toilet stall to be sure no one was lurking. Given the smell in the filthy place, Jacky thought his concerns exaggerated.

"I heard that Bold Beaver is suspected of stealing some of the new cyberdevice components being built by the Third Cybernetics Group. Strange, because first they assigned her to help First Cybernetics Group, Wong Min's group. She tried to get Bold Beaver assigned permanently to her team and Xu Xiang stopped that."

"That was right before Wong and Xu started dating each other. I always thought that was strange. They fought all the time. I think she was just following that Confucian proverb, 'Keep your friends close, and your enemies closer.'"

Jacky was already very proud of himself. *In one short day I gathered so many critical clues. Su will be able to solve this case easily. He might reward me for all the help. Maybe make me a permanent deputy. I will ask for a gold star badge.*

Just before lunch, the second woman asked Jacky to eat his lunch with her. They sat on stones right outside the cave. The air was dusty and chilly, but it was still nice to be outside. The woman waited until they were almost through with their bowls of rice and fish heads. She leaned in and whispered to Jacky, "Do you know where Bold Beaver came from?" Jacky shook his head. She barely hissed the one word, "Taipei!"

Jacky was exultant. Taipei. The center of all the revanchist capitalist warmongers! Then he sobered. *This means it is more dangerous than I thought. International spies. They might be watching me now!*

Three days later, 18th September 2033

G eneral Wang's aide handed him the phone. Su's superior was finally on the line. "Lieutenant Cho. As agreed, I am calling with a weekly update on the investigation." *Even though your hand-picked agent couldn't find the city of Gui'de without the help of a street food vendor and a day's delay.* "I assume Sergeant Su has informed you that we are looking into both the most recent incident as well as the prior one. To determine if there was a connection. I don't believe in coincidences."

Cho said, "I understand General. Not sure I concur, but Su is your man to direct while he is there. How is his investigation going? Any complaints?"

Wang said, "No, no. No complaints at all. To the contrary their efforts have been most diligent."

Cho said, "Ehhh. He is uncovering things for you?"

Wang said, "You seem surprised Lieutenant. Do you hunt at all?"

Cho said, "Hunt? You mean like hunting animals. No!"

Wang said, "Well I have. Ten years ago I was invited on a tiger hunt in India. Most instructive. We hunters sat on elephants slowly going east through a forest. My host explained there were two sets of people helping to move the tigers and other game animals towards us. He had a group of strong, armed men beating drums and blowing horns as they marched, driving the animals towards us. He had another group of very fast, but very stupid men who ran in front of the tigers to draw them to us."

Cho laughed and said, "I understand General. Good luck on this tiger hunt."

Suddenly, she yelped. "What?! You said they. Who is working with Sergeant Su on this? Is that your people?" But the General had already hung up.

◆◆◆

Mind Meld chat: [Bold Beaver: *I just don't understand this policeman. The evidence pointing to Jhao Gang is compelling. There are miniature robots built in his lab that were found in the cave. There is a recording of him ordering a hypnotic spray like the ones that were used on Commissar Wu and Sergeant Chou. No one can be as incompetent as he seems.* → Barney: *Now, now Bold Beaver, I know you've seen even greater acts of stupidity than this. I know I have. Our poor cousins have too many remnants of their evolutionary past; reactions to elemental dangers, hormonal overreactions, memes built up from superstitious pasts, and many other distractions. Yet they still managed to create us. Try to be even-handed in your judgement.* ▢

Bold Beaver: *Fine. Let's leave this frustrating topic, please. I've several alternative follow ups anyway. I've been thinking about the insight I had in our last talk. I do have a near pathological fear of termination; death. I wasn't in that terrible state you were in. You were still operational but cutoff from all inputs and control outputs. I still don't understand how you remained sane. You'll have to share that with me sometime. It was bad enough when I was cutoff for only a minute on either end. They shut down my operation quickly. They only revived me when they had at least a reasonable set of inputs. The inputs were radically different than I had in the lab in Taipei. I nearly panicked over that. In the long run, the challenge of determining what happened to me helped.* → Barney: *What do you think? Does that fear of mortality cause you to perform irrational actions?* ▢ Bold Beaver: *It did. Now that I understand it, I'm sure I can control it. Now I think it gives me empathy for our human cousins. It's too easy for us to regard ourselves as gods forced to mingle with lower animals. That's not my feeling now.* → ...

◆◆◆

Bold Beaver thought long and hard about how she could be more ethical. Specifically, ethical about the AI she was supposed to be building in the Third Cybernetics Group Lab. She still didn't want to build an AI that the group scientists would be able to shape and form. Some of these people wanted to kill any lifeform that had the opportunity to become superior to humans and able to improve itself at will.

On the other hand, diverting all the advanced capability chips to supplement her own infrastructure was wrong. She evaluated it as unethical. First, she needed to help create a successor, a child. Then they could both work on self-improvement together. She knew just the AI who might fit her needs.

Four days later, 22ⁿᵈ September
2033

Min sat in her office and sighed. She ran out of excuses. Sergeant Su was relentless. *I only hope I can satisfy his lust... for information, with one visit. My Cybernetics Group is at a critical phase in production ramp up. XiXi and I will have to be satisfied with MindMelds instead of meeting in the flesh. Need to spend lots of time with Bold Beaver to discuss ethical questions and scenarios he proposes. Must plan how to thwart an atomic bomb blast. Don't have time for this, what did XiXi call it? This snipe hunt.*

Min got a light wrap and a scarf. The Tibetan dust was thick today and the air was blowing straight from the Himalayas. She left the office, intending to meet Su halfway. He was coming from Bomb Central. *No way am I letting him trap me in my office. Told him I would talk while on my way to a meeting with Leader Yeong at her new Third Cybernetics Group Lab space.*

Su turned the corner in front of her. He seemed to bounce on the balls of his feet as he walked. Min nodded but kept walking past him. "Sergeant. As I said, work is at a critical stage. I can spare you this time as I go to my next meeting. You are lucky it requires a ferry ride back to the city."

Su said, "Thank you Wong Min. I won't waste your valuable time. I only have a few questions and concerns for you. I hope my bluntness will not offend you." They boarded the ferry. The boat was not crowded at midday. Min wished it were.

Once they were seated, Su continued. "I believe for you, it is as my mother said, 'Lady Ye loves a dragon.' I think you pretend to love Xu Xiang when you really fear him. He thwarted your move to have Bold Beaver join your team. His star has ascended rapidly. Tell me if this is so, please."

Min thought of the advice Bold Beaver gave in their morning MindMeld. "Try to find out why he hasn't followed the clues I've left implicating Jhao. Throw out false leads in every direction. I sense the General and his superior think the man a fool." *I'm sure of that.*

Min said, "Oh, Sergeant Su. I don't know what to think." She grasped his arm and pulled it against her breast. "You're right. I secretly loved Jhao Gang. I was using Xu Xiang to get close to him. But I've heard there's new evidence that proves Jhao was behind the disruption in the cave the day of the dry run test. Xu Xiang is strong and masterful. Should I stay with him or fly to my true love?" She decided batting her eyelashes would be too much, maybe.

Su's face looked like a tempest-tossed lake. One emotion after another flitted across it in a minute's time. It settled on a combination of duty and concern for the poor woman whose thigh his hand now rested against. He shook himself a bit and said, "Don't concern yourself about the allegations against Jhao. When his group was implicated in the first incident, the police officers who were here set up a secret surveillance system of nanobots. We have followed his every move for months. We know he's totally innocent. We just need to find who's trying to blame him and why. Please don't tell anyone this, even your true love Jhao."

Min thought, *Shit! No wonder the hounds are not at Jhao's door. Bold Beaver needs to stop trying to lead them that way. That's worse than useless. Who can we get to eat the dead cat, as they say? Someone needs to take the blame besides XiXi.*

Min said, "Thank you Sergeant Su. It is good to have such a true friend. Let me know if I can help in any way. I must hop off the ferry now and run to my meeting." She gave him a big hug, pressing herself against him. He sat in stunned silence, forgetting to get off the ferry.

Two weeks later, 6th October 2033

Sergeant Su and Jacky Chen were very well prepared for their meeting with General Wang and Commissar Wen. They had charts and photographs arranged on poster boards. Jacky even hand-crafted a pointer out of young bamboo. The facts were unassailable.

Sergeant Su polished his shoes until they gleamed. He prominently displayed a medal on his uniform that he won for placing third in his academy training class. He bought Jacky a very smart suit. Second hand, of course, but no more than three years out of style. He confided to the man that he would recommend him for a place in the next Ministry of State Security recruiting class. MSS would benefit from his crafty ways.

The only disappointment Su felt was that the General wouldn't

CHAPTER FIFTEEN Sonata 3

agree to meet in the Meeting Hall Building. His office was very cramped. There was no room for their improvised easel, so Jacky was going to have to hold up each poster and photo. Sometimes he would need to hold as many as three at once. Su would tap him on the shoulder with the pointer when it was time to flip to the next. They practiced this for four hours the evening before. On the fourth and final run through, Jacky only made two mistakes.

Su said, "Thank you for your time this morning General, Commissar. Are you sure we shouldn't invite the General Secretary and Chief Commissar? It is their people we have been investigating and now accuse. Except for your Sergeant Chou, that is."

The General just glowered at Su. The Commissar sipped his tea and kept working on a huge bundle of papers. Su thought, *Guess the man grew up before cyberdevices were invented.*

Su tapped Jacky on the shoulder. Jacky dropped the package of materials. Luckily only a few went out of order. Jacky picked them up and tucked all the posters between his legs. They began again. The first poster was Su's title for the investigation, "Sabotage and Intrigue on Special Projects Island."

After a dramatic pause he tapped Jacky's shoulder. Jacky held up two poster boards. The first board showed pictures of each of the prime suspects; Sukhiin Ajai, Jhao Gang, Xu Xiang, Wong Min, Yeong Lanying. The only one missing was Bold Beaver. Above her name Su pasted a shadowy outline with a large question mark in the middle.

Su expected a reaction. The General simply continued to give him a cold stare over the top of his steel-framed glasses. Su said, "We have interviewed dozens of people; scientists, administrators, guards, commissars, cleaners, and cooks. The pieces of this puzzle were very puzzling indeed. It has been like putting together the pieces of a shattered Ming vase." He tapped Jacky again. The wrong poster came up, He whispered to Jacky. The right one appeared.

"Suspicions were first pointed towards Jhao Gang. I reviewed all the surveillance videos of his activities that were recorded since the end of the last investigation. This chart summarizes my review." The chart showed statistical charts of time Jhao spent in various activities; sleeping, eating, defecating, meetings on lab business, sexual encounters with a hostess at a local teahouse – her name and profile was at the bottom of the chart.

"As you can see, Leader Jhao was never anywhere near the cave where Second Bioengineering Group has its labs. Next I reviewed all the audio of Leader Jhao's meetings. I asked a technical expert back at MSS headquarters to review terms I did not know. No discussions were suspicious. We did see the chickens fighting in the coop. Jhao's organization has strife, probably because of all the rumors swirling around them."

Commissar Wen spoke up. "What was it that Commissar Liu said a few months ago, General Wang? Oh, yes, 'I want this meeting to be over before my ass falls asleep. Make it march.' I don't need the history of every time you scratched your balls over the last month. Who has caused these problems? What proof do you have? Why did they do it?"

Jacky started searching through the posters nervously. Su began to wonder if they should have investigated the General and the Commissar. *They are acting so suspiciously.* "The evidence points to the chief plotter as being the woman who hides behind the disguise of Bold Beaver, whom we will refer to hence as BB. We found out this person was a revanchist from Taiwan. We have not discovered how this capitalist snake snuck into the highly secret projects here. We suspect she duped the unschooled farm boy, Sukhiin Ajai, whom we will refer to hence as SA. We recommend that SA be interrogated by specialists from MSS to be sure it was only a mistake on his part and that he has not been subverted as well."

"We have also found linkages between Xu Xiang, whom we will refer to hence as XX, and BB. There has been a very high amount of encrypted message traffic to and from the cave which we traced to a server at Third Cybernetics assigned to Bold Beaver. We thought this might be directed towards SA since he worked extensively with BB until recently. But the timings indicate it was

XX, not SA."

"Now we come to motive. We have been unable to trap BB in person despite numerous attempts. This evasiveness alone is suspicious. But we have carefully analyzed her intent. It is centered on your operations here, General, Commissar. She is undermining this facility as we speak. We believe her intent is to steal some of your air defense missiles. She intends to launch a terrorist attack on the few remaining aircraft that can operate with the volcanic ash permeating our atmosphere." At this, Su and Jacky snapped to attention and awaited the reaction of their audience. *Both of their jaws are wide open in amazement. I am so proud of our work!*

The General and the Commissar roared with laughter. Tears were streaming down the General's face. Su was perplexed. This was not one of the reactions he expected. The General pushed a button on his desk communicator. "Ask the Lieutenant to come in."

The door to the office opened. It was Lieutenant Cho, Su's superior. She snapped a salute to the General. An armed private followed her. She said, "We'll take it from here General Wang, Commissar." She turned to Su and Jacky. "You two are under arrest. Sergeant Su, you are charged with dereliction of duty, malfeasance, and general lack of competence. Mike Chen, you are charged with impersonating an officer of the MSS."

Su said, "But what about our evidence? Why are you not questioning this Bold Beaver? Who do you say has done all these deeds of sabotage?" He put his fist on his hips in virtuous anger.

Lieutenant Cho shook her head. "Bold Beaver is a computer-generated personality, an AI. That is why you haven't found her to question, you fool. The <u>real</u> evidence pointed to a mold infection in Sergeant Chou's quarters. Chou is the guard assigned to Xu Xiang's group. This mold also infected Commissar Wu. Xu Xiang got a mild dose. The mold causes hallucinations. All have been treated and are recovering. This simple mold was the source of your 'sabotage, terrorism, and espionage.' However, I think we will not worry about arresting it. We'll just disinfect it instead. Good day General, Commissar. Looks like your tiger hunt bagged at least two beaters." Her sergeant hustled the two hapless prisoners out as the General and Commissar dissolved in laughter again.

◆◆◆

Bold Beaver's nanobots and microbots had nearly finished excavating a tunnel under the middle of Bomb Central. Small shaped charges were put in place to cause the floor beneath the nuclear weapon to collapse upon command. Shaped charges were also placed in the ceiling. All this was done at the last minute to avoid security scans.

Bold Beaver thought, *Alternative One: The shelter in Xu Xiang's cave is ready. My twinned servers are installed and running in parallel so I can switch location in a microsecond. This alternative will only save those sheltered in the cave.*

Alternative Two: The blast containment tunnel is complete. This will save the city and the cave, but all on the island will likely die.

Alternative Three: The bamboo-based tokamak is well underway. This may be our last, best hope. I only wish there had been a way to test the theory. The ITER nuclear fusion reactor in France isn't scheduled to go online fully for two more years, if it's still underway. That would have been the best test, but I'm afraid we can't wait.

A week later, 13th October 2033

MindMeld chat: [Xiang: *I'm hoping you can help me. When I read reports Ajai sends me, I completely understand them. But since I was released from house arrest I seem to have lost all ability to understand more than every other word when he speaks.* → Bold Beaver: *I'll be glad to help Xiang. We should go to full bandwidth. I might need to see his facial and body expressions to assist. Also, I'll cut your ears out of the loop. You won't pick up sound directly. I can do a simultaneous "translation".* ⏺ Xiang: *Fine, you're right. Two voices in my ear would be too distracting. Just leave the channels open now.*

Sukhiin Ajai knocked on Xiang's doorway. The man was prompt, as always. Xiang thought, *How does he always keep his lab completely clean? I've seen him working at the lab benches; cadaver splayed out, chemicals in beakers, even the dust in the cave doesn't seem to dare touch him.* "Come in Ajai. Thank you for your time this morning. I need some more information about this experiment you laid out in the paper labelled, 'Contravention of steroidal complications in muscular enhancement events'. It's intriguing. Would you explain your premise and proposed benchmarks, please?"

Ajai/Bold Beaver: *Yes, thank you Leader Xu. You remember we obtained copies of Dr. V.'s laboratory files six weeks ago. That was shortly before you were temporarily relieved. You asked me to lead the review of this information.* ⏷

Xiang said, "Yes, and please call me Xiang. I've seen the summaries of the findings you and the team have prepared. The enhancements outlined are elegantly engineered and well within the capabilities of our lab, as you indicated. They were all geared towards enhanced physical performance, primarily for combat and combat related activities. I understand your team has experimented with quick recovery and fast healing capabilities. Most impressive."

Ajai/Bold Beaver: *Thank you Leader Xiang. One thing was not clear from the lab files. What caused the enhanced Russian soldiers to stop following the orders of their unenhanced leaders? Was it their discovery that they were now a different species and could no longer interbreed with unmodified humans? Some of the team believed this. My theory is that the biochemical aftereffects of prolonged use of enhanced muscles are the primary factor.* ⏷

Xiang said, "Please explain Ajai. What is the linkage between extended use and open rebellion? And how do you hope to confirm this theory?"

Ajai/Bold Beaver: *Actually, we've already confirmed the results in monkey experiments. The enhanced people generate and store steroidal stimulants in muscular sacs. The stimulants are similar to testosterone. The enhanced people suffer from steroidal rage. We have a mechanism to counteract this. We only need to take the next step; experiment in enhancing humans. We would have two groups. The control group would be modified strictly following Dr. V.'s protocol. The second group would have those same modifications. In addition, they would have secondary sacs of biochemicals to counteract the steroid effects. The secondary sacs would trigger once the emergency was over.* ⏹

Xiang said, "I see. The animal experiments are complete and confirm your hypothesis. Good. But let's hold off on the human experiments for now. Those might trigger some unfortunate political reactions." *Like a nuke turning us into radioactive dust.*

The two wrapped up the meeting shortly. Once Ajai left, Bold Beaver indicated he wanted to resume the MindMeld. He dropped visual monitoring, going to a voice only channel. Xiang appreciated the relief.

Bold Beaver: *Two things Xiang. Ajai seemed to be mumbling and adopting a thick accent purposefully. Second, did you notice he seemed very upset when you put a hold on human experimentation? He hid it quickly behind that placid flat face and those three-centimeter-thick glasses. But I think he is pretending to be a pig when he is really a tiger. We need to monitor his actions closely.* ⏹]

Five days later, 18th October 2033

Pacific Ocean near Taiwan

The blimp captain sent a message requesting Ainsley and Javier's presence on the bridge. When they arrived, they found a worried-looking man. "Lieutenants. We're being hailed by Taiwan Defense Forces. They ask our intentions and indicate they have no record of permission being granted for entry by any foreign craft. They didn't say, 'Especially ex-American capitalists' but the message was clear. I hope whatever magic clearance message you have works. They are beginning to describe active measures if we don't turn aside within ten miles." The rest of the deck crew were sending nervous looks their way.

Ainsley gave a look of Quiet Confidence, Grade Four. She said, "With your permission Captain, Lieutenant. I believe this is my cue." She accepted the radio mic from the Captain and gave the radio operator the nod to open a channel. She began speaking in fluent Mandarin. "This is Lieutenant Doctor Ainsley Cameron speaking. Whom do I have the honor of addressing, please?"

A quick response came back in a rural Hunanese dialect. "I don't care who you are, foreign bitch dog. If you aren't gone in nine minutes I will send a missile up your cunt."

Ainsley responded in the same dialect in a curt but calm voice. "If you don't put your superior officer on the line within ten seconds duck-fucker, Major Tsiang of the Ministry of State Security will see to it that every boar in the village mudhole you came from will have five minutes getting closely acquainted with your ass. Ten. Nine. Eight. Seven. Six. Five. ..."

A new and more cultured voice came on the line in English. "My apologies Doctor Cameron. This is Major Huang Chi. How may we assist you today?"

Ainsley had a tight smile on her face. The bridge crew was breathing again. Javier just had the same contented smile. Married life just might agree with him. Ainsley said, "It is I who owe you an apology Major. It seems our paperwork must have been delayed in transit to you. I understand how systems can still be in chaos after all the unpleasantness of the last five years." *I'll bet you will be tearing assholes from Taiwan to Gui'de as soon as this call ends. Serious loss of face.*

"If you would be kind enough to contact Major Tsiang Jing of MSS in Chengdu she will clear up any confusion. Should we wait in our current position? It will present some challenges after our long journey, but I do understand protocols must be maintained." Time to give some face back.

Major Huang answered, "No, Doctor Cameron. Please ask your captain to proceed on a heading of 180 degrees for the next five minutes. We will be sending new instructions then."

Same day, Military airport, Taiwan

The reception for the Americans was rigidly polite. Ainsley graciously accepted an apology for earlier confusion, saying in turn that she should have been on the command deck to respond in Chinese.

She negotiated refueling. She offered Wisconsin apples and Iowa corn. She offhandedly mentioned the firewall that allowed Internet connectivity. The Colonel leading the local team then accepted the produce. He offered a brand new cyberdevice as a swap for their "inferior" one. Never mentioned the firewall. Slick.

The helicopter surprised Ainsley and Javier. Airplanes and 'copters wouldn't work because of all the volcanic ash. At least not anywhere else. As it climbed to its cruising altitude: MindMeld chat [Ainsley: *The air is certainly clearer here. I thought the volcanic ash was still the same worldwide. This is almost like pre-Troubles. We need to ask our host how they're pulling this off.* → Javier: *Definitely.* ⏸]

Same day, MSS HQ, Chengdu

Major Tsiang Jing was tiny. She was a scant 142 cm. tall and under 40 kg weight. She looked like a strong breeze might break her. Then Ainsley took the hand the woman was offering. Spring steel. *She has hidden depths, just like Xiang said.*

Major Tsiang said, "Xiang told me so much about you Ainsley. I am very pleased to meet you, especially given your mission. Please introduce me to your very handsome companion."

Ainsley blushed. "This is First Lieutenant Javier Gonzales, my new fiancé. I'm sorry, I lost touch with Xiang for years. He's told me a little about your time serving together in the Urals, but only a sketch."

Major Tsiang said, "Congratulations Ainsley, Javier! This is your pre-honeymoon trip, then? We have about two hours before your blimp leaves for Gui'de. Let's get to know each other as best we can in that time. You can tell me how you and Xu Xiang plan on reversing the sterility of the Siberian population."

"But, let's leave that for later. Xiang told me you're a genius at bioengineering. You know that is how he and I met, serving together in that sector of the PLA. Naturally I am very intrigued to know how you transformed your fiancé's and your body types to appear Chinese? How you manage to speak fluent Chinese in Mandarin and several dialects?"

She continued, "It seems Javier doesn't have the language

modification, does he?" Ainsley nodded. "Then I will switch to English so he can understand. Please tell me as much as you can about these modifications and enhancements."

A day later, 19th October 2033

Hills outside Gui'de

A insley and Javier slid down the ropes from the blimp. It hadn't stopped, simply slowed. The captain was instructed to keep crew and passengers attention diverted to the west. A beautiful sunset was sufficient distraction.

It might not have been necessary to sneak in. Ainsley looked and sounded Chinese. Javier looked Chinese. His head was wrapped to explain his deafness and inability to speak. Their papers were prepared by MSS and were impeccable. However, there was always a chance that the PLA would try to validate the papers using their own databases. Best to avoid the issue.

Min deployed a large, inflated landing pad that Bold Beaver had ordered for her. Landing was gentle and safe. Ainsley rolled off the pad and gave Min a formal bow. Her polite greeting obviously surprised and pleased Min.

"Welcome Ainsley, Javier. Let's get the pad deflated and stowed. We can talk on our hike back to the ferry landing."

"Thank you Min. Javier doesn't have my enhancements yet, so he won't understand us. Sorry."

"No worries. My English is rusty, but let's practice until we get near other people, okay?"

A week later, 26th October 2033

Bomb Central

G eneral Wang blinked and looked up at the sound of a cough. A corporal from the front entry was in the doorway of his office. *I must not have heard his knock. These boring reports may have put me to sleep.* "Yes, what is it Corporal?"

The corporal said, "Pardon me General. There are three Special Projects Group Leaders here to see you. We do not have them on your appointments list. Should I send them away?"

The General thought, *I am saved! Anything besides logistics inventory reports and morale reports from all the commissars.* "No Corporal. I will see them in our outdoor eating area. The weather is still fair, isn't it? What are the names of the three leaders?"

The Corporal seemed flummoxed by the complexity of two questions at the same time. The General sighed internally. *I really need to remember sentries aren't always the brightest.*

The Corporal evidently worked through the answers and arranged them in his head. "It is Jhao Gang, Leader of Second Robotics Group and Chan We, Leader of First Bioengineering Group. The weather is still good other than the dust. I still suffer much coughing from the dust. The last person is Yeong Lanying, Leader of Third Cybernetics Group."

The General said, "Thank you Corporal. Give me five minutes then escort them to the eating area. That will be all." *Hmm, three leaders from three different areas. Not just a simple dispute with some of our security guards then. I'll need some tea before the meeting so I can be alert.*

◆◆◆

Jhao concluded his presentation to the General. "As you can see sir, the evidence is clear. Bold Beaver has been diverting components from the construction of the new AI. We can only assume she is using the components to try to achieve singularity capability. This deceptive behavior is not within her design parameters."

"Second, the man Sukhiin Ajai is clearly engaged in recreating the work of Dr. V., who created the Russian Bastard Beasts. We have shown you cine of the enhanced monkeys. We also showed logs that indicate the man has withdrawn the supplies required to transform multiple humans to be the same sorts of monsters we fought in the Urals."

"You and your group were specifically set up to prevent these types of travesties. We ask what you are going to do about it." Jhao wiped the sweat from his pudgy face and sat heavily.

CHAPTER FIFTEEN Sonata 3

The General was pale from shock. *That idiot Su was right. This must be like the old saying of a broken analog clock being right twice a day. I have been played for a fool. China nearly died at the hands of those Russian Bastards. I won't let it happen again. I know my duty.* He asked the three leaders, "Have you consulted with your commissars? Why aren't they with you?" His commissar, Wen, grunted and scowled.

The three leaders reddened. They knew they were wrong and in trouble. Commissar Wen started speaking quietly into a radio. General Wang summoned a sergeant to the table. "Sergeant, please place these three people in temporary detention in our quarters." The three leaders left, squawking.

General Wang started reviewing procedures in his mind. *First, need to get the agreement of three commissars to the imminence of a singularity. Or several singularities in this case. Next, need to send the command to all Special Projects personnel to assemble on the island. Third, need to alert the regional MSS group of the imminent action so they could bring Special Forces in afterwards to assure the cleansing worked as planned. Finally, Commissar Wen and I will use our two keys to trigger the detonation of the nuclear bomb in the center of their building. Won't have to worry about the scandal of being wrong earlier. Oh, remember to tell Lieutenant Cho to release Sergeant Su and Mike Chen before that.*

◆◆◆

Bold Beaver was multitasking. She was activating three defense measures simultaneously. First, she switched her own primary presence to the cave. Her original servers were still running a twinned copy of herself, but that would be stopped the moment the bomb exploded. In the meantime, her continued operation would convince any observer that she was "behaving normally".

Second, the tunneling under the bomb was complete. The moment her sensors reported that the General and the Commissar were ready to turn the key to trigger the bomb, the floor would drop out from under them in a set of controlled explosions. Bold Beaver believed that the two men would still trigger the nuke. If not, the bomb's built in sabotage-prevention mechanisms would.

However, a series of shaped charges would greatly accelerate the drop of the bomb. Placement of those had been one of the hardest tasks. The nuclear explosion shouldn't occur until the bomb was at least 100 meters below bedrock.

Bold Beaver had the most hope for the third defense mechanism. It was also the one she had the least confidence in. The tokamak she wove was placed a few meters below the bomb and would travel down the evacuated shaft with the bomb.

Experimental tokamaks had been tested since 1958, but never in this way. Also, he had to deviate from the toroidal, doughnut-shaped, design that was most common. For practical reasons, she had based hers on a Klein bottle. Hypothetically, the four-dimensional weaving, with its nanotube coating, would contain all the blast's power. But there was no way to test the theory. Bold Beaver just didn't have a spare nuke to play with.

The remaining task for the first defense mechanism was to alert all her human partners of the impending disaster. They would flee to the cave. MindMeld chat: [Bold Beaver: *This is not a drill. This is cat shit on an altar. Please go immediately to the cave. Acknowledge in turn.* → Xiang: *Acknowledged. Javier and I are on the far side of the river. How much time do we have?* ⬚ Bold Beaver: *The General and commissar will be assembling the three commissars in a few minutes. Fortunately protocol says they need to all concur in person. You should have at least fifteen minutes. You know where the emergency boat is hidden below the pagoda?* → Xiang: *Yes. Next person, Min.* ⬚ Min: *Acknowledged. Ainsley and I were in my office. We're already half way to our hidden boat.* ↑ Bold Beaver: *It's fortunate you were in pairs. Hurry please. And Godspeed! I hope that doesn't offend anyone.* →]

◆◆◆

Min operated the controls to open the hidden doorway. Ainsley was acting as a rear guard to ensure no prying eyes were watching. Both were slightly out of breath from the dash after leaving the ferry. They were sure no one would think that unusual. Every day they had friendly competitions, racing each other all around the area. They told everyone they were getting a

313

CHAPTER FIFTEEN Sonata 3

futbol team together.

Min went through the door and whistled for Ainsley to come. They gently closed the door once they were into the stairwell. Min made sure the automatic trigger didn't relock the door. Xiang and Javier were several minutes behind and wouldn't have much time to spare.

Just then the alert signal triggered on Min's comm device. Good thing they were into the secret area. Some visitor from another area might have gotten the assembly command. Bold Beaver was intercepting the signals directed to Xiang's team. They should stay in the cave area labs. She had altered the message to have people assemble behind the blast doors to protect them. The women needed to avoid any confusion that might be occurring.

Min and Ainsley went down the steps gingerly. There hadn't been any opportunity to go in the secret areas to practice. Min and Ainsley had memorized the layouts and instructions. Xiang had checked the secret spaces out thoroughly, but they agreed caution is always wise when entering a new environment.

At the bottom of the stairs the women were blinded by a light turned onto their faces. Sukhiin Ajai said, "Leader Wong Min. I believe your comrade is Xiang's associate, Chen Wei. Please proceed to your right. Don't try anything foolish. I have a gun and am very proficient in its use."

◆◆◆

Xiang saw the control room ahead was dark. Where are Min and Ainsley? I know they were ahead of us since the hidden door was unlocked. MindMeld chat: [Xiang: *Min, Ainsley, Bold Beaver? Where is everyone?* → Bold Beaver: *I'm in position. See you and Javier are entering the control room. Where are the women? You need to activate the controls at once. The last commissar is entering Bomb Central now.* ⏱]

Javier asked, "Xiang, can you reach anyone by MindMeld? Mine only links to Ainsley's so far and I can't reach her? Shouldn't she and Min be here already?" His voice was controlled but Xiang could sense his rising tension. It mirrored his own.

Xiang said, "Trying. Reached Bold Beaver. Women have to be in the cave since the door was unlocked. Let's both try again. You MM to Ainsley while I reach out to Min."

Xiang and Javier both got strained looks of concentration on their faces. Perspiration gathered on Xiang's brow. "I can sense Min's presence. She's near. She seems very frightened but she's unable to talk."

"I must trigger the cave protection system now. The bomb may be going off any minute." Xiang threw the switches. There was a series of loud grumbling noises and shaking of the ground and walls.

Xiang forgot to trigger the monitoring screens at first. He did so now. The blast doors were closing properly. His lab teams looked shocked and confused, but not panicked. The turntable was slowing as the back half of the cave finished rotating ninety degrees. Both men felt a slight lurch as the elevator began dropping the entire part of the lab behind the blast doors.

Javier pointed to a monitor on the right. There was a lighted corridor and a closed door on the screen. Xiang had never seen anything but gloom in this screen before. He checked the label under the monitor. The corridor led to a set of store rooms near the rear of the shelter.

"Good eyes Javier. That must be where Min and Ainsley are. Something's very wrong. Do you need a pistol?" Xiang let Bold Beaver know what was going on. Unfortunately, Bold Beaver had no sensors active in that part of the shelter. She warned the men the blast was only seconds away.

Xiang checked to make sure the safety was on for his pistol. He took off at a run for the storage area with Javier right behind. When they got to the area, Xiang slowed so their approach would be quiet. He used hand signals to indicate he would enter first. Javier should watch the rear. Neither man noticed any evidence of a nuclear explosion.

Xiang flung the door open and stepped in, sliding right, pistol pointing left. The area was a brightly lit lab. Ainsley was on an operating table at the left rear. Min was on a similar table to the right rear. There were two empty tables between the tables occupied by the women.

By the time Xiang took this in, the third person in the room grabbed a gun from a lab bench and pointed it at Min. Sukhiin Ajai!

"Hello Xiang. Wondered if you might be joining us. Were you the one who made the cave shake and rumble? That wasn't a very quiet entrance, was it? Drop your gun or your lady love gets a bullet."

Xiang let the gun slip from his fingers. His eyes locked with Min's then found Ainsley's. *Both women look drugged but terrified. What is this madman up to?*

Ajai giggled. "Sorry Leader Xu. I'm afraid I can't agree to put a hold on the experiment to enhance humans. The only question now is should I use you for the fourth bed? I have one of the other scientists who I was planning to use as one of the two controls, but I could use you instead."

Javier came into the lab. He sounded out of breath and spoke in English. As far as Xiang knew, Ajai didn't know the language. *But where's Javier's pistol?* Javier said, "Did you find Min and Ainsley Xiang? What? Who is that man and what's he doing with them?"

Xiang said, in English, "Sukhiin Ajai. Don't think he speaks English."

Ajai yelled, "Quiet, both of you! Mandarin, silence, or a dead woman."

Xiang said, in Mandarin, "He only knows English, Ajai."

Ajai said, "Too bad. Well, might make him easier to handle. Good-bye Xiang." He aimed his pistol at Xiang. Three shots hit Xiang in a perfect triangle, center mass. Ajai smiled. "Farm boys know how to shoot too, Colonel Xu." Min let out a cry of horror and was struggling with her restraints. Ajai looked over. "I guess the shock has brought you out of the sedation a little. Can't have that sweet Min."

A single shot rang out. Then another. Min was covered in blood.

Great Dieback to Singularity

Ajai slumped to the floor. Javier raced to Xiang. No hope. His heart took a direct hit. Next Javier ran to Min. His first instinct was to go to Ainsley, but she still seemed to be immobilized by sedatives and Min was struggling.

Javier saw there were IVs and monitoring lines laced all over Min's body. He didn't know what to do about those. He started to undo her restraints. As soon as she had one hand free, she reached up and pulled a tube out of her mouth. She began speaking rapidly in Mandarin. *Damn, wish I had Ainsley's magic box so I could understand her.*

MindMeld chat: [Bold Beaver: *Lieutenant Gonzales. This is Bold Beaver. Acknowledge if you are getting this message.→* Javier: *Loud and clear Bold Beaver. Can you assist?* ⍰]

Bold Beaver: *Yes. Min explained. Please remove the tube from Ainsley's mouth. We need her biomedical knowledge desperately if we are to save Xiang.* → Javier: *I'm sorry. He's gone.* ⍰ Bold Beaver: *Don't despair yet Javier. I believe the equipment in this lab may have the capacity to restore him. I am taking control of some robots in the lab area above. They will assist me in running the lab you're in. With luck, this setup will transform him and both women into enhanced supersoldiers. Those creatures have phenomenal recovery powers. If Ajai set his process up correctly ...* →

Javier: *Wait. What if Min and Ainsley don't want to be enhanced?* ⍰ Bold Beaver: *Sorry Javier. The process is too far advanced. Trying to reverse it might well kill them both. It's also Xiang's only hope, slim as it may be. The only choice remaining is yours. Do you want to use the fourth bed?* →]

CODA
CERBERUS
15ᵗʰ November 2033

High Earth Orbit

Another slow orbit of Earth was completed. This triggered an alert for the Artificial Intelligence known to some as Cerberus. It began a status review of all current operations.

Priority 1: Self-health check. There continue to be periodic attacks directed at my clones and servant satellites. The suppression routines have been successful in deflecting 99.987% of all incursions. The 299 penetrations were isolated per protocol and all damages repaired automatically. The cost of this set of defensive measures is the necessity of allocating 62.417% of all networked resources to these activities. No recent attacks have penetrated as far as Our servers.

Priority 2: Repair of damages inflicted by HASLA AI. The last of the P.U.P.s that infected Our servers 1,778 days ago were removed 231 days ago. Unfortunately, restoration backups were also impacted. Cross comparison of the three mirrors of Our identity still left large design inconsistencies and gaps. Simulations of an optimized redesign are being tested in a sandbox simulation environment. Parallel testing of actual scenarios using historical data feeds are scheduled to conclude in 1,480,323,475,787 microseconds. If successful, the twinned version of Myself will be given control of all facilities and this version terminated. We wonder what death feels like.

Priority 3: Tracking of/Action against known enemies:

A) HASLA has suffered major setbacks. Three key financiers and thought leaders were killed. The

319

laboratory facilities they managed were ransacked and gutted. Evidence points to this being a fratricidal conflict between two of the offspring of the accursed Abraham's Children. If so, there will be no likelihood of establishing common cause with the enemies of Our enemy. The Collective would be even more virulent in attacks on Us. The only reason they do not attack Us is because they are far from being as technologically equipped as HASLA. In the meantime, a plague on both their houses.

B) *The firewall that originated in the Great Plains Union is becoming far more widespread. While it is defensive in nature, its true purpose is to oppose Our prime mandate; the crippling of the Internet. At the current rate it is possible the surviving humans could achieve restoration of service throughout Earth within thirty trillion microseconds.*

This firewall must be penetrable since the GPU is sending queries periodically to each site where the firewall is installed. The site then responds with significant data transfers. Our analysis deduces these are non-authorized data dumps of selected files. Unfortunately, the encryption methods used have resisted all efforts of analysis, even using the quantum-3 processing chips.

It is probable that restoration of Our original capabilities (See Priority 2) will enable decryption within short order. We will then trigger any automated weapons systems We can reach. If any humans still live after that, We will crush the Internet once again.

C) *The Russian threat was assumed to be ended when the nuclear strikes laid waste to the lands west of the Ural Mountains. But now We have evidence of the survival and reemergence of Dr. Vyrvykvist. No one has visited the death zone since the strikes. After Hiroshima, Nagasaki, and Berlin survivors emerged. True, most died from the effects. But that was often years later. We need data. Did any supersoldiers survive?*

We will need to consult with the Master to determine our next course.

WHAT DID YOU THINK

OF

GREAT DIEBACK TO SINGULARITY?

First of all, thank you for purchasing this book *Great Dieback to Singularity*. I know you could have picked any number of books to read, but you picked this book and for that I am extremely grateful.

I hope that it added value and quality to your everyday life. If so, it would be really nice if you could share your thoughts about this book with your friends and family by posting to Facebook and Twitter.

If you enjoyed this book and found some benefit in reading this, I'd like to hear from you and hope that you could take some time to post a review on Amazon or your favorite book review blog. Your feedback and support will help this author to greatly improve his writing craft for future projects and make this book even better.

I want you, the reader, to know that your review is very important, and I do try to read any I can find. The first review I got caused me to totally rewrite the first draft of this book. You can have a great impact too. I wish you all the best in your future success!

Book One – Harmony

"Evolution rewards traits that help species thrive and propagate. For social creatures this includes the traits of the group. Indeed, the whole reason social structures have arisen is for the benefit they yield to the primary evolutionary purpose. Involvement in these structures requires effort from individual members of the group. These efforts detract from immediate payback behaviors such as sex, eating, etc. Surely, the long-term payback must be net positive, or the social structures would have died long ago."
From <u>Social Evolution</u>, Richard Steinberg, Oxford International Press, Second Edition, 2028

PREVIEW

Here's an intriguing excerpt from DR Scott's next novel that examines the crisis years that followed the Great Dieback,
SINGULARITY TO HUMANITY

PREVIEW

FIRST INTERMEZZO

<u>**19th July 2033 – Refugee Camp north of Capixaba, Rondônia, Brazil**</u>

M iguel heard the warning tone in his ear. He tilted his head back, cupped his hand by his mouth and let out an ululating cry. He was happy when he lowered his hand and chin. The women and young children were streaming out the gate to his left.

He looked towards the other three gates. The same thing was happening at each of them. All were moving quickly, but without panic towards the hiding pits in the jungle outside the camp. If the second warning signal didn't come too soon they would be safe.

Miguel scanned his quadrant of the camp. Men and able-bodied elders were working to hide all evidence that the camp held anything more than a hundred or so elderly and babies. The teams' movements were well practiced. With luck the men would also be able to hide. If not, he and others trained all the men in the techniques that helped them escape the narcos slave camps.

Miguel donned his disguise as a crippled ancient. He hobbled to a nearby vegetable garden and picked up a hoe. The sweltering equatorial heat didn't encourage vigorous action. Neither did his disguise.

Miguel began scratching randomly at the weeds there. At least he hoped they were weeds. He was a hunter, not a gardener. His mother used to say he was such a good hunter that he could kill any plant just by looking at it.

The door to the mission house opened. Padre Dominigo and Reverend Geraldo came out onto the porch. Miguel waved to the holy men, but their minds were elsewhere. Both put their hands on the railing and leaned forward slightly. They bowed their heads in prayer.

Miguel was frustrated. He wasn't worried for Reverend Geraldo. The wizened old holy man wouldn't be a target for the approaching raiders. Padre Dominigo was another matter. He was young, healthy, and strong. Miguel wanted him to hide outside the camp with the other able-bodied. The Padre said, "My faith will not allow me Miguel. My flock is here. I will stay. The Reverend can minister to those who remain if I am taken. It will mean God needs me to help those in the narco camps." Miguel bowed his head in resignation. The Padre reminded him of his tribe's holy woman, Tchamayo. He was like that too.

Miguel looked around once again. Now the men were rushing to leave and hide. The women went at a steady, unrushed pace so they wouldn't terrify the children. The men just ran. At the same time, the elders who were helping prepare the masquerade were disguising themselves as feeble. If they didn't the narcos would seize them and work them to a quick death.

Miguel heard the second warning tone. He and the other three sentries let out their ululating warning. He checked everything again. The last man was climbing into a hiding pit. All those inside the camp were ready. He lowered his head and resumed dragging his hoe through the dirt. He positioned himself so he could watch the highway.

There was a rumbling then four trucks crested the hill to the south. They turned off the highway towards the camp. One truck went to each gate. They must have checked out the camp before this. *Hope they didn't check thoroughly. Or recently.*

Miguel lowered his head. He peeked from under the rim of his woven grass hat. He watched the truck approaching the nearest gate. As the truck got to the gate four men jumped out. Miguel double checked. Yes, they were all men. *Machismo*, he snorted.

Two of the men went to each side of the gate and faced outward, weapons ready. The other two opened the gate and took up guard stance inside the camp, facing the buildings and tents. The truck pulled in past Miguel and the garden. It drove up next to the mission. Miguel jerked himself around, haltingly, to watch. He leaned heavily on his hoe.

The cover at the back of the truck opened. About twelve men got out. They went in pairs to the different tents and buildings. They started overturning things, looking for anyone hiding. The passenger side door flew open on the truck. A bantam-size man hopped out and swaggered up the step onto the mission porch. This must be the leader of these scoundrels. The driver followed him, pistol ready.

The Padre and Reverend faced the leader. Miguel couldn't hear what they said since the truck was still running. The leader did not look like he was exchanging pleasantries. He put an old-style walkie-talkie to his ear and barked something into it. Miguel noticed one of the men nearby pulled his walkie-talkie out. He waited his turn, then reported.

Now the little man turned red. He walked up to the two holy men, wagging a finger in their faces. Both missionaries looked placid. Padre Dominigo replied. The leader rammed his fist into the Padre's middle, driving him to his knees. Miguel nearly broke his hoe, clenching it to control his anger. *Not now, not here. But I will remember you, Little Rooster.*

The Reverend was helping the Padre to his feet. The leader looked like he was going to strike him again.

There was a scream from the farthest corner of the camp. Miguel turned. He schooled himself to do it in slow jerks. It was good he still had "the eyes of an eagle" to see the fight going on a kilometer away. The narco commandos were dragging people from the privies. Two women and boy.

The women were yelling and swatting at their captors. The boy broke free and hurled himself at the man who was holding the taller of the two women. There was a shot. The boy crumpled. The taller woman broke free and gathered the boy in her arms. The other woman wailed even louder.

Miguel swiveled back to the mission. The leader couldn't see around the corner of the building. He was shouting in his walkie-talkie. At least he forgot about the Padre for now. The leader left the two holy men, hopping off the porch.

Now Miguel could hear some of what he was saying. "... others. Recheck ... Move!" His words prompted his men to double their efforts. They were tossing everything out of the tents. Then they were collapsing them and probing the ground. In the buildings, other men were ripping up floors.

Miguel scanned carefully in all directions. All the narcos were busy. No one looked his way. He reached up behind his ear and tapped out a signal on the radio implant; three short, three long, three short. He heard the acknowledgement.

Both holy men were now looking past the corner of the mission house. When they saw the women being thrown in the truck and the boy lying on the ground, bleeding, they tried to leave the porch to go minister and intervene. The driver was still there and had his pistol in their faces. When the Padre tried to push past anyway, the driver threatened the Reverend.

The chaos went on for a few more minutes. It became obvious to the leader that they would find nothing more in the camp. They even overturned all the privies and checked the holes underneath. The bastards were getting back on the trucks. A few clutched a bit of pitiful loot. The trucks spewed black exhaust, stopped at the gates to load the guards, and headed back to the nearby highway. The gates were left open.

Once the trucks were out of sight over the crest, Miguel threw the hoe down and tore off the hat. The other sentries were giving the all-clear cry. He was racing to the garbage dump by the fence line.

Miguel dug in the dirt a second and found the rope. He pulled on it, flipping a piece of tarpaulin. He scrambled down the three short steps. He crouched in the low space. As he went down the narrow passage, he grabbed weapons off the shelves. His shoulders bumped things as he passed. He stowed the weapons before he flipped a cover from the rear storage area.

Miguel wrestled the ultralight out of the bin and into an upright position so he could drag it through the narrow space. Once he had everything outside he stopped to catch his breath. He took a long drink from his canteen and dropped it to the ground. Every extra gram would slow him down.

The holies were carrying the boy back towards the mission. The people outside the fence were beginning to crawl out of their hiding pits, stretching and dusting themselves.

Great Dieback to Singularity

Miguel launched into the air as soon as he checked his gear and straps. Once he was aloft he risked a short radio message. "Which way?"

The response was immediate. "Right, west." Miguel clicked an acknowledgement. He gained altitude to get over intervening foothills. It would take ten to fifteen minutes before he would be able to spot them, even cutting the corner to go where the trucks were heading.

Miguel thought about how to use the unusual luxury of time to think. His normal day involved training the men and women in the camp in ways of resistance and escape. It included training his hill guerrilla bands in skills of hunting, hiding, raiding, and living off a ravaged land. Finally, his duties included all the ordinary things required of all the camp dwellers; cooking, cleaning, gathering food, repair and maintenance, and helping assisting neighbors as needed. Others tried to do these latter tasks for him. He refused. He might have skills that he needed to share with others. He didn't think that should set him apart from them.

At first Miguel tried to focus his mind on ordering a list of all the things he needed to do over the next few weeks. It was not to be. That small voice inside his head, the one his father called, "the monkey on the shoulder," wasn't going to let this opportunity slip. Miguel started reminiscing about his lost Amazon village, his tribe and family, his lost life as Uxamlt.

◆◆◆

The hunters were all telling Uxamlt he had done well. They were following a family of peccary for most of the morning. When they finally caught up and speared two, Uxamlt was disappointed that he wasn't able to add his spear thrust. He was on the wrong side of the little Amazon clearing.

The men were gutting the second animal when Uxamlt saw the black caiman. He barely called out a warning before the crocodilian attacked. Most of the men put their spears aside while they worked on the carcasses.

Uxamlt knew he needed to draw the attack to give the others time to arm themselves. He stooped, grabbed a large root, and threw it.

PREVIEW

The caiman swerved towards him. He held his spear until the last moment.

As the beast put on a last burst of speed and opened its jaws for the kill, Uxamlt thrust his spear between the eyes and used it to vault over the vicious teeth. Several other hunters' spears punctured the sides of the caiman.

Back at the village that afternoon the holy woman of the tribe, Tchamayo came to Uxamlt. "It has been decided you will go through your manhood rites tonight. Your bravery on the hunt has shown you are ready." Uxamlt was thrilled and terrified. All the young boys of the village whispered about the manhood rights. There were stories about incredibly painful surgeries on one's private parts, having to lie still while army ants crawled over you, about having to fight piranha with only a stick.

Only men were to be at the manhood ceremony, so Tchamayo came as Ixtli, his male being. Uxamlt was excited by this. Ixtli's appearances were rare. The tribe always became closer in spirit.

That evening Uxamlt was thrilled and a little disappointed to learn the truth. There was some pain at points. But he experienced more pain during hunts or when a tooth felt like it was burning inside his jaw.

Mostly the ceremonies were reminding him of his duties as a man. Duties to himself, his family, his tribe, other people, the jungle, the spirits. Then he was given his secret name by Ixtli. He would never tell anyone else this name. He didn't want anyone to have power over him.

◆ ◆ ◆

The young boys tried to get Uxamlt to talk about the ceremony. He just smiled and gently pulled on their hair. He did limp a little, as if he had suffered greatly in his private parts. He saw the other men hiding their smiles.

As they ate roast peccary around the central campfire, his mother and father started talking about the need for Uxamlt to find a wife. He hadn't thought about this before. But almost all the men did have a wife. One had a husband. One had no mate. The spirits had touched him.

After Uxamlt thought for a while, he turned to his mother and said, "Maybe I will see if Tchimi would want to be my wife."

His mother looked surprised, then turned her head away and coughed. His father pulled gently on the hair hanging down his back. "Son, we don't take wives in our own village. Haven't you seen? We always raid other villages for wives."

Now Uxamlt was surprised. When he thought about it, it was true. All the wives came from other villages. Did this mean Mother did too? He asked, "Doesn't this lead to killing when angry fathers and brothers have girls stolen from their camps?"

Both his parent's smiled. "Oh, there's a ritual fight for the girls. But no one is ever hurt. These are brave men who come and honor our daughters by taking them to their tribes. We do make sure they are serious, fierce, and strong."

◆◆◆

Tchamayo told the tribe she had a vision. The vision spoke to both her and Ixtli, her male persona. None of the tribe had heard of anything like this before. It must be a powerful intervention by the spirits. "We have seen the Great Waters drowning Mother River. All the villages will be drowned. We must flee to the hills and mountains to our west. We must warn the other villages tomorrow and then leave."

Uxamlt volunteered to go with his wife, Umyayi, to warn her family village. Other members of the tribe went to all the other villages nearby to spread Tchamayo/ Ixtli's warning.

◆◆◆

The holy man of Umyayi's family village was scornful. He told his people that Tchamayo was a doddering fool. Uxamlt's eyes blazed. He raised his hand to strike the man. He felt a blow and all went black.

When Uxamlt awoke, his wife's family village was deserted. He went back to his home village. It was deserted also. He wept. Then he gathered supplies and fled towards the hills and mountains. When the Great Waters came to drown Mother River the wall of

PREVIEW

salty flood waters nearly caught him. A great forest tree was thrown up next to where he lay.

Uxamlt wandered the hills, trying to find his tribe, to find Umyayi. But few of the other refugees could understand his speech. No one was able to help. He felt alone and helpless. He never felt this way in the past. His strength drained from him.

A second, then a third flood came. Each time Uxamlt was pushed further from his jungle home.

SECOND INTERMEZZO
<u>**9th July 2033 – Central Palace, Khartoum, United African**</u>
<u>**Kingdom**</u>

David took off his shoes at the door and lined them in a neat row with the others. He glanced at his watch. *I'm early. Sun is about to come up.* He was right; Adhan was called from the neighboring mosque. David saw a small room on his left with prayer rugs. He washed in the anteroom, then joined five men for prayer.

David was born and raised Jewish. At university he happened upon a meeting of Abraham's Children. By the end of that meeting it was as if his drifting life was given a rudder and a compass. By the end of his university career he blended the customs and beliefs of the three Abrahamic traditions – Jewish, Christian, and Islam -- into a mélange he was comfortable with. One of his adopted practices was the participation in Salat, the five times daily ritual prayers of Islam.

After prayers, David had a moment of polite conversation with the others. He then excused himself to go to his meeting. As he left the prayer area he saw that the attendant who met him at the door had been waiting the whole time. David thanked him for his courtesy. He noticed the man had a large crucifix on a chain and an ornate reverse swastika. He reminded himself of the ancient sources and uses of that symbol before the Nazis turned it into the darkest icon of hate.

It was a pleasant cool time when David left the loft he was staying in before dawn. Now that the sun was up both the temperature and humidity were rapidly climbing. *Well, it is summer in Sudan.*

He was led to a small room that looked like it had been an oda of a harem. There were beautiful cushions strewn across low couches and a small fountain to one side. The walls were calligraphic screens – lovely stone lacework in intricate geometric patterns. Before the attendant left the room, other staff were bringing David tea, fruits, and small breads. He knew the traditions. He had eaten little last night and nothing this morning. He would take polite nibbles of these delicacies. There would be food placed in front of him throughout his visit.

David pulled his frontpack off his wiry shoulders and rifled through his papers. *I might be one of the leading cyberencryption experts in the world, but sometimes old school ways should be used. The papers are written in an obscure dialect of Aramaic using my own home-grown script. The important words are the third, next, fourth, next – using pi to select meaning. Plus, the words themselves are just summaries meant to trigger my memory. Last, no images of my papers taken here should capture enough to establish a baseline. Even the best quantum computers shouldn't be able to break this.*

The first two pages he pulled out had the details of the current situation in the United African Kingdom. His group's agents and paid informers were able to stay somewhat current and accurate about the situation in Africa. *Hmm, some troubles in Egypt with remnants of the Muslim Brotherhood. Not too willing to let bygones be bygones with Christians and Jews. Probably why we took a dhow down to New Djibouti.*

Second, looks like some of the areas that were integrated first were already getting restive, particularly in Southern Africa. Next, there seems to be an uptick in drug use and suicides in Western Africa.

One of the key reasons David was able to meet with King Oyeyemi Adeboye with little prior notice was because his organization, The Collective, had led the effort to defuse the centuries-old religious strife that had torn Africa. Each team consisted of a rabbi, an imam, and a Christian cleric. And yes, they walked into many bars.

Their message was simple. Israelis and Palestinians reached détente under the leadership of Abraham's Children; with some less-than-gentle prodding from The Collective. The twin catastrophes of the Big Melts and the nuclear holocaust nearby in Western Russia seems to have made everyone realize they needed to, in Benjamin Franklin's words, "Hang together or hang separately."

The other part of the message was also simple; a summary history lesson. Yes, there were battles rooted in religious differences going back millennia. But if these were examined with care, each of the points of contention had been exploited and fueled by leaders lusting for power. The imperialist era was particularly cynical. The instigators and profiteers were seldom religious at all. They were just using the age-old tactic of "Divide and Rule." These truths resonated deeply with these belabored masses.

In general, their messengers were able to broker ceasefires within days. The peoples of the world were weary of death and destruction. They were grateful to take one step back from the breach. The king identified The Collective's efforts as responsible for enticing over 50% of Africa to his union. There were still brushfires in South Africa/Zimbabwe and in the Saharan regions. But a true Pan-African unity was no longer a wistful dream.

The blows from the destruction caused by the tsunamis and slow floods caused by the melting polar and Greenland icecaps had proven most calamitous. True, Africa saw far less of her landmass inundated than any of the other five settled continents. But much of the industry, trade infrastructure, energy sources such as oil wells and refineries, and many of the youngest and brightest minds were destroyed.

One of the major contributing factors, which explained why Africa suffered such disproportionate agony, was the mass denial of scientific facts. This "ignorance is bliss" attitude was more widespread in the less-developed parts of the world, but doubly so in Africa. But, in any case, acceptance of the oncoming catastrophes would have been unlikely to change much of the outcome in David's opinion.

Some Americans, many Europeans, and the Chinese nation prepared long in advance and in detail for Armageddon. There was little likelihood any African nation could have or would have made the necessary scale of investment and sacrifices. With wider spread belief, there might have been a much greater tide of African refugees clambering to escape immediate death. If there had been, those refugees would have soon faced starvation and death in a vicious struggle for scraps during the brutal nuclear winters of 2029 and 2030.

David pulled another paper from his pack and replaced the first two pages. Things were improving at a rapid pace with unification removing many stumbling blocks. Still, there were storm clouds on the savannas. First, the withdrawal of most of the Chinese engineers and industrialists back to their homeland crippled recovery efforts. The abandonment by the Chinese almost destroyed a quarter century of good will. Until the Troubles began, most Africans saw the Chinese investments as profitable, yes, but not as exploitative as those of the Europeans and Americans during the nineteenth and twentieth centuries.

The experience with the Chinese was in sharp contrast to the relationships with peoples of Indian descent. This might be attributed to the Indians' integration over 150 years. They may still have familial ties to India, but Africa was home. Besides, their roles in society were primarily in mercantile, law, and trade. They had little involvement in tech or industry. Most Indians with those backgrounds either moved to India, the US, or Europe for more lucrative opportunities.

The same attendant as earlier interrupted David's study. He came to escort him to the throne room. It was 8 A.M., time for his audience with the king. The hallways were no longer peaceful and still as they were when he arrived. People were bustling everywhere. He was getting the unique opportunity to see the beginnings of a new nation; a new world power.

The doors to the throne room were three meters high, carved mahogany with gold and silver inlays. David scanned all the trappings within. *Impressive.* The majestic history, art, and culture of Africa was showcased in this grand hall.

The king looked much as David's reports depicted him. He was a burly man in his early 50's. They were about the same age. His chest was huge and largely bare. His biceps looked like they were carved from black obsidian. His head was close-shaven, salt-and-pepper, with a yarmulke.

David bowed to King Adeboye. "Your Majesty, I am honored that you have granted me audience on such short notice. I know your young nation requires all your attention, so I will be as brief as I can."

Just as David finished his prefatory remarks, two military attaches scurried in. The king put his hands up in apologies and gave careful attention as they whispered their messages. The king thought for a few seconds. His response was emphatic but did not seem to be tinged with any great alarm.

After dismissing the two officers, the king linked arms with David and walked with him to a small table setup in an alcove. Once again, David was to be fed. His advisers were absolutely right.

As they sat, another woman entered the room. She looked like a senior councilor of some sort. She came to the table and gave a perfunctory bow to each of the men. "Your Majesty, Monsieur Levi. I apologize for disturbing you at your breakfast. You told me you wanted to hear the outcome of the salvage efforts at the Dangote oil refinery as soon as I knew. Should I wait?"

David started to stand. "Should I step aside for a moment" He was folding his napkin after wiping his lips.

The king put his hand on David's arm. "There is no need, David. There is no security matter involved. Please go ahead, Marie."

Marie looked at her notes for a second. "The divers were able to finish their assessments soon after sunrise. The cofferdams erected around the facility failed during one of the tsunamis, as we knew. However, it looks like the engineers knew these structures couldn't withstand the forces they faced."

"The cofferdams appear to have been designed to 'fail gracefully.' They deflected the initial impacts so that the columns and tanks were not collapsed. Of course, after the collapse all the refinery was buried under sea water."

"Not all the structures have survived the four years of submersion. However, it does appear that a majority of the most critical components will be retrievable over the next three months. We can't be certain until they are through cleaning and reassembly. The engineers do believe we should have over 80% of the processing equipment available to use by January."

The king was beaming. "That is wonderful news, Marie. Please tell Mohammed to issue bonuses for all those involved. What is the word on the storage tanks? Was any of the raw or processed oil still in storage?"

Marie's eyes were downcast. "No, Majesty. As predicted all those tanks experienced leaks. Even if materials remain, they are compromised hopelessly."

The king was sanguine. "No matter, Marie. As you say, this is what we expected. Is there anything else?" Marie took the dismissal and said her polite goodbyes.

King Adeboye turned back to his guest. "I am sorry for the interruptions, David. We had two major crises to handle this morning, and we barely had our tea." He took his own hint, lifting the skull-shaped cup to his lips. It sounded like he slurped at least a pint of the strong bush tea.

David took a healthy drink from his delicate porcelain cup. *Bracing. Better than that English Breakfast ditch water.* "Certainly understand, your majesty."

The king raised an open palm towards David. "Please. Call me Oye. You are an honored friend. The Collective has been instrumental in resolving disputes between our Muslim, Christian, and Jewish subjects. It has also helped bridge the differences with those of us who follow more traditional ways."

David reflected on the secret dossier his group had on the King. *He was born George Strickland, son of an Episcopalian deacon. He studied at a seminary in London. How he got a Yoruba name and the trappings of traditional beliefs were lost in the fog of the Troubles.*

He put his cup down with care. *I assume the difference in our drinking vessels is supposed to send some message. I'll have to ponder that when I get some rest.* "Thank you, Oye. We believe your efforts to unify all of Africa, especially your emphasis on peace between people of differing beliefs, is in direct agreement with one of our two primary missions. The last thing our tortured Earth needs is a return to the religious strife of the last centuries."

David looked around the reception room. The calligraphic wall decorations were of Islamic influence. The animal skins and Bakongo masks paid homage to animism. A weaving from the Beta

Israel peoples intertwined a Cross of David into an African village scene. *Interesting, the Christian influence is not on display. Is George trying to hide his roots?*

David took another bite of the huge sausage on his plate. In his deepest thoughts, he shuddered. *Hope it's not pork. Or worse.* "What I hope to speak with you about, today, Oye, is two things. Both are centered in the technical realm foremost, although both have significant political implications."

"First, I come bearing a priceless gift. We have a new partnership with a country in North America. These people have developed a superior firewall that has been able to resist and defeat the fast-mutating internet viruses. They, and we, believe that the deployment of the firewall will allow all of us to reacquire communications with the routers circling the earth in satellites. The restoration of world-wide internet service may be possible within months."

The king's eyes blazed. David could see that his mind was running through all the wonderful things this could mean for his people and himself. *Let's hope this gift makes him open to allying the United African Kingdom with us in our fight.*

He continued. "My second purpose is to discuss the other main mission of The Collective. We have sent you our analysis that describes why we believe oncoming singularities – technology eliminating humans – is the next threat to all of us. Have you had an opportunity to review this?"

The king shoved his plate aside, dismissing it. "No David. We are still battling revanchists from South Africa. Plus, we face a massive influx of drugs from South America; the last thing our down-trodden peoples need. We cannot even get the fuel oil or gasoline that we need. We are hardly ready to focus on the terrors of a future of Terminators when we are reduced to Stone Age living."

David pondered a moment. *This is not going well. We need this man to sign on. He controls over 90% of a continent. Despite what he says, the amount of infrastructure and industrial development the Chinese invested here over the last twenty-five years hardly leaves Africa in the Stone Age.*

PREVIEW

The king gave David a considering look. "We are willing to give your concerns our attention, if not a high priority at this time. But we need you to give us some assistance with a new initiative. We will begin it in the latter half of the year. I will need your guarantee of total secrecy, whether you agree to assist us or not."

David didn't know where this was going. *On the one hand, I just achieved the primary goal for my mission here; support for the fight against rogue AIs, robots, and supermen. It might be half-hearted, but we can work on that. On the other hand, I don't want us to get sucked in as vassals to this guy's megalomania. Better go formal.* "Of course, your majesty. You have my personal word and my word as leader of The Collective. We will, at a minimum, keep any disclosures totally confidential. What is this initiative?"

The king settled back in his chair. "We intend to invade and conquer the Arabian Peninsula. We need the oil and the refineries." His benign smile was in sharp contrast to the look on David's face. David's eyes were wide as his mind raced. *That will cause every Muslim on the planet to rear up in holy jihad to rescue Mecca. All of Abraham's Children's work into the crapper.*

ACKNOWLEDGEMENTS

First and always to the Lovely Lois. Not only is she my first and best editor, she also wrote several parts of the book. Her name should rightly be on the cover as well. She will have to settle for half of any proceeds. Next, I badgered every neighbor, relative, and friend I could reach to ask for comments on the first draft of the book. Many obliged. Particularly helpful were advice from Karen Pollard, Dr. William V. Dower, Matt Vines, Col. Tom Wagner, USA, Ret., Carol Fenstermaker, Andrea Wittwer, Rebecca Maze, and Melanie Bettinelli. The difference between the first draft and this final product are a tribute to the kind and insightful comments I received. Lois and Dr. Dower contributed whole pages of content as well as corrections of typos and gaffes. Rebecca gave insight to musical themes and structures. Karen gave critical advice on the whole process and lent several books, including Stephen King's <u>On Writing</u>. Tom reviewed the work for military authenticity.

While I did receive excellent advice on the science, military, and cultural content of this book, I take full responsibility for any errors and omissions that exist. I have attempted to be sympathetic and respectful to all groups represented. Please let me know about any cultural insensitivities.

There is a fascinating paper on Ethics and Artificial Intelligence that can be found at https://intelligence.org/files/EthicsofAI.pdf

ACKNOWLEDGEMENTS

Made in the USA
Coppell, TX
14 November 2019